YOUNG FLAME

BOOK TWO

YOUNG FLAME

BOOK TWO

J. B. Oro

Podium

Published in 2025 by Podium Publishing
www.podiumentertainment.com

Podium

YOUNG FLAME

BOOK TWO

THE TITAN ALPS
JO
WASTELAND

PACT
NATIONS
THEOCRACY
ZADOK
NEW VETUS

CHAPTER ONE

Moving North . . . Again

Charred grass crunches under my foot as I step over the blackened land-scape. My bare foot passes through the ash and I debate removing my other shoe. After the fight in the Void Fog, I discovered much of my clothes in tatters. While I am immune to sword swings, the same cannot be said for what I carry. I've lost one shoe, the left side of my pants and much of my shirt. But all that means little because I lost Leal's jacket.

The general's sword must have damaged the heat resistance inscribed in the leather and left it to the mercy of the magma lake. My uncle's incredible work is the only reason the clothes from my tribe remain somewhat intact.

So, my first task is to find some new shoes and a jacket to keep myself safe should it rain again.

I try to ignore the lopsided gait caused by wearing only one shoe as I walk over the remains of the grassy fields after the pyre. The farther I walk, the prouder I become. I only intended to burn the area around the barn, but it went far past my expectations. I've walked dozens of kilometers and still haven't found the end to the charred remains of the grass fire.

My legs carry me away with haste. I can't stay here; even if I'm not being chased anymore, I still don't want to be around in the area when people come.

Maybe I should feel bad for burning someone's barn and all the crops in the area . . . but I just don't. I was able to give all the lost áed a better send off than anyone could have hoped for. It doesn't matter if they needed it; I needed it more.

As I breach the summit of a hill, the sight of a city comes into view. It's clearly an ursu city. There is just an obvious difference between the buildings of New Vetus and the ones of the Zadok Kingdom. While it's good to know the Void Fog didn't take me too far, it also means I have a long way to travel to reunite with the others.

I'll have to travel through ursu land, then that root forest again before trying to get past the wall north of Kelton. And that is just returning to where I started. It will be hard to find the others, but if I can do the same as Elder Enya, I'll be able to cover a lot more land than before. Before that, I need new clothes.

The city is far too quiet.

As I come up on its border, I'm confronted with the strange sight of . . . nothing. There is no movement, no wagons, no ursu moving around; heck, I can even hear the wind blowing around the buildings. It's so quiet.

Between the buildings, down a main road, the only visible change is the presence of wagons. Or, well, the remains of them. The Henosis's metal cars are aplenty, but not a single one is undamaged. Other Empire army supplies and fortifications line the street, but there is a distinct lack of life to go with them.

Were the Henosis beaten? Then where are the ursu?

Well, if there's nobody here, there's nobody to stop me looking through the homes.

I climb up the tall steps in the closest building and after searching only two homes, I find a jacket small enough to replace the one Leal gave me. It is still far too large, and only by tying it in half does it stop dragging along the ground. I don't even try looking for replacement shoes; there isn't a chance an ursu's would fit.

With something to protect me should it ever rain, I push on through the city. It doesn't matter where I look, there isn't a person in sight.

Only when I reach the central section of the city do I get an idea of what happened. Before me is something that can only be called a bloodbath. The plaza below the continae is painted crimson. Albanic bodies are everywhere, but not one is whole. Torsos and limbs lay scattered. The worst are the piles of mush pooling in craters.

It's a disgusting sight. I've seen people die before, many of them in horrible ways, but there has to be hundreds littering the area. What did this to them? It isn't still here, is it?

I twist my head at the surrounding buildings, eyeing each shadow and window in case it's still around. The city remains as silent as ever.

I sprint two full steps before I stop. My head turns back to the many, many bodies lying here, all untouched. The intoxicating satiety I experienced from the general's corpse digs into my thoughts. Can any of these bodies give me that same feeling?

Against my better judgment, I return to the massacre. My flames flick out, reaching for both blood and flesh. I attempt to ignore the texture as my fire burns through the area.

I twinge in frustration as none of the bodies satisfy that same need I'd discovered consuming the general. They all seem too . . . weak? It's like their flesh is of a lower quality. Like eating those twiggy shrubs when you want barrels of coal.

It just isn't enough.

I search through them all, cleaning each liter of blood from the ground until you'd be hard-pressed to even know the carnage was here. Nothing tastes even slightly filling and I realize I've wasted my time.

Only once I'm outside the city do I realize the flaw in my thoughts. I burned through the corpses of hundreds of people, but only cared that they didn't have enough energy to satisfy me. I haven't always been like this, right?

Unnerved by both the emptiness of the city and my own actions, I move out again.

Six hours of walking along a northerly paved road makes me wish I had a train. I'm not sure where exactly I am in New Vetus, but the country is huge enough that it will probably take me months to get anywhere.

I still have to test my improved binding and change into a bird, but I want to find somewhere safe to do so. How vulnerable I will be remains up in the air, and I don't want to risk getting caught unaware by whatever slaughtered all the Henosis.

On the road ahead of me is a caravan of the Empire's cars, also devoid of life. There are dozens of the heavy wagons just parked in the middle of the road. Abandoned.

Upon approaching, a scene not unlike that of the last city appears. Devastated landscape surrounds the cars, with crushed and dismembered bodies lying everywhere. The only things that remain intact are the cars themselves.

My flames give into greed and consume the bodies as I walk up to the first of the cars. As I climb up, I become aware of the many ursu corpses tightly organized within the storage space. Each body is arranged side by side, so tightly I don't think it would have been possible to fit more of them in.

What is strange is that the corpses are intact. Well, not exactly intact, as many have numerous bullet wounds and missing limbs, but compared to the albanic corpses around, these bodies are pristine.

Whatever attacked the Henosis obviously avoided damaging the bodies of the ursu. Is it targeting only the Empire soldiers or any non-ursu?

As I look over the ursu corpses tightly compressed in the Henosis cars, the temptation to pass my flames over them rises. The strength of the ursu has to make them more filling than the albanics, right? The feeling of the albanic just isn't enough. I'm tantalized by the possibility that the ursu might fill that hunger.

I shake my head with aggression to clear the dangerous thoughts. I can't risk it. Something intentionally avoided these corpses for a reason. If I so much as damage a strand of fur on their bodies, I could be painting a target on my own back. For now, I'll settle with the minimal satiation I can get from the albanics' remains.

I continue to follow the road until it curves to the west. So far, my travel has been incredibly quiet. Neither animals nor people disturb me as I continue forward, which is extremely odd. Many farmsteads and ursu homes lay empty. Most of the land seems fine; undamaged, but still abandoned.

Not wanting to follow the road to the wherever it travels in the west, I maneuver north and walk through the forsaken farmland. The organized nature of the crops makes passage far easier than it otherwise might have been.

The ursu have massive appetites, and massive appetites require massive farms. I've known intellectually that much of the ursu's land is used for farming. I've known that ever since Leal told me, but seeing the vast agriculture spanning between horizons is surreal.

And they just up and abandoned it all.

From the presence of the Empire's vehicles, I assume that this is a part of the land they have already captured, so it makes sense that they would have left before the area is ransacked. That also means I am closer to the isthmus, which is a lot farther away from Zadok than Morne was.

It will be fine as long as I haven't somehow landed myself on the completely annexed eastern half of New Vetus. If I have, then traveling north will do nothing but take me to the sea.

Even the thought that I might be stuck in the Henosis Empire–controlled territory doesn't worry me too much. They are obviously dealing with something far more threatening than I ever could, and even if I end up walking toward the sea, I can always walk back. It will take a long time, but my trip is going to take a while anyway. I have hope that flying might let me travel the normally months' long journey in a reduced time, but I'm in no rush.

I'm feeling great just experiencing my freedom while I have it, after months of being stuck in that cage. After even longer stuck in that furnace. Being able to fly excites me immensely, not just because I'll be able to travel freely, but because of the limits it removes. The wall in Zadok can't block me, oceans won't stop me, and mages will not catch me.

A giddy feeling rises in my chest at the thought of flying. Elder Enya once told me what it was like, but the wonder I'd experienced was subdued by disappointment when she told me it took all her life to manage it. Elder Enya was old.

To be able to twist her form enough to fly, she had to increase her binding with fire to a rank far higher than normal. She sacrificed all her time to raising it, neglecting the improvement of her control and temperature to focus solely on her binding with fire.

So, the fact that mine has risen to where it is in such a short time is odd. What exactly is the Void Fog to morph my very being so deeply? If it has changed me so much, what other beings might it have changed?

Now that I think back to it, I should have realized sooner. All the creatures I came across within it were far different from what I am used to. The sand-worms acted far more aggressive than normal, and they launched themselves out of the sand like bullets. It also explained why the colossal-worm was far larger than normal.

That ursu, the one far larger than any other I'd seen. He helped me. He knew what was going to happen, he must have experienced it himself. Is that why he was so large? The Void Fog twisted him to be far larger than normal?

The Fog didn't make me any taller, so how it decides what it changes must be something unique to each creature. The magpies too, other than there being millions of them, I'm unsure what was different about them. They didn't look physically different either.

A sudden thought slaps me and I'm ashamed I didn't think of it before. Is the big ursu the one going around killing the Henosis? He tore open the thick steel of the train capsule I was trapped within with ease; he would definitely have the strength to crush the albanic in the ways I've seen.

I'm conflicted about the giant. He broke me out of that train, and then helped me in the Fog, but the amount of damage I've seen left in his wake leaves me terrified of his strength. Even his presence had me freezing up, the sheer power he exudes is overwhelming. The Fog has enhanced me, but I don't believe I could survive for a single second if he ever directs his strength toward me.

I can turn my body ethereal now, but I still believe a punch from his enormous fist would be enough to end me, regardless of physicality. If I can do anything about it, I'll try to steer clear of wherever he is. On the small chance I come face-to-face with him again—and I'm unable to avoid him—I'll thank him properly.

Ahead of me, I spot the perfect place to hide away to try my change. It's an old-looking shed sitting beneath the shade of a couple of trees. The building looks decrepit and unused, perfect to hide away for a while when I have to worry about people coming across me in a more vulnerable state.

I pick up my pace, approaching the only door into the shed.

In an area where I haven't seen or heard any sign of life in almost a day, you can color me surprised when the door slams open and I'm suddenly looking down the barrel of a gun.

To think the only place I thought would be a good place to hide would happen to hide the only living soldiers I've seen.

CHAPTER TWO

Henosis's Regret

The dark interior of the barrel isn't as plain as I assumed. Inside the metal tube are visible markings curved circularly into the depths away from any light.

I raise my eyes from the gun aimed at my head to the soldier holding it. After surviving swings from the general's sword, guns don't seem all too terrifying.

I narrow my eyes at the albanics who walk out behind him, encircling me with their guns held upright, but keeping some distance between us. A total of eight were hiding within the small shed. I don't make any moves to startle them, nor do I cower under the threat of being shot.

Many of the soldiers' eyes struggle to remain on me for long, flickering over the horizon in all directions. It's as if they expect some terror to come out at any moment.

The first of the soldiers readjusts his gun to one hand and wipes his sweat on the leg of his pants. "Why are you here?" His eyes narrow at me.

"Corporal, she's a little girl. Should we really be holding our rifles at her?" one soldier asks from my right.

None of the other soldiers say anything, but a couple send glances at the first.

"Just because she's young doesn't mean we should forgo protocol. Wilhelm, August, restrain her."

"Don't do that." The words come out of my mouth before I even realize. The idea that I'll be trapped again does little but infuriate me.

Despite my words, there are still two who approach me from behind.

"The moment you touch me, you will burn," I warn. My eyes never leave the corporal in front of me.

His brows furrow, and I'm glad that my seriousness gets through to the man as he puts his hand up. "Stop."

The two approaching from behind do as he says, but don't back away.

The corporal stares at me for a long moment, his eyes flicker to the pilfered jacket and damaged clothing. "Why are you here?" he asks.

"I'm lost," I reply simply. He doesn't seem happy with my response. His frown grows and I hurry to continue. "I've been walking for days, but everyone has disappeared. I walked through one of the ursu cities earlier, but all I found was a massacre."

That seems to settle him some. "How did you get here? This is the middle of a battlefield, or well, it should have been."

I go to say I don't know, but the words don't come. Not because my lips won't spit out the words, but because I'm suddenly filled with an intense reluctance to lie. An intense desire to prevent trapping myself within my own false words.

I realize that not only don't I want to hide anything about myself, but I can't. Pretending I was an albanic in Zadok made me feel a sense of entrapment, and now that my mind has snapped into a single rope, I can't lie. Lying won't allow me to be truly free.

How annoying.

Maybe if I just tell bits of the truth, but not everything, will that work? It's worth an attempt. Even if I fail, none of these soldiers are mages and I doubt they have the same strength as the general. It's strange, but I don't feel afraid of them at all. I feel I can deal with each of them and barely take damage; those bullets will do nothing against my new, less physical body.

"I was traveling with some soldiers, but some giant killed everyone and now I don't know where I am." Okay good, no feeling of revulsion by omitting information. I just have to hope they don't ask why I was traveling with the soldiers.

"Why were you traveling with these soldiers? Who was the officer in command?"

Damn it. Why couldn't he have just left it there?

"Um . . . because . . ." I can't think of a way to answer. I can't even say *I don't know* as that would be a lie.

The corporal isn't impressed. "Continue with the restraints," he orders the two behind me.

I turn to glare at both of them. "Touch me and you'll regret it." Twisting back to the corporal, I give him a warning I think will make him respond a bit more intelligently, considering the still-wondering eyes of the other soldiers. "Be careful about firing your weapons, who knows which ursu might hear you."

His reaction is immediate, but still too late. The two lay their hands on me, trying to pull my arms behind my back. I don't give the opportunity. In but a moment, their arms are engulfed in flames and they are screaming.

The sight of the two behind me suddenly embroiled in a blaze must terrify the jumpy soldiers. Three of them fire on me, too late to hear the screaming order to "Hold your fire," from the corporal.

I barely feel the bullets as they pass through me, my body reforming around them in but a moment. Not moving from my spot, I wait until they all calm down and follow the corporal's order. I'm tempted to burn them all; they did attack first and are a part of Henosis. They are definitely not my favorite people, even if I've gotten some retribution from the general.

I pull my flames away from the burning arms of the two now rolling on the ground. As little as I care about them, I'd still like to get some information on where I am, and I could hardly do that after killing some of them off.

The corporal is panicking now, head spinning between horizons more than his soldiers. Looks like I'm close with my guess; they are hiding from the giant ursu. If those gunshots reach that ursu's ears, I don't want to be mistaken for one of the albanic. So, against the common guidance of my tribe, I let go of my control.

The Henosis soldiers stop their fearful searching and lock back onto me. My change has them raising their guns at me again.

It's surprisingly freeing to just let the world see me as I am, and I can now understand why the Agni tribes don't bother to hold themselves back. But, as good as it feels, it means too much to my tribe to ever permanently forgo controlling my flame.

The soldiers seem unsure how to proceed, so I figure I might as well take the lead.

"So, I don't actually know where we are. I know we're in New Vetus somewhere, but it's a pretty big country. Can you tell me where we are?"

The corporal doesn't answer immediately, instead his eyes flicker between the men cradling their burned arms behind me to the rest of the soldiers surrounding me. I don't care too much about how long he takes, but there's no way he will want this to last.

"Corporal. Your orders?" the man beside him asks, concern lacing his tone.

"I . . ." is all the corporal can manage, the indecision of his thoughts lacing his expression.

"Fuck this." One soldier to my left lowers his rifle to his hip. "I'm not waiting around here to be found by that monster," he says and storms off back toward the city I came from.

"Private Hermann. This is insubordination!"

"Fuck off. I'm not hiding in that fucking shed any longer. You don't have a clue what the fuck you're doing." Private Hermann twists on his feet to raise his middle finger at the corporal, continuing to walk backward as he does.

The wind stops dead and I suddenly get a really bad feeling.

The corporal doesn't notice, his face twisting in fury at the man walking away. He turns his gun from me and aims it at Private Hermann whose back is turned.

"No!" The man besides the corporal dives into him and a loud bang rings out.

Private Hermann drops, dead before he hits the ground.

The soldiers devolve into chaos. While the corporal brawls with the soldier that tackled him, a couple more jump in. I'm not sure whether they want to join the fight or separate them, but fists are quick to be thrown.

Two of the soldiers have taken for the hills, sprinting away as quick as they can while the corporal is stuck in the brawl. Most of the others stand around shouting at each other and only one approaches the downed Hermann to check on him.

The entire scene is an absolute mess, and I can't help but watch in shock as they all seem to even forget I'm here. The four men pile on top of each other, grappling and punching, their weapons all but forgotten.

I watch as the two running away reach a line of trees they use to hide from both my and presumably the corporal's line of sight. I guess things haven't been perfectly pleasant in that shed of theirs.

A cracking boom deafens me a moment before I'm showered in dirt. The air crackles as I turn to the source of the explosion, keeping as motionless as possible.

The dust settles around a crater in the same place the Henosis soldiers were brawling not a moment ago. None of them are there anymore, instead that giant ursu looms above. The dirt finishes falling from the sky as I watch him glower at the soldiers.

The Empire's men stand rooted to the spot, like me, unable to move in the presence of the being before us. The giant gives them no time to respond either, dashing toward them only a moment after arriving.

I knew he was strong before. I'd seen him tear a massive chunk of metal in half, but I never could have imagined this scene. He crashes through the first soldier, leaving nothing but a bloody vapor, while swinging the massive sword that blows a gust into me while slicing straight through the two other men unable to register his speed.

Again, he is gone, leaving me surrounded by blood-soaked soil. The sound of creaking has me turn to watch the tree the other soldiers passed not long ago collapsing from a large missing section at its base.

I hesitate to move. He never attacked me, but who knows what might turn his attention to me. I've never seen someone move so quick. Even the general hadn't come close to the speed and strength this ursu pulls off. How could he have ever believed he could compete, regardless of that weird sword?

The giant returns to my line of sight, stepping over the fallen tree and casually walking toward me. I want to do nothing but run and hide from his burning gaze. My flames burn stronger and with increased intensity as he closes the distance. Even I don't know whether I'm trying to act strong or if it's an appeal, telling him I'm not an albanic. I just hope his power isn't directed toward me.

His footsteps reverberate through the ground as he walks up in front of me. I can't move my feet, not while he looks down at me with such intensity. The air moves with each breath he takes. I have a better chance at survival diving into water than going against this ursu.

"You live." The deep bass of his voice fills my chest more than my ears.

I nod stiffly, not knowing what else to do.

"With your mind intact too," he says, quiet but clear. "Congratulations."

Even through the fear of the ursu before me, I realize it is because of him I made it through the Fog. Showing fear to a man who has helped me is nothing less than rude, but I can't help the instinctual terror I feel.

"Thank you," I manage, unable to look him in the eye.

"Is the Empire's general dead?"

I nod. How does he know I fought the general?

"Good."

Before I can blink, he is gone again. I look south to see him already far in the distance, and it only takes a few seconds before he is out of sight.

I release a staggered breath, finally relaxing. My form is pulled back under control, and I look around at the bodies he left behind. There is no doubt now what caused all the devastation in the city, and it's calming to know he doesn't want to hurt me, but his entire existence just seems so unreasonable. I don't care for the Henosis, but how is someone supposed to fight a monster like that?

From what I've seen so far, the ursu has single-handedly halted the invasion. Soldiers are scattered, petrified he might find them. But why did he take so long to fight back? Couldn't everything have been resolved if he crushed them when they first landed?

He's doing it now—and not holding back—so he must have his reasons. It's just sad things had to reach this point.

Well, now that I know what's killing everyone for certain, I don't need to be so worried. I can try changing my form for the first time and hopefully catch up with the others.

My gaze falls to the remains of the soldiers.

Maybe a quick snack first.

CHAPTER THREE

Flight

Now that I know the cause of destruction in the area has no intent to harm me, I feel more comfortable to stop where I am and actually try to become a bird as Elder Enya did. The more I think about what it might be like to fly, the more excited I get. The usefulness of flying doesn't even need to be stated.

It's a bit of a dumb worry, but I'm a little scared that if I change my form, I might be unable to change back. Like, maybe I stuff up the transformation and get stuck in a weird half-state between my current form and that of a bird. I know it's stupid to even worry about that. I have far too much control over my body for that to ever be possible, but the subtle fear remains.

My legs curl up underneath me and I sit on the grass a distance away from the once gruesome carnage left behind by that giant's massacre. I still don't know his name. If only I'd had the courage to ask after he'd saved me.

Now in a comfortable position, I close my eyes and try to picture the bird that Elder Enya became so long ago. My form flickers, scatters and moves under my will. I focus on the large wings that held Enya aloft, the bright undisguised flames constituting each feather. A weave of fire, rather than a single whole.

My arms morph, tugging and compressing me. I direct the shape in line with my memory, feeling the strange, yet not unpleasant sensation of my limbs twisting away from familiarity. It takes a while for them to fully form, but when they do, the oddness of not having fingers hits me harder than anything else.

I crack an eye open to peek at how different my arms look. In place of my arms are long, fiery feathered wings that look extremely out of place on my normal body. My arm . . . no, wing, moves and bends in places that feel extremely abnormal, like suddenly being able to move my elbow in the opposite direction it used to allow.

I'm not done yet. My eyes shut again and I focus on changing the rest of my body to match my new appendages. I try to change my chest to match that of Elder Enya, but soon find it difficult to transform myself any further. I can't push myself to grow any bigger. But a bird doesn't need to be big. I don't know why I didn't think to become smaller when growing my wings, but they are far too large as is.

With the new direction in mind, I shrink my wings and much of my body while forming my chest, legs, and head into the image of my elder.

Eventually, the reshaping of my body ends and I have the full, indisputable body of the bird from my memory.

I attempt to stand, but it is far different from what I'm used to. I struggle to even figure out how I should place these newly taloned feet underneath me. It feels like I'm a child learning to walk again.

I swing my arms wide, trying to keep my balance as I put my feet under me once again, but am surprised by how big these wings are. They easily touch the ground below me despite standing on my legs. I really shouldn't be surprised; avian anatomy isn't exactly familiar, after all.

I spread my wings wide and find that they far surpass my old height from tip to tip. My new height though, leaves me standing at about my old knee level.

I take a few hesitant steps with my wings pressed against the ground to help my balance. This is so strange, but I've done it. I've fully changed my form like Elder Enya. It took me a long time to do, but I'm proud to finally achieve one thing our tribe always considered an impressive feat.

Giddy with excitement to finally fly, I hop from foot to foot, trying to hurry myself to becoming comfortable with these legs. My balance still avoids me though, and even with a few stumbles, my patience is at its limit. I flap my wings like I've seen Enya do, like I've seen plenty of birds do, trying to will myself into the air.

Worse than being unable to get into the air, my flapping does nothing but send me off balance. My beak dives right into the soil before I can stop myself. I pull my head out with a squawk. Upon hearing myself, I let out a chirrup. I can't speak. I distinctly remember Enya being able to, so why can't I?

Disregarding that for now, I return to my attempts. It never seemed hard for the big birds to take off as long as there was some wind, and there's plenty of breeze today. I spread my wing tips as far apart as I can, breathing in the air as it touches every scalding feather on my body.

I push myself off the ground with a little hop and bring my wings down with strength.

My talons dig back into the soil. I don't rise even slightly. My wings cut through the air rather than pushing against it. Even now, with my wings held against the wind, I don't feel the resistance from the air I expect.

A short chirp drags my beak to the roof of the shed. I surprise myself by twisting my neck far further than I'm used to. A small bird, nowhere near my size, watches me with what must be amusement. Does it think my troubles are funny?

The tiny bird chirps, as if confirming my thought.

I screech at the creature, terrifying both it and myself with how loud I am. The bird scampers off, pumping its wings with gusto.

Even its terrified flying still annoys me. It flies, while I'm stuck on the ground, unable to figure it out.

I glance over my burning feathers, admiring the pattern woven by the flames. Did Elder Enya like hers as well? Is that why she never hid her flames while as a bird?

Wait . . .

I'm an idiot. Of course, I need to actually make my form physical before I can fly. Excitement returning with this new discovery, I try to return to physical and away from ethereal. My body resists me as I slowly force my bird form into physical flame, but it only takes a minute before I succeed. I push it further, trying to control my flames to hide them as I was taught to do, but it's far harder in the body of a bird.

I'm back to being a child, unable to control my flame. Is it really so much harder to do when I'm not in my natural form?

I ignore that for now. I don't think my flames need to be so physical that they can't be seen for me to fly. My wings lift once again and the difference is immediate. The wind rolls around my wings and gives an incredible amount of push. I stumble under the heavy weight the breeze places on me, only barely keeping my feet.

A single push of my wings is enough to launch me off the earth. I beat and catch as much wind as I can. My eyes almost slam shut as I fall to the earth, but I force them wide and aware.

The ground passes below me.

I'm flying.

I let out an involuntary screech at the achievement, interrupting my rhythm and nearly nosediving. My wings steady, locking in place, and bring me into a steady glide.

I fly for hours. The feeling of it is just too good, too freeing. I fly until it becomes as natural as walking and my wings ache from effort. Trying to head up toward the sun had been unfortunately disappointing. If I could get closer to the Eternal Inferno, I would get warmer right? Apparently not. Before long, the temperature drops instead of rising and I can't climb anymore.

I was also hoping it might have been possible to see my family in the Eternal Flame, even if that sounds stupid in hindsight.

After landing back at the shed, I return to my normal body. Surprisingly, it only takes a bit over twenty minutes to change back. Is my binding actually greater than what Elder Enya's was?

It doesn't take me long to set up a place to sleep in the shed and I'm out.

In the morning, I realize I don't want to be the same type of bird as Enya. I want to leave that as a memory of her and take on a form for myself.

The bird I decide on is smaller than the eagle Enya based her form on. Instead of the bulky legs and stocky body, I settle with a much sleeker appearance. It looks rather innocuous despite also being a predator of the skies, which I think is perfect for me.

My version of the bird turns out bigger than its inspired source, but there's only so much I can compress the flames of my body. Plus, I need to carry the huge jacket around with me, so a little extra wing size will help.

After wrapping my new talons around my things, I take to the sky. The breeze through my feathers is indescribable. How could Elder Enya not have spoken of this feeling more often? I've never felt something so freeing before. No one can cage me, trap me, or lock me away while in the air. I'm separate from everything.

My wings angle me north, toward the border between New Vetus and Zadok. At least this time I won't have to travel through the Wailing Woodland, I can just go over.

It doesn't take long before I find the edges of the area Henosis invaded. There are ursu walking around, sifting through the damaged remains of the Empire's weaponry and vehicles. I soon fly over a city, the largest one so far. An army of ursu flood the streets.

This is my first time actually seeing the ursu soldiers, I realize. Back in Morne, I'd seen the recruiters and official soldiers wearing full-body uniforms covering every portion of their bodies except their beefy hands and face. The soldiers below all wear sleeveless vests, the uniformity of it alongside their cohesive conduct clear indicators they are soldiers rather than normal civilians.

There is one thing I notice that tempts my curiosity. I swoop lower to get a better view of the ursu around. My appearance spooks some of the ursu and I note to myself how visible I am to those below. Only a rare few ursu hold any of the guns I've become so used to soldiers carrying. Both Zadok and Henosis had every albanic equipped with their own rifle, so it is strange to see the only guns held by ursu are pilfered. Even then, the weapons are deformed to allow their bulky fingers to reach the triggers.

Instead of guns, most ursu wield hefty weapons I am more familiar with: axes, some massive hammers, but mostly longswords. All of their weapons would be incredibly unwieldy to anyone except those of their height and weight. Seriously, I doubt three of me would be enough to lift the smallest sword.

Around the largest continae I've seen, even larger than the one within the Void Fog, is the heaviest congregation of ursu military. They swarm the open area like an aggravated ant colony. While most soldiers stand in orderly lines, there are many cheerful murmurs from the crowd as they chatter amongst themselves.

The attitude between a few arguing men at the foot of the continae is far more tense and distressed than the lax air of those surrounding them. It's plainly obvious that these ursu are the ones in charge. The way they hold themselves is enough of an indication, even while arguing they exude an unwavering confidence.

I'm tempted to go lower and hear what is being said, but there are already far too many eyes on me than I'm comfortable with. I don't want the big guy to have any reason to come after me and the best way to do that is to avoid the ursu as much as I can.

Fortunately, that is easy when you can fly right over them.

Now that I have wings, my travel speed is almost a nonissue. While I can't reach the speed that trains can manage, I'll be able to move around at unthinkable speed. It shouldn't take me more than a few days to reach the river border of Zadok.

Time I can use to get my voice to work in this form.

CHAPTER FOUR

Cleithrophobia

It took longer than learning to fly, but my voice is finally recognizable through my beak. Strangely, the sound of my voice is entirely determined by the shape of my throat and mouth. It was easy to replace the bird throat with what felt more natural, but it became a problem trying to speak without a mouth and lips.

Of course, I tried switching my beak back with a mouth, but that made flying far too annoying. The beak is surprisingly good at cutting through the air. Instead, I had to change my throat and tongue over the course of a few days until I felt comfortable that my voice was mostly identical to normal.

I now also have the ability to make my voice incredibly high or low pitch too, so that's fun. I might get a good scare out of someone one day. Leslie is definitely going to be my first target.

While I'm worried about how I might find the others, I'm excited to reunite with them. I know where they were planning to go, so as long as they didn't make any major deviations, I have a good idea where to start.

Amongst the northern states, there are two that border the Zadok Kingdom: the Kingdom of Joiak and the Vanguard. Joiak is a small nation that separated from Zadok a few generations ago. Supposedly, the kingdom doesn't discriminate against those with darker hair. The Vanguard, alternatively, is a nation with a well-known hatred for the Theocracy and is open to any immigrants that flee north.

That's about the limit of what I know, but Ash and the others were heading to the Kingdom of Joiak last time we were together. It's not much to go on, I know, but I'm feeling inexplicably confident I will find them. If I can follow their trail, surely someone will recognize their description.

After only a few days of flying—with proper nights of rest—I reach the river I've been looking for. With the number of ursu in these lands, it is obvious I'm in the west, but it is still relieving not to see the ocean. I may be able to fly now, but there isn't a chance I'm going over such a large body of water.

The Wailing Woodland never appeared. I guess it doesn't span the northern border as I'd mistakenly assumed.

I wonder what happened to the Zadokans that attacked the ursu. There was no sight of them in the areas I passed, so I can't imagine their invasion was successful. Did they retreat or were they slaughtered like the Henosis?

I look west along the river. There is no reason for me to pass the fort like last time. I can just glide over the river now, after all. But I want to see Finn again. I didn't realize it at the time, but he put his job on the line to help me out when he did. The reaction when the others in the caravan thought I was a darker-haired albanic was telling.

I want to see him and while I might lose a bit of time catching up with Leslie and the others, I am already a month or so behind them. A quick detour will hardly matter.

My wings sweep me west. I'm heading back to the original route through Zadok.

It takes a day to reach the familiar fort built over the river. Surprisingly, I find no other forts along the river. There are a few watchtowers, but even they are sparse.

My talons press down within the grass and I have to pull back on the fire that tries to spread from my touch. I could have flown right into the fort, but it will take me almost twenty minutes to change back and I'm not comfortable doing so around so many people.

I stand and walk toward the gate I passed only a few months ago. It feels like so much more time passed than reality. The building is the same, but even from a distance out I can tell there are nowhere near the number of guards manning the fort as before. There are none at the top of the walls and only two wait before me.

As I approach the final distance, the guards take longer than they probably should to notice me. Too busy talking between themselves.

"—ole just up and left. Ya think they'd notice if I took my vacation early?" I catch the end of their conversation.

I clear my throat. "Excuse me. Is Finn still around?"

The man who spoke flinches away from me with an "eek" while the other man looks me dead-on with annoyed eyes.

The first guard turns and lifts his musket right in my face. My eyes narrow at the threat and I frown toward the frightened man, who takes a hurried step back, keeping his gun pointed right between my eyes.

I'm about to step forward and burn the damn weapon out of his hands before his partner beats me to it. He grabs the gun by its barrel and jerks it out of his hands.

"I knew you were incompetent, but I never would have guessed you'd hold your weapon at a child."

"Oi! Give that back!"

The guard that snatched the weapon doesn't, instead he turns to me and furrows his brows.

"What's a child doing out here all alone anyway? Where did you come from?" His eyes flicker over my jacket—which is obviously too large for even an adult albanic—and to my hair, the blue not hidden by dirt this time.

I can understand his suspicions, but this time I don't have any intention to hide what I am.

My hair engulfs in a bright orange fire. I want them to know what I am, but there is no need to go against the standards of my tribe too much. Just enough that they'll know my hair color doesn't matter.

I successfully remove his suspicions. Unfortunately, they are replaced with hostility. He hefts his own gun right in the same position his partner did not a moment ago.

Irritated, I send out a quick burst to incinerate the weapon in his hand. Too late. The bullet pierces right through my head before I can burn the gun out of his hands. I feel a slight tingle as the shrapnel piece passes through me, but I'm left otherwise unaffected.

He throws away the weapon he's holding and lifts the one he snatched from the other guard. I didn't leave that weapon alone though, the trigger already red hot by the time he lifts his weapon. A sizzling finger is all he's left with as he jerks the second weapon away before even firing a shot.

"Back off," I growl.

My eyes flick to the first guard who stands there stunned, then back to the one who shot me. He's already tried to kill me twice; once more, and I won't be as forgiving.

I continue glaring and hold my ground as the man grabs at a knife on his belt.

"Hold! Stand down!" a familiar voice shouts, but the man before me doesn't hear.

He is just about to make his last mistake. My flames roil, prepared to end his existence the moment he touches me. But he doesn't reach me. His partner—the one who, until now, has done nothing but stand stiff after his own gun was snatched—grabs the albanic under the arms and pulls him away from me.

The man struggles against his restraint. "What are you doing? Let me go! Don't you see one of Chernobog's spawn right in front of you?"

Behind the two struggling guards, Finn and a couple of others run, wielding their own guns. He looks over me and I'm a bit disappointed he shows no recognition. I trust the situation will be handled properly now though, so I pull back on my primed fire, leaving only my hair aflame. That calms him and the guards beside him down enough that he turns his attention away from me.

"What the fuck do you think you are doing, firing against protocol?" Finn demands from the man still being restrained.

The guards flanking Finn watch me like hawks as he interrogates the guard.

"It's one of Chernobog's. Fuck protocol, it needs to die."

Finn glances over at me. "I don't remember fire ever being a part of Chernobog's domain. Would that not fall under the category of light rather than darkness?" His eyes widen as he looks over me. "Wait, Solvei?"

I give him a small wave. It's nice to know he remembers me.

Finn flicks his attention right back to the guard who shot me. "Even if there was one of Chernobog's spawn present, why did you not follow protocol and sound the alarm while they were still far off?" His eyes bear into the younger albanic still holding the man. "You weren't doing your job, were you?"

The young albanic turns to look away from Finn while his partner is indignant. "Fuck you, Finnigan! Bastards should've left me in charge instead. I've been doing this too long to be stuck on fucking gate duty."

"Calm yourself or I'll have you locked in the cells for the next week."

He scoffs. "You can't do that. This place can't function if you lose any more veterans."

"Sure I can. You three, take him to a cell. I'll deal with this one," Finn says and points a thumb at me.

"Wait, no. Stop!"

As they hurry to take him away, Finn calls after them, "And kid, don't think I've forgotten the negligence of your duty."

Finally free, Finn turns to me. "Y'know, it would have made my job so much easier last time if I'd known you weren't albanic."

"How so?" I ask.

"It's a strange thing. I can lose social status simply talking to a dark-haired child, but it becomes a complete non-problem if that child isn't albanic." He shakes his head. "So, you're an áed, right? Why come back here?"

"Yeah. I wanted to stop by and thank you for the risk you took helping me move to Kelton."

"Kelton? Gavin didn't take you to Serron?" he asks.

"No. He tossed me out of the caravan when found out how dark my hair was."

Finn kicked at the stone beneath his feet. "That bastard. He owed me." He glanced back at my still burning hair, reminding me to take control of myself again. "Like I said before, this would have all been solved if you hadn't pretended to be one of us. It's doubtful you could have integrated well in Zadok, but nobody would have stopped you moving to the northern states. We get the rare non-albanic trader through every now and then and they rarely have issues, far as I know. Well, so long as they're not ursu."

With those four other guards now out of sight, I realize that there really aren't many others around. Last time, the area within the fort was teeming with life, now it feels almost as empty as the ghost towns of New Vetus.

"Where is everyone?"

Finn looks around and sighs. "Our army was slaughtered in the invasion, barely a hundred returned. All the albanics in command of the fort fled, leaving the common guard to defend the border. Plenty of those deserted as well." He shakes his head before continuing. "Come. I'll get you something to drink while we talk out of the cold."

I follow him to the barracks. "No drink, thanks. But I'll have a snack if you've got anything."

"Dwight! Man the gate," Finn shouts across the courtyard before opening the door for me.

As I step through the threshold into the barracks, I'm overcome with a sudden inexplicable anxiety. My fingers tremble as I look around at the entrapping walls that seem far too close. Unsure why I feel this way, I take another step into the building, ignoring the tension in my chest.

The soft click of the door closing behind me changes everything. The trembling of my fingers spread across my entire body. Tightness in my chest grows until I'm choking, unable to breathe. I take in ragged gasps as my eyes flicker around me. Nothing has changed around me, but I can't contain the overwhelming fear of being trapped.

The brickwork walls are nothing but the bars of my cage. I'm trapped again. How did this happen? How am I here?

"Let me out! Let me out!" I slam my body against the door of this new cage, amplifying my heat until the handle and hinges melt under my assault.

I tumble out into open air again. On hands and knees, I scramble away from the cage they tried to trap me in.

I flop onto my back and look up at the sky. Each breath is a struggle and I can't get enough air with each pant. Numbness fills my limbs as they continue to shiver.

Soon, I get a hold of my breathing and my body stops trembling. It doesn't feel real. This feels like a nightmare. The blue of the sky distracts me from everything around and I lose myself in the sight of the Eternal Inferno. The blazing orb in the sky seems so inviting and terrifying all at once.

"Solvei!" I finally realize my name has been called a few times now.

Finn is standing over me, keeping some distance, but his voice is worried and I can't comprehend why.

"Solvei. You need to calm down and stop your fire."

What? I look around and see myself, the front door of the barracks, and much of the ground between us engulfed in an orange flame. When did that happen? I quickly extinguish it all before anything else can burn.

Finn kneels beside me, but still hesitates to come too close. My gaze turns back to the door, realizing for the first time that it's no longer attached to the barracks. It takes a few more moments for me to truly comprehend what happened. I panicked? I felt more fear than ever and lost control.

It is humiliating. Quickly rising to my knees, I stare at the ground between us.

"I'm sorry. I don't know what happened."

I don't understand. Why did I react like that? I've been through so much already, shouldn't I be immune to fear by now? Even looking back, I don't really know what I was so scared of. I just felt a nonsensical terror of suffocation and entrapment.

"Are you okay? Have you calmed?" Finn asks.

I nod, unwilling to meet his eye through the embarrassment of the display.

"Come, let's get you something to eat and a place to relax."

CHAPTER FIVE

Revisiting the Scar

I bite down on the dry biscuit and enjoy the feeling of it almost evaporating in my mouth. While waiting at the side of the barracks for Finn to return, I try to calm my trembling fingers. I no longer feel like I'm trapped and unable to escape, but my body refuses to calm down.

When Finn handed me a tin of his biscuits, my sizzling skin melted the paint right off the lid. He told me not to worry, but I still feel bad about it.

Thinking about what happened is almost as terrifying as the experience itself. I'd lost control of my body and thoughts. I'd gone into a panic trying to get out and I was lucky I hadn't hurt Finn in my haste to burn through the door.

Footsteps drag me out of my funk, and I look up at Finn.

"You feeling better now?" he asks as he sits beside me.

"Yep, your biscuits taste great." I hold my hands together to hide the shaking. "Sorry about the door. I really don't know why I acted like that."

"Don't worry about it. One of the boys will have it fixed up by the end of the day."

We sit in silence while I eat another biscuit from the tin. Eventually, Finn speaks. "What do you plan to do now? I don't know how long you've been outside Zadok, but the failed invasion has sent everyone mad. It'll be impossible to get through the wall now. I'm sorry, but I do not know where you can go."

"I'm gonna find my friends in the northern states."

Finn turns to me with furrowed brows. "That's going to be impossible.

There's no way north that doesn't have you passing the wall or through the Theocracy."

I fail to suppress my smirk. Finn is missing one small little detail.

"Oh, it'll be easy. I'll just fly over." I smile wide at him, knowing how impossible the idea of flying would have been two weeks ago.

"Fly? What?" He blinks at me.

"Yep. I can fly now!" I might have even transformed right there. Unfortunately, it still takes me a while to switch forms, so it'll be weird to wait around for fifteen minutes to show off.

"Right . . ."

What? He doesn't believe me, does he? Well, I wanted to avoid this, but I guess there's no choice now.

"Give me a few minutes and I'll prove it."

My body returns to the flickering of flame as I morph back into my falcon form.

"What are you doing?" Finn rises to his feet and takes a step away from my sudden blazing body.

He's unnecessarily worried. Really, it still surprises me how much these people are startled by a tiny bit of fire. It's not like I'm hurting myself. I need to remember fire is like water to them, just the presence can be enough to make them nervous.

A few minutes of awkward silence passes before the process is done, and my voice comes back.

"See? Easy." I flap my wings and fly up to sit on the roof of the barracks. "I can get over that wall, no issue."

"Huh," is all Finn can manage as he stares up at me.

In this form, I'm still readily visible; flames not being the stealthiest of things to have feathers made of. The only other guard in the courtyard other than Finn stares with a slack jaw. It's probably bad to feel this way, but I enjoy their awed looks as they observe the form I put so much effort into crafting.

"Right, well, that explains how you appeared south without passing through the fort."

"Ah, no. I only learned to do this a few days ago. Some things happened and I got tangled in the war in New Vetus." I don't want to go into detail about what happened, so I only give him a vague explanation.

"Thank you for your help, Finn. And thanks for the biscuits, they're tasty," I say from my ledge.

Finn finally snaps out of his daze. "Solvei, before you go, I should tell you it'll be best if you don't return to this fort. The ursu are bound to invade us in the coming days and when that happens, there is little chance this place will remain safe."

"You will get out before then, right?" I ask, now worried about his safety.

He smiles at me and nods. "Be careful out there, Solvei."

I smile back and wave goodbye, before realizing I can't smile and my wing probably makes the motion look odd.

"See ya." With a sweep of my wings, I'm once more soaring through the air. The wind against my feathers calming the remnant trembles.

It'll be annoying, but I might have to avoid going inside buildings again in case I have another panic attack like that. Rainy days are going to be miserable.

Shaking my head to clear the thoughts, I angle north, ready to fly as far as I can before night hits.

The wall is a sight to see. I never actually got a look at it when I was in Kelton last, but now that I have a literal bird's-eye view, it's thoroughly impressive. The stone wall extends as far as I can see from west to east.

Unlike the fort, the wall is not lacking in soldiers. It's almost to an excessive degree considering they had less than ten albanics manning the fort.

I glide over it with hardly a flap. It's almost anticlimactic how easy it is considering the past difficulty we had getting through. Would I be able to carry them over now? I doubted it. Even with the largest wingspan I can make, I'll probably not come close to lifting another person. Also, considering I don't have full control over my flames in this form, it'd be hard to say if I can refrain from burning them.

With the sun setting, I opt to search for a place to rest before I become even more visible in the sky than I already am.

I drop into a dive. The stables approach with thrilling speed. I pull up at the last moment and thread myself through a gap above a door. A pholo resting within startles at my sudden appearance, shrieking through the enclosed space. I land on a wooden beam and motion for it to calm down.

Maybe it was stupid to fly in without checking first, but the exhilaration of diving and my prioritization of not letting my sleeping space be discovered encouraged me to disregard my usual cautiousness.

The pholo won't calm down, so I launch myself back in the air before anyone can come looking. For now, I'm hidden well enough against the reds and yellows painting the sky from the setting sun, but if I take too long, I'll be a beacon to all as I try to find a place to nap.

I find another open air stable, this time with no pholos ready to screech my presence to all around.

Comforted by the many openings in the surrounding walls, I settle down and revert my form. As great as flying feels, being a bird just doesn't feel as natural as my normal form.

I curl up on a pile of straw, heating myself to ward off the cold. The days are getting colder. Soon, winter will hit with full force and I'll feel nothing but the lethargy as with most years.

I used to get sick every winter with my tribe, but hopefully I'm strong enough now that I won't need to worry. Even if I don't get sick, I still hope to find my friends before the torpid month arrives.

Winter was usually the only time in a year we would stop traveling as a tribe. We would set up with resources stockpiled in the months prior and rest. To keep our body temperatures from plummeting through winter, we would never leave our gers, sharing the warmth and limiting energy consumption.

I could always push through the cold with my own strength, but the amount of food I need to consume would multiply. With so many resources around, it won't be a problem, but I'd rather be with the others before the fatigue sets in.

Well, I still have a few weeks before the worst of the chill hits. That should be plenty of time.

The scar left by the Void Fog is quite the sight. From high above, I can see the extensive basin now half-drowned in water. Many of the edges where the Fog touched must have collapsed and slid into the scar, filling the once smooth surface with debris and loose rock. The remains of people's homes are visible amongst the stone and dirt.

I glide over the vast newborn canyon toward the stream of water trickling over the ledge. The creek where I last saw my friends comes into view. While I know there is little chance I'll find anything left behind of them, I still want to try.

The area where we separated was consumed by the Fog, but I fly low over the edge looking for something. I don't even know what I'm looking for. Old tracks in the ground, or maybe one of them dropped something that'll let me know they weren't consumed as well. After such a long time has passed, there is probably nothing to be found, especially considering I don't know exactly where they ran after we split.

A congregation of albanic in my peripheral vision pulls my attention from scouring the ground. Many stand around a sculpted wooden pillar in silence. Around them are thousands of tents. These tents aren't like the large circular gers I'm used to, instead, they are small things, at most enough to house two people. The triangular tarps look like they will topple with the slightest gust.

I glide down and land on the branch of a tree. Close enough to see, but hopefully hidden by the foliage.

An albanic approaches the pillar holding a ring of carved wood. They lift the ring and link it to a chain of near identical rings circling the pillar. Once she twists the ring into place, the albanic bows her head and turns to the rest. As she returns, another steps forward and does the same.

It's an odd thing, witnessing the albanic's funeral. That is what this is, without a doubt. The solemnity. The silence. The emotion that permeates the air. Nothing else brings that same feeling. It is almost enough to have me tearing up even though I don't know whom they mourn, simply because of the memories it dredges from within.

The people they mourn. Were they devoured by the Void Fog as well? Are they dead, or simply still trapped within?

Do these people even know it's possible their family might still be alive?

Well, if they don't, it's probably for the best. If they haven't escaped yet, it's not likely freedom will come to them soon.

My wings launch me off my perch and I fly over the tents. I consider transforming to ask around, but it'll take too long to do so and switch back for such a low chance that someone might have seen them.

I spot someone pointing up toward me and shouting to her neighbors. Well, it was bound to happen sooner or later. They've already spotted me, I might as well ask if they've seen Ash and the others.

I angle my wings to bring me down until I land on a table only a few meters from the woman. Her eyes are wide and staring as she backs up a few steps from me.

"Hi," I say. "Have you seen a group of . . . uh." I realize I didn't think about how I could describe them that might differentiate them from any other albanic in the area. "Did you see a lady traveling with a group of teenagers about a month ago?"

Unfortunately, the woman doesn't respond, her eyes widening further than I thought was possible. I'm about to ask again when a man runs around the side of a tent with a shovel and stands before the woman.

"Shoo, fowl. Shoo." He swings his shovel at me, but doesn't get close.

Fowl? Did he just call me a chicken? I look down at my carefully crafted fiery plumage. I'm obviously a falcon, can't he see that? A huff comes out of my beak as I glare at the man. I'm not a chicken.

Flames roil across my body at the indignation. I notice it happen and immediately clamp down on the annoyance I feel. Really, my control suffers when I'm not in my base form. It's not even worth getting angry about, anyway.

A sigh escapes me before I ask again to the gathering crowd. "About a month ago, did anyone see a group of teenagers and a woman walking north from here? It would have been right after the Void Fog showed up."

The silence following my words lasts only a moment before the raucous chatter starts. Amongst the conversations, the first woman I talked to finally gathers her wits and steps forward past the man with the shovel.

"Uh, there were many people who moved in and out of the town at the time, so it'll be hard to say," she says. "Miss birdie, what are you?"

"Miss birdie," I repeat under my breath. She could at least refer to me as something a bit cooler than that. Anyway, how often will I have to repeat that I'm an áed? I can imagine it'll be a lot considering that most who know of us—which there won't be many if my time in Kelton is indicative—don't know we can shift shapes. Elder Enya spent decades to do this much and I'm very much an oddity now that I think about it.

So instead, I want to have a bit of fun. "What do you think I am?" I ask with as smug of a tone as I can manage.

She and many of the others around gape at me, calming much of the chatter.

"You can't be, can you? One of his messengers?"

I have no idea what she's talking about, but it looks like they took the bait and took a—probably wrong—guess about what I am. I try to exude an air that I'm impressed they figured it out. Even if I'm not sure what they figured out.

Suddenly, each of them kneel before me with lowered heads.

Uh . . . that's a bit more than I expected.

I expected them to assume I was some animal that learned to talk, or at worst, think I was some monstrous creature. I was prepared to fly away if they got aggressive, but I wasn't prepared for this. Blatant worship. What exactly do they think I am?

"Oh, Belobog's messenger. Thank you for blessing us after such a disaster. It means the world to us that we remain in his heart."

"Uh . . ." What do I do? I can't tell them I'm not who they think I am; they'd be crushed. Or pissed.

"Well, I should be going. There's somewhere I need to be." I try to brush them off and take to the skies again.

"Wait," one of them calls. A middle-aged man with a strong build throws himself before me. "Before you leave, please take care of the void-touched. We can't reach our grain and the albicants refuse to send the army."

Void-touched?

"I really should be going, though," I say, trying not to be pulled into their mess. The words barely leave my beak with how limited the truth of them is.

Many more of the albanic before me throw themselves at my feet . . . talons. "Please," they plead, almost in sync.

Looking over them I can't help but feel sympathetic. I remember a time when I wished I was given a helping hand, a magic solution to my problems. I also remember my trust being betrayed. Gloria taking advantage of me taught me a valuable lesson; I'm not about to trust these people farther than I can throw them.

On the other hand, Ash and the others never let me down when I thought they would, so maybe it'll be fine to help just a little. I'll fly off as soon as something suspicious happens.

Really, the only reason I'm even considering this is that I don't have to worry so much about getting hurt anymore. Unless whatever it is has the same strange sword the general had, I'll be fine.

"What is a void-touched?"

CHAPTER SIX

Void-Touched

I really shouldn't have offered to help, but I felt this void-touched was something I needed to see. I have my suspicions of what it might be, especially as it appeared after the Void Fog left.

I fly low through the series of silos and warehouses. The albanics said the creature should be in the area. They spotted it a few times, but the townsfolk are too wary to approach. Considering how quick they were to slap a title of divine messenger on me, I'm not putting any confidence in the fearful descriptors of the being. For all I trust these people's judgment, the creature might be a wild dog or something.

Wary as I am of these albanics, I turn to watch them poking their heads over their makeshift barricade. Constructed of broken furniture and miscellaneous scrap, I doubt the short wall could stop anything they couldn't fight off themselves.

I should probably be annoyed that they are willing to let me go, yet don't take a step out themselves. They are quick to risk my life while they cower where they think it's safe. But if anything, I'm relieved. They couldn't do anything to me if they tried, but I still prefer not to have them following me.

The first sign that I'm dealing with something stronger than a mangy wild dog is the hole in the wall of the grain silo below. The lack of damage in this part of town makes it stand out.

I fly closer, careful of anything that might jump out at me. My caution is for nought as the silo is empty. A thin carpet of grain litters the ground both inside and around the silo.

A crash echoes through the deserted area. I regain height and glide toward the noise. It's not long before I come across what looks like a normal albanic, if more filthy than I've ever seen. The albanic, a woman, is hunched over and tears into a barrel with vigor.

As I circle above, I notice she's skin and bone. Ragged and torn cloth barely cling to her emaciated form. Rotten vegetables fall around her as she gorges on the contents of the barrel. Her arms continue to shove handfuls into her face.

I land on the branch of a tree behind the albanic. I thought I was quiet, but obviously not enough; she turns to me the moment my talons dig into wood. The creature that locks eyes with me is anything but one of the albanic. Despite the similar hair and body, there is no way that face and chest could be from the same race.

The creature's mouth nearly splits her head in half it is so wide. A fat tongue hangs between razor-sharp teeth. The most horrific part is that her chest is open, like her ribcage was pulled apart as if it was a set of doors. Crushed paste of half-digested vegetables mixed with a black substance pours out of the disgusting chest cavity.

There is no intelligence in her eyes. No comprehension of the pain she should feel. Only an insatiable hunger. Eyes filled with gluttony that judge whether I'm worth eating.

She turns back to the barrel before her, completely ignoring me. I guess she doesn't think fire will taste good. Wait, can she even comprehend what fire is? No, that doesn't matter. What matters is I've found the void-touched.

It's hard to look at the woman as she continues to force food down her throat. Not only because the sight is quite gruesome, but because of the idea I could have become like this. This is what happens to someone that doesn't focus their psyche when the hooks of the Void Fog change you. I can't pretend this creature is anything else. I can tell just by looking.

The Fog twisted any sentience away from her when it tore her open, looking for her strongest desire. The more I think about it, the sadder her situation must have been. Her scarily skinny body, her unending hunger, and even the changes to her mouth. She must have been starving before her changes; hunger was the desire the Void Fog latched onto.

If I had to guess, the changes made to her didn't include this tear in her torso. No. After the Fog had its way with her, she was left with such intense cravings that she tore her own chest open from the amount she consumed.

I can't help but picture myself in a similar position, had I not known to focus my mind, to tie my thoughts together. I really owe that giant ursu a lot.

Time passes as I struggle to figure out what to do. The pity I hold for the former albanic stops me from just leaving, but I'm unsure of what I can do to help her. With the damage to her chest, I can't imagine she'll live for long. Actually, I'm surprised she's still moving.

The moment she tries to eat the gruel that fell out of her own cavity is the moment I find my resolve. I can't let her continue like this. It's cruel.

My body morphs back to normal before I incinerate her body. She hardly reacts as her body burns away, simply continuing to gorge until her body simply doesn't let her anymore.

Like the other creatures within the Void Fog, her body is filled to the brim with energy, but there is no pleasure in consuming it. She isn't a soldier, nor has she done anything to deserve such a fate. Like myself and the other áed, she was brought into this without a say.

When nothing of her remains, I retake my falcon form and fly north again. As I fly over the heads of the albanics crowding the barricade, I can't help but be frustrated by their actions. Or lack thereof. The void-touched woman was in a pitiful state, but there was hardly much for them to fear. If they were courageous enough to approach her, they might have ended her suffering sooner.

I don't talk to them again, not in the mood to humor their misunderstanding. They'll have to find the courage to check the area themselves.

So I set my sights on the northern states, ready to find my friends. I kind of expected it, but there is nothing in the area to clue me to their presence. I'll have to trust that they went the same way we initially agreed on.

The border between Zadok and Joiak is a rocky expanse littered with canyons, valleys, and not a touch of arable land for leagues. Traversal through this geography must be a nightmare. The only path between the countries winds back and forth so often I wouldn't be surprised if one had to walk four times the distance I need to fly.

Have I mentioned how happy I am I can fly?

There is a surprising contrast between the northern and southern borders of Zadok. Down south near New Vetus, there is an incredibly dense population and defenses spanning the entire border. The north . . . lacks all of that. Villages are common enough in the countryside until the rocky valleys start, but from there all life peters out.

I don't spot a single defensive fortification along the northern areas I pass. It's rather odd. I guess they don't expect any attacks from Joiak. Or, more likely, they are just petrified of an ursu invasion. Not that I can imagine the ursu being ready for any attack in the near future.

Eventually, I come across signs of life again. Albanics walk the path below with their pholos laden with supplies. Roadside buildings gradually appear. Nothing more than traveler's rests, yet enough to signal that I'm close to Joiak.

As I close in on the first city of the nation, doubts infiltrate my thoughts. What if they never made it here? What if they got stuck in Zadok? Will I even be able to find them if they are in the city before me?

The city itself is hugged by the walls of a canyon, buildings crowd the limited space. They might be anywhere in the thousands of structures, or maybe they've already moved on. There is no way to know.

People waiting for entry flood the dirt road leading to the gates of the city. I guess my friends and I aren't the only ones wanting to get out of Zadok.

I fly back until I find a crevice in the rock out of sight and quickly change forms. The temptation to fly straight into the city is strong, but the people at the front gate processing the arrivals are the people most likely to have seen my friends.

With a glance over my form, I realize I forgot to find new clothes while I was passing through Zadok. The ones I have are in shreds, but at least I can wrap myself in the ursu coat. I'll have to find something more presentable in the city. Hopefully, they'll have a way for me to earn it without gid. Money is annoying when you don't have any.

Worst case, thievery always works.

As I approach the queue before the gate, a few albanics cast curious glances toward me, but refrain from approaching. I'm controlling my form so flames aren't visible, but I haven't doused my hair in filth, so the blue strands are apparent to any who look. To people with only white and shades of gray, I'm sure even that is odd.

I'm not about to hide what I am anymore, but if they can't tell by my appearance, then that's on them.

It took well over an hour before it was finally my turn to be led through. I follow a woman wearing a similar uniform to the guards in Zadok, but without the adorning weapons. She leaves her gray hair on open display, which leaves many of the crowd staring, obviously not used to the visage. I'm taken through an almost identical process to what I experienced when first entering Zadok, garnering at most a raised eyebrow when she asked about my race.

When she is done asking all her questions, I jump in to ask about my friends before she can run off to the next person to be processed.

"There's been a lot come through since the Zadok Kingdom's failed invasion. A surprising amount of high purity, too. There are many groups that match what you describe, so I can't say definitively where they might be now," the woman says, to my disappointment. "Though if they were struggling for gid when they arrived, your best bet is the worker's association."

It's not assured, but at least I have something to go on now. After thanking the woman, I rush down the street and ask the first person I see where the association is.

Soon, I walk through the large open doors of the worker's association, grateful that they remain open behind me and are one of many entrances left unblocked. The place is busy. Five albanics sit behind desks attending to the many people queuing before them.

Great, another waiting game. I just want to find them already and these interruptions are slowing me down. I complain and moan within my mind, but line up anyway. The stress that the doors might close at any moment has me checking behind myself repeatedly.

As I look around, I'm quick to notice that I'm not the only non-albanic waiting. In the line to my left is an odd lanky-looking being. Its short, round, and headless torso is held above the heads of the surrounding albanics by six long, flexible limbs protruding from its sides.

I'm not the only one staring either. It's such an odd shape for a creature and its limbs move with a fluidity that suggests a lack of bones. The being approaches the counter and speaks to the lady behind the counter. His voice is obviously male, but he has a strange, floaty speech pattern.

A cough snaps me back to the lady before me and I realize I'm at the front of the line and the woman before me is waiting expectantly. I step forward and try to pretend like I'm not embarrassed about being caught staring, but the raised edge of the woman's mouth makes me doubt my success.

"Hi. Did you see a group of teenagers come here a few weeks ago? Two girls and three boys, two of them twins."

"Friends of yours?" she asks. I nod and she flicks through the book before her. "What are their names?"

"Ash, Leslie, Kerry, and the twins are Demi and Medi."

She takes a moment to turn the pages. "Ah, here we are. Hired by Mr. Marshall's textile mill. They left for Valtin sixteen days ago."

They were here? They were actually here!

"Where is Valtin?" I ask, almost bouncing on my toes.

"It's four days' travel. Take the northern city exit and follow the road west. Good luck finding them."

I thank the woman and rush out of the building. It's so relieving to hear they got out safely. I had refused the possibility that the Fog had grasped them, but now that I know they reached Joiak, it is a weight off my mind.

In my excitement, I almost morph into a falcon right there and then, disregarding all those around. Almost. I still need to get replacement clothes, then I can go reunite with my friends.

I hope they are being treated well by Mr. Marshall.

CHAPTER SEVEN

Mr. Marshall's Mill I

Valtin is burning. Or at least that's what it looks like from a distance. Massive plumes of dark smoke rise over the city. As I fly closer, it becomes apparent the smoke comes from many towers spread through the city, rather than any actual fire.

The nearer I get, the fouler the stench of the air becomes. I would usually be attracted to the scent of burning coal, but there is something attached to the odor that makes me cringe in disgust.

It only took me a few hours to fly here. The winding roads continue through the nation, not limited to the border at the edge of Zadok. Mountainous landscape is hardly an issue when you can fly.

A train's horn blares as it departs the city, heading north through a tunnel dug in the mountainside. Didn't the ursu claim to have created the train? How did they get their hands on it so far north? Wait, the Henosis had a perfect understanding of how to use them. Did they have them too?

I shake my head. It hardly matters if the ursu created the trains or not. I'm here to find my friends.

As I land on the ledge of a building, I look down on the people walking the dark streets. Albanics are still the predominant species, but there are others now. I spot a few of those strange six-limbed creatures and several other beings completely alien to me.

Near constant banging reverberates from all around, overwhelming the sounds common in other populated cities.

Under the smoke darkened sky, I'm far more visible than I want to be. Before anyone spots me, I find a secluded place and regain my legs.

I brush my hand against the wall of the alley as I come out, only to bring back a thick layer of black muck. I scorch the lingering substance off my hand and look up at the wall it came from. The entire building is coated in it. Not just that, every building is. All right, no touching the walls then. I look down at the black road before me. Not the ground either.

This is hardly what I imagined after all that talk of a better place to live than the dredges of Zadok.

It took a while to find Mr. Marshall's mill. The people on the street weren't particularly willing to help, often ignoring my questions outright. Eventually, I got an answer and made my way to one of the larger factories in the area. A long brickwork building with two massive chimneys on each side.

The air reeks with an intensifying musk as I close in on the mill. I don't think I've ever smelled something I want to avoid burning as much as whatever is causing this stench. It's like something rotten, but at least I would be fine with burning a decaying substance. This just makes me retch.

I try to ignore the scent as I walk through the gate into the premises. The gate guards barely pay me any mind. I find it odd that they sit facing the mill rather than outward, but I'm not here to judge how they do their job.

As I approach the entry where many people, adults and kids alike, regularly pass through a narrow door, I feel tension rise within my chest. It's the same as back at Finn's fort. An irritating, illogical fear that I'll be trapped once I walk inside the enclosed space of the building.

I stand there, garnering stares from the passing workers as I bemoan the ridiculousness of being unable to walk into the building. The door is made of wood; there's no way it could stop me if I want to leave. I try to reason with myself, but the tension doesn't disappear as I watch the door.

"Solvei? Solvei!" Before I can turn to the voice, I'm tackled from behind.

"Oh, Belobog, I'm so glad you're okay. We thought the worst when you never caught up to us." It's Kerry.

I'm so happy to see her again. To know she is safe brings a smile to my face and I hug her back.

"C'mon, you have to see the others."

Kerry pulls me by the arm around the back of the textile mill toward a small outbuilding in the corner of the fenced property. A couple meters from the door, I have to tug at her arm to stop her from bringing me any closer.

"Can you bring them out here? Please?" I ask, rubbing at my forearm.

She gives me a confused look before agreeing and entering through the door. In the moment I have to look through the gap, I'm horrified by the conditions within. Dozens of kids lay beside each other in the cramped confines of what I'd thought of as a storage shed. Most of them look no older than eight or nine.

It's the filth inside that shocks me the most. That black muck I've seen through town is caked on every surface within. It'd be cleaner if they slept outside.

I don't have to wait long. Soon, they are rushing outside. Even the twins, who I assumed didn't really care for me, considering our lack of interaction. I'm quick to notice Leslie isn't there, and while Ash and the twins hurry to crowd me, they look exhausted. Filthy too.

"Solvei? You're actually okay? Thank Be—"

"We knew you weren't dead!" "We knew you were alive!" the twins say together as they crush me between them.

My smile is irremovable as we reunite. I feel bad that I thought they didn't care. It's a bit difficult to return the hug of the two taller boys, but I manage.

"You have to tell us what happened. Where have you been?" Ash speaks over the teary eyes of the twins.

I nod to him. "I will, but I want Leslie to be with us first. Where is she?"

The joy of the reunion wipes off his face, instead replaced by fatigue. His eyelids droop and arms flop at his side as he looks toward the main building.

"She's still working. They gave her more hours for an . . . outburst of hers a few days ago." His eyes fall back on me before he frowns. "You should probably leave while you still can."

"What are you talking about, Ash? If anyone can help us out of here, it's Solvei." Kerry glares at him before turning to me. "Right Solvei?"

I look between them, slightly confused.

Ash is about to respond, but is interrupted by another kid coming out through the door. "I know you lot are new, but you should really get inside before the overlooker comes out with his cane."

The girl, likely the same age as me, has deep discoloration around her eye. Deep hues of purple and red dye the skin above her cheekbones. As I look closer over her body, I spot many other causes for concern. Her body is skinny, far too much to be healthy. Her fingers have a similar level of bruising to her eye. Scabs and scars cover each digit.

"Okay. We're coming," Ash says as he, Kerry, and the twins move back inside.

I lower my eyes to each of my friends' hands, seeing much of the same bruising along their fingers. My jaw clenches and I have to focus to settle the sizzling within me.

Ash stops at the door. "Solvei, aren't you coming in?"

I turn to the large adjacent building. "No. I think I'm going to have a little look around."

"You can't! You'll get hurt."

I give him a glare that makes him take a step back.

"Don't get into trouble, okay? We still want to hear what happened."

I ignore Ash and walk toward the mill.

I'd have to be blind not to notice the foul nature of this place, even if it wasn't permeating the air. Horrid sleeping conditions, work that leaves them so exhausted, and the isolation and entrapment. Those guards were looking inward for a reason.

There are too many parallels to my time with Gloria.

I want to have a look at what it is they are doing inside the building. I'm still unable to just walk inside, but I should be able to get a decent idea looking through a window.

A huge machine takes up the entire open floor. From wall to wall is a large moving mechanism with thousands of strings connecting to other parts of the machine it moves back and forth from. Adults stand working on one side while the kids crawl after the moving apparatus under the suspended threads.

I watch for a while, but there are no breaks. They all just keep crawling back and forth, trying to keep their fingers away from the wheels that hold the machine. Eventually, one of the boys is unlucky; he screams over the constant banging within the building as he flinches back, holding his fingers.

I can't see their condition from where I am, and despite the other people inside watching the kid who looks no older than nine holding himself in pain, none move to check on him. After only two rotations of the machine without the kid underneath, the threads stop moving.

A door slams open at the far end of the building and a man thunders down the aisle toward the boy. I can't hear what he is yelling, but as soon as he reaches the kid, the man's cane is already swinging.

I have to look away. My inner flame is already bubbling within me. Should I watch any longer, I fear my anger would explode to the surface. It truly pisses me off to see this happening, and there isn't a chance I'm leaving it as is.

I approach the front door and burn off its hinges. There's no fear of entrapment when there's no door to close. The people around say nothing, but move out of my way regardless.

As I step into the mill, the reek of the air almost sends me running. Whatever they are burning is disgusting. The heat inside is rather nice, but isn't it too hot for albanics? Also, with the amount of dust floating about, I wouldn't be surprised if the air itself is flammable.

I rush over to where the man continues the pummeling of the young boy and stand between them. It's a struggle to hold myself back from torching the man, but I'm worried that might send the whole building ablaze.

"Leave him be!" I stand before him with clenched fists as the heat within me does nothing but intensify.

The man is momentarily stunned by my presence, but is quick to regain his composure and scoff in my face.

"Who do you think you're talking to, child? He's not done his job properly, so he must be punished. As shall you for the backtalk."

He raises his cane and swings it at me. I stare him dead in the eye as the stick passes right through my head. It's hard to clamp down on my flame before it ignites the air, but I manage.

Shock and confusion are plastered on the man's face. The first attempt isn't enough of a warning for him, though. He tries to whack me again, only to receive the same outcome.

"Don't you dare move! The owner will be out to deal with you in a moment," the man declares as he scurries back the way he came.

Once he's out of sight, I look down at the boy hugging himself on the floor with pity. This is horrible. Once I get everyone out of the building, I'll burn it to the ground. First, I need to find Leslie.

Another door blocks the way to the stairs, and with a careful application of cinders to the hinges so that only the wood of the door burns, I have another door lying on the ground. I don't know what I'm gonna do if I need to enter a place where I can't cause such property damage, but I'll worry about it then.

I tear into the second floor and immediately spot her along the side wall. She looks far too tall to be crawling under the machine with the other kids. Leslie, of all people, I couldn't imagine taking this sort of treatment sitting down. And of course, as I approach from her side, the consequence of her resistance becomes apparent.

A brace is locked around her leg, connected to the wall with an iron chain. Her back looks horrible; much of the cloth and skin is torn off in alarming gashes. She doesn't notice me even as I stop behind her.

"Leslie . . ." I start. It's hard to even look at her in this state.

She jerks at my voice. "Solvei?" She looks up at me. Before I can even process it, she has me in a death grip. Tears streak down her face as she presses into me.

"You're here to get us out, right? You'll save us," she sobs.

Leslie was always such a strong person, never backing down from a fight, even against the adults we stole from. Now, she's like a different person. To see her pleading for help like this is just wrong.

"Of course. Once everyone is out, this building is cinders. The people who did this to you will wish I am as quick when I deal with them."

CHAPTER EIGHT

Mr. Marshall's Mill II

E veryone!" I call out over the banging of the machine. "It's time for you all to leave."

These people can't stay here if I want to freely use my flames. They especially can't stay considering I plan to burn it to the ground. As irritated as I am that these workers don't protect those being beaten right in front of them, they aren't the ones I want dead.

None of them so much as stop their work at my demands. I can tell they are listening. The glances out of the corner of their eyes are proof enough. But they ignore my words and continue as if I'm not here.

"If you don't leave, you'll be trapped in my inferno as it annihilates the building." I give my warning, and yet they don't move.

Why is this so frustrating? I'd give them a display to prove I'm not joking if only I wasn't so worried that the air might explode in the presence of a flicker.

Well, so be it. My priorities are my friends first. I'll get them out and come back to give the owner and his overlookers what they deserve.

I grab the chain linking Leslie to the wall and, with barely a thought, melt right through the metal. My arm reaches under her shoulder and I try to help her to her feet.

It's not until I've taken a few steps with her toward the exit do I realize what I've just done. My eyes widen as I turn to the remnants of the chain lying on the floor behind me.

I burned through iron.

The major adulthood milestone of my tribe.

A sad smile graces my lips as I move toward the stairs with Leslie. Not like it means much now.

I bang on the door to the shabby kids' sleeping quarters before pulling it open. Now that I'm not stuck in that dusty mill, I freely let out my flames. I need to be taken seriously. I refuse to be disregarded by those I'm trying to help. So, if that means a bit of intimidation, then so be it.

With my frame now outlined by fire, I raise my voice to be heard by all. "Everyone out! We are leaving." I probably should explain in more clarity, but the anger and frustration of everything I've seen leaves me impatient.

My friends are quick to follow. Ash and Kerry encourage the younger children to do as I say.

I approach the gate with far less following than I hoped. It seems the fear beaten into them exceeds the impact of my intimidation.

The gate guards scamper to block our path as we near.

"What do you lot think you're doing? No leaving without the master's permission," one of them says.

"Move aside," I growl, not bothering to restrict the raging inferno from bubbling to the surface any longer.

The man hardly hesitates to step forward with his baton raised. It's all I need to wrap chains of scorching embers around his ankles. Muscle melts off bone in moments.

His shrieks send the other guards stumbling back, but my chains follow and disable each of them like the first. I'm not allowing a reprieve until I know they've atoned.

I turn to the kids following me. Most have an awed expression of shock as they look over the downed men that no longer block their escape.

"Well? Hurry up!" I don't have time to deal with all these kids, so I turn to Ash. "Lead them out. Once I'm done here, I'll catch up."

Now, I have to figure how to get all those workers out of the building so I can bring it down.

"Oi! Stop them!" A shout comes from the now missing door to the mill.

Oh? I guess I don't need to go looking for the owner. A man in a suit that lacks the wear and tear of the other men's storms out of the mill, four others following close behind. This must be Mr. Marshall and his overlookers.

They chase after the children who ran the moment the owner's voice reached them.

The first one gets within a few meters of me before I act. It looks like he was intending to ignore me, which is simply foolish. My flame wraps up his leg, burning through flesh and sending him tumbling amongst the pile of guards still screaming in pain.

I leave my eyes on the owner even as the overlooker collapses behind me.

"What do you think you are doing?" he shouts, but halts his run together with his last three overlookers. His eyes flicker between me and the escaping children with frustration.

"Sir, this is the girl." I recognize the overlooker at the owner's side as the one who swung at me earlier.

"Mr. Marshall, correct?" I stare down the aging man. "I hope you are ready to pay for what you've done."

"What I've done? And what have I done, little missy? Everything here is perfectly in line with Joiak Kingdom law." He looks down at the men I've crippled before addressing the overlookers at his side. "Back off, boys. Let her go. I'll have the mercs chase her and those children down."

Let me go? I almost laugh. "I think you are confused, Mr. Marshall. I'm not going anywhere." Fire bursts out from me and I let my form completely shift to enhance the point. "And neither will you."

The overlookers don't react quick enough. All three of them scream as my flaming tempest engulfs their bodies. The fear that rises in the owner's eyes is the exact thing I was waiting for. A grin crawls across my face as I relish in this scum's terror before I give back the same pain he inflicted upon my friends.

"The Mercenary Order won't let you go if you do this," he says as he stumbles away from the writhing overlookers. "You'll regret it if you kill me!"

Does this man think spouting nonsense will help him? Even if this Mercenary Order has the strength to come after me, it would have been worth it to end this monster.

"She might, depending on whose pockets you've layered." An unfamiliar voice says over the whimpering of crippled men.

I turn my head to see one of those strange six-limbed creatures standing just outside the gate of the mill. Large expressive eyes are visible through the membrane of his orb-like torso. He lacks any of the other physical characteristics I would normally associate with a face; ears, nose, not even a mouth. Even without all those features, his eyes express a distinctly amused nonchalance.

"So? Who is it? Which official will seek vengeance for you?"

"You! You're a merc, are you not? Deal with this brat. I've paid Mr. William a fortune for his services."

"Mr. William. Mr. William . . . I'm unfamiliar with that name. Are you sure you weren't scammed?" the odd being's cheery voice questions. "Oh! He told you he was above third class, correct? I'd hate to call one of the lower officials a scammer, but that would explain why I don't know his name. Either case, this Mr. William doesn't have jurisdiction over me."

The owner seems flustered by his words, but they are nothing other than a distraction to me. I step over the body of an overlooker, the man shivering despite the body-wide burns. With each step I take, I gather my flames around me. The owner's brows furrow and a scowl wrinkles his face as I stand right before him. I hold my flames back from touching him; I want to try something different.

Almost predictably, the man doesn't just stand there. He reaches a hand into his pants pocket and pulls out some short metal thing. The owner flicks his wrist, exposing the blade, before plunging it right into my chest.

I hear that odd creature at the gate behind me shout but ignore him. I pull my hands up and grasp at the hand holding the blade. The skin sizzles under my touch, but I push his hand deeper, showing just how futile his attempt is. And ever is it worth it. The scowl morphs. His eyes widen in horror as he jerks his arms away. They slip out of my grasp with ease, but I still have more for him.

Flames explode around us, trapping the owner with me inside a dome. Again, I'm careful to keep my fire from touching him directly.

He deserves worse.

I grasp the blade and pull it out of my chest. I inspect the piece as I slide the blade back inside its handle. Ornate patterns carved into the steel make it look like a fashion accessory rather than a weapon. I pocket it; he won't be needing it soon.

The owner has finally realized there is no escape without pushing through flames hot enough to melt skin.

"Fine. Take the children, take all of them, just let me go."

I ignore him and slowly begin rising the temperature in this enclosed space.

"Do you want money? Is that it? I'll give you a million gid if you let me go." He is sweating now, the drops stream down his face. The sweltering heat not yet reaching the temperatures of a furnace, but it will be soon.

"What do you want?" he pleads as he tears off his suit and shirt, desperate to escape the intensifying heat.

"Nothing. Not from you."

Strangely, the sweating on the man's body stops. His skin flakes and dries. He gasps with each breath like he can't get any air and his eyes shrivel in his head. His body isn't burning and other than the drying skin and eyes; there is no clear sign it will end any time soon.

At least, until he collapses. With a clutch at his chest, the owner stills on the ground.

I really expected him to last longer if it was just heat.

No sense wasting energy now. I pull down the dome surrounding us and head toward the mill again. As I'm getting my fire under control, the six-limbed man from before—still standing just outside the gate—calls out.

"Yo, kid, you probably shouldn't burn down the mill. The country won't care about some replaceable manager, but they'll care a lot if you destroy one of their biggest manufacturing plants."

I glance back for a moment, considering his words. But only for a moment, because I realize I don't care. Any place like this should burn to the ground, regardless of how many people want it operating.

I turn and head inside.

The workers have obviously been watching the events outside through the windows and yet so many of them still refuse to leave the post of their work. The machine never stops. A long leather belt connects the machine to a spinning wheel sticking out the side of the wall. I place my hand over it and snap the belt moving the contraption, all the while careful to stop myself igniting the very air.

The spinning threats and rolling wheels come to a stop. With no more work, these people shouldn't have any more reason to stay.

"It's time for everyone to leave if they don't want to be roasted like Mr. Marshall." I don't spare them another glance as I walk up the stairs and do the same for the next three floors.

Leslie wasn't the only one locked in their working position. Many children on the upper floors seem to live in their workstations if the filth along the floor was any sign. It takes some time to get through each of their chains.

I wait on the top floor until I feel everyone should have escaped. Any deciding to stay after has nobody but themselves to blame.

As I light a flame before me, my concern for the dust in the air is more than validated. At the touch of a small flare, the air explodes around me. The sound of glass shattering overwhelms the roar of the inferno for only a brief second. My flames spread to each corner of the room in a moment, engulfing everything in its way.

I walk down the stairs, prepared to ignite each room individually, but there is no need. The fire spreads without a need to help. Really, how had this place not burned down before I showed up?

I'm glad to see they took my warning seriously and none of the workers remain.

I leave the mill before it can start collapsing on top of me. The crowd of workers stares with open mouths as I walk through the fire engulfing the building. They move aside for me as I approach the gate. Strands of flames branch out and end the lives of the overlookers and guards still prone on the ground. Some of them crawled some distance away and some find themselves as the punching-bags to many of the children once locked up. Even a few of the female workers join in.

The large eyes of the tentacle-limbed man follow me as I walk toward my friends. A small rodent not dissimilar to a jerboa now sits upon his head . . . body . . . whatever. The tiny creature wears an incredibly formfitting bit of clothing. Is that his pet or something? It's strange to dress up an animal, isn't it?

As I walk down the street where I can see my friends congregating with the other freed kids, I notice the six-limbed man following me.

I spin on my heel. "What do you want?" I don't want to deal with any more people. I just want to talk with my friends again.

"Oh, you know, just curious to know what an áed's doing so far away from the wasteland. You're quite strong for your age, y'know," his chipper voice chimes.

The rodent sitting on his head scoffs. "A bit more than that; she took a cane right through her head. Acted like she didn't even feel it."

Ah, so the rodent isn't a pet. Some other sapient species? I feel a little bad for making the assumption.

"Ah, yes, that is a bit hard to believe. I don't recall any other áed being able to do that. Donk 'em hard enough and they fall like anything else."

I narrow my eyes at that statement, preparing to fight if I need to.

"Chill, girl, chill. I'm not here for conflict, even if I would have rather you not burned the mill. I'm not gonna stop hearing complaints from the brass if they find out I was in the area. No, I want to make an offer."

Somehow, I can tell he's grinning even without a mouth.

CHAPTER NINE

Remus

Y ou see, my group and I find ourselves in a bit of strife at the moment. Due to some unfortunate events, our trusty and reliable mage is gone. Left. Now, we flounder as she searches new horizons."

The being puts on a dramatic display as he walks by my side. I want to walk off and leave him behind, but he doesn't seem to understand I am ignoring him.

"Without a mage, our most eminent role, our team ceases to function. What is the point of fighting if you cannot advance, after all? We cannot simply take any odd mage either. No, they must have at least the minimum capabilities of self-defense against the atrocities we face. But, for shame, uncovering capable mages not chained down by prior obligations is an arduous undertaking."

His eyes roll upward in his head, like marbles in a jar, until they lie right underneath that tiny sapient rodent.

"Jav tells me you have what it takes. You may not be a mage, but both áed and áinfean can bend hyle to their will. Which means it would be no issue teaching you how to operate the ritual. My only concern is whether you are skilled enough to survive our battles. I trust Jav, but you are younger than my great-granddaughter."

We turn a bend in the road and I finally see my friends ahead. I run off from the rambling man to rejoin them.

"Oi, aren't you listening?" is the last I hear from him before I return to Kerry's embrace.

She laughs as I return her tight grip. They won't be forced to work in that horrible place again. I want no one to experience what Gloria put me through. To know they spent an entire week in that mill is saddening. As I look over some of the bony bodies and hollow eyes of the kids around, I can't help but feel glad I got here before things got worse for my friends.

I feel bad for the other kids, of course, but knowing that they are in pain just doesn't hit the same as my own friends' pain.

"Thank you, Solvei," Ash says as Kerry and I separate. "I never knew you were so . . . capable. Sorry for doubting you."

I shake my head. "It wouldn't have been so easy the last time we met."

Leslie stretches and enjoys the open—still murky—air. She must have been stuck in there a while.

I drop to my knee beside her and, using my hand to separate the metal cuff from her leg, I melt it off. The heat must have still gotten through to her as she flinches and I almost fail to stop the hot metal from sizzling her skin. Thankfully, she settles down and lets me eat through the heavy anklet.

Now I know why my elders never went for wood and coal themselves. They may say it's for the sake of the younger áed, but there is no way the taste isn't the largest factor. This is amazing. It's more of a heavy flavor than the sweetness of wood, if it even makes sense for a taste to be heavy.

I have to remind myself that the iron is still around Leslie's ankle, so I don't just scorch my way through it.

Once done, I let go of her leg and take the remaining pieces for myself.

"Thank you." Leslie shakes her leg, a grin rising to her face. "What now? I don't know about you guys, but I'm about to pass out."

I look to Ash. As much as I got them out and everything, I never really thought about what to do afterward. Where are all these kids going to go?

Ash returns my look. I guess he expected me to have some idea what to do? I shake my head and shrug.

He sighs and drops his head. "I guess we tell them to form groups and find a place for themselves. We might have to resort to old methods if we can't find a trustworthy place." Ash pauses for a moment to look around the black muck–covered city. "I think we should move away from here first."

"Good plan. Good plan. Well, it would be if Joiak wasn't disgusting everywhere you go." The six-limbed man steps into the conversation with his small partner still on his head. "Ya see, that business you just burned down, little lady, was not the exception. That is the norm in this country. Real unfortunate, actually, you got a bunch of kids like yourselves trying to find greener pastures outside Zadok, and Joiak is all too willing to put them to use.

"Now. I have a proposal," he says and turns to look directly at me. "I can pull some favors and get each of these little kiddies and your friends into a far more friendly country within the pact. There won't be any working to exhaustion like here. Heck, some of the younger ones might even be adopted into loving families."

He doesn't turn, but the eyeballs in his head move out of my sight and he strides away from me as if that is the new front of his body. Jav, on his head, remains facing me.

"I could do that, but it would be incredibly inconvenient for me to do so without reason, don't you think?" His eyes once more swivel in his head to lock on me. "So here's the deal. You join my team for a bit and I'll make sure everyone here gets nice and safe. What do ya think? Good deal, yeah?"

Is he serious? Can I even trust him? He put no effort into stopping that bastard of a man mistreating all these kids . . . but I guess he also didn't stop me from tearing through the owner and his men. What is so important about this ritual thing that they need me?

"Look, kid," the little jerboa-like person says, "I know my friend can be a bit . . . overwhelming when he's trying to make an impression, but we are desperate for the help you could bring. I promise we mean no harm to you or your friends."

I guess it might be fine if it's just for a little. But I need to make sure I'm not being trapped in some contract or environment like my friends had been.

"Okay, but only if I'm allowed to leave if I don't like the way you do things."

"Splendid. Now, we need to confirm if you're actually qualified." The man flicks his limbs outwards, away from my friends, creating loud cracks through the air as each limb extends.

"What?"

"You didn't think it would be that simple, did you? You still have to prove to me you can survive the things we face."

Jav jumps off his head and surprisingly, a couple of flaps extend from his small suit, letting him glide to the ground.

With his flicking done, all six tentacles rest on the ground to keep the man upright. Unlike bipedal or quadruped creatures, his limbs all seem equally capable of attacking and being used for mobility.

"So little lady, are you ready for a spar?"

I nod to him and give a last glance at my friends watching over us in silence. Leslie has passed out on the black road and Kerry kneels over her. Ash and the twins watch.

"Just don't get hurt, okay?" Ash says and the twins nod beside him.

I smile at them. It warms my heart to know they care.

Bringing my attention back to my opponent, I walk some distance away from my friends so I can let loose without worry. If this man wants to test me, I have no intention of holding back.

I don't wait until he's ready. Immediately, I lash out with a torrent of fire. My inner flame grasps at his torso and I try to burn through his thick, rubbery skin. The heat now able to melt iron hardly does anything. Like with my fight with the general, his skin doesn't burn under my assault.

"Disappointing heat for an áed, but I guess you're still young."

Is he mocking me? I feel for any openings and find his mouth at the bottom of his head. My flames rush through, pushing to burn him from the inside out.

With a flick of a limb and a slide backward, I find my flames losing their grip on his body. Knocked aside as if they are but a pest.

"I do like your willingness to take what advantage you can, but you'll definitely need a weapon to focus your flames in the future. There's just no oomph in your attacks."

He's definitely trying to irritate me now. I swipe at him again, raising my temperature as far as I can.

But I don't come close.

With a push of his limbs, he flies to the side at a speed I cannot follow. I'm unable to turn my body fast enough to keep up with him as he springs off the ground without stopping.

I jump away from him, expecting an attack. But it doesn't come; he is gone. I twist on my feet and find him behind me. His eyes smaller than before.

He glances off the side to his small partner. "Jav, are you sure you weren't mistaken?"

Jav grins back at him, razor-sharp teeth peeking through his tiny mouth. "Just attack her already, you'll see."

He sighs, his torso drooping with the slackening of his tentacles. "Sorry, little lady."

As soon as he finishes his words, alarm bells go off in my head. I throw myself to the side as his limb cracks through the air right where my hand had just been.

I hadn't seen him move at all.

"Oh? Nice reaction speed," he compliments, but it isn't enough to stop him from following up.

A second tears right through my hand. It is forced into wispy flames before reforming after a second. The feeling is uncomfortable, but not painful. I blast him with my fire again to regain space.

He stands there observing me with widened eyes. "Amazing. I see what you mean now, Jav. Let's see how far she can go."

I don't have time to retreat. Warnings blare in my head from each direction. He's attacking so many times at once I have nowhere to go, so I brace myself for the onslaught.

Arms, chest and legs; he tears through them all with nary a delay. My body splits open in places for moments before snapping back together. I hear one of my friends scream my name from the side, but I'm too busy to focus on that.

Each impact is an annoyance, but I have no way of stopping them like I did when fighting the general. I don't have the Void Fog and its creatures to help me this time. What can I do to fight back? Do I just stand here and take the abuse, hoping my body can handle it indefinitely?

He's stopped holding back now. He freely goes for my head as much as he can. I stop trying to pull myself back into a physical form and leave my body's flames visible to all.

I don't want to leave this as is. I need to fight back. My flames swirl around me, obscuring my arms and legs while he continues his onslaught. In a few seconds, I've done what I need to.

My body straightens under the assault. He can't hurt me, so I have no need to be afraid of getting close. He is too fast for me, so I just have to hope his arrogance lets me get close enough to do what I plan to do.

When I dash forward, I'm glad he doesn't move. He's ready and willing to take whatever I throw. I don't know if even this will be enough, he can brush off my flames after all, so it might be hopeless. But it's worth the attempt.

Pouncing forward, I latch onto his torso with my newly grown claws. They don't cut into his rubbery skin, but they give me enough grip that I'm able to hold on when he tries to flick me away like he did my inner flame.

I grow claws from my hands and feet to give me the grip that I just couldn't hope for with fingers. Well, I hoped to tear into him, but I'll have to settle for this.

Hugging myself around his head, I struggle to remain in place as he dashes around the area with speed I can hardly comprehend. Once I stabilize myself, I engulf the both of us in flames. I've already been shown I can't really burn through him, so I intend to burn through all the air before it reaches him. Doesn't matter how strong he is, he'll suffocate if he doesn't breathe.

Through my flames, I notice his tentacles reaching for small pouches hidden between the base of the limbs and the torso. From within each pouch, he pulls a metal encasing for the ends of each tentacle. The metal is some alloy I've never felt before and no matter how hard I try to melt them off his limbs, they remain cold.

I feel the difference immediately when he hits me with the metal plates. The ethereal flames of my body spread far from my body with each impact. Too far to reform myself with any haste.

It's not long before I lose my grip around him and I'm sent flying off his back to the filthy pavement.

"Wow, I'm very impressed. The name's Remus. Welcome to the group."

"Huh?" What?

Remus puts the metal gloves back in their hidden pouches and walks toward me.

We're not fighting anymore?

"That was amazing, little miss. I've never seen an áed with such a close relationship with fire. Please, what is your name? I mean, I heard your friends say it, but I would like to hear it from you."

"Uh, Solvei." Isn't this a bit too quick of a transition? I thought he was trying to kill me a second ago. I definitely was trying to do the same to him.

"Well, Solvei, I look forward to working with you."

CHAPTER TEN

Leaving Joiak

It only took a few days for the people Remus organized to arrive. The large caravan contains many unfamiliar species. Plenty of dohrni—which is what Remus's race is apparently called—as well as creatures with strange bone-like growths make up most of the group. Only a couple albanics stand amongst them.

I'm surprised Remus put this much effort into supporting a bunch of kids he doesn't know, even if it is for a deal with me. Really, I wouldn't have been opposed to work with him even if he didn't help. Once my friends are safe, I'll need a way to improve myself. Strengthen myself. Remus has already made it clear we will find ourselves in positions to grow. Dangerous as they may be, these opportunities could be invaluable.

My fight with the general and Remus has shown me I can never truly be free to do what I want unless I have the strength to back it up. If Remus will bring me to places where I can consume creatures to enhance my strength, then I'll jump at the chance.

It's a bonus that he's willing to go this far to bring me in.

Of course, I've experienced the despicable side of too many beings to trust outright. I'll be careful and keep my eyes open, but I won't assume he has bad intentions from the start. My friends have taught me the error of that line of thought; paranoia isn't helpful.

"So, what is this ritual you need me for?" I ask Remus now that we are on our way out of Joiak. He was in a hurry to leave, and planned to have the kids move with the people he organized rather than with us, but I am adamant about staying with my friends until I know they are safe. So now, the eight of us move away from the other kids. I'll check in to make sure they reach somewhere safe later, but for now, I think it's fine to leave them.

"Hmm, have you ever met an enhanced? People like myself with greater strength than their bodies naturally allow. Remember how your flames struggle to burn my body? Well, that's a good indicator for someone with a body pushing the limits."

I nod. The general must have been one of these enhanced. And if he was, that ursu giant was surely one as well.

"The ritual is the only way those without an extremely high connection with an element can enhance their bodies beyond all limits. Áed and áinfean can directly consume the dead, making the ritual unnecessary. Technically, us fleshy creatures can take on the strength of the creatures we eat, but I'd love to meet the person able to scoff down the immense bodies of some of the beasts we fight."

"Is that what Henosis and New Vetus do? Fight monsters to get stronger?" I ask.

Remus's eyes shrink at my words. "No. I don't think the ursu have bothered enhancing themselves for over a century. There is a reason they are losing the war. Henosis have the entire eastern ocean to hunt, but that isn't enough for them. They power their conquests with something far more despicable."

More despicable? Oh. I guess it isn't a huge leap to use the corpses of your enemies to empower yourself.

Should I avoid telling Remus I ate the dead albanic soldiers?

"New Vetus isn't losing the war anymore," I say.

"Huh?" Both Remus and Jav on his head turn to me. I guess they didn't know.

"Some giant ursu slaughtered the entire army. I wouldn't be surprised if the remnants are fleeing back to the Empire right now. Assuming they escaped his wrath."

"Fu . . . damn. Hund is still alive then. And I'd thought the old fella finally croaked after not appearing in a century."

"You fought him?" I can feel my eyes widening.

Remus laughs at my question. "Fought Hund? I'm still alive and well, which is not something anyone who Hund has laid eyes on can say. I've seen that ursu fight though, and he felt more like a Titan hiding in ursu fur than anything else I've seen. I still have nightmares from that day."

Jav stares at me. "You saw him, didn't you?"

"Yeah." I look over at my friends listening in as they stuck together. I've noticed they've been a bit withheld around Remus and Jav, I'll have to make some time for us to talk alone soon. "Some Henosis soldiers were fighting amongst themselves and he showed up. The soldiers didn't last long."

"Wait, how long ago was this?" Jav asks.

"A bit over a week ago. Why?"

"You made it all the way here in a week? How?"

Oh, right, they don't know yet. A grin grows over my face and I glance at my friends. The curiosity in their eyes makes my smirk widen. "You'll just have to wait and see."

I laugh at their dissatisfied expressions.

Remus is looking at me with his wide eyes I can just tell are smirking. He doesn't know, does he? He hasn't seen me do any more than grow some talons, that wouldn't be enough for him, right?

"Hey, you've met other áed before, right? Not many know about us this far from the wasteland." Maybe some have pushed out from the wasteland before me. It'd be nice if I could meet some in the northern states.

"Yeah, I have," Remus says. "But it was fifty years ago when I traveled into the wasteland. I'll tell ya, that place really ain't friendly to anyone but you áed. If you don't take a water mage with you, you're done. Any liquid disappears from your bottles no matter how tight they are."

"So you've never seen any áed in the northern states?"

"Nope. Honestly, I'm surprised to see you up here in pact territory. You lot stick to your own far more than most."

"Pact territory?" I ask.

"Yeah, what you call the northern states. Most of the nations amongst the pact lay next to the Titan Alps, which regularly has powerful creatures descend. The pact is an agreement between these countries to share military strength, the Mercenary Order. Which is what you'll be joining once we introduce you to the rest of the team. The politics of sharing the mercenary force between so many nations creates problems, which—"

"Which is not something she should worry about." Jav rises to his feet on Remus's head and glares down. "The only thing we should worry about is getting these kids somewhere safe before we take their friend out to climb the Alps. Don't forget how young she is, Remus."

Okay, that irks me. With everything I've gone through, being treated like a child again is not something I'm happy about. Just as I'm about to protest, Jav speaks again.

"I've had enough of this chat for a bit. Remus, launch me." Jav stretches his small arms and tail as one of Remus's limbs wrap around his torso.

In a moment, the air cracks as Remus's tentacle whips through the air. Jav is nowhere to be seen.

Did . . . did he just throw Jav?

I try to look through the air for the little rodent, but it's as if he's vanished.

"I wouldn't bother looking, you'll never find him," Remus says.

"Did you just throw him?" I'm incredulous. Why would he do that?

"Of course." Remus looks at me oddly. "How else would a volan get the air they need to fly? They're not birds, you know."

"Volan?"

"Yeah. You know: Jav's race. Despite not naturally having wings, they love flying."

I'd seen the guy glide before with that suit of his, but the idea that he would use it to actually fly is baffling.

"How far did you throw him?"

"Hmm . . ." Remus raises one of his limbs before his face in a thinking pose. "We've never measured it, but Jav complains about how hard it is to breathe when I throw him too high, so I usually hold back a bit. So . . . maybe a dozen kilometers?"

Eh? He's joking right? But as much as I try to find the humor in his eyes, it's not there.

This enhancement is quite something. I don't have any other answer to how Jav could survive being flung like that.

I slow my pace to let Remus walk ahead, and I rejoin my friends.

"Solvei, what kind of weirdos do you have us traveling with?" Leslie asks. It's good to see her spring back to her old self. The state she'd been left in when I found her was horrible and I hope she never has to experience something like that again. I hope none of them do.

"Are you going to be okay with them? It feels wrong that you're the only one that needs to pay for our safety," Ash says.

"It's hardly paying. I get to know you're safe and, well . . ." I lower my voice so Remus can't overhear. "I see this as an opportunity to grow, to gain strength for myself."

Ash watches me closely as we follow a good distance behind the dohrni. "You still need to tell us what happened after we lost you."

"Yeah, you mentioned it only took you a week to get here. What were you doing in all that time? How did you get here so quick?" Kerry asks.

I scratch at my arm, not sure where to start. "I couldn't outrun the Fog and got trapped inside for a while. Eventually, I got out only for the Henosis to catch me."

"Wait, the Void Fog didn't kill you?" Kerry gapes.

"No. It's an indescribable place, but nothing it passes is destroyed, simply taken somewhere else," I say. "Anyway, I was imprisoned by the Empire for most of the time I was gone before this giant ursu went and killed them all. He was huge, like six of me tall."

"He's the one you and Remus were talking about before, right? Hund?"

"Yeah. I didn't know his name was Hund, but it was terrifying just being near him."

"So how did you get back as quick as you did?" Leslie asks and, upon seeing my growing smirk, she groans. "C'mon, you can hardly keep us in suspense forever."

"Hmm, fine. But it'll take a while to show you, so no peeking until I'm done." There's nothing worrying around us, so it should be fine to change while we walk.

I want to keep it a surprise until I'm done, so I create a wall of my flame to cover me as I start the transformation. The time I take to transform has lowered a lot, but I still can't manage much faster than fifteen minutes for a full-body change. I wonder if I'll ever be able to change on the spot?

When I'm finally done, I compress my flames into myself, but stop before the outline of my form becomes visible to any outside observers. I can be a bit more creative with this, right? I might as well put on a show for my viewers.

I twist the flames around me, hopefully dragging the eyes of any not already paying attention. The vortex of flames spins around me so fast it roars in my ears. With a flick of mental control, I explode the flame in all directions. I fly hidden within a flare as it shoots out from the eruption of spinning fire, leaving the space I was just standing empty.

I fly high enough that I can use the sun to hide my body from my audience below. Below, the faces of my friends are shocked. I laugh a little as they search around for me as the remnant flames disperse.

My amusement halts as my attention turns to Remus. His humored eyes are locked on mine. Was he able to see through my display? I can't help but groan. At least I still have my friends to surprise.

I control my flames so they won't burn and am careful of my talons as I glide down to land on Leslie's shoulder. "Hey," I say as I touch down.

She screams and stumbles away, leaving me to flap to regain my balance and land safely on the ground. I laugh at her reaction, my giggles drawing the attention of the others.

"Solvei?"

"You like?" I spread my wings wide to show them off. "Some things happened, now my binding is far higher than before."

"Binding?" Ash asks, but Leslie interrupts.

"That's so cool. Damn áed get the best abilities."

"This isn't a normal thing for áed. Well, at least not for most," Remus says as he approaches me. "I'd say you're closer to the threshold than anyone I've met. I don't know how you managed it, but I can't wait to see what happens when you increase your connection more than you already have." His eyes twinkle. The lack of familiar facial features do nothing to hide his grin. "I'm sure it'll be spectacular."

CHAPTER ELEVEN

Motivations

Once we made it out of the twisting roads of Joiak, our path became far more direct. Good thing too, even though I've only been able to fly for two weeks now, going back to walking is nothing more than a pain.

"So, I should have probably asked this earlier, but where are we going?"

"Haven't I said?" Remus asks. "We're going to the Meja Matriarchy. It's our group's home and once your friends get settled in, you'll be able to see them between jobs."

"How far is that?"

"Well, it's far, but it shouldn't take long once we reach the train station. Really, it's quite annoying that Joiak doesn't allow passenger carriages within their borders."

Ah, so not long at all. I groan and look up at the sky. Why didn't he tell us that sooner?

I catch movement from the corner of my eye. It looks like Jav is back with dinner. The small creature lugs behind him a fully grown deer. Even if I've seen it a few times before, it still looks odd to see him carrying something probably fifty times his weight. Well, maybe carry is the wrong word; Jav drags the deer along the ground, leaving a long trail of blood from wherever he killed it.

"Jav, why don't you ever call for help? I'm sure some of us could carry it back much easier than this," I ask.

He glares at me over the hoof in his grasp. "I don't need help to get dinner sorted. Why don't you mind your own business," he says before going back to tugging.

I'm a bit put off by his response. Why is he so hostile? I just want to help.

"Don't worry about him. He just gets cranky when people assume he can't do something because of his size." Remus walks up behind me.

"I do not!"

Remus chuckles as Jav cuts into the deer. Again, it looks odd because of his diminutive size. I've always been the smallest amongst any group of people, so it is strange to be on the other end now.

I leave him alone for now. Even as I watch him struggling to start a fire that I could have roaring in moments. He wants to do it all himself, right? It's best I don't butt in, no matter how slow and pitiful his attempts to start a fire are.

I return to my friends, who have their own stockpile of wood ready for a firepit. A sudden gust of wind brushes over us, making me shiver and amplify my heat. The others don't look any better, each of them rubbing their hands together for warmth.

They look up at me expectantly as they sit around their gathered bundle of sticks. I consider playing dumb for a moment, but the cold is already making me burn through double the amount of food I'd usually need. I can't imagine what it'd feel like for them; they have no way of heating themselves, after all.

Soon everyone is cramming around the warm campfire. I'm really glad for the bountiful resources around, there's no way I could have kept moving like this through the lowering temperatures if this was the wasteland.

I hope this winter doesn't last long.

As I look over my friends, I realize I forgot about someone.

"Hey, what happened to that woman who led you to Joiak? What was her name? Ivory?"

"After all that happened with the Void Fog, she sent us north on our own. I can't blame her though, she had family lost to the Fog. She stayed to look for them," Ash says over his shoulder but doesn't move away from the heat.

"Oh, right. We were staying in her cousin's backyard, weren't we," I murmur. How was I so lucky to escape and receive help when uncountable others died within its grasp? Even those who escape the Fog are twisted beyond recognition.

Against the Void Fog. Against the Titan. What can be done besides hope for survival when such otherworldly disasters strike? Will I ever be strong enough that such events no longer worry me? Or will I always be trapped by the endless fear that an incomprehensible disaster is waiting right around the corner to devastate me and all I care for?

Even taking Remus's deal, can I gain the strength to fight off such night-marish existences? Beings that can annihilate much of the world itself.

No. It will never be possible. I can't even conceptualize ever contesting Hund's strength, no matter how much I think I can grow. But does that matter? There will always be something greater, something to be a source of terror regardless of strength. But if I never put in the effort, I'll never be able to fight for the things I want when they are within my power to take.

It is impossible to advance to where nothing can entrap me. But if I don't push forward, I'll be trapped in a world of my own fears. If I don't grow, I'll never be able to escape the paranoia of the intent of those around, never able to freely exist amongst those I want to consider family.

It's something I've been worrying about; I might have to leave my friends behind if I want to join this mercenary group. They'll hardly be able to follow me and there is no guarantee I'll get to see them often. Remus has been rather casual about it, but the areas we will go and the creatures we'll face are not something to be taken so carelessly. The bird from the Wailing Woodland, the colossal-worms, and so many other creatures I've seen come nowhere near the strength of the Titans, yet they pose a great danger in and of themselves.

If I hadn't been gifted with such a perfect means of escape by the Void Fog, I never would have considered joining them, even if Remus had thought I was capable without my intangible-flame defense. But I have the capability. Maybe it's arrogance, but I now feel like nothing can hold me. As much of a lie as that is, the feeling permeates my being. I want, no, I need to spread, like the growing cinders of an incipient fire. Intensifying my flames until they can no longer be extinguished is something I truly want.

I look over at the five I've grown close enough to call my friends. They huddle together, chatting around the campfire. I think of Leal, my first friend outside of my tribe. How might she be doing? Now that New Vetus is taking back lost ground, are she and her mom doing better? Will I ever be able to see them again?

I now have new people to live for, but simply living isn't enough. I don't want to have them taken from me like my tribe was.

As I am now, I can protect myself. I can escape most things that might do me harm. But my friends can't, and I don't have the strength to protect them. If I lose any of them, I have no way of finding them. Should they be trapped—like they were by the owner of that mill—they have no way of escaping.

I need to be strong enough that I can stop that. I need to be capable enough to find them, to find Leal again.

I can only do that if I press forward. Consuming the general has opened my eyes to how much strength can be gained by felling the strong. I'm certain his death and Teine's sacrifice are the only reasons I'm already able to burn through iron.

If Remus and Jav hadn't appeared, I would have decided on the same course. Now, I simply have someone to direct me, rather than an unguided search for beasts to hunt.

I should enjoy the little time I have left with my friends before we have to go our separate ways.

"Not long now and you can meet the team. Our place is just a bit farther down the road," Remus declares as he points with one of his long, boneless limbs down the path breaching the thick forest vegetation.

We had not long left the fortress Baansguard. From the outside, it didn't look like much. Reminiscent of a large slab of stone or maybe a rocky hill, it was only once you entered its core that you could see the true magnificence of the city within.

A large central area of open space inside gave a perfect view of the layers in which hundreds of thousands of people lived. Carved into the rock were large platforms that held innumerable buildings. The ceiling visible above the large central chamber of this huge fortress glowed bright like the sun; the heat it gave off felt similar too.

I struggled a lot in the city, and I refused to leave the entrance area where I had a clear view through the ten-meter-tall tunnel leading directly out. As long as I had a clear view to the outside, I was able to hold in my anxiety about being trapped. But it still made my goodbyes with my friends frustrating.

Thankfully, they seemed to settle into their newly given lodgings rather easily. It was some building with a bunch of other teenagers. A trade school, Remus had called it. They would be taught a profession, along with the other orphaned kids.

I am satisfied that they will be treated well, but I'll only truly know for sure when I next meet my friends.

The long tunnel out of the city had been a rather long walk. There had to be somewhere near a hundred meters of stone separating the city from the outside world in every direction. It really couldn't be considered anything but a fortress. What exactly did they expect to need to protect the city from?

As we left, I'd asked if I should fly so Remus could move at a faster pace. I'd seen him move in our spar. There's no way this was his normal traveling speed. But he seemed content to continue at the slow clip, so I reluctantly followed by his side.

Two hours of walking from Baansguard and only now are we getting close. If I'd flown, I could have been here in ten minutes. No, maybe even five.

Baansguard is the westernmost city in the Meja Matriarchy, and for the sapient races, is also one of the closest dwellings to the Titan Alps.

There is no way you could miss the mountains here.

It doesn't matter where you are in the world, from the western edges of the wasteland to the southern portion of New Vetus, the mountains are always visible. Most of the time, they are a part of the background. Like the moon during the day—always there, but only paid attention when navigating.

Not here, though. We are so close that a third of the sky is dominated by their height. No longer are the mountains dimmed by distance, their feet are right before us.

There is a reason they are called the Titan Alps. Like the Titans are incomprehensible beings, thousands of times larger than normal creatures, these Alps dwarf all mountains as if they are nothing more than pebbles.

Through any gap in the canopy, the Alps remain visible. Ever looming over all.

Soon, we enter a clearing and Jav throws himself off Remus's head, the wings of his suit gliding him through the open window of a wooden cabin. A large veranda extends out of the other side from where Jav flew in through, furnished with couches, tables, and an entire outdoor kitchen.

"Bloody rat! Use the front door!" a voice shouts from within.

I look up at Remus beside me, his eyes grin back at me. "Well, it's time to introduce you to the team."

CHAPTER TWELVE

Team Luis-Eight

Remus walks right through the heavy front door. I push into the doorway and block it while the yelling within grows more audible.

"Damned fucking rat, how much damage do you have to cause before you stop using the window as a door?"

"I didn't break anything this time. Why don't you learn not to put your things under the window I enter from?"

"Which window don't you use? I can hardly keep this place smelling fresh if I can't use the windows. You lot drag in enough muck as it is. You didn't even wash the blood off your wingsuit before coming in, did you?"

Without moving a step further inside than the doorway, I watch as Jav stands on a countertop exchanging verbal barbs with a bone-growth man wearing an apron. I'd seen plenty of his race—the khirig—in Baansguard, seemingly the most populous in Meja.

If you look closely, his central, fleshy body looks similar to an albanic's, except incredibly thin and without the limbs from elbow and knee down. Antler-like protrusions across his body remove any similarity one might see between his race and that of an albanic.

From his spine, the antlers wrap around his chest, protecting his soft skin in a way reminiscent of a bony rib cage. The protrusions also pierce out of the back of his arms and legs, creating branch-like limbs that reach beyond the protective cage. Short antlers rise out of his head like a crown.

The variation I've seen between the khirig is incredible. The man before me has thin, workable fingers made from the bony antlers, and his cage is tight around his vulnerable body. Some in Baansguard had huge antlers with thick cages that prevent you even peeking at the body within. But those large khirig lack visibly working hands, so I don't know how beneficial it would be for the added defense.

"Stop it, you two, you're putting on a bad first impression." Remus turns to me while wrapping a limb around the khirig with the apron hanging off his cage antlers. "Solvei, this is Ossian. He takes care of our home while we're out."

Ossian brushes off Remus's tentacle. "I also take care of these slobs when they're here."

Remus laughs, his eyes squinting in humor. "Yes, and we're grateful for all you do."

"Not all of you." He turns to glower at Jav already digging food out of the cupboard.

"Anyway, this is Solvei. She'll be joining our team."

Ossian focus snaps to me. "This one? Are you sure? She hardly looks out of her preteens. Where are her markings? You've gone senile."

"I'm not *that* old," Remus rebuts.

"She's not an albanic, Oss, she's an áed. I promise she can handle herself," Jav cuts in before returning to stuffing his face with biscuits he found.

"An áed? Like from your stories?"

Remus nods at his inquiring eye.

"Well, if you're sure." Ossian lowers himself to my level before whispering just loud enough so the other two can hear. "Hey, they didn't kidnap you, did they? You're not being forced?"

Remus rolls his eyes and Jav throws the now-empty container at Ossian's head.

While he rubs at one of his head antlers, I shake my head. "No, I came here willingly."

"Well, if you're sure." He rises to his branch feet again and storms over to the cupboard. He pulls Jav by the tail and tosses him to the other side of the room.

Jav gracefully glides to a stop, still eating a slice of cake he found.

Something nudges my back and I definitely don't squeak when I see what has gotten so close without my notice. A huge panther, almost too big for the door, stares down at me from its excessive height. Without thinking, I try to slam the door in its face, but the heavy door comes to a hard stop against the creature.

With a huff, it walks inside before laying on a large couch that I'm surprised doesn't collapse under its weight.

Still grasping the door, I move back to the doorsill.

"So she's the one?" a new voice asks. It doesn't take long to realize it's coming from the panther now relaxing on the side of the room, its head tilted in my direction.

Okay. With all these new intelligent beings around, I should hardly be surprised anymore. From now on, I'll assume it's smart until proven otherwise.

Still . . . even if it's a sapient race, those teeth are huge. Massive sabers exposed outside its closed jaw tell of a naturally predatory species.

"Yep, this is Solvei. Solvei, Grímr. He's one of the portian."

"Portian?" I ask, unfamiliar with the race. Well, I'm unfamiliar with a lot of the races, so it isn't surprising I don't know.

"Yeah, they're a race of —"

"No!" Grímr interrupts. "No, she doesn't need to know."

Remus looks at Grímr with concern. "Are you sure? She's an áed, you know. Like the áinfean, there shouldn't be a problem if she knows."

"She is?" The big panther's eyes scan over me. "Even still, I'd prefer she didn't know." He tries to smile at me, but with a maw lined with teeth bigger than my hands, I don't think it gives the same image I think he intends. "Solvei, you can just think of me as a big cat. It's good to meet you."

"Uh, sure." If they'd had that conversation without me present, I'm sure there wouldn't be any issue. But now my curiosity is piqued. What about his race does he want to hide?

"So, where are the ladies?" Remus casts his gaze around the room as if they'll pop out of thin air.

"Where else do they ever go? Bunny is training and Doe is probably at the Order offices in Baansguard," Ossian says.

"Oh well, I guess we'll have to wait until they're back." Remus drops into a chair across from Grímr before looking over at me. "Solvei? What are you standing over there for? Come in. Relax."

I shake my head a bit too abruptly. "No. I'm fine over here."

"Well, you're letting in the cold," Ossian says. "At least shut the door."

Rather than doing as he asks, I pump up my body temperature. The room quickly heats from proximity.

"Oh! Ha, I guess that works too." Ossian turns to Remus. "I see why you chose her now, finally had enough of the chill up the mountain?"

Remus sheepishly scratches at the top of his head. "The thought may have crossed my mind. But no, she is definitely capable enough to join us. For now, we'll have her only fill the role of ritual technician, but I think she will be able to join in on the fights after a bit of training from Bunny. If we didn't already have Jav, she would have made a perfect scout."

Ossian's head nods in understanding. "Wouldn't want the little guy to lose one of the few things he's useful for."

"You know I can hear you. Do you want to wake sharing your bed with a snake?" Jav's voice yells from another room.

Ossian's smile becomes strained and he remains quiet.

Remus's eyes rotate beneath the surface of his head until they land on me. We stare at each other for a moment before he rises from his chair.

"Y'know what? I think we should go introduce you to Bunny. If we leave her alone, who knows how long she'll stay out?"

"Are you sure?" Grímr, the large panther, asks. "You know how she gets when interrupted." He climbs off the couch and follows close behind Remus.

"Who said anything about interrupting? We are only going to observe."

I step aside before following them into the forest on the other side of the clearing. Thankfully, there's no more pressure to go inside. I can't handle the anxiety and fear I know will explode should the door close on me. I'd rather keep my issues to myself, even if it may cause issues when night comes. How I'm gonna tell them I'd rather sleep outside, I'm not sure.

As we move between the trees, the sound of rushing water reaches my ears. "Where are we going?" I ask.

"There's a space beside the river where Bunny does her training." Remus casts his eyes back at me. "Don't worry, we won't go near the water."

Loud footfalls and panting sound out as we move through the last of the dense tree line. My eyes immediately catch the albanic woman that must be Bunny. She is nothing like what I expected, considering her name.

Bunny obviously notices us, sending a glance our way, but continues her . . . training.

Hefted above her head with both arms is a boulder that must be larger than I am. She sprints back and forth between the line of trees and the river's edge, pressing the heavy rock off her shoulders at each turn.

She's the strongest looking albanic I've ever seen, her muscular arms could compete with an ursu's.

Seriously? Her name's Bunny?

"This, Solvei, is Bunny." Remus answers my inner question. "She's a weapon master and by far our best fighter."

I definitely don't doubt she's a good fighter.

Bunny drops the boulder and the ground shakes from the impact. Instead of acknowledging us as I expect since she's stopped running, she unsheathes a thin blade from her waist and takes a stance.

The dance that follows seems far too elegant for such a heavily muscled woman. The gusts created from her swings don't seem as strong as the general's had been, but her strikes are far more deliberate and are delivered with swiftness the general couldn't hope to compare.

"In the future, I believe she can help you learn a weapon. You'll need something with impact for the times your flame won't be enough."

"Shut it in the peanut gallery," Bunny yells. "If you want to watch, be quiet. I'll be done soon."

And so we stand there watching as her blade slices through the air, audibly tearing through it with intense strength. Few in my tribe focused on the sword, but the movements remind me of the fluidity my elders expressed while wielding their respective weapons.

With a final flourish, she sheaths her blade and relaxes. "So, you finally found someone?" Bunny turns and walks up to us. She scrutinizes me with her gaze.

Cover her in fur and add a little height, and she'd be indistinguishable from an ursu. She's already taller than most albanic by a good head.

"Yep, meet Solvei; an áed we met in Joiak of all places. Solvei, this is—"

"Tetsu." She grasps my shoulder in her firm grasp. "Call me Tetsu."

"You might as well accept it now. She'll be calling you Bunny soon enough."

"Tetsu," she repeats, glaring down at me and squeezing my shoulder.

I'm uncomfortable being held like this. I can feel the tension rising the longer she takes to remove her hand. The stare and squeezing intensifies to a point where I can't handle it anymore. My shoulder loses its form and wraps her arm in flame as I jump a few steps back.

Tetsu looks down at her hand with a frown. Like with Remus, my flames do nothing, and she brushes them off with ease. "I see why you were willing to choose one so young."

I glare back as her eyes dig deep into me once again.

"Now that we have our replacement, we can finally go hunting again, correct? Tonight?"

"Whoa, whoa, whoa. I still need to show her how to work the ritual."

"You can do that as we travel."

"I'd prefer she knew what to do before we get in any trouble. I also wanted you to train her in a weapon."

"Sure," she says nonchalantly. "I can do that as we travel."

"At least let us wait until Doe returns."

"Why?"

"I want to introduce her to Solvei."

"Why?"

"Because she's a part of the team."

Tetsu raises an eyebrow at him. "No, she isn't. Doe's a part of the Order's bureaucracy. She isn't one of us."

Remus hesitates, looking uncomfortable for the first time since I met him. "Maybe not, but we can at least try to be civil."

The two stare down for a moment before Tetsu speaks. "We leave at midday tomorrow at the latest. If she doesn't arrive before then, too bad."

"Fine." Remus sighs.

Tetsu eagerly turns to me. "So what weapon did you want to learn?"

I don't even need to think about it. "The spear."

CHAPTER THIRTEEN

A Quick Hunt

It didn't take Tetsu long to find a couple of spears for us. She holds out the long pole of steel, and I wrap my fingers around it in the same grip I remember Auntie Kay teaching me. The familiarity is enticing and I can't help but stare.

Tetsu releases the spear into my grip and I immediately get pulled to the ground under the unreasonable weight of it. The thing has to weigh as much as I do.

I crouch and lift the spear in my hands, but it is insanely heavy and I struggle to do more than hold it against my thighs.

"Stop," Tetsu says and takes the spear out of my grip.

She stabs the base into the ground, leaving it standing upright, and sweeps her hands under my elbows. Tetsu lifts me into the air, sending me into a panic. I'm already becoming incorporeal and scorching her arms when she lets me go.

I try to calm my tense body as I glare up at the woman who held me without warning.

"You weigh nothing," Tetsu says and jogs back to her weapon stash.

"Hurry and teach her the ritual while I make a stick," she shouts to Remus as she runs to the line of trees, lugging an axe over her shoulder.

Remus and I watch as Tetsu slaps her hand onto trees, one after another, until she is no longer in sight.

"Well, Bunny won't be long, so we best get started." He turns and leads me back to the cabin.

As I wait outside for him, I hear a loud crack echo through the forest. A more subdued thump follows it.

"Looks like Bunny found a tree she likes." Grímr's voice startles me. I'd completely forgotten he was behind me. Something so large shouldn't be allowed to be so quiet.

I wonder how she got the nickname *Bunny* of all things. I just can't see how it fits her. It's not like she introduces herself like that.

Another crack echoes around us as Remus comes out holding a scroll.

"Wow, she's impatient." Remus turns to the forest at the sound of another thwack.

"She's been stuck waiting for months now and you bring someone she can share her art with. Of course she's excited," Grímr says.

"I guess we better hurry, then." Remus unrolls the parchment in front of me. "Solvei, your task for the next while is to memorize this ritual. Usually, I have a mage run their hyle through the inscription to show how it works before they attempt to craft it with their element, but fire and paper aren't exactly good friends."

On the scroll, the inscription is configured with a large and small circle. Inside each circle are thousands of lines detailing what look like completely random patterns.

"The large circle is the placement for the target. We'll place the remains of our hunts within. The small circle is the output, where the receiver will take in the energy transferred from the target. Please be careful with it. Getting another copy will take a long time if it gets damaged."

I nod and carefully take it from him. It looks hard, but I need to do my best to memorize it.

"So, do I just make this shape and it'll work?"

"I think so? Most mages I've met have been able to power it without any issue. Even those who'd never seen it before. I'm not a mage, so I can't tell you if there will be any differences between using the inscription and creating it with your fire."

My flames come to life in the air, attempting to mimic the intricate pattern as close as possible. But it's slow work; it takes much of my focus to recreate the complex lines. I quickly lose myself making it match.

"Hey. I'm done. Let's get back to it."

I look up in time to catch the pole thrown at me. Tetsu is already striding toward the clearing where we found her. The wooden pole feels smooth to the touch and perfectly straight. A spearhead is expertly affixed to the end of the wood.

I'm downgraded to a stick again.

It's not all bad. The stick weighs about as much as the spears back in my tribe. Not so light that I can swing it around freely, but I can pick it up with no problem. I swing the weapon experimentally. It feels good in my hands. I'm happy I can finally get back to learning Mom's weapon.

"Hurry up!" Tetsu snaps from ahead.

"Right. Coming."

Doe never showed up, so as per Tetsu's wishes, we leave the moment the sun reaches its peak.

Remus is the only one who seems resistant to leaving so soon. Jav jumped at the chance as soon as he heard, and Grímr was fine to go along with everyone else.

"Okay, so who's holding the kid?" Tetsu asks as she jogs on the spot.

Why would someone hold me? Is it for speed? I already know three of them can move a lot quicker than me and it wouldn't take much to assume Grímr can move quickly too, considering his body. "Should I change? Flying will be quicker."

"No, I want you memorizing the ritual. Grímr should be a stable enough ride," Remus says.

Grímr looks at me oddly, but lowers to a crouch and lets me climb onto his back. As soon as I'm comfortable on his neck, Tetsu is already running off.

"You ready?" Grímr asks as he rises to his feet again, the others already out of sight.

"Yes."

The scroll almost slips out of my hands as Grímr dashes after the three. He dodges and weaves through trees as I try to stabilize myself with the fur at his nape. When I said yes, I didn't expect him to hit a sprint right away. I'm lucky I didn't fall off.

We catch up, and if not for the trees whipping past us at insane speeds, I would think this is a casual jog with the lackadaisical effort they put into their movements.

It may not be any faster than I can fly, but the trees passing at such speed makes it difficult to focus on anything but grasping at Grímr. I try to unroll the scroll, but it flutters in the wind like crazy. I'm only barely able to keep it steady by pushing it into my ride's fur.

This is a horrible place to do this, but I have to try anyway. I don't know if I'll be able to focus on the parchment enough to achieve anything, and I would really rather spend my time flying than in such close proximity to someone who is still a stranger.

"What did you mean before?" Grímr's voice reaches me. "You said you can fly? How?"

"Remus hasn't told you? I can transform my body. If I become a bird, I can fly just like one."

"Is that something only áed can do? Remus has spoken of your people before. He described you as similar to the áinfean, but none I've met could change their forms."

"It's not common. My elder was the only one other than me who I know could do it. Who are the áinfean? I've never—" I'm interrupted by a branch whacking me in the face. I try to duck, but I'm not quick enough. Grímr's movement around the trees is too fast for me to react while focusing on the parchment.

Fortunately, the branch passes right through my head, only leaving me a little disoriented.

Unfortunately, Grímr snaps to a halt, sending me flying over his head. I crash into the forest floor amongst roots and leaves.

I groan and check the scroll in my grasp, making sure it wasn't damaged.

"I'm so sorry! I'm still not used to this b . . . uh, I wasn't thinking. Are you okay?" The large panther stands over me.

I give him an annoyed glare as I rise to my feet. It didn't hurt or anything, but I'd really rather fly under my own strength than be thrown around like that.

I see this group as a strong and capable bunch, but how can one be that clumsy? Did he forget I was sitting on top of him? Mid-conversation?

"I'm fine," I say and climb onto Grímr's back again.

If it happens again, I don't care how quickly Remus needs me to learn the ritual, I'm flying.

"Uh, you asked about the áinfean right?"

I unroll the scroll again, intending to ignore the large creature under me so they might not become distracted and send me flying again.

Grímr runs along in silence for a few seconds before my reluctance to speak becomes clear. He doesn't take the hint, though.

"The áinfean are another energy race like yourself. Similar to how you áed are bound to fire, they are to lightning. We portian owe a lot to them for what they've done over the centuries. The other races have a tendency to see us as their enemy, regardless of our intentions. Most stick to the north at the edge of the ice plains, but there are plenty living within pact territories."

As much as I try to ignore him and focus on the inscription before me, I can't help but listen as he talks. It's always interesting to hear more about the world. I wonder what he's hiding about his race that makes most sapients hostile? I mean, these big panthers look threatening enough as it is, and if it weren't for Grímr's open secrecy, I'd assume it was just because of their appearance. There's obviously something more.

"They're good swimmers, did you know? But they refuse to touch the water unless it's as fresh as can be. Glacial rivers are their favorite. When I was a kid in the . . . uh, when I swam with them, I was always impressed by the speeds they could reach."

It looks like Grímr is a fan of these áinfean. While he continues to blabber about his experiences with them, I cast my sight toward Tetsu running ahead of us. She carries a massive pack strapped to her back that one might assume is filled with camping gear and whatnot for our travels, but is instead loaded with nothing but weapons.

I watched her pack it. Half the weapons she shoved in there I've never seen before. The spear she made for me, along with many other pole weapons, are tied in bundles and strapped to the sides of the pack. I haven't a clue what she could need them for.

Spear training with Tetsu had been eye opening. Only after fighting against her did I realize that Auntie Kay had been soft with me. I knew Auntie hadn't been putting in her all when teaching me, but when I compare her to the no-holds-barred attitude of Tetsu, I realize just how careful she'd been.

Tetsu is a monster. I hope it's because she knows I won't take any lasting damage from her strikes, but with the way she acts, I can't rule out that she simply doesn't know how to hold back.

She was nice enough to guide me on my forms. She told me that most of the forms she knows for the spear would be useless for me because of how little I weigh. If I am to use my weapon effectively, I need to learn how to move quickly and always deflect rather than block. She was familiar with all the forms I remembered and told me which would be better to focus on at my current size and weight.

It was after her guidance session that she invited me to a spar. I don't know how she considered that a spar, every second of that fight I spent trying to recover from a spear piercing or cutting through me. Tetsu might as well have used me as a practice target for all I accomplished trying to hit her back.

There is one important thing I learned fighting her though; I'm not truly as invulnerable as I'd assumed. The faster and harder she hits me, the further my intangible body flames are sent. If an impact spreads my flames far enough, it becomes hard to pull myself back together. I found the actual sharp blade of the spear to be easier to deal with than the shaft. If the sharp edge cuts into me, my form simply bends around it. But if a blunt edge like that of the shaft hits me, it makes it a lot harder to keep myself together.

It is something I'm incredibly glad to find out now, and not somewhere it might get me killed, but I'm also stuck with Tetsu knowing. There is no way she didn't spot how much slower I recovered when she used her shaft, especially considering she only used the blade after the first few times.

The same thing happened when I grasped at Remus during our fight. The impact he caused with the metal gauntlets dispersed my body enough that he could simply brush me off.

I'm suddenly not feeling as safe and assured of myself as I had been yesterday.

Well, whatever. There are still worse things to worry about.

Like water.

Like ice.

Like the snowcapped mountains we are currently sprinting toward.

We're gonna stop before we reach the snow, right?

CHAPTER FOURTEEN

Snow

It's rather strange. We put all this time and effort into climbing the mountain before us, and yet the ridgeline beyond is no closer.

I cling tight to Grímr's fur as we run through the snow-laden slope. An icy gale rolls over us and I increase my heat to push away the cold.

Why are we moving through here? Couldn't we have stuck to the areas without such a deadly carpet? They aren't trying to put me in danger on purpose, are they? I cling tighter to the fur and consider changing to give myself flight and escape any possibility that Grímr might toss me off again.

"You look like you're enjoying yourself, Grímr," Remus muses. "If only we could say the same about your passenger."

"It's incredible. She's like a living heat pack. The higher altitudes won't be a problem if she can keep this up."

All right, stuff this. I'm not going to put myself in danger to be someone's back warmer. I change my legs first and dig my talons into Grímr's hide. Besides a curious glance back, he doesn't complain. I press in hard, but the sharp points on my feet don't pierce through.

By the time my transformation is complete, we are approaching the summit. The mountain is probably tall in its own right, but the speed at which we scaled it and its position beneath the Titan Alps makes it feel like nothing more than a hill.

The moment I take wing, we surmount the peak. I ignore the sigh of disappointment from below as I stare in amazement at the view before me. The

Titan Alps have always been a constant companion. They are always visible. Always present. To see them so close and clear is incredible.

Snow covers the Titan Alps as well, but unlike the mountain underneath me, the snow only reaches the lowest rung. While still far above me, the white sheet eventually ends and unmarred black and gray stone blocks out the sky.

"From this point onwards, Solvei, is where we hunt," Remus declares with three limbs raised toward the vast mountain ranges before us.

The land between here and the Titan Alps gradually increases in altitude, leaving most of the ground white.

"You never said anything about the snow." There isn't any way I'll be working with them if I'm constantly in danger.

"Don't worry so much, as long as you control the heat you give off, like I've seen you do, you'll be fine until one of us pulls you out."

I give him an incredulous look as I circle above. That's hardly reasonable. Am I supposed to just let myself freeze out here? I'm already burning through far too many resources to keep myself warm in these icy conditions. I'll tire myself out in no time if I try to keep a temperature difference so that I'm still warm on the inside while forcing my exterior to be cold enough not to melt snow.

I can do it somewhat when I'm trying to lower my outer temperature to interact with others, but it's almost impossible to force my body to be that cold. Why does he assume I can do that?

"There's no way I can do that. Do you know how hard that is?"

Remus just looks up and tilts his head . . . body at me. It looks odd.

"Don't think about it too much." I almost jerk out of my flight as Jav appears beside me. "Remus expects the best in everyone. If he believes you can do it, then there is a good chance you can. Even if you don't believe him, you only need to get through this trip. I've put an order in with my sisters to get you proper snow gear to fit. You shouldn't have to deal with those oversized clothes after we get back. And trust me, their work is so good, you won't get a drop of water on you even if you decide to go swimming. Although, probably best not to try it."

I guess it'll be fine just this once. "I'm not changing back, though." I'd rather keep flight available to me than be susceptible in my normal form.

"That's fine. Do what makes you comfortable." Jav glides down to land on Remus's head again.

Tetsu is already charging down the mountainside, too impatient to wait while we argue. The rest of us are soon to follow behind. I glide above while they sprint their way down and cast my sight across the valley. Most of the area is blanketed in snow, with the exception of the lower altitude of the valley that drops into a river. But, to the west, an almost perfectly circular region along the mountainside lacks the white cover entirely. The area, half a league wide, sticks out from the surroundings.

"Hey, can we hunt over there?" I call to Remus and direct my beak to the area I won't have to worry about the snow.

"No," Remus answers immediately. "We never go near there. That's the home of the Ice Glutton."

"The Ice Glutton?"

"It may not be in the realm of a Titan, but it is still far from anything we could hope to take on. As long as we leave it alone, it'll stay near its home and only come out to gullet some snow."

"It just stays here? A mountain away from people?"

"Yep. Hasn't moved from the spot since it arrived over a century ago. Good thing too, cause the last time a hunting party was formed, none survived."

I send one last glance toward the only extensive area without a buildup of snow. It's annoying. The only place that looks at all appealing to fly toward just happens to hold some unbeatable monster.

"What about above the snow? Do you ever go there?" I nod toward the Titan Alps above.

"We've certainly tried, but no. I don't think you would want to try either. If you think it's cold here, I don't think you could imagine the chill up there. It takes months to prepare for a journey to the Middle Elevation, and that's not accounting for the time it would take to traverse. Sorry, but you'll just have to learn to work around the snow." Remus picks up his speed and we close the distance on Tetsu.

"Has anyone tried to climb over the Titan Alps?"

"Plenty. If any have succeeded, they never made it back. It's the biggest cause of death for Beith-class mercenaries. They tend to get bored after a long time without a good fight and go looking over the mountain. Well, that or they hassle the Theocracy and Empire."

"So, does anyone know what's on the other side of the mountains?"

"Nope. But people like to guess—"

"It's a land of endless conflict. Men and women fight for their lives every day with weapons and talents unheard of." Tetsu stops dead in her tracks to interrupt.

"Don't you already have that here?" Remus asks.

"Hardly. Most people cower in their cities, not even knowing what a monster is until it butchers them."

Remus sighs at his teammate. "Like I was saying, people like to guess at what might be over there, but nobody knows for sure. I like to think it's just the same as over here, with plenty of people trying their hardest to live the best lives they can."

"It's definitely the home of the Titans over there, why else would they name it the Titan Alps?" Jav says.

I look at Grímr, expecting him to give his thoughts as well. He takes a moment before he notices my gaze.

"What? I don't know what's over there. I couldn't guess."

"Now that you mention it, Jav," Remus says. "Maybe that Titan who climbed the Alps near two years ago was trying to meet its family?"

"Don't even say that," Grímr says. "I don't want to think of the chance that those things aren't perpetually sleeping. Could you imagine the death that crocodile Titan could have inflicted should it have passed through inhabited land rather than the wasteland?"

Ah, yes, all the lives that were saved by it choosing to devastate my tribe instead.

No longer in the mood to talk, I fly higher. The air seems to get colder with every extra meter I rise, but I just burn through it. I'm getting hungry from how fast I'm expending energy, but I can wait. I just need some time to myself so I don't fall back into a slump.

I'm not even given time to clear my head, though. Remus launches Jav into the air and soon the little volan flies beside me.

"Remus sent me after you. Is something wrong?"

"I'm fine." I don't mean to snap at him, but that's how it comes out.

After a moment of silence, Jav speaks. "You know, you're a part of the team now. So if there's anything you need help with, just ask. We'll be waiting for you."

I watch him glide back to his resting spot on Remus's head. I guess making space for myself without being noticed was too much to hope for.

Will I really be able to hunt out here with them amongst all this frozen water? When I agreed to work with them, I never expected to be thrown into such a hazardous environment. I instead pictured fights with wolves or colossal-worms where I'd have no need to worry about their claws or teeth. In my head, there never would be any genuine danger.

Now the question is, do I still want to go forward knowing it will actually be dangerous?

I need to grow, and if all creatures strong enough to enhance my growth have the same resistance to fire as each member of this team has, then I'd have no chance of bringing them down. If I could even find creatures outside the Titan Alps without their help.

Remus has already organized a home for my friends and all the other victims of the mill. If I don't at least put some effort in to help them, then I haven't done my half of the deal. Worst-case scenario, Remus might even go back on his promise to provide them safety.

For now, simply following along seems like the best course.

I can't stay away from them any longer than I already have. I'm hungry, but all the trees in the area are covered in white slush.

"Hey," I call as I get close. "Do you mind shaking the snow off that tree?" I ask Remus.

He gives a glance to Tetsu, who is already approaching the tree ahead of her.

She places her muscular arms around the thick trunk and shakes. If it was anything but a tree, I'd assume she was trying to strangle the life out of whatever she'd caught in her grasp. Cracks and groans from the tree accompany the sight of falling snow.

Tetsu brushes the powder off her shoulders as she steps away from the deep arm shaped depressions left in the cracked wood.

"Thanks." I land on a branch and enwrap the tree in flame.

"Well, I guess now is as good a time as any to take a break," Remus says and takes a seat in the snow under the flaming tree.

Tetsu looks annoyed. I can understand the impatience that comes with getting so close to something you've missed. Even if the thing she misses is fighting.

"So how far until we reach wherever we're going?" I ask.

"Not long at all. Only a few more hours until we reach the roach colony hotspot. They're the perfect creatures for you to practice the ritual on; they aren't too dangerous, they're close to home, and best of all, you'll never run out."

"I don't know how you could ever consider that a good thing." Jav cringes. "They are ugly things and their meat tastes disgusting."

"You're the only one I know who has tried to cook them," Grímr says.

"What? Not all bugs taste bad. Crickets are delicious."

"Normal crickets or blood crickets?"

"Both. But you have to slow roast the blood crickets for a good five hours before they are edible. Usually not worth the effort."

While I take my time to burn through the tree, Tetsu has pulled out some chain weapon with a knife linked to the end. The blade tears through the trees as if they are paper. How does a single person get so good with so many weapons? None of my elders ever branched away from the single weapon they learned.

"Not gonna practice forming the inscription while you have the chance, Solvei?" Remus calls up to me.

Oh, right. I still need to do that, don't I? I can hardly take the parchment back from Grímr's pack where I left it while burning through the tree, but I can try forming it from memory.

I create the two circles and try to fill them in with as many of the lines as I remember. I don't get very far. A good portion of the smaller circle is filled, but I'm not sure I got them perfect. Trying to fill the larger circle is too much for me; I can't remember a thing.

I look down at Remus, expecting to see disappointment, but he stands there holding the parchment up above his head for me to see. "Good job on your first attempt, but you still have quite a bit to memorize."

A breath escapes me. Yeah, I do.

CHAPTER FIFTEEN

The Ritual

It's time to move," Tetsu says the moment I finish burning through the last of the trunk.

She'd been so focused on her weapon practice, but still must have been paying attention while I ate away at the tree. I'd consumed it slowly, to give myself a little extra time to practice the ritual, but I guess there is only so much I can delay her impatience.

There was no need for me to eat the entire tree, but I wanted to have enough energy to last a good long while in this chill. I should also be good to expel quite a bit of energy in any fight we take.

I take to the skies again as the rest continue their run through the valley between mountains. Remus flings Jav far into the skies ahead of me, but he quickly disappears in the distance.

Thirty minutes later, he returns and I fly low enough to hear as he lands on Remus.

"They've moved farther north since we last came through, but they definitely need a bit of population control. They're overflowing at the moment."

"Wonderful! We can hit three birds with one stone." Remus's eyes grin. "Anything to worry about in the area?"

"Nothing on the surface, but I did spot signs of burrowers to the west. River flow is too low for anything threatening to be hiding within. And I didn't see anything in the skies. Should be all good."

"Good, good. I'll stick with Solvei. You three enjoy yourselves."

As if waiting for those words, Tetsu dashes ahead without a word. Grímr and Jav follow behind her. I try to speed up, but I can't reach their speeds even with flight. Remus matches my pace.

Time passes and I almost think I might have passed them or gone off track when I crest the ridge and finally find what I'm looking for. The slope beneath me flattens into a plateau between mountain ranges, and standing out from the snow covered ground are hundreds of thousands of brown critters crawling over each other. It would be a disgusting sight even if they were tiny like normal bugs, but no, these things are as long as my legs. Bigger than I am as a bird.

A mountain of the bugs are blown into the sky, and I spot Tetsu wading through the endless roaches with a grin as she swings dual sabers. Jav is flying ahead of me and Grímr is sitting off to the side, the both of them letting Tetsu have her fun and doing as much as they can to avoid touching the bugs.

Tetsu is dripping in some foul, brown-black sludge. The same goop that bursts out when she cuts through the roaches.

"We left a pile of carcasses over there." Jav flies close and nods toward a mound of the unmoving brown bugs.

"Perfect, we can get started right away then," Remus says.

I bring myself down to land on Remus's head and prepare myself to get through this. I can hope it'll be quick, but I have a feeling it won't be as easy as Remus keeps saying.

It takes me a while, but I feel like I've formed my flame to match perfectly with the inscription held by Remus. The shape doesn't make my fire any different from normal. No extra effect occurs simply by holding my flames in this pattern as Remus said it should.

I compare my suspended flames to the parchment for the hundredth time, but I can't spot any differences. Everything looks identical. So why doesn't the ritual work?

"Are you sure this thing is supposed to do anything? The shape is right, but it doesn't react in any way more than I'd usually expect."

"Hmm." He leans over and inspects my flame spread above the ground. If he spots any issues with it, he doesn't say. "I think you might have to use that scroll, after all."

"I thought you needed it? Wouldn't I destroy it?"

"Well, yes. The hyle of fire is still fire, so the paper won't last long. But if you can understand how it works before you incinerate the page, there shouldn't be anything to worry about."

"What is hyle?"

Remus's eyes roll in his head to look up at me. "Er, well I can't give you the technical details because I don't know enough about it myself. What I do know is that it's the form that any element can take to flow freely through physical materials. Have you ever seen a mage's tattoos glow? That's the hyle of their respective element cycling through their bodies. To my understanding, hyle is the only reason you can have stone or water mages and inscriptions."

So the hyle of water was what Leal had running along her tattoos? Is there a hyle of everything? If you converted an element to hyle, can you send it through walls?

Huh? I've done that before. I've made hyle when I interacted with those inscriptions; at Leal's mage academy, the manor in Zadok, and Henosis's weapon. The inscriptions for each passed through walls, but I had no trouble passing my flame through them without needing to burn through the buildings.

I can do it. It shouldn't be any harder than controlling fire normally.

I reach for the paper, ready to figure out what it is I'm doing wrong, but Remus pulls it away before I can reach.

"Don't be hasty. You still need to memorize it before we should risk running your flame through. We have plenty of time while Bunny enjoys herself."

I groan, but do as he says. This is gonna take forever.

Two days have passed and only now do I feel confident I can completely recreate the inscription from memory. After the vast majority of roaches were wiped out and the rest scattered to the horizons, Tetsu took off to the west. The group seems wholly unconcerned about her actions, so I can only assume she does this often.

Maybe it's because of the difference in the way we taste, but I find the roaches to be rather good. With all Jav's talk about how disgusting they are, I expected worse. Their outer shell is resistant to my flames, not so much that I can't burn through, but enough that their gooey interior incinerates the bug before they lose the exoskeleton. I wouldn't call them sweet like sand-worms, but they definitely taste similar.

While the energy within each bug comes nowhere close to the creatures in the Void Fog, the sheer quantity makes up the difference. Unfortunately, I still need to keep them for practice with the ritual, so Remus only lets me eat a relatively tiny portion. A tiny portion that may have been about a hundred times my body weight, but compared to the plateau buried in the roaches, it is nothing.

"So, ready to do this?" Remus brings the roasted thigh of some creature Jav hunted to his concealed mouth.

"Are you sure? You'll lose the scroll." I want to confirm it's okay for the last time. I'd hate to have him regret his decision after it's gone.

"Yep, no worries. It'll take some time to get another, but I might squeeze a more efficient ritual out of the upper brass."

Remus lays the scroll on the hard soil. With all the fire I've had over it in the past few days, it's no surprise the snow melted away. Even the ground dried out enough for me to land without issue. I still remain a falcon, as the ability to fly away at a moment's notice is just too important.

Remus picks up a roach carcass and places it so it is touching the center of the large circle and places the tip of his own limb in the little circle.

"Should you really be touching it? What if I do it wrong and the inscription doesn't do what it's supposed to?"

"Well, you better get it right then." He grins at me. "How else are we going to see if it works if we don't have a target?"

Does he really have to add more pressure than I'm already feeling? Well, if he thinks he'll be fine, then that's enough for me.

I place a talon on the page, careful to not tear through the paper or burn it. With a deep breath, I push my flames through the lines of the inscription. I try to keep them as cold as possible and watch as the lines light up in a deep red.

Around the glowing lines, the scroll burns away. The burning inscription remains suspended ever so slightly off the ground, but it does not break down like the rest of the scroll. My flames flood through it and I finally see that I never could have achieved this simply by replicating the shape. The lines are unimportant. It's the action that each line represents that matters.

A straight line reduces the heat from one point to another, while a three-pronged star with curved lines uses two points to create an empowering effect at the third. There are so many of these unique tiny shapes that create different effects. Only when the ritual actually starts do I realize I've felt this sort of reaction before. Those odd actions the Henosis had me perform to power and activate their weapon. It's not identical. Actually, it's not even that similar, but it gives me the same feeling when my flames run through the inscription as each little shape reacts and plays off each other to create the effect of the dissolving roach before me.

Small, hardly visible motes float off the carcass toward the inscription where they are condensed and directed toward the smaller circle and into Remus's tentacle. It doesn't take long for the roach to be torn apart by the ritual, but I've already seen what I need. With nothing more to tear apart, the inscription falls away from my control, crumbling into ash.

"So, figure anything out?" Remus asks.

I nod, but don't acknowledge him any more than that. In moments, I have the recreated inscription from my memory formed in flames before me. As fast as I can, I find shapes in the pattern and give each their respective action that I felt during the ritual. There are many shapes, but I think I successfully created a replica of each one. Now, I just need to reproduce the effect of each shape within the inscription with what they should have.

The inscription is not simple at all, so I don't imagine this will be a quick process. I'll need to memorize the changes as well. I sigh to myself. Hopefully, this won't take long.

"Is she done?" are the first words I hear from Tetsu upon her return.

"She's doing well," Remus says behind me.

"No. Now go have a bath, you reek," Jav says.

I turn to the group lazing around behind me. Except for Tetsu, they are all laying in the snow as if it's a comfortable couch.

"I'm done. I was done a while ago now. I just wanted to memorize it properly."

Tetsu's eyes light up, as do the others as they rise to their feet.

"Finally!" Tetsu is covered head to toe in the blood and muck from whatever she'd been fighting. Maybe I should have waited until she'd washed to announce I'm done.

Remus grins. "That's great, Solvei, I knew you could do it."

"We have a mountain to get through." Tetsu nods to the roach piles. "No time to wait."

"No, Jav's right. You need a bath first," Remus says.

"Wha—? But . . ." Tetsu looks to her other teammate, hoping for support, but Grímr holds a paw over his nose and pointedly doesn't look her way. "Fine, but don't you start without me." She runs off to the nearest river.

"You might as well start," Grímr says. "She won't be long."

I barely even spread my flame over the area when Tetsu rushes back. "Wait!" She's dripping wet, but still looks filthy.

"You didn't even wash yourself," Jav says.

"Sure I did. I dove in and everything."

"What, for a millisecond?"

"It was at least a second."

Groans resound amongst the team.

"After the first round, you're going to scrub yourself properly," Remus says.

"Uh-huh, sure," Tetsu says dismissively, already looking over the inscription burning in the air as wide as I can make it.

I'm unable to spread it to the nearest mound, so I wait until they've piled up the roaches beneath the large flaming circle. With how excited Tetsu is, it doesn't take long for everything to be in position and they stand underneath the small circle.

For the final time, I look over my work. I make sure there is no missing line and each has the appropriate effect attached. Nothing is out of place. With a deep breath, I connect the last few pathways. Immediately, I feel my fire flowing almost without my input. I could pull them back if I need to, but for now, I leave the inscription to guide me through the intensely complicated process of breaking down the dead bodies and direct their energy to those waiting in the receiver circle.

It's an incredible sight. The blood and ooze around the roaches are the first to dematerialize. The hard shells don't seem to provide all that much defense against the ritual. Despite their resistance to my flames, they break into pieces and disperse into the air as they rise toward the burning inscription.

The sound is not something I expected. My flames roar in a repetitive, deep thrum. It's not a noise I thought I could ever have associated with flames. Each thrum shakes the very air.

The shell and inner flesh of the roaches continue to flake and separate, being sucked through the inscription and charging into the bodies of the three in the circle.

Wait . . . three?

I look around to see Grímr sitting off to the side. Why didn't he join them?

He catches my inquisitive gaze. "The ritual doesn't have as much of an effect on me as the others. They help me out in . . . other ways."

Okay. He's being vague again. I'll worry about him later, I still need to focus.

Eventually, the last of the bugs are gone and I feel the inscription powering down, taking the heavy sound with it.

"That was beautiful, Solvei. Good job!"

Jav jumps on Remus's head. "Yeah, that's gonna be a lot more convenient than having to wait for someone to draw it out every time."

Draw it? "Didn't you say mages create it with their element?"

"I did," Remus confirms. "And technically they do. They combine their element with the paint they use on the ground. I've seen áinfean and some of the better mages create inscriptions in the air like that with their element, so I figured it would be easy for you. Also, much more convenient for us; we don't have to wait while you prepare."

I just stare at him for a moment. "Isn't that too much of an expectation to have?"

Jav snorts. "You'll get used to it, kid."

CHAPTER SIXTEEN

Katobles

The katobles is just over this hill," Jav calls over the strong wind.

It took us all day to get through the remains of the roaches. Even then, there were still thousands remaining by the time Tetsu became impatient and encouraged us to get back to hunting. Remus gave me the go-ahead to fly around burning the leftovers.

Now that I can effectively create the ritual with a wave of my hand . . . or wing, the others are keen to push farther up the Titan Alps.

Remus makes sure we stick close together as we move through the mountainous ranges, not letting Tetsu run off on her own again. "Bunny, hold back a bit this fight, will you? Let the others get into the flow of things, it's been a while since we've all fought."

He does that weird thing with his eyes, where he looks at me through the top of his head without actually turning his body. "Solvei, it's up to you whether you want to participate or not. You know what your job is. As long as you do that, you are free to sit out. If you want to fight, be careful. Katobles might look tough, but their true danger is in the toxic fumes they breathe. I don't know if they are effective on áed or not, but watch out."

I fly over the hill and it's not hard to spot the creature. A massive, gray, stocky beast stands tall over the line of trees a few hundred meters ahead. Its four legs give it a distinct similarity to the pholos used to pull wagons. The only visual differences I can spot—other than the obvious size difference—are the long, trunk-like legs and the extended neck that hangs its head below the white canopy.

For now, I gain some altitude and watch the others sprint toward the beast. At about a hundred meters out, Remus flings Jav toward the katobles. The small volan's wingsuit stabilizes him and a glint reaches my eyes. He moves too quick to see, but as I watch the beast, small lacerations appear all along its neck. A hundred cuts, each with barely a trickle of blood.

I catch sight of Jav again. At an insane speed, he spins around the ankle of the katobles. Short, barely noticeable blades extend from his suit, continually cutting into the leg of the creature. Each pass barely digs into the skin, but the volan spins around hundreds of times a second, cutting ever so slightly deeper through the tough skin.

The katobles cries out in a low-pitched bellow as it pulls its leg away before slamming it down on the earth. The beast grunts with aggression as it backs up. With his remaining speed, Jav joins me in the sky, watching over the creature as the other three move toward it.

The katobles curls its head up between its front legs until it touches its underbelly, using its trunk-like legs as protection.

In the time Jav was cutting through the creature's neck and leg, Remus, Tetsu, and Grímr position themselves around it. Tetsu rushes in from the front with a long halberd and strikes at the back of its head. The blade pierces cleanly into the neck of the beast, and it lets out a deep bellow. The katobles brings one of its thick legs down, attempting to squash Tetsu, but she dodges by millimeters and springs up the other leg. She looks like she's about to bounce even higher off the leg when Remus calls out.

"What did I say, Bunny? No taking it on yourself."

She looks disappointed, but acknowledges by letting herself fall back to the ground. She dashes back to her position in front of the creature.

The katobles doesn't seem to want to let her go, though. It lowers its body and lets out another bellow before charging after her.

Tetsu dodges the beast's large body with ease. Each dodge, her arms twitch, as if physically struggling not to strike as the beast continues its charge. It knocks down a good few hundred trees before it slows to a stop.

Remus and Grímr don't give it time to prepare another charge. Remus's whiplike arms slam into the katobles's front leg where Jav sliced deep into the skin, while Grímr barrels through its rear one. With the legs on the right side of its body knocked out from underneath it, the beast falters and tumbles to its side. The resounding crash shakes trees while the creature grunts and bellows.

The two are quick to capitalize on their downed foe and rush in to strike at its head. The metal gauntlets on Remus's limbs pound into flesh with repeated cracks of air. Grímr takes full advantage of his claws and teeth by tearing through the thick skin protecting its skull.

"Gas!" Jav shouts from above.

"I see it!" Remus yells as he and Grímr dash away from the uncurling head.

Laying on its side, the katobles's head moves away from its chest, breathing out a deep, opaque purple mist that soon hides the creature from sight. Trees wither and die as soon as the gas touches them. None dare approach the toxic fumes.

I fly closer to Jav as I hear the heavy thuds of the katobles rising to its feet.

"How do you deal with that?" I ask.

Jav glances at me before returning his sight down below. "We wait it out. It's only dangerous when it's dense enough to see. The wind will disperse it in a few minutes."

I look down at the others below. Tetsu walks off to practice her stances with the halberd, and Remus is flinging stones into the obscuring fumes to little effect. Grímr lies beside him as if now is the perfect time for a nap. They are all very casual about this. Do they fight these katobles often?

I'm curious about this toxic breath that stops even people as strong as them from pushing through. I fly low over the cloudy purple gas and send down a small ball of my inner flame. If need be, I'm prepared to expel it, but I've never seen poison able to taint my flame, so I'm not too worried.

My flame lowers until it touches the fumes. I tense up, expecting it to be painful or for something unexpected to happen, but none of that comes. My fire burns right through the gas without resistance. Well, that's good. It feels a bit anticlimactic considering how seriously the others treat the toxic mist.

I might as well make myself useful. I spread my flames wide around me, then fly through the purple gas, scorching through as much of the substance as I can. It doesn't take long before I can make out the katobles within the remaining fumes. My wings sweep the air beside me and I fall into a dive. I curve under the beast's body and cover as much of it as I can in my flames before pulling back above.

The toxic gas sits in pockets around the area. While I can burn through the substance, it is not naturally flammable, so my flames don't spread unless I'm close enough to do it myself. I rush down each of the remaining patches while my flames spread over the head and forelegs of the katobles. The creature snorts and grunts as it rubs its head against the ground, trying in vain to remove my fire.

This far above the creature, I don't have full control over my flames, but I can still feel as it spreads over the thin, wiry hairs that cover its body with my minimal directing nudges.

When the last of the purple mist is gone, Remus and Grímr dash toward the exposed beast. The tall creature limps on the leg attacked by both Remus and Jav, while it continues to rub its head into the dirt below. It doesn't notice the returning attackers until they throw themselves onto its head and start pummeling through its skull.

The katobles intensifies its efforts, now slamming its head to the ground and rubbing its forelegs over it, trying with the desperation of a cornered animal to remove those tearing into it.

Not much longer does the beast last. Both Remus and Grímr's skillful avoidance of being squashed—and their continual beating and clawing—has the katobles bellowing its last as it collapses.

I land on Grímr's back as they approach to confirm its death.

"Good job, Solvei. Knowing you can burn through that toxic gas will be lifesaving next time a katobles wanders into inhabited land."

I look at Remus walking beside us. "These are common?" That thing was harder to take down than a colossal-worm.

"Not common, but there are incidents every year. We don't cull their numbers much because they eat the roots of many poisonous plants in the lower portion of the Stepps often frequented by people. Sometimes the katobles follow the scent of pollution right back to the cities. Joiak is the country most commonly hit by katobles."

"C'mon, we're burning daylight." Tetsu rushes to my side. "Start up the ritual already."

I go to complain about her constant nagging and impatience when I see Remus and Jav giving me pleading eyes themselves. I guess the energy they'll get from this beast is a lot more than the roaches we dealt with before.

My flames quickly spread over our heads. I won't be able to cover the entirety of the katobles with the inscription, but I can position it in the center of its body so it will hopefully still take it in. It takes a little work to make sure it's all correctly made before I start the ritual.

The heavy pounding through the air as it powers up is irritating, but I ignore it and focus on the inscription as the energy redirects from the disappearing corpse into the bodies of the three mercenaries.

As the ritual progresses, I notice that only the parts of the katobles directly underneath the large, burning circle are vaporized. Within the remains of the corpse is a massive cylindrical hole, cut cleanly through its chest.

So the ritual won't take in anything except what is directly placed over or under it, even if it is a part of another whole. What would happen if I angled it to the side? How far would it be able to dissipate corpses?

As the first round of the ritual comes to its conclusion, I prepare to try it out on an angle, but I'm stopped by Grímr's voice.

"Blizzard incoming, we'll have to give up the rest."

Everyone turns toward a distant covering of white as it crawls over the mountaintop to the north. Remus and Jav immediately start trekking away from the corpse and I'm surprised to see Tetsu follow them with hardly more than a groan of disappointment.

Not wanting to waste any of the leftover katobles, I pass my flames over it and try to eat through it as quick as I can.

"Solvei!" Remus calls with concern lacing his voice. "You of all people should be worried about the blizzard. Hurry!"

Quick to abandon my attempt, I fly to the others, their pace set much higher than on our way up the mountains.

I cast my eyes back on the wall of white that appears to build up on the top of the mountain for a while. It doesn't move any closer to us, instead growing over the entire ridge of the mountain. Much of the Titan Alps above the blizzard disappear behind the buildup of white.

Then it falls.

In moments, the mountain rising high above and behind us is gone, consumed by the snowstorm as it tears down the slope. The terrifying speed at which it tears down the mountain reminds me far too much of the ocean fog. I look away and pump my wings as hard as they'll move.

Loud rumbling slams through me and sends shivers down my back. I don't focus on anything but getting away as fast as I can. My head doesn't turn away from the open air before me as the deep rumbling intensifies. I don't look at the others running, nor do I turn to watch the frozen water barreling toward me.

What am I doing? I'm not a terrified child anymore. I should think about this properly and not let myself fall into a blind panic. Forcefully dragging my head down to the group below, I see they are sprinting off to my left together. My head turns behind me and I have to suppress the panic that tries to overwhelm me as I feel my stomach drop.

The blizzard will be upon us in moments.

The top of the snowstorm catches my eye. I take far too long to realize I can just fly up and avoid it entirely. But the moment I change my course from flying away to gaining as much altitude as I can, I hear Jav's voice shout.

I'm barely able to turn my head in his direction before an impact slams me out of my flight. I flail, trying to get my wings straight again before I realize I'm being pulled along by something. My flames shoot out on instinct, trying to incinerate whatever is grabbing me.

"Stop it, you idiot. Stop fighting me!"

It's Jav? I hate the feeling of being pulled along, but I hold myself back from burning the volan.

"Have you never heard of the Matron of Winter? Never fly over a blizzard."

Jav finally lets go of me, and I crash into the fur of Grímr's back. They are all still sprinting as fast as they can move and Grímr doesn't acknowledge my presence.

"Solvei, we have only a couple of seconds. Cover yourself with your jacket and don't let go!" Remus shouts over the intensifying rumbling.

I scramble to pull my jacket over myself and cling to Grímr's back. My wing tips slowly begin their change into taloned fingers so I can better hold the coat around myself.

The blizzard hits.

I can feel the heavy impact as a wall of snow almost knocks me off my mount. I cool down my body as much as I can, hoping anything that lands on me won't melt as we move.

A few minutes pass with constant pelting through the jacket. My body shivers from the freezing temperature, but I don't dare raise my heat. The cold might be bad, but water is a thousand times worse.

The rumbling calms and the thrumming against my back stops. I wait, still grasping the jacket tightly around me as Grímr's repetitive steps shake through me. Minutes pass until Remus gives me the all clear.

"Solvei, you should be fine now."

I peek out before shaking off the buildup of snow covering my jacket. With the snow gone, I heat myself up again, reveling in the warmth after freezing for so long.

Behind us, the blizzard has slowed at the bottom of the valley. It still moves up the side of the mountain we are climbing, but at a far slower pace than before.

What a relief that's over.

CHAPTER SEVENTEEN

End of the Hunt

What the fuck were you doing? Everyone knows how stupid it is to fly over a blizzard. You're better off freezing to death inside the snowstorm than trying to move over one." Jav lands beside me, scowling.

"What?" Why wouldn't I go over? It looked like the safest place at the time.

"Ja-a-av," Remus calls with a singsong tone. "She's no volan, did you forget? Your bogeymen and fairy-tales mean nothing to her."

"Oh . . . Right. Uh, sorry." Jav looks away. "Look, the frost specters that follow above blizzards are some of the most dangerous creatures you can come across. We have a children's story told amongst us volans. The Matron of Winter. She was the mightiest mage of her time, able to bend blizzards to her will. She wiped out armies and monsters alike with the ice storms she conjured. But it wasn't enough for her. She wanted to see more of the beauty that lay in snow."

Jav points up at the mountains behind us. "She climbed the Alps and made their blizzards her own. With her mastery over ice, she flew high through the storms. She pierced through the heights of the blizzard in order to view it all. Nobody knows whether the sight she saw was as beautiful as she hoped. The Matron of Winter froze to death."

"While nobody is sure if the Matron of Winter was a real person, or even if the frost specters are real," Remus starts. "It is true that there are things in this world that are impossible to take on, no matter how much strength you gain. Every culture—especially those along the Titan Alps—has stories warning against the arrogance of challenging the unknown. Even that which you think is your strength, might become your end."

After that scare with the blizzard, we ended our excursion and headed back to the lodge where I met Grímr and Tetsu. I was surprised to see Tetsu not fight the idea of ending the hunting trip. Her constant, one-minded focus on fighting and growing had me forget she was also training me in the spear.

Once we are far down the mountain enough that snow no longer covers the ground, she addresses me. "Solvei, change to normal."

She, nor any of the others, slow at her words, so I land on Grímr's back and morph. As soon as I'm done, I look up questioningly at Tetsu, only to barely catch the thrown spear in time.

"From here on, you are going to practice your forms."

"On Grímr's back?" I ask incredulously.

"Yes, on his back. You need to be prepared to fight, no matter where you are."

I look down at the wooden spear in my hands. My hands move to their proper placements along the shaft as I move my legs around the sides of Grímr's neck. I take a swing, trying to get comfortable with the panther's movement.

"No. Stand up," Tetsu's gruff voice commands from behind.

"What? But I'll fall off."

"That's fine. If you lose your balance, I'll put you right back on."

I glance behind me, hoping she's kidding, but she retains the same seriousness as always.

With one hand grasping my spear and the other a handful of Grímr's fur, I drag my knees underneath me. Once I feel steady enough, I try to place one foot on his back. I'm lucky Grímr's back is so wide; there's plenty of space to stand.

It's only when I let go of his fur and try to rise that his pace falters. Grímr dashes over some felled tree and sends me tumbling off his side.

Before I reach the ground, Tetsu has me in her grasp and places me back on top of the portian.

"You have very little heft, so perfect balance and speed is a must if you want to fight. Weapon or no," Tetsu chides.

Grímr looks over his shoulder at me. "Sorry."

"No apologies," she snaps. "Don't make it easy for her. Dash around as many trees as you have to."

Grímr snaps his head back to the front, but I'm thankful he doesn't start making it impossible for me. In fact, I can feel him straighten his back. It doesn't help much, but I appreciate the sentiment.

Once again, I lift myself to my feet. The wobbles in my legs don't disappear as I try to rise, so I fall back into a crouch. I remain there for only a moment to catch my bearings, but that is a moment too long for Tetsu.

"Stand up now or I'll add dodging practice to the exercise."

A glance back reveals her juggling a stone the size of her fist. She goes to throw it upon seeing me look, so I scramble to rise. Thankfully, the stone doesn't come, but it's still a challenge to keep standing as Grímr dashes through the trees.

"Don't just stand there, swing your spear," Tetsu shouts in my ear.

I can't keep my balance, even when I focus my everything on doing so, and she wants me to swing? It's impossible.

Impossible, it may be, but Tetsu still waits behind me with that stone ready to throw. I grasp the spear in my other hand and try to do a basic angled slash, but as expected, what little balance I gained is lost and I fall off again.

This time Tetsu doesn't catch me. She lets me hit the ground before scooping me up.

"If you don't think you can do it, then you'll never be able to do it."

"But how can I think I can do it without actually doing it?" I shout back, frustrated at her and her methods.

"How can you improve, if you don't believe you can improve? How can you fight, if you don't believe you can fight? How can you continue to live, if you don't believe you have a chance?" She sets me back on Grímr and looks me in the eye. "Sometimes, you have to ignore what you believe, and just do."

She slows her pace until she's right behind us again.

Just do, huh? Well, what's the worst that can happen? I get knocked off and winded when I slam to the ground. A bit of breathlessness means nothing if I can improve myself.

So, I suppress my doubts, tying them up in a bundle of threads, and shove them out of my mind. With the experience I have from the Void Fog, doing so is far easier than it otherwise might have been.

My mind is clear. No doubts. No beliefs. Nothing except the intent to rise to my feet and swing my spear as Tetsu instructed.

I stand. My feet are steady. I grasp the spear in both hands and swing. Once. Twice. Grímr jerks to the right and I try to adapt to the sudden movement. My feet slip out from underneath me and I slam headfirst into the trunk Grímr was trying to dodge.

I groan as I sit up. I hear Tetsu let out a giddy chuckle as she grasps me by the shoulders and spins me to face her.

"I've never seen anyone learn to suppress their thoughts so quickly. Oh, you're going to be a pleasure to train."

I won't say it to her face, but her grin scares me.

I lay facedown on Grímr's back as we come into the clearing around the team's cabin. I'm so exhausted I can barely look up as the line of trees clear.

I thought she was just trying to scare me when she threatened to throw rocks at me. Nope. After I'd shown her I could restrict my thoughts, she didn't go easy on me. Which is strange, because I thought she'd already been over-working me.

She had me trying to dodge her thrown stones while continuing my practice swings standing on Grímr. I figured I'd ignore them at first and let them pass right through me. But each time I did, she would strike me with the large steel ball of something she called a modified flail. Despite being incorporeal, the weapon still disturbed enough of my body to send me flying off the panther.

After a hundred times of slamming into the ground at intense speed, Tetsu raised the difficulty again. I hadn't been able to stand straight on Grímr's back for over ten seconds yet, and she wanted to add more for me to do?

She made me send out a wave of flame with each strike of my spear for the next two hours until we finally made it back to the cabin. Exerting as much energy as I could with each swing.

I'm tired and starving. Expelling that much flame in such cold temperatures drained me of all the energy I have to spare. I eye one of the large trees surrounding the cabin as Grímr slows to a stop. With what little I have left, I crawl toward it and torch the thing.

As my fire chews away at the tree, I idly wonder what cobalt might taste like. I haven't really tried to eat any metal or rock since I found out my flames are hot enough to melt iron. I wonder if I could get the team to get me some?

"Where the fuck were you?" I hear a raging voice from the cabin.

I turn to watch a khirig—the same race as Ossian—march out toward Remus. Her antler-like extensions are far more enclosed than Ossian's, almost hugging the soft flesh of her torso hidden within. Her arm and leg antlers are slender, with barely more branching bones than she needs to stand.

"What were you thinking? Not only did you stand around with your tentacles up your ass as one of Joiak's major factories burned to the ground, but you organized trafficking for everyone to see? Joiak has slashed their funding and the top brass are pissed!"

"Those were children being mistreated. Do you really think I should have stood by and watch as their lives are ruined?" Remus remains calm, but stares down this new woman.

"I don't care if they are Actaeon damned pixies. What? You don't have the authority to decide the laws and morals of another country. Especially not one that contributes so heavily to funding the Order." She looks past Remus toward me. "Uh, you have a tree on fire."

Remus's eyes spin to me for only a moment before spinning back. "Don't worry about that. It's only Solvei."

"Solvei? As in the girl who burned down the mill and killed a bunch of the factory's managing staff?"

"Yep." Remus's voice returns to its usual chipper tone. "We took her in as the new member of the team."

The woman looks at him before sighing in exasperation. "Is she at least worth it?"

"Very much so. I don't think it's possible to find a better fit."

The khirig nods and walks past him, heading toward me. With my back against the tree, I watch her curiously.

With a short bend of her leg antlers, she introduces herself. "Solvei, I am team Luis-Eight's manager. My name is Doe."

I just nod to her, still too exhausted to bother with talking.

"Now, Solvei, I'm not too familiar with how your people do things where you're from, but here you need to follow the laws set by each country you enter. You cannot go around burning people and their property. I need you to promise me you won't do what you did in Joiak again." Doe looks down on me as I sit on the ground.

Despite the tiredness permeating my body, I rise to my feet. I approach the woman, keeping my flames burning the tree behind me. When I'm a single pace from Doe, I glare up into her eyes. "I don't care who they are; if someone wants to lock up and abuse others, they don't deserve to live. I will never make that promise."

I keep my eyes locked on hers as she takes a hurried step back.

Remus rushes in between us and wraps a limb around me. "Don't worry, Doe, we'll make sure she doesn't get into any trouble."

"Uh, yeah. Okay." Even as she responds to Remus, her eyes keep flicking back to me. There's an odd, worried look to her as she backs away.

Is she . . . scared of me? I don't know how to feel about that. What does she have to fear if she hasn't treated anyone horribly? I narrow my eyes at the thought. I'll have to keep an eye on her.

Turning away from me, she continues addressing Remus. "The brass isn't happy with you. They've assigned your team to the Breach defense until they decide what to do with you. Now that the Titan's path has cooled, monsters are descending the mountain at an accelerating pace. You should probably expect to be sent in deep after this mess." With her piece said, she rushes back inside.

A chuckle behind me makes me jump. "Good one, Solvei. I always love watching that bitch squirm," Tetsu says.

"She's a part of the team. Stop calling her that," Remus half-heartedly chides.

"No, she isn't."

I zone out their bickering and return to my seat against the burning tree. I don't think I've felt like this in a long time; exhausted, but not tense.

It feels nice.

CHAPTER EIGHTEEN

Bleed

We left the cabin early the next morning.

They'd been fine to let me sleep under the veranda on a comfortable, woven-thread couch. Grímr slept across the table from me on his own couch. I'm thankful they haven't questioned my reluctance to enter any buildings. I can't tell them I'm petrified of being trapped. It's unreasonable to think I'd be trapped inside a building entirely made of burnable timber, I know that, but I can't help how I feel. They will think I'm weak if they know. So for now, while I can't lie to them, I'll refrain from telling them.

Thankfully, we left without Doe. Although she's apparently going to join us a few weeks after we arrive at our destination, I'm glad I don't have to see her. Maybe I'm being too quick with my judgment, but anyone who's okay with what the people at the mill were doing is not someone I think I could ever like. It is especially bad that she wants to stop me helping anyone in those circumstances.

I fly low over the heads of the others as they run through the vast plains toward the base of an enormous black trail that winds up the entirety of the Titan Alps.

"So, where are we going?" I'd been a bit too tired last night to listen as they talked about the plan going forward.

"We're joining the garrison at the Breach. They've been experiencing an uptick in attack frequency for months now. We expected to be sent there as soon as we found our new team member," Remus says.

"We'd have been there months ago if you'd accepted one of the mages the Order offered." Despite the accusative words, Tetsu's face remains indifferent.

"You know if I had, I wouldn't have been willing to push our team into the riskier fights."

Tetsu affirms his words with her silence.

"You said there were attacks. What's attacking?" I ask.

"Well, until a few months back, it was just heat-based or fire-resistant creatures. Beings that could traverse the molten rock left by the Titan. Now, not only are Lower Elevation creatures descending, but Mid Elevation ones too. Not a good sign."

"I don't know about you guys, but Doe said the brass was angry." Grímr's claws tear through the soil as he runs beneath me. "I somehow doubt we'll be sitting on our laurels with the other Luis rank teams."

"Oh, absolutely," Remus cheers. "We'll be sent right into the Titan's nest."

Tetsu cracks her fists. "Not much of a punishment, if you ask me. We haven't had a good challenge in a long time."

"Hmm? It was only six months ago we pushed to the Middle Elevation. Was that not enough for you? Even though it scared away poor Dyani?"

"Six months is a long time, old man. It was really unfortunate Dyani turned out to be such a coward. I'd hoped with her arrogance she might have thick enough skin to stick with us."

"That's a rather unfair statement, don't you think? She stuck with us through all the Lower Elevation."

"I agree with Bunny," Jav says. "Dyani was fine to gloat while her spells were effective, but the moment she faced something too much for her, she broke down. Nothing wrong with that; everyone faces their inferiority eventually. But she quit. Didn't even attempt to try anything new. She didn't want to learn to work around the creatures her markings couldn't hold."

I'm assuming Dyani was the mage they had before I came along. No wonder Tetsu has been dying to fight; six months is an eternity to be doing nothing but training.

"Still, you shouldn't bad-mouth the efforts she made."

"Wasn't that the main reason we went looking for a replacement rather than taking one from the Order? You didn't trust their personality judgment," Jav says.

Remus doesn't respond. He looks away with a playfully guilty expression.

I ignore the team and turn my attention to our destination. The Breach is somewhere at the base of that thick, black line that winds up to the top of the Titan Alps.

It is insane to think that the impossibly tall Titan I'd seen collapse an extensive range of cliffs with its sheer size could be considered tiny next to the Alps above.

Why did the Titan climb the Alps? It's not going to come back over while we're here, is it?

The Breach is a horribly devastated area, but not an unfamiliar sight. The Titan's once molten path left hard black rock in its place. It made a surprisingly convenient road for walking. Which is fortunate because none of the surrounding land remains stable after the creature's passing.

I'd already seen how the Titan flattened the cliffs down in the wasteland's southern coast, but to see the same has happened with an entire mountain is something else. The ridgeline that stood in the path of the Titan is now a valley. A three-hundred-meter depression in the mountains where the rock liquefied and flowed anywhere it could. If any trees or plant life had been in the area, it is impossible to tell.

The garrison had been established a couple of kilometers from the extensive black path, far from the unstable, fissure-ridden ground. It is a simple-looking place. Many large log cabins make up the living area. There are no stone walls or defenses surrounding the camp. Is this really the central command for defense against an influx of creatures?

Considering all the talk I've heard of the danger this place poses for the nearest nations, there doesn't seem to be all that many people here. Only a few hundred, if the number of buildings is any indication. Compared to the armies both New Vetus and Henosis fielded, this is nothing. I understand that those with enhancement can achieve so much more than regular soldiers, but it's still odd to see a defensive position with such a minimal force. Said defensive position doesn't even look like it's meant to defend against anything, unlike Baansguard.

As we approach the outer ring of the encampment, I hear chatter from the center. We walked the last five hundred meters to the garrison. Remus says it is good manners. I even changed back to my normal form while we took our time approaching. I figure it will be easier introducing myself and talking to the people in the camp with my normal face than that of a bird.

As we pass through the first row of buildings, a door slams open, making me jump and instinctively bring flames up around me.

"Remus, you old fuck. Good to see ya." Some khirig with the thickest antlers I've seen wrapped around their body storms out through the door.

A quick look around tells me I was the only one who apparently didn't know he was going to jump out of nowhere. I calm myself and hide my flames away.

The khirig's long arm antlers wrap around Remus, trapping the dohrni's limbs under his spheric body. Remus's head wobbles around as he tries in vain to free himself. I can't help amusement at the sight. I know he can probably get out if he wants and none of the other team members are hurrying to free him.

"Oho, who is this little one? A bit young to be out here, ain't ya?" The man sends a curious glance to Remus, who has finally wormed his way out of the man's grasp.

"It's good to see you too, Hirsh. Solvei here is our replacement for Dyani."

Hirsh looks me up and down before frowning at Remus. "I'm disappointed Remus. When did you become a baby snatcher?"

Snorts erupt from Tetsu and Jav before he continues.

"We don't have to worry about some furious parents laying siege, do we? We've already got enough to deal with from the mountain."

I catch Remus's eyes narrowing at Hirsh and the two that laughed before returning to his normal cheerful expression. "Nope, no parents to worry about. But Jav and Bunny did convince Jelena to stop by."

That immediately snapped the smile off Hirsh's face. "You didn't. You're kidding . . . right?"

"You'll have to ask those two. They're the ones who talked to her." Remus turns to me. "Come, Solvei, Grímr. Let's leave them to it."

As I follow Remus deeper into the garrison, I turn to watch Jav backing away from a furious Hirsh. Tetsu stands there trying very hard to pretend like she can't hear him.

"Who is Jelena?" I ask.

"His sister. They're a loving family, but she can be quite . . . intense."

As we follow the cacophony into the central section of the garrison, we come across a diverse congregation. On one side, there are many tables with people either talking and drinking or crowding around, cheering and shouting. The other side has a training area with a weapon shed that seems almost unused in comparison.

"I'm going to talk to the defense manager. You two get comfortable," Remus says and walks toward a building with large open doors with many others frequently moving in and out.

I follow Grímr, feeling the eyes of some people watching us across the open area. I expect him to join the raucous crowd near the tables. Instead, he walks off to a secluded corner near the training field and lays down, content to relax and not interact with the other people around.

That's not something I want, though. I'm curious as to what has everyone's attention at the table. They sometimes quieten down, only to be followed by a chorus of cheers or derisive shouts.

I leave Grímr's side and approach the table, feeling his eyes on my back the whole way.

A small bit of space is left for me to peer over the table. I get a few odd looks from those who notice me, but the majority leave their focus on the game before them.

There are six people holding cards with twice as many watching over their shoulders, trying their best to peek at the cards the players hold. In front of each player are three cards with numbers one through six and varying patterns drawn. Players keep their hands on three separate cards, some hiding them from the people around and others freely showing them off.

They sometimes remove a card from either the upturned or hidden ones and throw it in a pile while picking up another to replace it. Each time one of them does so, they place a coin on the table. The coins look like gid, but their design is different. Most likely, it's another form of currency.

Once each player has finished replacing cards, the men and women standing behind them throw coins in front of a player of their choosing. I notice most of the money lands before the player with a four, five, and six on the table before him.

The players each reveal the three hidden cards to everyone and resounding groans fill the silence. A woman at the other end of the table—and the only person who put a coin in front of her—cheer as the pile of money is pushed toward them.

I watch a few more rounds as money quickly changes hands until a player who loses each round since I started watching stands up for the next person to take his place. A dohrni moves to take his seat, but his eyes catch mine.

"Hey, kid, do you want to play?"

"I don't know how."

"I'll teach you."

Someone in the crowd groans. "C'mon, don't slow the game down."

"I promise to keep her moving."

I push around the crowd and sit in the chair, legs pulled up under me to get more height. The man places his tentacle on the back of my chair and leans over my shoulder to guide me.

He directs my cards for a few rounds, telling me which card combinations are better than others and betting in my stead. He introduces himself as Ligo; a member of team Fearn-Thirty-Two.

The game turns out to be rather fun. I even win the fourth round.

"So, whose kid are you?" At my questioning look, Ligo rephrases. "Who are your parents? Did one of the team managers bring you?"

"I'm no one's *kid*." I stress the word. "I came here with my team."

The table goes quiet. I guess more people have been paying attention to us than I thought.

"Right. And which team?" he asks with amused skepticism.

"Luis-Eight," I answer and swap out one of my hidden cards. I just need a four and I'll have a mid-set; five of a kind.

The card bends under my fingers as I take a peek at the one I just picked up. A grin threatens to overtake me, but I clamp down on it. Everyone is looking at me; I don't want to let them know I have a winning hand.

"Uh-huh, okay. And how did you get on Remus's team?"

It hardly matters to me if he doesn't believe my words. "He asked me to."

That seemed to get a round of chuckles from the mercenaries around the table. It doesn't matter what they think, because I win another round. I grin as the pile of coins is pushed toward me. Ligo and those who bet on my hand take their winnings.

Ligo places some coins in my hand. "Here. You've had a pretty lucky start. You should use your own to play."

I play a couple more rounds until a familiar face lands on the table beside me.

"What ya doing, Solvei?" Jav asks.

"I'm playing, uh . . ." I turn to Ligo, who's eyeing Jav. "What's this game called?"

"Bleed."

"Really?" That's an odd name for a game.

"Yes."

I turn back to Jav, who's peeking at my hidden cards. "I'm playing Bleed. How'd it go with Hirsh?"

"Prick wouldn't believe me when I said I didn't tell his sister to come. Well, I see you've made yourself comfortable amongst this lot. How about I join ya?"

Jav walks across the table to the seat of the player to my right and takes the cards out of the tip of the dohrni's limbs.

"The fuck! What do you think you're doing?" he shouts, rising to his full height.

"Taking your place." Jav sits with his tail hanging off the edge of the table, paying the man no mind.

The dohrni, enraged by Jav's attitude, reaches forward to grab at the volan.

Someone grasps his shoulder before he can and leans in to whisper. The bluish color of his skin turns clear gray at whatever he heard and takes a few steps to the back of the crowd.

"You weren't lying, were you?" Ligo says behind me. "About being a part of Luis-Eight."

I look curiously back at him. "No. Why would I?"

Jav laughs.

CHAPTER NINETEEN

First Mission

Jav and I walk away from the game table with heavier pockets. I won a couple rounds and leave with more than I started with, which is not exactly surprising considering I had nothing. I have no clue to the value of these ten coins, but it feels great to win.

Jav is really good at Bleed. After he came in, he seemed to win at least half the rounds. His own bag of winnings makes mine look minuscule. I'm not sure how he did it, but he seemed to always know exactly what everyone else had and would only pay to replace cards when he would win the round.

Of course, I wasn't the only one to notice this. The other players backed out of buying cards whenever Jav did. The crowd also placed their bets on him whenever he did so. It made his wins less profitable, but he still came away with far more than anyone.

I place one of the coins in my mouth and taste the metals inside. There are two incredibly distinct flavors that fight for domination of my taste as I burn through the metal. I recognize one ingredient from that knife in the Cano manor. It tastes a thousand times better now that I can actually burn through it and I relish as it melts over my tongue.

Jav is staring at me.

"What?" I ask.

He stares at me a moment longer, before lifting a paw to his face. "First, don't put coins in your mouth. Who knows where they've been? Second, that coin was worth far more than the metals that make it. If you're hungry, we can buy you some."

I look down at my remaining coins. "Where?"

"Come, there's bound to be some greedy merchant brave enough to risk their life for a bit of gold."

Jav leads me to an area with three large wagons. Other than the group of five sitting around a campfire, the place is empty.

"Hey, do any of you lot have metal or ore?" Jav calls out.

At once, the people crowding the campfire perk up and dash toward the wagons. A pair of khirigs open up a wooden door to show the many wares inside. A duo of a dohrni and a volan do much the same with their own wagon.

It's the last one that catches my attention. It isn't a race I'm familiar with. They have a stocky body with short arms and legs. Their skin is a brownish-green coloration with bubble like texture, more wart than skin. The head is as large as its chest and is split by a wide mouth.

The being's large, bulging eyes watch us as it unloads a crate from its wagon.

The khirigs are the first to speak. "Metals and ore, for decoration or weapons?"

"Neither. It's for this one to eat." Jav points my way.

Befuddlement paints their faces.

"To eat?" the dohrni repeats, his tentacles freezing in the motion of unpacking.

"If it's for consumption, do you want to try a selection, or is there a specific metal you're after?" The wart-man is quick to adapt; I'm not even sure he hesitated for a second unlike the other four.

He quickly brings a heavy crate in front of us and I realize he's waiting for my reply.

"Uh, the selection?" I say, unsure how much these coins are worth.

He nods to me and pulls out a leather-bound roll of finger-length rods.

"It's strange to see a heqet this far from the seas," Jav says as he observes the trader unloading the range of metals. "It's even stranger to see a heqet not trying to tear the throat out of anyone in their vicinity." Jav looks to the four that had shared a campfire.

"Well, you know how it is. Gotta break away from tradition sometimes." The heqet laughs as if he said something funny. "Go on, kid, see which ones you like."

With his encouragement, I pass a flame over the metals. Not enough to burn through them, but just enough to get a taste.

"So, what brings you here, anyway?" Jav asks.

"I came to sell the weapons I collected in Riparia."

Jav's eyes widen. "You have Riparian weapons?"

The heqet shakes his head. "Not anymore. They sold quick. Now I'm stocking up on unique creature parts before heading north. It's rather frustrating that most mercs prefer to waste those resources on themselves instead of sell them."

"Well, we have to improve ourselves somehow."

"Yes, but is it so much to ask just to save the odd claw or two?"

"Usually, yeah. It's a pain in the ass to carry that stuff back with you unless you have someone dedicated to the role."

As I taste-test each of the metals, I come across one that makes me salivate more than any other. The silvery-white metal tastes absolutely amazing. There isn't a single thing I've ever had that even comes close.

"Oh, you've found one, have you?" His grin spreads across his entire face when he sees which one I've focused on. "You have good taste, young lady." He laughs to himself again. "What you have there is quality platinum. That quarter-kilo rod, I can part with just for you at eight hundred paccs."

I'm not sure how much that is. It sounds cheap compared to the prices in Zadok. I turn to Jav to see his opinion. He's narrowed his eyes and scrunched up his brow at the heqet.

"Why exactly do you have that much platinum on you?"

"Oh, it's a favorite inscribing material for the Riparians. But if we are talking about using a metal for consumption, then I admit it's unnecessarily expensive. I can sell you as much cast iron for one thousandth of the price."

As if they were waiting for the opportunity, the other traders push themselves into the conversation. "If it's cast iron you want, we have plenty to sell. We'll give you a good deal?"

At the interruption, the heqet's protruding eyes narrow dangerously. He turns and pulls an axe I hadn't seen from behind his back.

"Back the fuck off my deal!" he screams, aggressively stepping toward the other merchants with axe raised.

Jav tenses, ready to jump in, but the heqet stops himself.

"No, calm. They're not worth it. Calm. Calm," he murmurs to himself, only barely audible to my ears.

"Sorry about that," he says, turning to us with his cheer returned. "Never easy fighting nature. So, where were we?"

I walk away three iron ingots heavier and three coins lighter. I bought one from each of the trader groups to make it fairer. It's an incredible challenge to carry each of the two and a half kilo chunks, but I'll be having a massive feast with this. I'll have to see if I can get someone in the team to carry an ingot for me when we travel.

My eyes lock on Grímr.

I walk up beside him and drop the heavy ingots on the grass. With a sigh of relief, I drop to the ground next to him. How did my tribe carry cartloads of this stuff? I struggle even with this much.

"Hey, Grímr, do you mind carrying my dinner in one of your bags when we travel again?"

"Sure, what did you get?" He turns to see me pointing at the ingots. He blinks before letting out a short laugh. "No problem, but you'll have to tell me how it tastes."

"Thanks!" I smile at the portian.

It's a shame I couldn't get any of that platinum. Seriously, it was too good. I'm definitely going to look for some in the future.

I don't get to sit for long. Remus finally comes out of the command building and rejoins us.

"We'll be heading out right away. Where is . . ." He looks around before spotting Tetsu alone in the training area. "Bunny! Let's go!" he shouts over the background chatter.

We follow Remus as he strides out of the garrison. "Solvei, if you want to fly, you better change now. We'll be moving quick."

I jump on Grímr's back and do as Remus says. If ever given the option, I'd rather the freedom of flight than being carried. The moment my change finishes, Remus increases our speed to my maximum flight speed. It's a challenge to keep the pace, but I manage.

"So why are we out so quick? Don't tell me the brass sent their orders for us already?" Jav asks.

"No, the defense manager had no knowledge we were coming until I stopped by. We'll have to wait until after this job to see how bad I pissed them off. Let's just hope it isn't another Mid Elevation incursion."

"So, what's the mission?" Tetsu asks.

"Got a young Fearn team on scouting duty four days late with their report. The six other Luis teams they have on site are already watching major choke points with the highest frequency of attacks. Command needed to wait a few more days before they could shuffle one of the Luis out to investigate. We came at a convenient time for them."

"Wait. What about the Beiths? They don't have any on the roster?" Jav asks.

"There were supposed to be two, but both have gone missing. They aren't the only ones either; a third of all Beith mercs have disappeared without a trace. Another third refuses to move from their home posts and the rest are already busy."

"Damn, you'd think with how much they're paid, they'd have some urgency to do their job," Jav gripes. "Well, how far off are they? Is it worth me having a look yet?"

"I'll give you a boost in an hour. They should be watching over a deep gulch farther up the Stepps."

This isn't the first time he's mentioned some place I'm unfamiliar with. I lower my flight until I'm right above Grímr. "What are the Stepps?" I ask.

Grímr strides behind the rest of the team. "It's the lowest series of mountains along the Alps. Above that is the Lower, Middle, and Upper Elevations. Beyond that is the Summit Line. We usually hunt in the Lower Elevation."

Oh right, the Middle Elevation was where their last mage quit. "So, the Lower Elevation is where we went last time?"

"Oh no, far from it. That was still the Stepps. We would never have taken you to the Lower Elevation without making sure you're properly equipped. It's not exactly as easy to traverse above the Stepps, even if you can fly."

If creatures like katobles are common in the lowest and weakest region, then what kind of terrifying monsters hide up at the summit? Titans? Is there anything that even comes close to them?

Well, it's not like I'll be going that high up the mountain any time soon, so there's nothing to worry about.

"The scouting team we are looking for, what do you think happened to them?" I'm still mostly unsure of what these Alps hold and even if the Stepps are the lowest, the blizzard shows there are still things to worry about.

"Uh . . ." Grímr hesitates. "I'm not going to lie; usually when a team doesn't send their report on time, it's likely they are dead."

I nod. I figured that would be the circumstances. "But what could have killed them?"

Grímr glances up at me with a concerned look, but answers anyway. "Anything, really. But Remus specified the youth of their team, which usually means they let their strength get to their head. A scouting team is not supposed to engage anything unless they have a hundred percent certainty of victory. The fights they may take are supposed to be of no challenge. If I was to guess, I'd say their ego pushed them to fight something out of their league."

"What are we supposed to do if they are dead?"

"We confirm each of their deaths, hunt down what killed them, and return with their bodies. If that is not possible, we bury them on the mountain."

"Bury them? Why would you bury the dead?"

Grímr gives me a strange look. "Why wouldn't you?"

"Isn't it better to give creatures and people a purpose after death? To let their lifeless bodies support those still living rather than decay into nothing."

A deep, throaty growl rumbles from Grímr's chest. "People are not like animals, they should be given proper respect as they move into the afterlife. Perverting their bodies once they are no longer there to defend themselves is the most despicable of acts."

That goes against everything my tribe has ever taught me. I cannot agree with the willful misuse of life. They may no longer be alive, but it would be a greater disrespect to them if they meant nothing to the world after their death.

Áed may not leave bodies behind after death, but our flames are returned to the Eternal Inferno to be cycled back into the world. The thought of being buried after death, of being isolated with no way back to the Inferno is horrifying.

"No, you can't do that!" I can't help but raise my voice at the image. "Don't take away their freedom to return to the world. Burn them, feed them to creatures, or use them in the ritual for all I care. Just don't lock them away."

I glare down at Grímr and he returns it with a low, rumbling growl.

"Hey, hey. Stop it, you two." Remus smacks Grímr on the back of the head. "Everyone has their differences in culture and beliefs, but don't you think it's a bit early to be writing off those kids as dead? You can fight over what we do if it ever comes to that point, but for now, let's not act like children, all right?"

I flap my wings and gain some height, intending to ignore the one that treats the dead with such cruelty.

A few minutes later, Remus throws Jav far ahead of us. We'll be coming up to the scouting team soon. Whether they are still alive or not is something we'll need to wait and see.

CHAPTER TWENTY

Missing

It took Jav a full fifteen minutes to return from his flight ahead. The volan lands on Remus's head as per usual, so I lower my altitude to hear what he found.

"I couldn't find them anywhere. Except for their camp equipment, there is no sign of them anywhere. The camp doesn't seem to have been used in days. No sign of battle. No beast presence. Unless they dug their own grave . . ." Jav looks my way. "Uh, sorry." He turns back to Remus. "I have no idea where they've gone."

"All right then, we best have a look at their camp first."

I follow above the others as they run along a ten meter depression at the bottom of the V-shaped valley. The smooth walls of rock that surround them have strange lines running across it that make the land look almost like it has layers. I wonder what causes it to look like that?

Soon we reach the scouting party's campsite. It sits up the slope of the valley, away from the depression at the bottom. There are a few tents abandoned and a burned-out fireplace that hasn't been lit for a week.

"It definitely looks like it's been unused for a while. All their hunting gear is gone, but their rations are untouched, so we can assume they at least left the camp without issue. But the problem is they shouldn't have gone far from their camp in the first place." Remus brings a tentacle up to scratch the side of his head. "For now, we search individually for any signs of a fight. Solvei, I want you to stick with Bunny."

With his orders given, Remus throws Jav and rushes farther along the valley toward the Alps. I fly over Tetsu as she climbs the slope to the left and Grímr takes the opposite side.

"So . . . what are we looking for?"

"Bodies, blood, broken trees or branches. Anything that might result from a fight. Even creatures known to eat people whole leave signs of their presence behind."

There is sparse tree cover through this valley, so it's unlikely we'll miss something should we come across it. It's strange that Jav hasn't seen anything. Where could they have gone? What might have happened that nothing is left behind?

Maybe they're not dead and instead trapped somewhere, waiting for help. I shiver at the thought. Not much could be worse than that.

Tetsu reaches the ridge overlooking the entire valley and I rise only so high that I can still see the ground below in detail. I don't know where to look. Everywhere just looks the same to me, but I keep at it.

A series of shrill whistles echo over the hills, making me look back to the gulch, trying to find the source.

"Solvei," Tetsu shouts from far below. "They found something, let's head back."

I drop to her side again as she descends the slope. I hope they haven't found anything too horrible. It would be nice to find the scout team unharmed, but I know how unlikely of a scenario that is. Really, we can only hope to find that they didn't suffer when they died, or at least determine what caused their death.

We meet back with Grímr at the depression. Without a word, the three of us rush after Jav and Remus. Even speeding through the flat-bottomed gulch, we take a good half an hour to catch up.

The two stand off to the side, waiting for us. In the middle of the depression is another old campfire. There are no tents to accompany this one, but the leftover bones of some roasted creature are piled in the cold ashes.

"As you can see, our scouts have pushed quite a bit farther than they should. The fire is cold, but considering their report was due four days ago, I'd say they were here at least a week ago," Jav says.

"Five days," I interject.

"What?" he asks, everyone's eyes falling on me.

"The fire. It died five days ago."

"Really?" Remus asks. "But that would mean they were pushing up the mountains with only a day until their deadline. The shortest time a Fearn team could cross that distance would be two days. A young Fearn team? Closer to four. Were they late coming back from pushing up the mountain? Then what happened to them between here and their camp?"

That can't be right. "The fire back at the camp went out seven days ago." It's more likely they were heading up the Alps.

"That doesn't make sense." Jav crosses his tiny arms and furrows his brow. "I can see a bunch of arrogant kids pushing above their rank, but complete negligence of their duty? Something isn't right."

"Well, there's no point pondering it here. We'll move forward, see if we can find anything else."

Four hours later, deep in the snow wrapped mountains, we still haven't come across any sign of the missing team. Jav is constantly in the air, coming back every five minutes for a boost through the air. I can only imagine how much ground he's covering with the speed he moves.

Do we even have a chance of finding them if Jav hasn't spotted anything yet?

"All right, this is far enough." Remus seems to agree with my thought. "We should have seen something by now."

Tetsu casts her gaze over the surrounding horizon. "There's something that's been bugging me. Where are the fauna? This is supposed to be a hotspot, so where are all the descending beasts? Where are all the creatures that inhabit these mountains?"

I look around. She's right. Even in that hunting trip, there was plenty of wildlife that lived in the areas alongside the more dangerous beasts. Now? The area feels dead. If there were any in the area, they are long gone. That, or they're hiding.

"Yes, I noticed that as well." Remus's eyes flick to the Titan's path on the Alps above. "I think, for now, we should head to the Titan's trail. If we're to find anything, I'll bet it's there."

I'm tired from hours of flying at top speed, but it doesn't look like we'll be taking a break any time soon.

"Tetsu, do you mind if I rest my wings a bit?" I refuse to go to Grímr. I'm still annoyed at his horrifying treatment of the dead. At least for now, it's only words, but I don't know how I could stand it if he tried to bury a body in my presence. I hope we don't find that team, simply to avoid the possibility they'll have their bodies prevented from reentering the cycle.

"Sure." She lifts her arm for me to land.

Her thick biceps don't budge as I drop my entire weight on her. I know I don't weigh much, but still, it must be uncomfortable to run with your arm extended out like that. I scoot onto her shoulder so she can drop her arm again.

"What could make the area as bare as it is?" I ask once I'm settled in the nook of her neck.

"Strong beasts. For an area as large as we've experienced, we're probably facing one from the Middle Elevation. For everything to be in hiding means that whatever it is hasn't been hiding its presence. Which makes it all the more strange that we can't feel it."

"Could it already be gone?"

Tetsu frowns. "I don't know what would be worse. If, as you say, it has already moved on somewhere it might cause irreparable damage. Or it is hiding its presence only from us."

"You think it might ambush us?" I twist my head, looking for something that might be hidden.

"That might be a possibility, but it's not what we are most concerned about. A creature that has enough strength to confidently exude a presence, but stops itself around us, means it isn't some stealth-focused ambush predator. No, it shows the most dangerous quality you can find in a beast; intelligence."

"I thought you liked a hard fight?" From what I know of Tetsu so far is that the more challenging the fight, the better.

She glances at me out of the corner of her eye. "Of course, but when a beast avoids the fight because it believes there is a chance it might not win, that makes them annoying. The smartest can hold grudges. My father used to tell me of a time he was hunting one particularly intelligent creature, only to find it had skirted him and left the city behind him in rubble."

So there's a creature like that around here? Once more, I involuntarily cast my gaze around the area.

"If there is a creature in the area, the best scenario is that it does attack us. We are far better equipped to deal with a Mid Elevation beast than most other teams down below. No need to be worried."

I'm not worried. But as I go to tell her as such, I realize how childish they might seem. Instead, I jump off her shoulder and take flight.

It'll probably take up to an hour to reach the Titan's path from here. Maybe we'll get lucky and find a proper explanation for what's going on.

As we near the path of the Titan, the quantity of beasts does a full reversal. Instead of none as far as we can see, we struggle to move for more than a few minutes before stumbling upon some new creature.

Each beast is quickly dealt with and I'm surprised we don't stop to use the ritual on their bodies as we pass. Instead, we barely even slow to confirm the kills.

The most common creatures we brush through are wolves. Identical to the ones I struggled against in the Wailing Woodland. Many of them are larger than the biggest of those I faced, but somehow seem far less intelligent. They throw themselves at us, regardless of how many of their brethren we cut through before them. At least the wolves from that woodland were smart enough to cut their losses.

Is that what Tetsu meant about the more intelligent beasts? They could have attacked me at any time after they retreated into the woodland, but they'd learned to avoid me rather than attack. I couldn't imagine if creatures like the roaches had that sort of intelligence. They may not have much individual strength, but they could cause immense damage if they coordinated their numbers.

The devastation that is the Titan's path comes into view before us. It's almost unthinkable how much rock and earth has been gouged away from the being's passing. What must it be like to be so large, so heavy that you leave trenches in the land hundreds of meters deep anywhere you go? Does it even notice the ground caving in under its immense feet?

I peer down into the wide expanse of black rock. While there are a lot of creatures down there, I would hesitate to say it's a horde. The beasts keep their distance from other creatures, growling or screeching at those who get too close. They seem content to remain in proximity while they follow the long, descending path.

"Why do they only go down?" I ask. Most don't even attempt to climb the edge of the path, they stick to the easy road down the mountains.

Remus steps to the ledge overlooking the path. "These are the common residents from the Lower Elevation. It's instinctual for them to strive to reach for lower altitudes. They know—even if not intellectually—that it is safer down here. The predators of the Alps are not something they can protect themselves from. The barrier between the Stepps and the Lower Elevation is usually too much for them to breach, but now they have a way."

"Unfortunately for these creatures, they need to be culled," Tetsu says. "They will destabilize the ecosystem if they carve too much of a presence in the Stepps." She casually places her foot out over open air and falls down into the deep recession of the path.

Remus sighs but nods and falls after her.

"Solvei, wait." Grímr approaches behind me.

I angle myself so I can hover in the wind with only a few quick beats. I don't want to land on his back at the moment.

"Solvei, I'm sorry for my aggression earlier, and I've thought about our . . .

conversation. I can somewhat understand your reasoning to refuse burials, but for my people, using the body of sapients is the worst taboo." Grímr turns his head toward the others already rushing through the extermination. "I hope it doesn't come to this, but should we ever have to deal with the remains of a person, would it be fine to cremate them *without* you consuming them? Just let a natural fire take them."

I still feel like that's a bit of a waste, but I can agree to that. With a nod toward him, I drop down into the path to help the others.

As long as he won't go burying people around me, I think everything will be fine.

CHAPTER TWENTY-ONE

Overzealous

It didn't take long to clear the immediate area of life. It's really quite unfortunate for these creatures; they try to leave a place of danger, to create a safer life for themselves, but we cut them down for the sake of maintaining a preestablished status quo. Even I can tell these creatures aren't worth hunting for their energy.

Is it not possible to integrate at least some of them into the local wildlife?

"All right. If there ever was a higher-tiered beast, it never came through here. It might've left from closer to the crevasse, but we don't have the time to go that far. For now, I think it's best to head back. See if we can spot anything we might have missed," Remus says.

"Don't you think it'll be better to clear the path on our way down?" Jav asks. "I doubt we'll find anything heading back the same way."

"There's no sign of anything too dangerous heading down the path. We may as well let the Fearn teams earn their pay."

As we travel back to the abandoned camp, it becomes apparent that whatever terrified the wildlife is long gone. Signs of local wildlife have returned. The whistling songs of birds, the rabbits dashing to their burrows, and the chirping of crickets. They aren't exactly frequent, but it tells us that whatever was here has moved on.

The issue is that we don't know what the creature is, nor where it has gone.

For all we know, it's some unthinkable horror heading right for the garrison or some undefended village.

We arrive at the Fearn team's camp, still as untouched as we left it. They haven't returned while we were looking for them. It was unlikely to happen—considering how wide Jav's search range is—but I still hoped for an optimistic resolution.

At least we don't need to worry about dealing with their bodies, as horrible as that sounds.

I've been thinking about Grímr's apology. Thinking about my own feelings. While it is true that burials go against my tribe's teachings, no one in my tribe would have reacted with as much hostility as I did. Upon reflecting, I realize that it's my fear of entrapment messing with my thoughts.

I still think it's one of the worst ways to treat the dead, but if I think of it as an eternal, impassible entrapment, then that would mean my tribe is still stuck under that cliff.

I cannot accept that.

They had their funeral pyre. There is no way that wasn't enough to guide them to the Eternal Inferno. There were plenty of cracks through the earth for their deceased flames to escape.

The fleshy bodies of most creatures, on the other hand, would have no way to break free of their tombs in death. Their bodies would not be found useful for those still living, and therefore, they would be forever trapped with their decaying bodies.

Grímr's proposition to cremate the corpses without making any use of them goes against my uncle's teachings, but it doesn't horrify me as much as burial. I can begrudgingly agree to this middle ground, even if I'm not happy with it.

Remus lets out a deep sigh at the sight of the camp. "There's no way around it. We'll just have to report their disappearance and the presence of a strong beast in the area. We can't delay our return any longer than we already have."

It's rough. To know our efforts were for nothing is depressing. As strong as the members of this team are, if there's no fight to take or road to follow, then nothing can be done. The Fearn team is missing, likely dead, and we have no explanation for it besides a few animals going quiet.

Is there some creature now roaming the Stepps that leaves no trace of its passing and can kill without dropping any remains? I can only hope other teams don't go missing as well.

* * *

It is dark when we finally return to the garrison. Remus and Jav head for the command building while a khirig guides the rest of us to the house we'll be using for our stay here. It's smaller than the cabin they have for themselves near Baansguard, but still plenty of room for the five of us. Fortunately, there's a porch running around the front and side of the building. No couches like the team cabin's veranda, but the few wooden chairs will be fine to sleep on.

The loud chattering from where the mercenaries collectively drink and gamble echoes off the buildings. Even as late as it is, there are still plenty enjoying themselves.

As I take a seat, Grímr eyes me from the front door. He seems to hesitate for a moment before lowering his head and moving inside.

I relax back into the chair and look up to the glowing red sky as Eldest Ember declares her presence. From here, the moon is hidden by the Alps, but Ember's light still reaches us. Half the sky remains in the shadow of the mountains, leaving darkness above and a burning red to the east. The summit ridgeline is enveloped in the crimson light, silhouetting it from the sky above.

My fingers brush over my chest, where Mom's marble normally rests. I buried it back at the cabin; if I'm going to be fighting, I'd rather be reassured that I won't lose it.

I wonder what they would think about where I am. About what I've done. Mom, Eldest Ember, the rest of my tribe. Would they be proud that I've come so far? Might they be disappointed that I haven't returned to the wasteland?

What would they think of all the people I've killed? Gloria, the Henosis soldiers, the Empire's general, those at the mill. Would they think everyone I've killed was justified? Or say I should have found another way?

I don't regret what I've done at all. But the thoughts of my family mean a lot to me. If they were to label what I've done despicable, I don't know how I'd react. I'd be devastated, at the very least. After all that has happened in my struggle to survive, will they still welcome me when I return to the Eternal Inferno?

These doubts are pointless. I'll never know until I die, and I don't plan to find out for a long time.

I continue watching the Ember Moon.

The Alps make it seem higher in the sky than I'm used to.

"Hello."

I lower my gaze to the khirig rising the steps of the porch. It's that man from when we first entered the garrison. I forgot his name.

"Hi." I expect him to continue past me and knock on the front door. Instead, he drops into the chair next to mine.

"You've been on the tip of everyone's tongue recently, you know? Nobody can stop talking about the young mage that Remus found out of nowhere."

I'm unsure how to respond. It doesn't really matter whether people are talking about me or not. If anything, it annoys me they think I'm a mage.

"So, Solvei right?" At my nod, he continues. "From one mage to another, tell me. Where did you learn? How do you hide your markings? You must have an excellent teacher to have caught old Remus's eye."

I look over the black markings etched into his antlers. Right, a mage. If it weren't for the clear indication—and him saying so—I never would have thought he was one. His antlers give him immense size, far taller and bulkier than Ossian back at the cabin. Compared to the thinner stature of the mages from the Empire and even Leal's scrawniness—for an ursu—he doesn't seem to fit the mold.

"I'm an áed," I answer simply. Being so far away from the wasteland is rather inconvenient. At least in New Vetus the ursu knew of our race, even if the knowledge was limited.

"An áed? I'm sorry I'm unfamiliar with the term. Is that some albanic family?"

A bubble of irritation rises in my chest. I'm fine with him not knowing what I am, but being mistaken for an albanic bothers me.

"No! It's my race." I wreath my fingers in flickers and pull back on their physicality.

He stares for a moment before lighting up. "Oh! The fire people from Remus's old stories. Damn, kid, you're far from home. He used to tell many stories about his travels when I was your age. Your people were one of them."

I look the khirig up and down. He calls Remus old, but I got the impression this man is old himself.

"How old is he?"

"Oh, he's an absolute fossil. Been around for at least a good century and a half, at the very least. We suspect he's long past two hundred, though."

A hundred and fifty years? I thought he was old, but that's insane.

I sit in silence for a moment, just considering how much he could've done in such a long life before my attention is dragged back to the khirig sitting next to me.

"What was your name?" I ask.

"What? Am I not interesting enough for you to remember after our first meeting?" His smirk is the only indicator that he's joking. "I'm Hirsh, mage of team Fearn-Three."

"What type of mage are you?" Please be anything but a water mage.

"I'm a water mage."

Damn it.

"Do you want me to give you a little showing?"

"No." I scoot a little farther away from him.

"Nonsense. My nieces and nephews love watching what I can do. I'm sure you will too."

He rises to his feet and I stumble to my own not a moment later. Whatever he wants to do, I don't want to be anywhere near. He walks down the steps and stands before the house, while I scamper off in the opposite direction and climb over the porch railing.

I crash into the ground. As I pull myself to my feet, I cast my sight back to watch an immense volume of water pouring out of the ends of his antlers. His markings glow a bright white-blue illuminating the waves of water rolling off his body. In the dark, post-Ember-Moon night, the water is both as mystical as it is terrifying.

It seems to almost float as it leaves Hirsh's antlers, but gravity soon takes hold and pulls it to the earth, with the rest pooling around his legs. A mound of the liquid amasses around the khirig. It collects under his feet before lifting him off the ground, raising him on a pillar of water higher than the building.

I want to be ready if he does anything, so I scuttle backward while keeping my eye on the water flowing around him.

The water stops gushing out the ends of his antlers and at the same time, several bright lines cease their glow. There are still other markings lit, unaffected by the dimming of nearby patterns.

He lifts his arms and new lines shine. Immediately, spinning discs emerge from the column of water. A grinding hiss rings out from the many rapidly rotating blades. Several of them spin around the water pillar, but most rush down to the puddle surrounding him. The blades of water tear through soil and rock as they speed away from his central water concentration.

I notice that each of the blades stop before reaching the end of his puddle of water on the ground, but they still cut through air and earth as they spin around his suspended body.

Calm, still, unmoving water is too much for me, so why do there have to be people able to wield it so terrifyingly freely like that?

The latest activated marking dims and the buzzing water discs fall into the puddle below.

"Solvei? Are you watching?" Hirsh turns to see me backing away on the far side of the house. "Why are you so far away? Come on, I'll give you a ride."

Another set of markings light up, this time much closer to the constantly lit ones. The water bunches up underneath him and carries him forward on a wave. He speeds after me at nearly the same pace as team Luis-Eight travels.

I twist and launch into a sprint, but without my wings I'm nowhere near fast enough. I've put some distance between us already, but it wouldn't be enough.

"Stop it!" I shout desperately.

Is this really going to be my end? Not to the Empire responsible for hunting many of the áed. Not the Titan that tore my tribe from me. I'm going to go out not to some terrible evil, but to some overzealous idiot too excited about showing off?

No, I refuse. There must be some way and I will not give up until I've found it.

Droplets of water splash over me from the wave closing in on me. My oversized jacket stops most of it, but the water that breaches the exposed areas burns on contact. I ignore the stinging pain and pump my legs.

Jets of flame blast back into the wall of water closing on me. I pull back my inner flame so it isn't myself touching the water. Hopefully, it scares him back from chasing me.

I hear his laugh from behind. "So you want to play, do ya? All right, I'm game."

He's an absolute moron.

Instead of backing off, it only encouraged him more. My flamethrowers spearing into his wave do nothing but billow out steam. I only have the time to glance back for a moment to see him activating another set of markings.

I wish I could change my form in a second; that would solve everything right now. But I'm still stuck with a fifteen-minute limit. I can't switch to a bird for an easy escape, nor can I think of anything else that might save me now.

My only chance is if I can get into the building ahead of me. I'm still terrified of being locked inside. My arms stiffen even thinking about what I'm going to do. But it's that or death.

Maybe if I hadn't been so afraid, I could've hidden inside our team's home instead of running away, but I'm already too far.

It feels like I've been running for ages, but barely a few moments have passed since he began the chase. With each step I take, he cuts the distance between us, but I also close in on the door to my safety.

Something speeds by out of the corner of my eye. I turn to watch as a wall of water speeds around my side and curves ahead of me. Another from my other side does the same. Before I can react, they close in and seal off my only escape, completely encircling me and the khirig water mage.

I never made it inside the building, but the overwhelming pressure of being trapped burns in my chest.

I turn to face down the coming wave and the imbecile with it.

My flames smolder around me, prepared to incinerate the khirig who will kill me, even if it's the last thing I'll do.

The droplets are agonizing as they splash against my face, but I hold my glower at him.

"Fuck you!"

CHAPTER TWENTY-TWO

Departing

The khirig and his towering wave of water close in on me. A secondary wave extends out of the one holding Hirsh aloft and reaches for me as if it were a hand.

I look into his oncoming eyes with overwhelming disdain, ready to explode and tear him apart.

For the first time, I see him hesitate. His eyes widen as they lock on mine. But it's too late. The water is almost upon me. He won't pull back in time.

A world-shattering crack pounds through my chest and a visible shock-wave slams the water flat into the ground. Before I can even process what happened, I feel an impact in my back and the world spins around me.

My chest slams into the earth. I hadn't even realized I'd been flung through the air. My body is quick to twist back to the khirig and the mass of water behind me, but it's not there anymore. Water floods the ground, but not near me.

In place of the wave stands Remus. He is unmoving, looking down at something in front of him. I follow his gaze and see Hirsh, his body buried in a crater.

"What the fuck! Remus?" the khirig groans and tries to move, but he can't seem to get up. "What the hell are you doing? This'll take weeks to regrow." He tries to move again, but one of his large antlers cracks and snaps off.

Remus remains still. Unusually quiet.

I feel something touch my shoulder and turn to see Jav.

"You okay?" he asks.

It doesn't feel like I should be; my arms still shake and my face aches, but I nod anyway. "Yeah. Thanks." I turn back to Remus and Hirsh.

"Ah, fuck. That hurt, you old fool. What was that for?"

I can only barely make out the narrowing of Remus's eyes. "You attacked my team. One of my own." His voice is cold. Far from the ever cheery tone he always maintains.

"What? No. I was just showing the kid what I could do. I do that with all my brother's and sister's kids. A little ride around the camp is all." I can hear the worry entering Hirsh's voice. It seems like he hasn't seen Remus like this before either.

Remus takes a step toward the downed khirig before a crack of thunder rings out and Hirsh bellows a scream. The dohrni's tentacle pulls back from the pained man.

"You didn't stop when she ran from you? You didn't stop when she pleaded? I did not watch you grow up to be so inconsiderate. Be thankful I don't tear your horns from their roots." Remus's tone remains flat and quiet, but there is a fury barely hidden beneath the surface.

Another crack thunders out, followed by a scream. With a final glare, Remus turns and walks to me and Jav.

"Are you okay?" he asks as he bends down before me. His cold gaze returning to cheery as if it were never gone.

"Uh, yeah." I'm put off by the jerking of my emotions. I still haven't calmed down from the overwhelming fear. How can I be more fearful of being trapped than water? I'd prepared myself to dive into a building, but when I was confined by the wall of water, it felt far worse than the agony of water sizzling away at my flames.

"Thanks for the help," I say.

"Naturally." He rises to full height again and addresses Jav. "Get her ready. I'll get the others."

I jump to my feet immediately, trying to hide the shivers running down my arms. I don't want them to think I'm weak. They can't know my embers ache with terror.

Will I ever get over this fear of being caged? No matter how much strength I gain, will water always be an impossible hurdle for me? If a water mage was to attack me and I didn't have my team around to help me, could I ever compete?

My team . . .

It was strange to see Remus get so mad for me. Until this point, everything had been so casual. They'd all been too welcoming. So much so that I assumed they were just happy to have someone who could fill the role. I didn't really think they considered me a part of their group. A part of their team.

But they protected me. They got mad *for* me. They already considered me one of them and I'd just not noticed.

A sigh escapes my lips. I thought I'd resolved myself to be more trusting after Ash proved me wrong, but I fell into some of the same doubts. Even when they showed patience in teaching me and a willingness to work with me.

"We got our mission orders from the brass. There are quite a few bits of bad news, most relevant of which is that we'll be heading out immediately. No time to sleep." Jav eyes me as I finally calm myself properly. "Are you sure you're all right? We can help, you know?"

"Yeah." I should probably tell them of my issue with entrapment. I've wanted to hide it to hide my weaknesses, but if tonight has shown me anything, it's that I might need to rely on them to cover those weaknesses. If Remus and Jav hadn't appeared when he did, I would be dead. "I'll tell you later."

"All right." Jav then unstraps a satchel from his back and presents it to me. "Here. We were lucky my sisters got your outfit here before we left. You can use the bag when you want to fly."

I pull out the gift to inspect it. The cloth is a full-body piece that seems will cover every surface of my body except my hands and face. Hardened boots are sewn directly into the outfit, leaving nowhere for snow or water to drip down into.

"There should be gloves, goggles, and a mask in the bag. You should be able to zip them into the suit and leave you entirely covered. As far as I know, it should keep you safe from snow. And maybe water too."

I stare in amazement at the workmanship of it. This is amazing. It would be an incredible thing to bring back to the áed tribes if it holds back water as well as Jav says.

"How do I put it on?" It's all one piece, so I can't see where I'm supposed to fit in unless I flex myself in my incorporeal form and worm my way in. Which won't be quick.

Jav steps forward and unzips the front where I hadn't even noticed a seam. He shows me the same type of connection at both the sleeves and the hood, where they would connect to the gloves and mask.

This is really too good to waste with the temporary flame resistance inscription I'd been using up until this point. I need proper materials to give this outfit the proper protection it deserves. "You think that merchant will still be awake?"

"Merchants out here are always ready for a sale. But we shouldn't take long; Remus expects us out in five minutes."

The heqet merchant didn't have one of the metal types I remember my uncle often using for the inscription, but silver—the metal in the kitchenware I'd stolen from the Cano mansion—turned out to be a decent replacement. It was costly, but in combination with copper and aluminum, I think they will work great.

I also had to get a ceramic bowl that can withstand the heat of the melted metals while I mix them.

Now that I have everything I need, I just need to wait until we stop for a rest and I can write out the inscription into my new suit. I can't wait to throw away these worn-out rags.

Jav and I leave the garrison to find the others waiting. As soon as he notices, Grímr rushes to my side.

"He didn't hurt you, did he, Solvei? I'm sorry, I should've stayed outside with you. I should've noticed when you were in trouble." His ears lie flat on his down-turned head.

With this level of concern he shows, I feel foolish for holding a grudge against his opinions.

"Yeah, I'm fine. Do you mind if I ride with you for a bit? I'd like to get some sleep before we reach the snow again." Nobody has said it yet, but there's no doubt in my mind we're heading back up the mountains.

The big cat's ears flick up, and he raises his head. "Sure! No problem." He then lowers himself for me.

Remus speaks loud enough for us all to hear. "The brass have given us our orders and we are to head out at once, which is a good thing, because if we were to stay at this moment, I may be tried for murder come tomorrow morning." He laughs, but there is no humor in his tone.

The khirig water mage isn't dead . . . yet. I don't feel the same burning wrath for him as I did for Gloria, or the general. I'd rather just leave than think about him.

"We have been given the unreasonable task of following the Titan's path to discover the source of previously unseen species that have been attacking our defensive positions for the past months. They are expected to originate somewhere in the Middle Elevation."

"You're kidding? No prep?" Grímr exclaims.

"Nope."

A silence hangs over us for a time. I'm still new to the dangers of the

Alps, but everything I've heard points this mission to being unreasonably difficult.

But I have no issue with that. As long as it gets me away from this garrison right now, I don't care how difficult the coming days will be. I never want to be near Hirsh again.

I am lucky enough to get some sleep before we reach the snowline. After our first hunting trip together, Grímr runs a tad smoother. His thick fur coat is rather easy to nap on, even with the constant movement.

I requested we break before the snow and now that we are here, I can't help but feel giddy. Not only do I have this incredible new outfit, but I'm going to recreate one of the enhancements I'd only seen my uncle inscribe, never helped with. As I couldn't melt metals on my own, it had been all but impossible for me to perform any of the more difficult protections for our clothing.

I lay out the suit and accompanying equipment and prepare the bowl along with the metals I bought. I don't have a perfect memory of how much of each metal I need to use, but going off feeling shouldn't be too bad. Uncle specified that the mix of metals used only really affected the efficiency and maximum temperature a small percentage. The jump from using no metals to what I'm doing is huge, so I'm not too worried about getting the best ratios. A perfect mix of metals would only increase the max temp by maybe five percent.

I can tell by the way my fire interacts with the silver that it will be the most important part, so I melt down the entirety of the silver I brought. Next is to add enough copper and aluminum to give me enough total volume to work with while limiting the loss of efficiency a smaller portion of silver would cause.

A pure sample of silver wouldn't work, but as it's the lowest quantity of metal I have, I need to be careful not to dilute it too much.

"Wow. Jav really didn't cheap out on your welcome gift." Remus inspects the outfit in front of me.

"Huh?" I look down at the cloth. How much did this cost?

"Oh, don't worry. It's good you'll have something to protect you."

Back to my project; I hold both the copper and aluminum bars in a hand and slowly melt them into the bowl. Once I have only half of each metal bars left, I stop. The silver has solidified at the bottom of the bowl, leaving the other two metals to sit on top. I can only see the aluminum on the surface, but mixing the bowl with my finger swirls some of the copper color into the mixture.

Uncle told me that once the metals melt and are mixed for a few seconds, the drawing process needs to be done immediately. The pattern requires the metals to be together, but not truly combined. If I spend too long heating and mixing them, it might not work.

So, while keeping the metals from cooling into solid, I use the tip of my finger to paint the patterns into my new snowsuit. If I was with my tribe, I could have used a proper tool for this, to make the strokes perfect, but I'm limited by what I have on me and what that trader could sell.

As I paint, I realize that while the concept is similar, our inscriptions have almost no fundamental similarities to those common in these eastern nations. I don't know how it works, but the patterns I learned from my tribe don't follow the same logic of the lines in the ritual. Actually, I can't seem to see any form of logic for ours other than the pattern that repeats both horizontally and vertically. Also, unlike the ritual inscription, there are many parts that are not touching. The logical lines of eastern inscriptions always connect to each other, these patterns from my tribe do not.

Eventually, the process is complete. Only a tiny bit of the liquid metal remains in the bowl. I bring forth a flame to test it, ready to pull back if it damages the cloth even slightly. My fire touches the suit and I jerk it back.

There is no damage.

I let out a sigh of relief and put my flame back over the outfit, waiting for any part to damage. My tribe's pattern does its job though, and even if I have no idea how it does so, the snowsuit is protected.

The goggles were the hardest to do. There wasn't enough surface area on the rims and band to draw the pattern, so I had to write over the clear panels. It might obstruct sight slightly, but it's better than burning them in the heat of the moment.

With my work complete, I don the outfit. It fits surprisingly well; even the sewn-in boots don't slide around and fit tight.

"Looks good." Remus gives his usual eye grin.

I can't help the smile that rises in return. "I'm ready."

CHAPTER TWENTY-THREE

Centipede

The path remains clear until the first major checkpoint. No creatures swarm this far down; the teams farther up the trail are thinning them out. We pass several other teams as we head up the mountains, but never share more than a passing greeting.

The others have obviously been holding back for me. Now that I am willing to ride with Grímr again, the others don't need to slow themselves to my flying speed. That, and they have a reason to push through the Stepps as fast as possible.

A gradually growing influx of creatures has put a strain on the Mercenary Order's defensive positions. These beasts are varying, but each is of a type never seen prior. The most worrisome issue is that it apparently takes five Fearn teams at the very least to assure a kill without losses.

That there are so many of them is a cause of concern for all relevant parties. The upper brass of the Order would have sent a few of the Beith mercenaries to investigate under normal circumstances. Due to a combination of Remus and I having pissed off the Order's management, and a lack of available Beith mercenaries, we are stuck investigating instead. Alone.

It's not the worst, though; at least we'll get to consume stronger beasts than we've yet faced. Luis-Eight—our team—also happens to be amongst the strongest of the Luis rank.

I'm feeling far more confident now that I have this snowsuit. Maybe I can actually learn to participate with my spear without worry of the snow under my feet.

I've hardly had the time to practice, so I doubt the time I can fight with a spear alongside the others will be any time soon. Tetsu might continue teaching me as we travel, but for now, the team seems far too keen on moving up the mountains as quick as possible.

Jav glides back to his perch on Remus. He'd been flying ahead, scouting the path we'll be taking.

"We'll be getting our first look at one of those creatures soon. It moves at least as fast as us, so maybe fifteen minutes until intercept."

"Anything you can tell us?" Remus asks.

"Yeah. It's a big fucking centipede."

"How big exactly?"

"Bigger than a centipede should ever get; about the length of a house."

"All right then, I guess we're about to see just how strong these things are. Bunny, you take front. Solvei, want to go for a flight?"

He asks it like a question, but it feels more like a request, if not an outright order. I'm disappointed to put away my new outfit already, but I do as he says and start my change.

As soon as the icy breeze flows over my body once more, I realize how good the suit is at keeping my heat contained. I hardly needed to strain to keep my body temperature high. Now in my falcon form, the frosty wind forces me to burn hotter.

In the air once more, I have a better view of the path before us. I can see the centipede approaching at an incredible pace. Its yellow legs almost look like they are rolling backward as the creature speeds down the slope with its jagged, zigzagging skitter.

It's hard to get a good idea of its size at this distance, but it is obviously fast. The ground passes underneath it from tip to end in a fraction of a second.

I look down at my team. Tetsu is charging head on toward the creature, with Remus and Grímr spreading out from her sides. Jav still sits with Remus, but I imagine as they get closer, he'll be thrown again.

A hiss announces the centipede's awareness of us. Jav flies toward the creature, closing the vast distance in but a moment. His short wing blades slice through several legs before it can react. But when the centipede does react, it is with lightning speed. A razor-tipped leg thrusts toward Jav faster than my eyes can follow.

Jav twists around the sharp leg and curves through the air to cut off another leg before letting his momentum pull him high into the air, expertly dodging the next six bladed leg strikes.

Even as it strikes at Jav, the centipede never stops moving. Both it and our albanic charge head first into each other.

Tetsu brings down a massive war-axe on the head of the critter as they collide. Four of the being's front legs lift to hold back the swing just enough that the axe slams into the creature's exoskeleton, but doesn't cleave through. Tetsu abandons the axe now stuck in the creature's head and holds her arms out to grasp the two large fangs snapping closed around her.

Their impact has Tetsu sliding back twenty meters from the momentum of the creature before she gets enough of a grip under her to grind it to a stop. The fangs come so close to the sides of her chest, but with her strength, she keeps them from snapping closed.

The centipede doesn't just sit there trying to win a battle of strength. It curls its body around, trying to stab or grasp the woman while she is stuck fending off its fangs.

Before it can do so, Grímr charges in and slams into the center of the centipede's trunk. The creature jerks away from Tetsu as Grímr's heft lifts it into the air before flipping onto its back. The panther is quick to mount it and use his large teeth and claws to tear into the softer-shelled underside of the centipede.

The bug curls up around Grímr and jabs a number of its sharp legs into his side and back. He snarls and continues tearing through the wound he'd created. Gray blood gushes out and covers Grímr's fur.

The familiar thunderous sound of Remus's limbs cracks through the air as he impacts the axe already lodged in the creature's head. The axe cuts clean through the centipede, splitting its head in half, but the creature still moves.

It writhes and coils, stabbing its legs into Grímr, and tries to crawl out from under him.

Jav and Tetsu return to the fight. Jav continues cutting off as many of the legs as he can, prioritizing those stabbing into Grímr and avoiding what must be instinctual reactive strikes from the centipede. Tetsu steps forward and grasps the remains of the creature's head, pinning it still and halting its constricting.

With an unmoving target, Remus has an easy time crushing through the exoskeleton with his whiplike tentacles.

It is only a matter of time now until the centipede dies. Maybe I should have helped, or participated somehow, but I didn't know how I should. They all work so well with each other that I would only get in their way. If I were to engulf the area in flame, I'd just be limiting my team's line of sight. I know how ineffective my flames are against beasts like this.

The body of the creature finally slows. Its legs still twitch and move as if walking, despite its body being overturned.

Remus and Tetsu help remove the centipede's legs lodged in Grímr. Crimson blood flows from the wounds and mixes with the blue of the centipede's coating his hide. He barely seems to mind what look like grievous wounds.

"So, what do you think about one of them?" Remus asks Grímr with an amused tone.

"Please, don't even consider the thought." He seems to hardly notice the many wounds lining his back and sides.

"Are you going to be okay?" I ask, looking at his bloody fur coat.

Grímr looks up at me, then back at himself. "Huh? Oh, don't worry, this is nothing. I'll be back to perfect shape in an hour."

"That felt rather weak for a Mid Elevation creature," Tetsu says as she retrieves her battle-axe. "You don't suppose it's a swarm type, do you?"

"Don't you dare even put that thought in our heads, madwoman," Jav says.

I catch a small upward twitch at the corner of Tetsu's mouth.

My flames spread out over the centipede to shape the ritual while I change back to normal and hop back in the comfort of my outfit. Its insulation feels amazing.

"It is good that they aren't that strong," Remus says. "If we're lucky, they come from somewhere in the Lower Elevation and we won't even need to go through the effort of reaching the Mid."

"How long will it take to reach the Lower Elevation?" I ask.

"We'll likely have to fight a few more of those things, so three days sounds right."

"What should we call them?" Jav asks as the last motes of the centipede disappear into the inscription.

"Bugs." Tetsu ties her axe back into the side of her pack.

"Oh, yeah, why not?" Jav rolls his eyes. "I'll just tell you we're facing a bug anytime I scout something. Good luck if it turns out to be a swarm of blood crickets or a thermite hornet."

"Sounds good." Tetsu grins.

"No, no. You won't be doing that, Jav; we don't need any unnecessary confusion. Just call them centipedes for now. I doubt anyone here would mistake them for the regular-sized ones. Let the teams back home decide their name," Remus says.

I burn through the small portion of centipede left over and remount Grímr. In no time, we are sprinting through the mountains again. Plumes rise behind us where our speedy movements disturb the snow.

In the next few days, we tear through many of the centipedes. The higher we move, the more often we come across them. They aren't the only creature, but each we come across is far easier dealt with. It is hard to believe considering the immense amount of land we've covered, but apparently we are still only on the Stepps.

"How far is the Lower Elevation from here, anyway?" I ask.

Jav stokes the campfire. An array of fish sit above the flames, simmering under the volan's careful eye. "About another day. You'll know when we're there."

I wait a moment, expecting him to elaborate, but he remains quiet with his attention entirely on the burning fish before him.

"Why? What's there?"

"You'll just have to wait and see," Remus butts in, his eye grin more teasing than usual.

That's annoying. Can't he just tell me instead of messing around? My annoyance must have been visible on my face as he lets out a chuckle.

"I heard you did pretty well in Bleed for your first game. How about we all have a game?" Remus materializes a deck of the cards out of thin air.

Tetsu's eyes narrow. "Is Jav playing?"

Remus turns a questioning gaze to the small cook.

"Of course," Jav says.

"I'm out."

"Nope."

Both Grímr and Tetsu immediately refuse to play.

"Oh, come now, we don't have to play for bets. Just a nice friendly game." Remus tries to encourage them.

"It's never a friendly game with Jav," Tetsu says.

"You're just scared of losing," Jav says. "The battle of strategy is the only battle you're not confident in."

The internal conflict Tetsu feels is as blatant as a charging beast. "Fine. I'll beat you this time." She frowns, but sits with us.

Jav grins at her and turns to Grímr. "You're not going to be the only one to sit out, are you? How lonely." Despite his words, Jav is grinning ear to ear.

Grímr sighs and, without more prodding, drops beside Tetsu.

"Excellent. We have a fifth player now, so do we move up to three decks or stick with two?"

"Three," Grímr and Tetsu say in unison.

"Oh, look, the fish is ready." Jav proceeds to apply some sort of powder to the fish before handing them out to everyone.

I'm surprised I'm even given one; I still have my iron to eat through. The thin metal stick that skewers the fish rests in my hand as I inspect it. Fish come from the water; I watched as Jav dove after them earlier. They are a strange existence, completely opposite to me. Each of these silvery blue creatures can only survive in the water. The idea just seems so bizarre.

I poke at the charred scales of the fish, expecting to be burned like I'm touching water. But I don't feel any pain, instead it feels soft and springy.

Remus eyes me as he deals out the cards. "There's no water in the fish, if you're worried. Well, no more than any other animal, and you have no problem with them."

I take it in my hands, and slowly raise the fish to my mouth. Hesitantly, I take a bite. It's delicious. As surprisingly good as it is, I can't see myself ever willingly putting myself close to water to get some for myself.

My cards in front of me are horrible, there's no way I'll win this round. I look around at the others to see if their public cards are any worse than mine. Everyone gorges on their own fish. Both Tetsu and Jav savor their meal while the other two dig in without care.

"So," Jav starts after everyone has finished eating, "I know Remus said there wouldn't be any bets, but the game just isn't the same without. How about just a tiny wager?"

An hour later, Jav finds himself with another pile of coins before him. Grímr and Tetsu are both deflated in depression. Remus, despite having lost more to Jav than anyone, seems more happy than usual. He packs away the cards, whistling all the while.

"Never again," I hear Tetsu groan, getting a grunt of agreement from the big cat next to her.

It's getting late now. I crawl on top of Grímr's back, away from the snow-laden ground and snuggling into his comfortable fur. It surprised even me how quickly I'd become accustomed to sleeping on Grímr, but when the alternative is the cold ground, I find his thick fur coat far more appealing.

"Enjoy your last night of peaceful rest," Remus says. "From tomorrow, we won't be able to be so lax."

CHAPTER TWENTY-FOUR

Crevasse

My wings stretch wide, floating in the breeze high in the air. I look down at my team below, bare pinpricks in the distance. Sailing through the skies with nary a sound, I wait for my target to move within range.

These winged beasts have incredible hearing, which I've noticed in my past attempts, but this time I plan to catch it by surprise.

It flies underneath me with its leathery black wings, and I decide it's now or never. My wings pull into my side and I nosedive. The wind whipping past and the ground rushing toward me is exhilarating, but I focus on my target.

Ever so slightly, I spread my wings to angle myself toward the flying creature. It has yet to notice me, but my past attempts prove that it only needs a moment to twist the situation to its advantage.

My talons jerk forward just in time to pierce into the creature's back. A perfect landing, if I say so. My impact—right between the base of its wings—sends us spiraling, but I dig my sharp claws deep and clamp down with my beak.

The bat screeches, vibrating my flames right to the core. It disturbs my fire and threatens to rip my body back to incorporeal, but I hold on. The first time I experienced their ultrasonic screams, I hadn't expected it at all and dropped from the sky when my wings lost their form. I know now to defend myself against their screeches, but it is still an extremely odd feeling to have your body try to ripple away from you.

The black wings spread out again as the creature tries to regain its stability.

As it does, I reach out my flames and begin burning through the rubbery wings. Another screech rings out, shaking my flames as it tries to twist on itself and bite at me.

I fail to pull my wing back in time, and it tears straight through it. Unfortunately for the bat, it hurts him more than it does me. I use the opportunity to shove my flames down into its gullet, careful to only push in tongues of fire not laced with inner flame to avoid any pain its saliva might inflict. While not nearly as dangerous as water, the bodily fluids of creatures can sting.

It snaps its jaw closed, cutting off the flames within its maw. The bat slaps its wings back, knocking me just enough to dislodge my grip. My talons tear through the back of the creature and I let go with my beak. I've already burned through its wings enough that it won't be escaping this free fall.

My wings snap wide, immediately slowing my fall to a crawl.

The bat struggles to flap its wings and regain control, but the air does nothing except tear through the already damaged membrane. As the beast cries upon realizing the inevitable, another ultrasonic screech slams into me, a noise only audible through the feeling it makes in my chest.

A thump is the only sound that comes from the bat's unimpressive collision against the ground. Snow gets blown everywhere, but it doesn't look like the creature would have died from the fall. Sure enough, the crippled bat crawls out of the snow crater.

I don't have to worry about fighting it amongst the snow, fortunately. In moments, my team tears through the beast, leaving it no time to fight back.

These bats are another of the new beasts that have been descending the mountain since the cooling of the Titan's path. Nowhere near as strong as the centipedes, but their flight has been a cause of worry for the Mercenary Order. It's hard to stop creatures like these that can completely ignore the defensive choke points set up to funnel the descending monsters.

I rejoin my team, smoothly gliding onto Grímr as the others finish the bat. It went rather well this time. I wasn't discovered until I'd already latched onto its back. Last time, my wings caught the wind a bit too audibly and it was enough for the bat to hear me coming. I'd been completely unable to catch the creature, even spreading my flames after it. Jav had to come and knock it out of the sky instead.

"Nice job, Solvei!" Grímr glances back at me before turning to the dead mammal. "What made the brass think that these creatures are coming from the Middle Elevation? There's no chance they could survive long that high up, right?"

"Apparently it's one of the older Beith mercs that believe they are coming from the Middle Elevation. It's not too hard to understand why; there aren't any known ecosystems in the Lower Elevation or on the Stepps that these creatures might be coming from. Mid and above are the only places unexplored enough that there might be some region we haven't seen."

"Sure, but if that's the case, then do we even need to worry? If some previously enclosed ecosystem lost its barrier to the outside world, then why don't we just let the mid-tier beast wipe them out?"

Remus casts an eye our way. "It's rather rash to assume they are all weak because of the few we've seen. In any case, our job is investigation; even if they are overwhelmed by the surrounding species, we still need to confirm it."

Regardless of their origin, we still need to move out of the Stepps. We are getting close now. What looks like a massive wall of ice extends far to the distant horizons, an obvious representation of the change between the ranked regions.

The air is thin now. At this height, not only is the air freezing, but it makes breathing far more difficult. It's been fine for now, but whenever I fly at any significant altitude, I have to spread my flames wide to reach as much air as I can.

The others don't consider the bat's corpse to be worth the time it takes to perform the ritual, so I wrap it in my fire and take it for myself. I wonder if there's a way to speed the process up? Not that I care too much; anything the others don't want, I can take for myself.

With the bat eaten, I go to take to the skies once more. The more bats I knock out, the more I get to consume after all.

"Hold on, Solvei." Remus stops my launch. "The skies get rather treacherous from here on. I want you to stick with us."

"Okay." My wings relax at my side. "Should I switch back?"

"No, being able to fly will make the transition between the Elevations easier."

I peer up at the looming glacial wall. "Do we have to climb that?"

"Yep! But that's not the tough part of making it into the Lower Elevation."

I glance at him curiously, but his innocently smiling eyes give nothing away. I turn back to the massive wall ever so slowly getting higher above us. Despite their incredible pace this entire journey, they slow down the closer we get to the Lower Elevation. Right now, we are moving at half my maximum flight speed, which is far slower than what we'd been traveling for the last few days.

The Titan's path cuts right through the glacial wall ahead of us. Unlike the rest of the path that we've followed until now, there is no black rock remnant creating an easy road for us. Instead, a forest of massive jagged, vertical shards of ice lies ahead, likely formed by the melting of the ice wall. It doesn't look any easier to traverse than the frozen precipice.

I can't help but stare in awe whenever I look at the incredible geographic change such a disaster has brought. Anywhere except where the Titan has passed, the glacial wall remains the same height. Nowhere else is there a blemish.

A powerful gust of freezing cold wind blows into me from the deep abyss below.

I vigorously beat my wings until I'm back amongst my team. A large chasm drops far into the earth before me. Nervously, I approach the edge once more. This time I fly only a few meters away from my team.

The extensive opening between the ground beneath me and the wall of ice ahead drops into nothingness. It is too dark to see how deep it is.

If not for the mound of black stone bridging the gap along the Titan's path, I'd have no idea how my team might pass this crevasse. Actually, how did they? I cast a glance at my land-bound teammates strolling leisurely across the last stretch of black rock. They've said they usually hunt in the Lower Elevation, so how do they get across this chasm?

Flying away from the edge, I follow close behind the others. We move slowly across this auspicious igneous rock-pile of a bridge. Unlike before, we have slowed to almost a crawl as we move over the filled ravine.

The wind picks up the farther we cross into the crevasse. Despite only fly-ing a couple meters off the ground and the curved edge being far to each side, I find my flight buffeted almost to an uncontrollable degree. The chilly wind pelts my wings, threatening to send me far into the sky before I can resist.

I crash into Grímr's back and warm myself from the cold. Grímr's fur gives an appreciative shake at my warmth. If the wind was this bad here, covered by hundreds of meters of stone, what would it be like out over the chasm itself?

"The Alps become treacherous from this point on, Solvei," I hear Remus call over the loud whistling of the wind. "We won't be able to travel as fast as before. Make sure you are always beside us. Even teams as experienced as us need to be wary here."

"How do you cross this thing normally?"

"The only way you can; down and back up again. It's only something like a thousand meters down." Remus is far too casual for the words he says. "Well, that's how far down you need to go. You can usually find a fallen glacier shard bridging the gap. Below that, the ravine can go much farther down."

"Fortunately for us," Jav cuts in, "there are many fractures and caves run-ning through the glaciers. They're hard to see from here, but there are always thousands of interconnected passages through the ice. They make the climb up much easier."

Caves running through the ice? I do not like the sound of that. It definitely seems like something that'll knock me back into another panic attack if I can't see a way out.

I really need to tell them about my fear. I should. They deserve that much. But as I open my mouth to say something, doubts run through my mind. How can I tell them about something so debilitating? Will they think poorly of me for having such an unreasonable fear?

Even as I cling to Grímr's back, being saved from a gust blowing me away, I can't say it.

The unnatural bridge unfortunately doesn't reach the entire length of the chasm. From where we are, it curves downward into the glacier. We got to skip most of the trip down, but it looks like it won't be completely without a climb.

I struggle within myself to say something about my fears to my team as we walk the last stretch of igneous rock. I peer at Remus walking at the front. Jav, like me, clings to his ride. The wings of his suit stored away, but the wind still knocks around his light body.

I look down slightly and catch Remus watching me. I snap my head back into Grímr's fur. Why was he watching me? Does he already know? He can't read minds, right?

No, Solvei. Stop being stupid. He was only looking at you. It means nothing.

"Oh? How convenient," I hear Tetsu say. "Looks like we won't be needing to climb today."

I pull my head out of the thick fur and look forward. At the end of our bridge, in the wall of ice, is a cavern. Wide enough for each of us to pass through with ease, but I can't help but feel apprehension at the sight of it. The glacial cave curves away from the entrance after only a few meters. There is no way I'll be able to enter without falling into an involuntary panic.

I catch Remus's eyes boring into mine. There is no doubt he knows something, and yet he hasn't judged me poorly . . . I think. I don't have a choice now. I have to swallow my doubts and just tell them.

"I'm sorry. I should have told you this earlier."

CHAPTER TWENTY-FIVE

Glacier

I tell them my fear. My crippling apprehension for being in apparent positions of helplessness and being trapped. I tell them what caused it. Everything about the Void Fog and how I had to twist my consciousness to stop myself going mad like the void-touched.

I sit there, expecting anger or disappointment, or at the very least irritation. I don't meet any of their eyes as I fidget with my wings in front of my body.

"Huh. I always thought there was something more to the Void Fog than everyone assumed. The monsters it spits out are always incredibly unique," Remus says, not even mentioning my fears.

"That explains how quick you were to learn to suppress your thoughts."

Jav joins me on Grímr's back. The large cat doesn't complain about his passengers. Jav takes a few steps until he's right in front of my beak. I try to turn my head away, but he puts his paw out to stop me.

"Look me in the eye," he says, and I have no choice but to do exactly that. "I don't care what sort of misunderstanding you have about this phobia of yours. As long as you put the effort in to help yourself and find workarounds, it doesn't matter how crippling it is. Your team is here to cover your weaknesses, just as we do for each other. Now, are you going to let this stop you?"

How else can I answer that? "No."

"Good, because if the caves are too much for you, we'll have to climb. I hope you're ready. Oh, and you should change back for this; you really don't want to be flying around here."

I twist my head to the others and see none of the irritation I'd been expecting.

Huh.

I guess I have been overreacting. But it's still embarrassing to speak about something that makes me so weak. To hide from the humiliation, I take Jav's advice and begin my transformation.

It is interesting to see how each of my team approaches the vertical climb. Tetsu has pulled out a pair of curved knives and stabs each deep into the frozen wall for leverage. Grímr looks incredibly odd walking up the vertical slope as if it were normal ground, his claws slicing into the ice under his feet. Jav has it the hardest; I can't tell if he feigns sleep, or he's actually taking a nap on top of Remus. The dohrni doesn't mind his passenger as he fits his boneless limbs in any thin crack he can find and pulls himself up.

My arms wrap around Grímr's neck. I'm unable to reach my hands with how thick his neck is, but his thick fur is a good enough handhold anyway.

The heavy cracks resounding with each stab of Tetsu's blades into the ice do nothing but stress me out, and for good reason too. Another swing of her blade fractures much of the surrounding ice. A section of the glacial wall dislodges and tilts away, taking Tetsu with it. Only a quick reaction from Remus saves her; he jumps off the wall and, with a crack of his whiplike limbs, shatters the dislodged ice before pulling her back to the wall.

This has happened four times now.

You'd think Tetsu would learn to be softer with her blows to the ice. But no, she continues to slam her arms into the wall without so much as an acknowledgment that she was close to plunging to her death.

We only have another three incidents before we reach the base of the forest of ice pillars. This region of the glacier—damaged by the passing Titan—isn't as easily traversed as I'd hoped when I'd seen it. The massive shards of ice are like the walls themselves, but there is no ground to stand on between them. The space between each spike leads down into the extensive tunnels and fissures running through the ground underneath us.

Instead of a—relatively—easy climb up a single slope, we need to jump from one pillar to another. Maybe that wouldn't have been an issue if these shards weren't ten to twenty meters away from each other.

Yet Tetsu hops between the pillars with ease that even Remus couldn't hope to mimic. She launches off the ice with both legs pouncing together, not even bothering to use the knives to get a grip before hopping off once more.

Oh.

Bunny.

I can't help but let out an involuntary laugh. A laugh which attracts her attention.

"What?"

"I get it," I declare, smiling up at her.

"You get what?" she raises an eyebrow.

"Bunny!"

She scoffs and jumps away as a round of guffaws erupts from the rest of the team.

A satisfied sigh escapes me as I gaze at those around me. I was foolish to think they would think less of me for my phobia. It is good to see that the team has quickly returned to their usual camaraderie.

Tetsu . . . no, Bunny has never complained about their nickname for her. Of course, she reacts upon hearing it, but if she truly had an issue, I'm sure she would ask the team to stop.

I hold tight as Grímr pounces to the nearest pillar. The heavy cat's claws dig deep into the ice. Deep gashes follow the movement before our momentum comes to a halt. He lifts his paw to continue climbing when an intense crack reverberates through the area.

More cracking sounds out until an echoing crash washes over us. I can feel the rumbling vibrations in the ice even through Grímr.

There's no sign of where the loud noise came from, but as I look around, one of the tall ice shards we passed only a few minutes ago cracks and topples into its neighbors. The base of the pillar cannot hold its weight and shatters, dropping the collapsing ice down into the tunnels underneath. The second tall shard cracks from the impact and slams into the next pillar. It comes to a rest, dangerously ready to fall, but not quite dropping.

Despite the visible collapse of a pillar we only just passed, that isn't what I'm worried about. The initial crashing noise was far heavier than the collapse of the pillar right behind me.

"What was that?"

"Part of the glacial wall collapsing," Grímr says, before continuing up the ice.

"Is that normal?" How do they know it won't happen while we're climbing?

"Unfortunately. In the past, they've tried building bridges across the crevasse, but having a few million tons of ice fall on any structure is a quick way to destroy it."

"What do you do if it collapses when you're climbing it?"

"You fling yourself as far away as you can and hope you don't die from the fall." I can't tell if he's joking or not. "Of course, Luis teams like us won't have too much of an issue if it happens. And there are well-charted areas that are monitored for stability to allow the lower ranked teams passage with little risk."

I hug myself tighter into Grímr. The very fragile structures around me are added to the list of things I'm not thinking about. Along with entrapping caves below and the unbelievable amount of frozen water around me.

Yes, definitely not thinking about any of those things.

Not thinking about them.

Not thinking about them.

Damn.

After a while of climbing through the forest of spikes, we come to the edge of the Titan's path and pull ourselves up the last wall of ice before we are on flat ground again.

A plane of wavy glacier extends far as I can see. A constant upward slope of ice peppered with holes and fissures. Looking back down into the Titan's path, the pillars of ice extend through it until I can't make them out anymore. There is a distinct lack of mountains or rock, leaving the far-extending glacier as the only thing in sight beside the peak of the Alps that hulk beyond.

We don't stand around long. While not inside the path anymore, we actually have stable ground on the outskirts of where the Titan has traveled. The path itself is almost three times as wide and five times deeper than back in the Stepps. I guess the heat of the Titan melted the ice much easier than it did rock.

My team speeds into a jog, but nowhere near as fast as I'd become used to in the past few days. I also notice the team is more structured in their relative positions as we run along the inclining ice. Even when Remus throws Jav, he isn't gone for thirty minutes each time like before. Now, I can see him even at the maximum distance he travels.

That playfulness I've felt amongst the team until now isn't gone exactly, but it feels subdued. More serious. I follow their lead, keeping my eye out for any of those creatures we're supposed to be following.

"So . . . how are we supposed to find where the beasts are coming from if they all use the glacial tunnels? I have yet to see any on the surface," Jav says as he comes back from his most recent flight.

"For now, we continue on," Remus says. "We still have a reason to believe they are coming from the Middle Elevation. If we cannot find a sign of them once past the worst of the glacier, then we can come back and search through the tunnels."

Grímr grumbles beneath me. "Let's hope it doesn't come to that. We have more than a few reasons for that to be less than ideal."

We continue our gradual trot alongside the ledge, heading up the slope. Hours pass and I get lost in the fascinating reflections of the sunlight through the ice. It is mostly transparent, so the patches of glacier that aren't covered in snow give me an incredible view of the intricate weave of tunnels and fissures below. The light distorts the image and the blue tint eventually stops me seeing any lower, but it's an enrapturing sight.

I notice Grímr's ear twitch and a moment later he shakes his head and I feel a shiver run through his body. The temperature is horribly low now. I'm glad I stopped flying; my snowsuit is incredibly warm. I feel bad for Grímr out in the open to this cold. After having been on my ride for so long, I feel I owe him.

I unzip the connection, locking my gloves to my suit to allow my inner flame to engulf Grímr's fur coat. The chill and lack of air make spreading my flame incredibly difficult, but I burn through a good portion of my energy to heat the portian up.

I snap my gloves closed once more to keep the chill out while keeping control of my flame. It is almost the limit of my ability to keep my flames burning with such little air. I hope we don't have far to go until we reach the Middle Elevation; it's extremely difficult to breathe already, I can only imagine it getting worse the higher we go.

Despite the warm blanket I've given Grímr, he ignores it. His ear twitches again, and he picks up the pace until he's right next to Remus.

"Comfortable?" Remus asks with smirking eyes as he notices my flames.

Grímr doesn't react to his comment. "We're being followed," he grunts, almost too quiet for me to hear.

We are? I'm just about to turn to look around, but Remus's words stop me.

"Solvei, stop!" he says hurriedly. "Don't let them know we know." He turns his sight back ahead of us but addresses Grímr. "Where? How many?"

"A few hundred meters directly behind us. Just one. It sounds like it's crawling through the tunnels."

"Beast?"

"Can't tell; the sound isn't distinct enough."

Remus pauses for a moment. "All right, we'll continue as we are for now. Tell me if it closes the distance or you lose track of it."

Even though everyone walks the same as before, I can tell they are far more wary of their surroundings now. Each depression in the ice possibly hiding an ambush.

There is something out there following us, but that it only follows and doesn't attack is worrying; is it the only one? Are there more waiting ahead and the one behind is readying to pincer us?

The most dangerous thing is the lack of information we have. I can't help but feel the worst possibility is being surrounded, so why don't we engage the thing following us while we have the upper hand? I don't know, Remus is the most experienced with these things.

I've only known him for a month, but I trust his judgment.

CHAPTER TWENTY-SIX

Portian

It is incredibly hard not to turn and look for our tail. Even harder to not let the silence get to me. Now and then, I notice the flicking of Grímr's ear. I've come to realize it's a subconscious reaction he makes whenever he hears something from whatever is following us.

I strain my hearing, but I can't pick out anything from the constant groaning and cracking of the ice underfoot. As far as I can tell, the entire glacier is empty. There are no creatures in any direction. I don't know if that's normal or not here, but it is definitely different from the high number we've come to expect in the Stepps.

Is the thing following us some beast stalking its prey, or is it something intelligent? Could it be someone from the races following us? If so, what reason could they have?

My wild guesses are baseless, but with no information other than Grímr hearing sounds behind us, all I'm able to do is speculate as my team and I walk in silence.

How good must Grímr's hearing be if he can not only make out a sound from over a hundred meters away, but can distinguish it from the background noise and determine that it's caused by something following us?

We travel for hours with barely any change until Grímr finally informs of our pursuer's actions.

"It's creeping up on us now. Maybe ten minutes until contact."

"All right, in a minute, I'll send Jav out. We'll continue on as we have, but the moment it breaches to the surface, Jav will call the attack."

When Remus flings the small volan through the air, I notice he doesn't go directly up as usual. Jav flies far ahead of us before curving around behind us. He stays within a hundred meters of the ice, taking long sweeping circles in the air to retain his speed.

I wonder why he doesn't rise any higher.

"Fuck." Grímr's sudden curse pulls our attention. Under our curious gazes, he is forced to explain. "I heard it. It's a mountain panther," he says, hesitating.

"Oh." I catch Remus's eyes flicker to me, before laughing. "Well, I guess you'll be talking earlier than you expected."

Grímr grumbles in response. Is this about that secret of his race? It's definitely that. What does it have to do with the creature following us?

"It's only fair. She was willing to share her fears; about time you reciprocate," Bunny says with hardly a glance our way.

"Oh? And you'll offer your own fears?" Grímr snaps.

"I fear nothing." She flicks her head around to glare and he returns in kind.

I don't have time to ponder what the secret might be. A whistle cuts through the air behind us and we all turn at once.

A large panther—identical to Grímr—is crouched not twenty meters from us. A portian? Why was one of Grímr's race creeping up on us?

Jav drops from above, cutting a deep gash in the side of its neck. He curves in the air, ready to strike at the other side. The panther is quick to react now that it's aware of the volan, moving its head out of the way and swinging a clawed paw at him. It strikes nothing but air.

The three with me are quick to dash toward the portian, ready to engage it while it's distracted.

Remus arrives first and whips a gauntlet-wielding tentacle forward. The panther notices the new threats just in time, leaping away as the metal encased limb tears through the air hardly a whisker away.

It's a thinking person. Why are we attacking without even trying to talk first?

The panther backs up, eyeing each of my team as they surround it. It scrunches up its muzzle as if it smells something horrible and snaps its head to Grímr. The portian growls, losing sight of anything around it beside Grímr. Its eyes hold a murderous tinge.

Not caring for the other threats, the panther dashes forward before crashing into Grímr. I'm sent flying off his back, but my suit is enough to keep the thin layer of snow from touching me as my back slams into the ground.

Both panthers tumble down the slope of ice, rolling over each other as they try to bite and claw at each other. Tetsu and Remus follow close behind the interlocked pair, striking whenever they find an opportunity.

Grímr lets out a guttural roar as the long saber-teeth of the panther dig deep into his neck. The other portian doesn't get away with any less damage; Grímr's claws tear through much of its chest while gauntlets and sword damage its flanks.

They roll to a stop with Grímr pinned underneath. The panther continues to receive more damage from the two attacking its sides but ignores them. Its entire attention is on tearing Grímr apart.

I don't get it. Why does it have such a one-minded aggressiveness toward one of its own kind?

With a jerk of its head, the panther tears a chunk of flesh out of Grímr's neck. He hisses in pain as Remus's tentacle slams into the being's face, sending it flying down the glacier slope.

Grímr rolls back to his feet and coughs up blood. More gushes out the huge gash in the side of his neck. A choking, gurgling sound escapes his throat as he tries to breathe through the blood. He doesn't look all right at all, but he turns toward the panther rising to its feet again ten meters away.

One of its hind legs is limp, bent the wrong way, while deep wounds cut up much of the other flank. Despite the damage taken, it still pays no attention to the two at the sides of Grímr.

Another deep growl rumbles from its chest as it begins its desperate offense. With one leg completely useless, it struggles, but still dashes toward us with speed far greater than it should be capable of.

Jav drops in from behind it and cuts through the tendon in the back of the panther's leg just as it tries to push off, sending it tumbling across the ground.

It howls with its murderous gaze continuing to burn into Grímr. Despite the loss of the use of both rear legs, it continues to crawl forward.

Bunny's sword swings down and cuts halfway through its neck. The panther stops for a moment, but even as the focus in its eyes fades, it resumes its desperate crawl.

The sword is jerked out, only to come down once more, decapitating the beast.

There was no intelligence in that creature. Nothing but a murderous desperation I hadn't seen since the chthonic. What exactly caused the portian to act as it had?

Maybe that's the wrong question. My team had been unhesitating as they engaged the creature. So what is it that makes Grímr different?

I turn back to the portian, but my thoughts are put on hold as I'm reminded of his injury. Grímr's laying down and pressing his paws into the wound as a river of blood continues to gush from the wound where a chunk of his neck is missing.

I hurry to his side. "Should I cauterize?" I ask as I avoid the blood pooling on the ice.

He chokes out a gurgle, but upon hearing himself, settles to nod.

I push my flames into his wound, quickly burning closed the tubes of blood. After that, I take more care to only lightly burn areas where it feels like blood is gushing.

With how open his wound is, it's far easier to stop the bleeding than it had been for Ash's leg, despite the far greater area of damage.

"Doing all right over there, Grímr?" Remus asks jovially.

I turn to see him calmly walking past the headless corpse. Isn't he being far too casual when his friend has such a grievous wound?

Grímr nods to Remus, equally carefree. As if he isn't missing a third of his neck. He's acting like it doesn't even hurt.

"What?" I blink at my teammates.

For now, I'm going to ignore the wound that Grímr seems to have almost forgotten about, if the way he stares at me is any sign. He seems far more interested in watching me with concern than his own mortal wound. Or at least what would normally be.

If he doesn't care about it, then why should I? I try to tell myself, but really I just need a distraction from the deadly looking wound.

"Why did a portian attack so mindlessly?" I ask, but everyone looks toward Grímr.

I turn on the injured panther. "What is it that everyone knows about you that I don't?"

He opens his mouth to speak, but coughs, and blood trickles down the side of his maw. My anger subsides slightly at the sight, but he hardly reacts to what must be incredibly painful.

After coughing and spitting out a globule of congealed blood, he finally clears his throat enough to speak.

"Um . . . Would you believe if I said that was my ex?" he says with a nervous grin.

He gets a round of snorts from the others, but I just glare at him.

"Okay, sorry." He points to the dead portian. "That is a mountain panther, not a portian. In some very specific and difficult-to-achieve circumstances, us portian can, uh, repurpose the bodies of beasts."

He ducks his head as if expecting me to lash out.

Repurpose bodies? Doesn't everyone do that? He specified the panther wasn't a portian, so does that mean he, what . . . took their bodies?

Bunny sighs. "He's skirting the topic. Portians are parasites that live by taking the bodies of other creatures."

Grímr jerks at her sudden revelation. "But we never take sapients." He turns to me. "And I'm sure áed are immune, anyway; I know áinfean are."

That's it? That's the big secret? I don't see why he would care about hiding it. It doesn't seem much different from how I would burn a corpse or we enact the ritual or even simply using a corpse for parts. What was he so worried about?

There are a thousand things in the world more terrifying than someone that can wear another being like armor. Although, it is a bit gross.

"That's it?" I can't help but say.

Grímr stares at me uncomprehendingly.

"What did I tell you? Nothing to worry about with the áed." Remus claps two of his tentacles together before rubbing them. "Now that all the drama is over with, we have a panther to sacrifice. Solvei, start up the ritual. Do you want the head, or a leg?"

I follow Remus and proceed with the ritual as I burn through the head for myself.

I wonder how Grímr takes over a creature? Is there a limit? Could he take over a Titan? I doubt it, but how big of a creature can he control? Do they have to be alive? Or dead?

So many thoughts run through my head about the possibilities. As they do, I realize why he'd been so concerned about my reaction. If he could take over a beast, then what might stop him from taking over the body of a sapient? I'm sure the very thought causes a lot of tension between the portian and the other races.

Strangely, I find myself not even worried about the possibility of it happening to me. I don't even know how the portian might control the bodies, but I somehow, almost instinctively, know that the control of my own flames can never be taken from me.

After I've finished running the ritual for the team, I turn to Grímr, only to see that the entire gash in his neck has recovered. Replaced with a furless patch of unblemished hide.

I'd seen it after the first centipede fight, but at the time I'd just thought the wounds weren't as deep as they looked. Grímr regenerates incredibly fast. No wonder he didn't consider it an issue to take the damage he had.

As I inspect his newly grown neck, I catch him glance my way before turning his head and pretending we hadn't locked eyes.

I guess he's still worried about what I think. As much as I wish they hadn't left me in the dark, I can't say this new information has changed my opinion on him. The fact that he likes to bury people is still far more shocking.

I jump on his back, ready to continue moving, but Grímr jerks under my touch.

I raise an eyebrow as I look down at him. "You're fine if I keep borrowing your back, yeah?"

"Of course." He hesitates. "You're not afraid?"

I laugh. It's such a strange sight; a massive predator of a beast being so concerned over how he is seen by others.

"No," I say. "Should I be?"

He shakes his head as he trots along the ice. I swear I heard him purr for an instant. If he did, he clamped down on it immediately.

Well, at least he's happy.

CHAPTER TWENTY-SEVEN

Dahu

A week has passed since we climbed into the Lower Elevation and only now do the mountains breach through the glacial plains. The steady slope of ice continues undisturbed around the peaks that breach the surface.

Despite what should have been the easier path—following the rather flat glacier—the Titan never veered from its line. As the number of mountains increases ahead of us, so too have sections of glacier been carved away. Whenever the Titan passed a mountain, it left an immense amount of molten rock to melt through the surrounding ice.

Due to the vast alteration of the landscape, we can no longer travel beside the path.

No creatures have blocked our way since the panther tried to sneak up on us. Most likely, it's sticking to the tunnels in the ice. I'm surprised even the bats do so; they have wings, so why not use them?

Every so often, Jav flies over the path to watch for anything that might be too big to take the tunnels. Considering how long we've already gone without a fight, I feel like he might be wasting his time checking.

My team has warned about how we'll likely come across Middle Elevation creatures on the way up, but so far, it's been disappointingly quiet.

The panther that tore Grímr's neck apart was a Lower Elevation creature that populates many of the higher mountains of the region. I'd asked Grímr about his body, and while he'd been hesitant, he told me he had taken the panther after he lost his previous body in a fight seven months ago.

He didn't specify many details beyond that, but it must have been from the same time they lost their mage. I wonder what they faced that split the team as it had.

Bunny readjusting her pack draws my attention. She takes out another unique weapon and stores the short axe she's been holding for the last few hours. The new weapon has two short, curved blades protruding from a central grip.

"What is that?" I ask. Not for the first time either. I've asked so many times now that I swear she chooses the ones I don't know simply to show off.

"This is a haladie. The Wyle kin created them in Laverna long before the Henosis Empire absorbed the country." She spins the blade in her hand. "These blades aren't the best in a direct confrontation, but they are great for techniques relying on deception and trickery."

Well, either it's to show off, or give herself the opportunity to talk about the weapons she loves.

"Martial styles using the haladie rely on feints and sleight of hand to breach an opponent's defense. I would love to meet the people of the Wyle kin, but since they lost their homeland, they've been impossible to find."

"Why do you carry so many different weapons, anyway?" I ask. "Couldn't you take only two or three and not worry about that massive pack?"

"No." She twirls the curved double-blade in her fingers. "Who knows when I'll need a specific type? It's better to be prepared and not need it, than need it and not have it."

I mean, I understand what she's saying, but as I look at the bag, I can't help but feel she is a bit too prepared. Exactly what kind of situation would require one type of blade over another?

"Then, if you could only have one weapon, what would you choose?"

"Don't ask such impossible questions."

"You don't have a favorite?"

"I have too many favorites."

"There has to be something that sets one weapon apart from another, right?"

"Of course. The quality of make means everything. I've learned how to craft my own weapons, but nothing beats a true professional at their craft."

I remember Jav's reaction when he heard that heqet trader had been trading—what was it again?—Riparian weapons. Were they made by professionals?

"Are Riparian weapons good?"

"In a sense. The Riparians are abhorrent weaponsmiths, but their inscriptions are unparalleled. It is almost impossible to get your hands on one of their weapons. The Riparian clans aren't often open to trade with outsiders."

"Huh. I guess that trader must have been lucky to get his hands on some," I ponder aloud.

"What?" Bunny stops dead in her tracks. "What trader?" She turns and pulls me off Grímr's back, holding me in her grasp.

I just barely hold down the pressure screaming at me to burn her arms off, to escape her grasp in whatever manner I can. My body doesn't lose control, but I still feel an intense anxiety rise the longer her hands grip my shoulders.

"Where did you meet a trader selling Riparian makes?" Her eyes are as intense as her tone, boring deep into me in her desire.

Remus's tentacles slap her arms off me, letting me drop to the thin layer of snow. Once again, I'm grateful for Jav's gift as it blocks out the slush of frozen water. Bunny appears confused by Remus's actions before she looks back at me and has the decency to look embarrassed.

"Where is that trader?" she asks again. This time keeping her hands to herself.

"Jav and I met him back at the garrison."

"Jav knew and didn't tell me?" For the first time since I've met her, she actually looks angry. She clenches her fists so hard I can see the muscles in her arms bulging.

"Oh, I can't wait till he gets back," she says as she turns her attention up the Alps.

Almost as if summoned by her words, Jav flies over a mountain crest ahead of us. After noticing him, it is only a moment until he rejoins us. As soon as he touches down, he's speaking.

"We've got a—"

"Why didn't you tell me?" Bunny is immediately in Jav's face, glaring at the volan.

"Huh? Tell you what?" Jav blinks at her.

"That you met a trader with Riparian weapons."

Jav glances my way with annoyance plastered on his face.

I raise my arms in question. How was I supposed to know I shouldn't have told her?

"The trader only had words to show, no weapons. He was a heqet; no doubt in my mind he was lying."

"You still should have told me." Bunny huffs and steps away from Jav. "If there's even the possibility of meeting someone in with the Riparians, I need to try."

"He was—" Jav cuts himself off as he looks toward the mountain ahead of us where he just came from. "This isn't the time. We have a dahu ahead of us."

That gets a reaction from the team. Bunny immediately cuts her complaints and digs through her pack while Remus and Grímr's stances grow straighter.

Bunny returns the haladie and takes the large hammer from the bundle. She drops her pack on the ice behind her and swings it experimentally. One side of the hammer's head is flat while the other concentrates into a sharp point.

"Solvei, sky again," Remus orders. "Try to stay over the ice. Don't fly near any earth you can see."

I begin the change while he hurries to organize the rest of the team.

"To think the first mid-tier we come across is a dahu," I hear Grímr grumble underneath me as my wings form.

"Are they that dangerous?" I ask.

Grímr drops his own packs to the ice beside Bunny's. "Yes. They're slow and have weak bodies, so they aren't exactly the worst. But reaching them is a pain in the a—ah, behind."

Remus jumps in as he tightens his gauntlets at the ends of his tentacles. "Fortunately, we have the benefit of ice below our feet, so we'll have more time to react to its attacks." He looks up at me as I take to the sky. "Solvei. This is your first time seeing what something from the Middle Elevation is capable of. I want you to stay far from the fighting, all right? This isn't a beast to be taken lightly. Oh, and remember; don't fly more than a hundred meters above the ground."

I hold eye contact with him for long enough to know how serious he is.

I want to at least try to help them. To prove my worth, not just to my team, but to myself. Against Hirsh, I'd been unable to do anything, and he wasn't even intentionally trying to fight. How will I ever get strong enough to defend myself if I don't fight?

I need to find ways of dealing with my weaknesses, both water and my fears. Currently, both are crippling. Even the smallest of either takes me out of a fight.

Consuming strong beasts will only help me so much. I need to discover for myself ways to improve. Bunny is teaching me the spear, but I'm nowhere near ready to use it.

Really, the only way I can think of improving is to participate in fights like this, but as I look at Remus, I see he won't budge on his position.

Reluctantly, I nod.

My eyes pass over the mountain looking for the dahu we are waiting for. It takes a few minutes, everyone patient and unmoving until the creature crests the ridge of the mountain protruding from ice.

I don't know what I was expecting, but a small goat-like creature was not even close. It treks down the mountain, either paying us no mind or not having noticed us.

My team below me stands as still as they can, ready to rush forward at Remus's command. Before he can though, the goat halts its steps. Unnervingly, its head swivels toward us. Glowing amber eyes are clear even from such a distance.

"Go!" Remus shouts as he flings Jav straight toward the dahu.

The goat bleats. The sound isn't loud, nor does it echo, but I can hear it as clearly as if the creature were right next to me. Its mouth opens; each tooth has the same amber glow as its eyes. The dahu's eyes turn away from my team as it lowers its head to the earth underneath it.

Jav tears through the air, closing the distance before I can blink. His tiny, bladed wing tips angle to slice through the neck of the goat as its teeth dig into the ground.

Just when I expect to see blood gushing, the earth around the dahu explodes. Massive spikes of stone throw dirt and loose rock far into the sky as they pierce out from the ground in a ten meter radius of the goat.

Jav glides back amongst the rest of the team.

"Sorry, I wasn't quick enough," he says as Remus wraps a limb around him once more.

"It's fine. We'll just do this the normal way." A flick of the limb sends Jav above the dome of stone spikes.

The dahu has encased itself in interlocking jagged stone. It can control rock? At least it seems limited to only a ten meter radius around it.

Nearly the instant I think that, towering spikes tear through the ice right below where my team is running. The glacier cracks and groans as the stone breaks through it with little resistance.

Fortunately, my team's reaction is quick and each of them is out of the way of the incoming spikes. They don't slow for a second.

The dahu doesn't seem pleased that its attackers aren't dead. The blue tint of the glacier darkens to gray. I can hardly comprehend what I'm seeing, but thousands of giant pillars spike through the ice. An irrefutable jungle of stone rises from beneath the glacier.

My team evades the spikes nearest them, but they can no longer charge toward the dahu with the speed they had. Grímr slows the most, his large body unable to move between the dense congregation of pillars. Both Remus and Bunny take to using the very pillars to traverse. Remus slings himself from pillar to pillar, but Bunny takes the lead, rocketing off each pillar with powerful kicks.

Above, Jav glides, waiting for an opportunity to strike and keeping an eye for any unexpected occurrences.

They seem to have no issue. At the pace they're moving, they'll reach the goat's protective dome and shatter their way through in no time. Even with hundreds of meters to climb, Bunny is preparing to swing her hammer already.

Her feet press into the stone pillar, ready to bounce forward. As she does, her foothold sinks away, burying her leg deep in the spike. Bunny is off balance for only a second before she brings her hammer down on that which holds her leg.

She bounds forward the moment she touches the cracked ice below. Each time Bunny or the others come into contact with the stone, it crumbles, trying to grasp them. Her hammer swings remain effective. Even as the stone tries to collapse in on itself before the impact, the pillars still shatter.

The dahu somehow knows exactly where my teammates are. I'm not sure how, considering it has blocked its own sight with the dome it built around itself.

Things change the moment Bunny reaches the border between the glacier and mountain. She charges through the last of a thousand stone spikes and sprints up the steep incline. The forest of pillars lean toward her, fracturing the ice as the thousands of tons of earth force its way through. A constant deluge of shattering and groaning resounds.

"Volley incoming!" Jav shouts over the deafening sound, but loud enough that Bunny hears.

She abandons her climb and throws herself back down the cliff just as the entire forest of stone spikes throw themselves out of the ice toward her.

They hardly travel fast, but the insane mass behind the volley of stone projectiles leaves a terrifying image as they curve through the air.

Below, where the spikes once were, is a devastated region of glacier. Much of the ice drops into a new depression, a mimicry of the Titan's path.

Neither Grímr nor Remus remain below.

I only barely spot them amongst the airborne spikes as they smash into the mountainside. An explosive bang slams through the air from the impact. Each spike splinters against the cliff with such force, the ground appears to ripple.

Somehow, Remus and Grímr escaped that. They roll down the mountain before coming to a rest beside Bunny. Did they get swept up in that barrage or did they intentionally ride it? I'm not sure which is worse.

They all seem okay, even after having toppled a hundred meters down the slope.

A rumble echoes through the air as they begin their sprint up the mountain.

Despite only having restarted their run, they are forced to split and run for the sides. Above them, the cliff face the volley shattered against destabilizes. The entire stone shelf moves.

A massive rockslide bears down on my team.

CHAPTER TWENTY-EIGHT

Rockslide

The entire cliff face slides down the mountain. A moment is all it takes for fractures to crack through it. The falling cliff crumbles into enormous boulders as the rock accelerates. Each boulder speeds down the slope, indiscriminate of what is below. As fast as my team is, there's no way they can get away in time.

Grímr runs to the left, while Remus and Bunny try to escape to the right. Already, shrapnel rains down on their heads. It's incredible to watch as they dodge the boulders rushing past them.

Their luck doesn't last. With the massive amount of rock still falling on their heads, a single mistake is all it takes. Bunny stumbles, the ground collapses under her feet as she tries to dodge another rock the size of her body. Unable to react in time, the boulder collides against her back, slamming her into the ground.

She doesn't move, even as a shower of debris falls on her. The worst has happened. Is she dead? She can't possibly be. A rock like that couldn't be enough to kill her, right?

She is only prone for a moment before Remus has her legs grasped in his tentacles. With a spin and a flick of his limbs, he throws Bunny far to the side. Out of the way of the rockslide. She crashes hard, but out of danger.

Remus lost all the momentum he'd gained by launching her to safety. He cannot regain his speed before the rock engulfs him. I lose sight of him in the immense landslide.

Grímr escapes out the other side . . . well, not safe, but in far better shape than the other two.

Despite Remus's orders, I fly to the mountainside. I can't just sit out while they are hurt. Bunny rises to her feet and I'm flooded with relief that she's okay. She holds her chest and I'm sure the impact really hurt her, but she's alive. That's all that matters right now.

Bunny looks down at the rockslide as it slows into the devastated area of the glacier, then turns to me. I'm trying not to think what might have happened to Remus. There's no way anyone could have survived that.

"Go find Remus. He should be fine; a bit of rock won't hurt him as long as we deal with the dahu." She turns her attention up the mountain, where the dome hiding the dahu sits right on the top ledge of a new vertical cliff face. "I'm going to stop it causing any more damage."

I look down over the fallen cliff. How exactly does she think he'll be fine buried under a million tons of rock? But if she has confidence in him surviving, then I guess I should be hopeful.

Bunny is already sprinting up the mountain again when I leave for the churned up sea of rock. I don't have a clue where I should start my search.

As she rushes toward the fortified dahu, Bunny dances around the stone spikes piercing out from below. They aren't as tall as they were before, but they jab at her with far more speed. She twists, jumps, and slams her way through the rapid spikes as she closes in on the stone dome.

Grímr is slowly making his way up to the dahu from the other side, but he doesn't seem to face the same aggressive defense that Bunny does.

Both Grímr and Bunny reach the dome within a second of each other. The portian charges head first into the dome, leveraging his weight to smash through the wall. Bunny does much the same on the other side, swinging her hammer into the stone before her.

Both breach their respective barriers. The stone collapses under the immense impacts.

The dahu bleats. Once more I hear it clearly despite the distance. The loss of parts of its defensive wall unnerves the creature. Neither of my teammates can react in time as the entire rock dome slams into them. The goat forgoing its defense to send them away.

The stone spikes knock them back. Bunny scrambles against the ground, her momentum dying just as her feet slide over the ledge of the cliff. The goat already has pillars of stone rising to wrap its body in a dome once more.

Both regain their footing and rush back toward the dahu. They won't reach it in time before the dome is rebuilt.

Jav drops through the air. I realize I forgot about him until now. He glides right through the open space in the stone and falls out of sight behind the rising walls.

The spikes interweave and close in defense around the creature, locking Jav in with it. I can understand the others being able to take some blows, but I'm pretty sure Jav doesn't have the same thick skin as the others. I retain hope. If, as Bunny says, Remus is fine even with a mountain falling on him, then why wouldn't Jav be? I'll have to trust Jav has some way to keep himself safe.

Movement below has me drop amongst the rock. He's actually okay. I can't help but be shocked. Remus climbs out through the rubble he'd been buried under. Deep purple discolorations cover his usually blue skin, but he's alive!

I drop to his side to help him, but in my bird form there's little I can do. He pulls himself through the gravel, pushing aside boulders as easily as smaller stones.

A couple of bangs ring out, which lifts my attention to the dome atop the cliff. Bunny and Grímr have breached through. This time, there is no reaction. The dome doesn't explode outward, nor do any more stone spikes emerge.

Remus laughs as he looks up. "I hope you like goat; it's one of Jav's favorites."

So they killed it? Not a moment later, my question is answered. Bunny walks out with the head of the dahu and raises it above her head for us to see. Its eyes and teeth glow amber even in death.

"So, is that normal for the Middle Elevation?" I ask, shocked by the power put on display by the beast.

"The ground there is a touch more stable. Ignoring that, then yeah." The amusement in his eyes is clear.

I hear a crack in the distance as a portion of the glacier fractures. Seriously, the collateral damage from that goat is insane.

Jav takes the best cuts from the dahu and leaves the rest for the ritual. Despite the obvious power wielded by the creature, the team seems more interested in Jav's cooking than taking in that strength for themselves.

It doesn't take him long to get the steaks sizzling over a fire.

Turns out, when Jav dropped on the dahu, he'd been able to slice right through its neck with only a few spins. How something capable of so much damage could be killed so simply, I don't know. Then again, the creature didn't make it easy.

After being left to watch them struggle, I feel frustrated. Frustrated that I'd been left out of the fight, but mostly because I know I couldn't have helped, regardless. The head of the dahu sits there with the rest of its corpse, teeth glowing and waiting for the moment we use it as fuel for our growth. The others may be patient, but I want to get stronger sooner rather than later.

I'm tempted to just take the head for myself, hoard the energy I can burn out of it and enhance my flames. The thought runs through my head, but I can't do that. Not after all the effort the others have put forward to welcome and help me. It's the same as when I was with my tribe; I'm protected, but can never help when it truly matters.

I grab my spear from Bunny's pack and walk off to practice while the others relax after their fight. With each thrust, I think about the force behind the dahu's stone spikes. Each swing, Remus's cratering whips overwhelm me. I look at the strength behind my own attacks and see nothing. When my flames don't burn and my strength can't compete, how will I ever stand by their side?

For now, my only use is the ritual I provide the team. I won't say it, but after such an intense fight, the fact that they would rather put off the part that I can actually contribute . . . well, hurt isn't the right word. It makes me feel unneeded; like the ritual isn't as important as they've led me to believe.

Even as I swing my spear to unleash my frustrations, I know I'm overthinking things, but I can't help but feel like nothing has changed in the two years since I've been without my tribe. Despite everything I've been through, I'm back in the same position of being protected by others and not able to contribute.

These thoughts cycling through my mind will do nothing but continue to frustrate me. So I channel the emotion into my movements and attempt to blank my mind.

The next few days pass rather uneventfully. Well, as uneventfully as it can be now that creature encounters are increasing again. The glacier still passes through the valleys between mountains, but the Titan's path continues straight, uncaring for the mountains it left half molten.

Now that it is a direct path once more, we no longer avoid the creatures that might have followed the tunnels in the ice. At least we know we didn't miss some hidden biome under the glacier; the bats, centipedes, and other creatures we are following have shown themselves again.

I keep up my spear training, dedicated to improving in any way I can while I can. Bunny is all too keen to help. This high, the snow seems to lack the same powdery feeling to it. Instead, it is nearly as hard as ice itself. I can walk along it without fear of sinking in. Even if I fall over, I'll probably be fine.

It goes to show how much heavier Grímr and Bunny are; they fall through the hard snow to their knees. Jav, Remus, and I walk along above the two with hardly an issue.

Grímr's regenerative speed seems to be unique to himself. After the fight, he'd had a few bumps and bruises that cleared up in a matter of hours, but Remus and Bunny are less fortunate. The purple color has darkened and spread over much of Remus's body and Bunny fractured a rib being crushed by that boulder.

It's hard to tell if they don't feel pain from their injuries or if they're just really good at hiding it from me. Even with the damage they've taken, we continue moving.

We have yet to face another mid-tier beast, fortunately. Or, maybe that's unfortunate. The dahu's body was dense with compressed energy, the teeth were especially energizing. As much as I want more of that empowering feeling I get while consuming those creatures, I shouldn't wish another fight of that scale upon the others. Not until I can fight as well.

We are here to investigate the source of the new monsters, not to hunt. I should be grateful for the creatures I get to consume on the way and not hope for more from the Middle Elevation.

As we move farther up the Alps, I can't help but notice that each mountain is far less . . . whole. If I look beyond the damage caused by the Titan, there are still sweeping regions where land just ceases. A series of deep gouges in a mountain appear to be terrifyingly large claw marks when viewed from far away. Craters hundreds of meters wide disfigure much of the landscape.

Plant life has also diminished, leaving only the most resilient to thrive in the cold, thin air. Air which has been doing a number on me. Even with my new snowsuit, the cold permeates everything. I'm able to push it off by eating beasts and the iron in Grímr's pack, but every day I feel myself growing more exhausted. The thin air is difficult to breathe and leaves my flames weak.

"Hit me!" Bunny commands as she jogs backward.

The landscape has become treacherous enough that the team has slowed to my speed. If they continue at their previous speed, they are apparently far more likely to fall prey to the ambush predators common in the Middle Elevation. We haven't come across one yet, but Remus believes it is worth being careful.

I sprint toward her and swing with an overhead diagonal slash before jerking my arm back and thrusting forward with as much strength as I can manage. She falls for my feint, but I'm not fast enough to get the thrust through her guard before she reacts.

Her overwhelming strength knocks my spear to the side. Brushed away as if less threatening than a gust of wind.

"Your technique has improved by leaps and bounds," Bunny says as she jumps over a protruding rock without turning around. "But your strength hasn't improved since we started. Normally, strength is the easiest to improve; all you need to do is train, but it doesn't seem to help you."

I lower my grip on the spear and sweep at her legs with as much force as I can muster. Bunny simply lowers her body and catches the spear right below the blade, not showing the slightest of having felt the impact. She jerks her hand and I can do nothing as she pulls the spear from my grasp.

"Even with all the energy you've taken, your strength is not increasing. It feels like I'm being hit by a five-year-old." She throws back my spear and turns to Remus. "Hey, you've dealt with her kind before. How do they improve their strength? I know they are supposed to be rather deadly once they've mastered their weapon, assuming those old tomes on southern weapons weren't filled with misinformation."

I glance his way as well, curious about anything he might know about my people.

He shakes his head. "No, I traveled with them for some time, but I was always an outsider. Anything they considered important, they kept to themselves. That includes everything about their growth and weapons." He looks at me. "Sorry, Solvei, you'll have to figure it out yourself."

I nod to him as I think about what I might have to do. I'd been following Bunny's guidance until now because she said it was the best way, but if an áed's strength comes from somewhere else than these flesh people, then it's understandable she can't help.

My first thought is covering my spear in flames to somehow enhance my strength. Even before the flames extend the weapon's length, I realize it won't work. Auntie Kay never engulfed her spear in flame when we trained, yet she still could manage far greater strength.

I try to think about what my elders had done in all the times I'd seen them fight. Nothing other than them wreathing their weapons in fire comes to mind. What else could they have done?

A stray thought comes to mind. What was it that my tribe emphasized training over all else?

Well, it was easy enough to try, I might as well see.

"Can you tell me if this is weaker than my previous strikes?" I ask Bunny before I prepare myself.

I lower the control I have on my body, letting it return to its natural, unhidden flame. My body reaches for a state more incorporeal than the physical form it usually is. Not so far that I can't hold my spear, but enough that the results should be obvious to Bunny.

I step toward her and swing with all the strength I can manage. It's hard to tell, because my strike is stopped just as easily as before, but I think it was weaker.

"Yeah, that one felt like an infant tapped me."

I glare at Bunny for her comment, but it confirms what I need to do; it's time to get back to training my control.

"Uh, guys? Did anyone see where that came from?" Jav says as he lowers from the sky.

At the edge of the Titan's path is a centipede crawling over the ledge toward us.

"No?"

"Well, it wasn't there two minutes ago."

CHAPTER TWENTY-NINE

Meltdown

After making quick work of the centipede, we climb to the ledge of the Titan's path to see a large fissure in the ground. It's not an unusual sight along the unstable earth parallel to the path, but I don't think any of us expected anything to be down there.

"You don't think . . ." Grímr trails off as we all stare down into the darkness.

We're not on the glacier anymore, so there shouldn't be anything underneath us. Well, as far as I've been told, there shouldn't be. I look over at Remus to see what he thinks.

"Whelp, only one way to find out." He winks back at us before throwing himself down into the depths.

Both Jav and Bunny follow soon after, but I can't do it. I can't push myself to jump into the earth like that. What if it caves in on me?

Grímr stands by my side, not even taking a step toward the crevice. He lays by my side and fakes a yawn. "You know, I'm kind of tired. I think I'll take a nap here while the others do all the hard work down there."

Whether he's playing around or is just a poor actor, I'm not sure, but I don't think I can express how appreciative I am for his consideration. I don't want to go down there, but I don't know what I'll do if I'm left alone up here.

I sit down and lean into his fur. My body pushes its heat to warm the both of us, even though doing so burns through far more energy than I should. The frozen air leaves a dull ache through my body the longer I'm exposed. Even burning hot, I can feel it permeating through me. Ever so slowly getting worse.

I really hope they find nothing down there. Hopefully, the centipede just fell down into the crevice and we only saw as it crawled back out.

As I huddle in close, I look out over the land below the Alps. It's incredible how high we are. A carpet of clouds dot the land as far as I can see. We have come so far already, but as I glance up at the peak of the Alps, it only feels like the mountain has gotten higher.

The world below me is serene, beautiful even. Despite the danger, there is so much more to the world than the empty husk that is the wasteland. So many curiosities to see. Simply being here, taking in the sights, fills me with questions. Is the horizon curved or is it a trick of the eye? Why are the Alps bigger than normal mountain ranges?

I glance down the fissure my teammates descended.

What lurks where we cannot see?

Despite the dangers to my kind, I really think the áed should explore beyond the borders of our wasteland. If I could survive out here, there is no reason the adults can't. The world may be dangerous, but there are far more resources to be found. We would never find ourselves wanting again.

Eventually, the resources in the wasteland will dry up, and when that happens, all áed will be forced out regardless of how fearful they are of what is outside.

Grímr and I continue to wait in a comfortable silence until the others come back.

"So? Lead anywhere?" The vibration I feel through his fur as he speaks makes me want to lean into him more, like a soft bed, but the others are back so I give up on comfort and rise to my feet.

"You won't believe what we found," Remus says. "There's a tunnel, about ten meters wide, that follows under the path."

"Really? How far does it go?"

"Don't know. We walked for a while without finding an end. It's definitely where those creatures are coming from; the tunnel was crawling with them."

"So we've found it then?" I ask. "We can go back and report it now, right?"

Remus shakes his head as Bunny approaches my side. "Unfortunately, we still need to investigate. We need to know what's at the end of that tunnel."

"But we can continue on the surface, right? Go down and check every now and then. You said it follows under the Titan's path, right?" Grímr asks for my sake.

"We could, but now is a good time to help Solvei through her fear before we climb any higher." Remus looks at me as he says that, and my chest clenches.

"But, Solvei . . ." Grímr turns to me with concern.

"We will ease her into it, don't worry. This is something she needs to overcome."

Is it really something I can just push through though? I'd love to move past the phobia, but such a thing is impossible. Even thinking about going down in that hole sends shivers through my body.

Bunny places her hand on my shoulder. It's light, barely touching, but I still hate the feeling. "I'll carry you down. The moment it is too much, yell." She crouches and shows her back, inviting me to climb on.

I really, really don't want to do this, but what is the point of me being on their team if I don't try to improve. I just . . . I wish there was some other way to do this.

"All right." I climb onto her back, holding myself around her neck. It doesn't feel that bad as long as she doesn't grab me.

Bunny rises to her feet and trots to the edge of the fissure. She makes no sudden movements and slowly crouches by the edge. Her first step goes well, all things considered. My chest tightens, but that's it. Each meter she lowers us makes the pressure worse, but I hold on. I don't give up.

It is only when I look up and realize I can't see the sky beyond the bend in the fissure does everything collapse. The tightness explodes and I can't breathe. Completely without my control, my flames spread around me, engulfing Bunny as I clamber over her shoulders in a desperate attempt to find the sky again.

"I can't do it. I can't. I won't." This is too much.

Thankfully, Bunny kept her word and in hardly a second, the sky returns above. I scramble away from her and the edge of the fissure. My fingers dig through the earth, dragging myself as far as possible as I try to regain my breaths.

"Good work, Solvei," Remus says, appearing above me. "Rest for a few minutes and we'll try again."

He wants me to go down there again? Impossible. "No. I can't."

"You'll be all right. You can do this."

"No," I don't budge.

He hesitates before sighing. "All right. We'll rest here for the night, then figure out what we're going to do."

It took a while for me to properly calm down again after that. Grímr's comfortable back made for great stress relief, though. It's shameful that I showed the team such a cowardly side of me. I want to stand up and show them I can walk down there just as much as they can, but even glancing toward the fissure terrifies me.

Going below isn't just difficult, it's downright impossible.

I know I'm holding them back right now, and I feel bad, but no matter what, I can't push myself to go down. Jav circles above, only a dozen meters in the air, and refuses to wander off too far from the rest of the team. Bunny and Remus discuss something off to my side, but I can't focus enough to listen in.

Remus will want me to try again, and I'm not looking forward to telling him no.

I close my eyes and listen to the wind. The constant creaking and cracking of the glaciers are long past, but every now and then there are some odd cracking or echoing noises that reach my ears. Grímr doesn't react to them though, so I doubt they're anything to worry about.

Despite how close I listen, I still don't hear what causes Grímr's ears to twitch and his head to raise. A few moments later, Jav's whistle rings out over us and we're on our feet in an instant.

The small volan shouts from above. "We need to move now! Massive blizzard."

By the time he'd finished speaking, the rumbling reaches my ears. All across the ridge of the mountain we're climbing a blanket of white appears. Unlike the one we experienced a few weeks ago, this one doesn't build up at the peak. It overflows, and immediately swathes half the mountain. The sky darkens above us long before the rushing weather reaches us.

I quickly pull my mask up and strap my goggles, not wanting a repeat of last time.

Remus's eyes flicker between the blizzard, me and the fissure. Something screams a warning in my head. "Bunny, grab Solvei. We're going under."

"What? But there's no need—" I hear Grímr arguing, but Bunny is already at my side, wrapping her arms around me.

"Sorry." My body tenses at her words, but she has me in her grasp and in moments we are falling into darkness.

My arms lash out, trying to free me from her iron grip. I kick and wriggle. Nothing makes her let me go. My chest writhes and my form abandons its physicality. She is already sprinting through the tunnel, my bright yellow flame illuminating the walls of the cavern as we pass through.

I struggle in my outfit, feeling far more trapping than I had a minute ago. My breath comes in ragged gasps and my eyes flicker all around me, looking for some way out.

As my panic rises, I worm my way out of the snowsuit. Flames claw their way out the arm and neck holes. I feel a strange sensation of extreme calm as my body splits into three. It doesn't last long. My body pulls back together, and with it, a sledgehammer of overwhelming pressure sends me sprawling.

I feel the hard rock under my fingers. Without thought, fire explodes from me. Searching for the way out. Any escape I can. My feet kick at the ground and I'm sprinting away from Tetsu. Flames scorch the walls of the tunnel. Where did she bring me? Where is the way out?

I run and run and run. The walls around me close in, squeezing at my sides. The darkness gets darker. Rock beneath my feet grasp at me with each step, trying to hold me down, to keep me locked away. But I will not give in. I'll keep running until I'm free.

A crack!

A tiny fissure in the tunnel's side. Without a moment's hesitation, I throw myself into it. The incorporeal nature of my form the only thing letting me through. I scamper through the tiny opening until it ends at a wall. My fingers dig into the stone, melting right through. I claw my way up the wall, scampering to reach the sky as fast as possible.

Rock digs into my back as I climb. If not for my arms able to bend around the tight curve between stone walls, I wouldn't be able to move them. Molten rock from where my fingers dig flows down the wall in tiny cascades. I glance up, but I still can't see the way out.

It's here. I know it is. It has to be.

My hand hits something. I try to put my hand above me again, but I hit rock again. A ceiling? My body trembles as I send my arms to the sides, looking for the path up that has to be there. Not only don't I find any way up, the walls clamp down on my sides.

I scream. Fire detonates around me as I push everything I have into burning through the rock above. I dig at the rock, scooping it away as it melts on contact.

Everything around me glows red. I scrape at the ceiling with desperation, but I slip. The rock above my head falls out of range as a feeling of weightlessness overcomes me.

Dread. Horror. My escape evades me.

My arms slam to the side as an impact devastates my back.

It takes until a drop of molten rock lands on my face for me to realize I've fallen. The glowing earth above still searing hot.

I'm tired.

My flames rage at the surrounding walls, soon engulfing me in a flood of lava, but I don't move. I can't. I'm unable to tell which way is up. Am I on the ceiling? Floor? Maybe I'm stuck to the wall? It doesn't matter; the darkness encroaches almost as fast as the rock. It's hard to breathe.

I'm exhausted.

What am I doing? I'm not free yet. I need to do everything, anything I can to stay free. Never again shall I stay trapped, even if I die trying.

It's hard, but I rise to my feet again. My hands try to find a grip in the wall, but the molten rock keeps me from getting a good grip. Regardless, I keep trying. I push my arms deep into the stone to get as much of a hold as I can. Ever so slowly, I pull myself to the ceiling again.

Aches ripple through my body from the exertion, but I'm so close to my escape. I burn. I burn so hot it hurts. The rock liquefies at a touch, so I have to dig in with my legs just as much as I burn away with my arms.

The darkness is terrifyingly close now. Everything except what's directly in front of my eyes might as well not exist. Each scrape brings me closer to escape, but I feel the walls clamping down on me now. I push my arm forward again, only to miss.

What? I'm falling again? But I can feel the walls hugging me. Squeezing me. Crushing me. Why is my escape leaving?

Everything is dark now.

"What the fuck were you thinking?"

"I never thought her reaction would be so severe." Tetsu peered into the tight crack Solvei somehow wedged herself inside.

"She told you how terrified she was. Did you not consider how she might feel for a second?" Grímr snarled, glowering at her. "We didn't need to dive down here. We had time to escape the blizzard."

"Just shut up and help me get her out. I can't hear her struggling anymore."

This hadn't been what she wanted. Tetsu thought there might have been a bit of panic—it was all but certain the girl would lash out—but if it helped her get over her fear, then it would be worth whatever anger she might receive from the girl. They would have eased her into it if only the blizzard hadn't come.

Magma flowed over Tetsu's arm as she tore off a chunk of rock, widening the opening. It surprised her how much heat she could feel from within. It exceeded what Tetsu thought the girl could manage.

"That was more than the desperation a simple fear could incite. It seems the Void Fog is quite insidious." Remus stood behind Tetsu as she continued to tear away at the wall. "I'm sorry, Grímr, don't blame Bunny for this. If I had known it would be this bad of a reaction, I wouldn't have made this decision."

The fissure widened enough for Tetsu to get a view at the glowing cavern.

There wasn't a spot along the tight crevice that hadn't liquefied. Magma rolled down the walls and pooled below. Solvei wasn't in sight; likely submerged in the molten rock.

"Remus, can you get her out?" Tetsu asked as she pulled out of the tight passage.

Better to have the most flexible of them in the tight passage.

Without a word, Remus did as asked. He squirmed his way through and came out with the young áed in a moment. She was limp in his limbs, lost to unconsciousness. Her body flickered in flame, no longer hiding what she was. Despite the damage she just caused to the chamber, her flames were weak. She gave off far less heat than normal.

"Grímr, pass me her iron."

The portian was quick to pull his packs off and rummage through them. With precision that would have been impossible for a normal mountain panther, he pulled out the metal ingots between his claws.

Remus took them and held them against the child's chest. It looked strange to Tetsu, but Remus was the only one on the team that knew anything about the áed and their biology.

"So what now? We can't exactly take her back to the surface?" Jav asked.

"We move on," Remus said. "I want to find where those creatures are coming from."

"Then I'll take Solvei and wait for the blizzard to clear." Grímr moved to take her from Remus, but the dohrni raised a limb to stop him.

"No. We're not splitting up. I don't want to risk you two having to face a mid-tier alone." His eyes moved back toward the tunnel with impenetrable darkness. "Besides, we'll need our full strength going forward."

Grímr growled. "How could you be willing to put her through that again?"

"I like it as much as you do, but we'll be stuck down here until the blizzard passes." Remus looked down at the sleeping girl. "We'll use that time to search, then return. Hopefully, she will stay asleep until then. If not, we can only do our best to help her work through the fear."

Grímr snarled, but said no more. He walked to the wall of the tunnel and struck out, his claws slicing deep through the rock.

Tetsu understood how he felt, but Remus was right; Solvei needed a push to overcome her fear. The girl refused to enter buildings, for fuck's sake. If she didn't get over her phobia, she would never be able to live in civilization. Not to mention how unfair the world could be sometimes. If she continued to push for more strength, there was no doubt in Tetsu's mind Solvei would face challenges that wouldn't be so kind as to only leave her with fear.

Thoughts of her father and the near vegetative state he'd returned in after his ultimate battle dug their way into her mind before she could shake them. She didn't want to think about him. Too painful to imagine the imposing weapon master she'd always idolized reduced to what he'd become.

Luckily for Solvei, she slept for the subsequent hours as they ran through the tunnel. The wide cavern often had cracks in the side, leading to fissures on the surface. Plenty of places for the bugs to crawl their way to the surface. The farther they traveled, the more dense the population of their targets became.

Solvei's sleep was anything but pleasant. She would toss and turn in calm moments, then lash out in a panic, her flames trying to burn at anything they could grasp. Grímr had relieved Remus of taking care of her. The portian clearly saw many of his old áinfean relatives in the girl. He was usually far more reserved around people, especially those he hadn't known for years.

They eventually came across the source of those creatures. The tunnel's black rock underfoot changed to a smooth gray stone that sloped upward until the tunnel they'd been following pinched off. In the center of this new stone floor was a hole large enough for Grímr to fit in lengthwise.

Tetsu jumped down first. The ground under her feet was made of the same stone as above. She looked around, only to be shocked at how far she could see. A low-ceiling cavern extended before her at a slight upward slope. It was dark, but in the low light Solvei gave off, the two layers of stone kept an almost perfect, three-meter separation for as far as she could see. Not just in one direction, but all around her.

Just where in the Grand Champion's name did this lead?

CHAPTER THIRTY

Illness

Pain.

That's the first thing I notice through cloudy thoughts.

My body aches and screams for me to return to the void of nothingness. But a part of my mind lashes out, refusing to stay still any longer. I feel like I'm being pulled at both ends, stretched to my limit.

It's hard to think through the intense migraine, and my body refuses to move when I try to open my eyes.

I'm familiar with this feeling. I haven't felt it in years, and I'd hoped never to again, but it looks like the cold has been too much for me.

Grímr's footfalls thump through his back and into my chest. We must still be traveling, then. I wonder if we've gotten close to the Middle Elevation yet?

Sudden memories of Tetsu forcing me into the entrapping grasp of the underground tunnels slam into me. My mind forces my eyes open, ignoring my body's resistance. The smooth, gray ceiling confirms my greatest fear and I jerk, trying to escape. A pained gasp leaves my throat, but that seems to be all I can do. My body is exhausted and refuses to move when I command it.

The tension in my limbs amplifies the aches of sickness. My body shakes involuntarily and I try my hardest to force a reaction. Anything that might get me an escape. I spread my flames, but they flicker and die, refusing my commands.

I'm running on fumes, I realize. All the energy I had is gone. Now, I barely have enough to survive and my body won't let me kill myself.

But . . . but trapped down here as I am, I might as well be dead. I try to roll over, to open my hands or send out my flames, but nothing does as I want. I choke and struggle to breathe from my desperate attempt to move.

"Solvei, you need to calm down. It's all right. You're not in danger."

I hear a voice. Grímr? I can't tell. There's too much haze over my mind. It's hard to think straight.

With enough struggle, I eventually twist to my side. I pant and try to catch my breath, but I can now see the cavern is long. I can't see the end, but the walls aren't closing in on me. It's too much effort to turn my head, but in no direction does the cave end.

Somehow, I slow my breathing, but my body still shakes from the pain and fear.

"Solvei, you are not trapped. Calm down and regain yourself."

Remus is in front of me now. He wants me to calm down? Doesn't he realize how horrifying this situation is? If I don't do everything I can to get out, then . . .

Then what? I don't really know what happens then, but I know it is bad. Terrifyingly bad. Why doesn't he understand that?

"I know this is hard, but you have to try to work through this. You will never overcome your fear if you let it overwhelm you."

I try to deny him, to shake my head or tell him that being confined like this is the worst thing imaginable, but I can't even manage that.

My migraine intensifies. I can't fight off the growing darkness any longer.

I awake again, this time without the haze over my mind. The body tremors start as soon as I realize where I am, but I can at least think straight.

My body is still resistant to what I tell it, but I can open my eyes. We are still traveling under the ceiling of gray stone. I gasp for breath and feel a writhing compression in my chest.

I'm about to struggle again, to push my flames out and try my hardest to find any way out, when my head is grasped in two firm hands. My head is tilted up to face Tetsu.

"Get a hold of yourself," she snaps. "There is nothing for you to fear. There's no reason we can't make our way out. You are not trapped."

For a moment, I'm stunned. She was the one who brought me down here. She forced me into this situation. It was Tetsu who trapped me and she has the nerve to yell at me?

A well of anger bubbles within me. I glare at her with all the spite I suddenly feel. She betrayed my trust. I told her my fear, and she abuses it.

"How could you?" I try to demand, but my voice is barely audible to my own ears.

She hesitates, visibly backing away from me. Remus jumps in before she can answer.

"Don't blame her. It was my idea," he says. "At the time, I thought it was for the best."

I narrow my eyes at him before looking up at Jav, who turns away from my gaze.

"Couldn't we have run from the blizzard, like we did last time?" I ask incredulously.

I feel a low growl underneath me. "Yes, we could have." Grímr glares at the others.

My chest burns, but I don't know whether it's the overwhelming fear, the sickness permeating my body, or the betrayal I feel.

"I trusted you." I twist my head away from them as far as the aches will let me.

"It worked, didn't it? In your anger, you ignored that fear," Jav says.

Is that what he thinks? I'm not trembling in fear while I rage at them? No, I wish that were how it was, but I just don't have the energy to scream and thrash despite how much I feel I should be.

It'll tear me apart if I continue to focus on these emotions. They've betrayed me, but Grímr didn't. I focus on that. Grímr is still on my side, even if the others might not be. His fur is warm under me and I take comfort in the proximity. As much comfort as I can manage while my body writhes in anxiety.

I focus on my breathing, pulling my mind into myself to keep my eyes away from the stony cavern. It's all I can manage not to scream. I know, logically, that this is unreasonable. Just because I'm in an enclosed space doesn't mean there isn't a way out.

"Can we leave?" I plead into Grímr's back, only loud enough for the panther himself to hear.

"I'm sorry. I want to as well, but I need you to hold in there."

Even the only one I thought was on my side won't help me. I force my eyes closed and try to relax enough to fall asleep. Hopefully, by the time I wake, we'll be out.

. . .

I can't sleep.

The tension continues to strangle me every time I think about where I am. Nothing I do can remove it from my mind. I focus on the thuds shaking through Grímr's chest, the faint beats that come every few seconds, and the repetitive lifting and falling underneath me. Anything that can distract me, I latch onto.

We better not be down here long.

We've been down here so long.

Without the light of the Eternal Inferno, I have no way to tell how long has passed, but it must be days. The pressure squeezing me never gets better, but somehow, I push through. My exhaustion recedes enough that I can move my arms and flames again. It is incredibly difficult to hold myself back from lashing out again, but I manage. I don't want to be stuck unable to move my body again.

While some of my energy is back, my sickness pounds me as intensely as before. Through the dizziness, I sometimes hear the team speaking, but it's been mostly incomprehensible through my headache until now.

I have some strength back, but I keep my head firmly in the fur before me. I'm in control of myself now, but who knows what might happen when I look at the walls enclosing me once more. I'd really rather not lose myself to another panic attack.

I can hear the others arguing now, their raised voices flaring my migraine. The most that filters through my foggy thoughts is that they can't decide where to go. Some change must have happened and now there is conflict on our path going forward.

I refuse to lift my head, so I can't know what has changed. Whether it's a change in the landscape or some monster, I don't know.

They soon settle down though, to the relief of my psyche.

Time passes in thankful quiet. Except for the occasional sound of some unfortunate creature being crushed, the journey is about as pleasant as I can hope for. I feel horrible and my body fights against me at every moment, but I'm able to close myself away in my tiny world on Grímr's back that definitely is not trapped under the earth.

It hasn't worked yet, but if I keep telling myself we are running along the open mountains with sunlight bearing down on us from above, I'm sure I'll eventually calm down.

I feel something touch my back before I hear a voice.

"Solvei." I can't tell if it's Jav or Remus, my mind slow to recognize the voice in its lethargic state. "You are doing great. You've held on for so long. I need you to work with us here, all right? I need you to open your eyes."

I shake my head with vigor, only to worsen my migraine. There's no way I can do that. It'll make everything worse again; I won't be able to think past the fear.

"If you can't do that, please hide your fire. Just for a bit, okay?" I can pinpoint the voice as Remus's now.

I'm not controlling my flame? A flush of embarrassment runs through me as I feel it out in the open without even realizing. The feeling is muted against the pain and tension consuming my body.

I consider for a moment to keep myself as I am, simply to spite Remus after he put me in this position. But doing so would be going against my tribe for the sake of an inconsequential defiance.

I don't reply, but I force my body back until it's physical enough to hide my flames.

"Thank you," he says before I hear him scuttling off.

All is quiet for the next few minutes. Quieter even, than it has been for a while. Their steps are near silent. Only what I assume is Tetsu's footsteps can be heard, but even they are muffled. Despite his size, Grímr is deadly silent.

What are they doing? Why are they sneaking?

I'm answered by a deep growl rumbling along the cavern and through my chest. It isn't loud, but it shakes the cave regardless. An intense presence screaming its power to the world. If I hadn't already been ensnared in anxiety, I'm sure the terror of this familiar feeling would engulf me.

Only two beings have ever made me feel like this. A presence so intimidatingly absolute that even as my eyes snap open for the first time in days, I am frozen. My body screams to escape my confines once more, but a deeper, more primal part of me refuses to move.

In the darkness, I can barely make out the team members huddling close together. Everything is silent. Nobody makes a noise, nor is there any sound from whatever that thing was.

As the seconds tick by, I wonder if it has left. Whatever it was gave me the same instinctual terror as Hund. A similar all-encompassing sensation to the Titan.

Without warning, the cavern rumbles.

I hold tight to Grímr as an earsplitting bang rips through us. A heavy grinding joins the clamor of rocks falling to the ground of the cavern. Something big is scraping against the stone ahead of us.

None of us dare move. The grinding quietens until all I can hear is tapping. The sound you would expect from hitting stone with a metal pole. It echoes along the low ceiling without rhythm.

We all shrink away from the noise, hoping the source won't notice us.

The tapping stops. The sound of something massive grinding and tearing apart the stone returns, but only for a short time until it quietens again. A wet, splattering noise replaces it. Hardly even audible after the intensity of rock being pulverized.

Minutes pass as the sound continues. I look to my side, wondering if any of the others are planning to move away yet. It's nearly impossible to see them with how dark it is, but from what I can see, none dare move a muscle. Even Tetsu, who I'd assume would charge in to a challenging fight without restraint, remains frozen. Her eyes glued to the origin of the unsettling noises hidden in the dark.

The wet noises eventually stop, only for both the tapping and grinding to return as whatever is before us moves away.

I'd probably feel relieved if I was anywhere but in this cavern. The rest of the team doesn't have the same reservations. Each of them lets out a breath and their bodies loosen as the tension leaves them. I watch as Remus flops down onto the ground, his limbs spread wide around him. A touch of envy mixes with the tension I still feel. Even with the fear of that monstrosity gone, my terror of this simple enclosed space still has its grasp on me.

I've been doing well. Maybe it was the instinctual feeling that forced me to freeze, but even with the creature gone, my panic doesn't escalate more than I can manage. I don't strike out randomly at my surroundings.

"I guess we now know how that other hole was made." Jav's voice echoes from ahead of me.

The beast only just left. Why is he over there already? Does he want to bring it back? And what other hole? Against my wishes, Grímr approaches the volan. As we get closer, I spot him through the darkness looking down at the ground before him.

Grímr stops by Jav's side and only then do I realize what he's talking about. Before us, a massive section of the stone floor is gone. But instead of another tunnel, it drops into another cavern a hundred meters below. A blue glow carpets the cavern below us, its dim light hardly enough to make out anything in the area below us.

The biggest shock is that the stone under our feet isn't half a meter thick. Assuming that what I see on the other end of the hole continues on our side, we've been wandering over this massive cavern without knowing.

"Solvei, sorry to ask after everything, but could you give us some light?" Remus stops beside us.

I almost refuse, but he's not looking down with the rest of us. His eyes are locked on the ceiling ahead of us.

Begrudgingly, I do as asked. The light from my arms is enough to light up everything before us. A hundred white orbs the size of my arm stick to the ceiling with a slick paste.

Are they eggs?

CHAPTER THIRTY-ONE

Convalesce

So . . . should we destroy them? I'm not sure I like the idea of more of whatever that was running around," Jav says.

"No," Tetsu says. "Did you not feel that presence? We don't have a chance if it comes back."

I look down at the glowing base of the cavern below. Large swathes of the blue glow go dark in areas silhouetting . . . something down there. The light isn't bright enough to actually see what the shadows are, but if there is more than one of those things down there, I really don't want to stand around here. Actually, even the one is too much.

"Bunny's right." Remus stares up at the eggs on the ceiling. "This is our limit. Thanks to whatever that glow is, we know there is an entire unexplored ecosystem down here. We won't have to search that last hole we found. Now is the time to report back."

As he takes a step back, the familiar skittering sound of a centipede comes from the other side of the hole. I pump my flames a bit to get a better look, feeling exhausted even from this slight effort. The creature is already digging into an egg, eating whatever undeveloped creature it finds inside.

"Well, that's not good," Remus says as I hear more critters all around us. "On the off chance that thing actually cares about its babies, we should probably run."

And like that, we are off. Grímr lunges after him, and the rough motion immediately flares the aches in my body, reigniting my migraine. I shut my eyes to try and push away the pain, but it isn't helpful.

There is no sound of grinding rock nor the tapping from earlier. All I hear as we run is the scuttle of many centipedes rushing for a free lunch. Whatever left those eggs, thankfully, doesn't return.

We slow after Remus decides we are far enough from the hole.

"All right," he starts. "Where's the way out?"

"You weren't paying attention? Again?" Jav says, exasperated. "Just go east."

At the blank looks he receives, he sighs and points in a direction. "Just walk that way."

Again, we are back to walking through the endless flat cavern. I am capable of looking around without losing my mind in panic. So . . . progress.

I don't know how Jav can tell where we are. It looks the same no matter how far we travel.

Regardless of how he does it, he exudes a confidence that doesn't make me doubt his ability to find the exit for a second. That is until he has us stop where there is no hole in the ceiling and looks around in confusion after hours of walking with confidence.

"It should be here."

"Oh my, what's this? Jav lost his touch?" Remus gasps. "And to think he was so confident all this time."

"Not the time," Jav snaps, looking along the ceiling as if it will pop into existence. "I'm not wrong. It should be here."

Remus sighs. "All right. Everyone fan out and see if you can find it."

Grímr and I rush off. With my body as reluctant to work with me as it is, it's a challenge to brighten my flames. I push them so we have a decent amount of light to work with, but despite that, we find no signs of our entrance.

We search for a long while, covering several hundred meters from the point Jav claimed the exit should be. Not a hint of the entrance to be found.

But that's not to say we find nothing.

"Everyone," Tetsu calls through the dark. "Get here now."

Grímr and I arrive to see her standing over what looks like a golden brown, flat-bottomed bowl.

"What did you find?" Remus says as he approaches.

"Not sure. It looks like a pastry, but I've never seen one so hard." She pokes the toe of her boot at the offending bowl and it clatters along the stone as if it were rock itself.

Jav is off Remus's head and scoops the pastry off the ground. "Old man, I didn't realize you ate these. I thought you hated acting your age?"

"What?" Remus's eyes widen as he gets a closer look at the bowl. "That's not mine."

"Then this is concerning," Jav says, putting strength into his arms until the thing cracks apart.

"What is it?" Grímr asks.

"A pie. Not like the ones you'll find back home, this pastry is hard enough to survive some abuse. It's used to contain meat for safe consumption while traveling. They're an outdated practice as the inedible crust wastes a lot of space." Jav pauses as he looks around the cavern. "Someone else has been down here."

"But . . . why? Did the Order send someone before us?" Tetsu asks.

"No. They shouldn't have. Even if you ignore the fact that this was more of a punishment than a mission, they sent us alone because nobody else was available." Remus rests his head on a curled-up tentacle. "I think for now we should just focus on getting out. We'll trust that Jav's sense isn't off and that the Titan's path is above us. Bunny, can you please?"

Without a word, she pulls out her war hammer and swings it so the spike smashes into the stone above our heads. The loud clang sends a jolt of pain through my head. Her hammer does nothing more than bounce off the stone. A thin scratch is all that marks the spot she hit.

After watching her smash through thousands of tons of stone against the dahu, it is shocking to see her swing cause nearly no damage.

"Wha . . . ?" She obviously feels the same way.

She lines up her strike again, but is no more effective than before. In fact, the ceiling seems to have damaged her hammer rather than the opposite. The sharp tip on the back of her hammer is ever so slightly dulled.

Remus shoos her out of the way and dons a gauntlet. His tentacle moves too quick to see, but I hear the thunderous crack reverberating from his swing. Even his attack leaves nothing more than a dent the shape of his gauntlet in the ceiling.

"Well," he starts. "This is worrisome."

Each of the team casts their gaze around the cavern in obvious concern. It seems I'm the only one who doesn't know what's going on.

"Is that . . ." Grímr pauses. "Is all of this . . . ranked stone?"

"It appears so."

"Well, shit. It looks like Solvei was right to be worried about being trapped," Jav says.

His words feel like a spike being nailed into my chest. When there was a way out, I hadn't been able to stop the panic attack coming on. But now they say we are actually trapped?

I can't stop the delirium that envelopes me. I go to lash out but find no energy responds. Darkness takes me.

* * *

My eyes open to a wall of blue light. I blink and groan from the pain that assaults me. I guess it's too much to ask to sleep until I feel better.

As I look around, I realize it isn't a blue wall, but a thousand blue glowing dots around me. Tiny little flying insects that weave in amongst themselves a meter or two above the ground.

Wait . . . we didn't go down into the home of that monster, did we?

I can't see the ceiling. Not a good sign. The ground under Grímr's feet is uneven soil with protruding jagged rocks, not smooth stone. The glow-flies must be the source of the blue glow I saw looking down that hole.

Despite possibly being in the home of some Titan and being trapped underground, the panic that has consumed me ever since they dragged me down here has calmed. I still feel horribly sick and lacking energy, but the overwhelming desperation is gone.

The fear is still there, but I feel like it is manageable. It's both more natural and yet somewhat subdued. Maybe it's because the cavern is much larger, or I've just burned through all the effort I'm willing to go through in my efforts to escape.

Something about these options doesn't seem right to me, but I'm grateful to think with a clear mind again. Now, I can figure out how I'm going to get out of here. If this team tries to stop me from getting out, then it might be time to separate from them.

"You're awake!" Grímr says as I readjust my position.

"Yeah," I manage, still feeling tired.

"You've been out for weeks. We were worried."

The team comes to a stop and surrounds me. It is uncomfortable to have everyone's attention solely on me. Especially as vulnerable as I feel right now.

Remus steps before me and dips his head until it's below mine. "I am deeply regretful of the actions I have made. I apologize for not treating your concerns with the sincerity they deserve. My actions were intended to help, but that is no excuse for the suffering I have inflicted on you."

He tilts his eyes up in his head until he's locking them with my own. "I talked about the arrogance within the younger teams, but it was my own that landed us here. If I had listened to your fears, I would not have put you in such a dangerous place. For that, I am sorry."

I don't know how to react. I turn to the others to see their reaction. Both Jav and Tetsu bow their heads to me as well. Even Grímr lowers his head underneath me.

"I am sorry," Tetsu says stiffly.

Jav nods at her words. "You should have seen Grímr's outburst. I don't think I've ever seen him so angry. He made sure each of us regret what we did."

I don't know if I should believe their apologies are sincere. What if they're trying to bait me in with a false sense of security only to betray me once more? Just as Gloria did.

Well, regardless of their intentions, if I can use their intent to make up—genuine or not—I'll use them as much as I can to find a way out.

I give them a small nod to appease them.

"What happened?" I ask.

Grímr takes the chance to jump in. "After you fainted, we spent a week walking through the flat cavern, looking for any sign of a way out. We had no luck; the cavern was identical almost the entire way through except for the holes created by that large egg-laying monster and a few other insignificant oddities. We found nothing in our search, so we decided it was best to look down here."

"So, how do we plan to get out?"

"We hope to find a path down here. There was nothing for us to find up there. The entrance we came through has seemingly been replaced by ranked stone," Remus says.

"You want to find your way out . . . by going down? Won't we just reenter that cavern if we climb up again? And what's ranked stone?"

"Ranked stone, or any ranked element, is the enhanced version of that element. Think how we are strengthened people of our own race; it is like that, but for stone. That cavern above us is entirely made of ranked stone. Which, I should be clear, is insane. Many of the stronger Middle Elevation beasts can only create or influence a small amount of the stuff. Imagine all the rock the dahu manipulated, all of that compressed to the size of your hand."

I look down at my hand and struggle to comprehend the exact magnitude of what he is talking about. All I know is that this ranked stone is strong.

"There are few things that can break through ranked stone. None of us can. So we come down here on the assumption that the area acts like the Middle Elevation; there may be paths that shouldn't exist if you mapped them out. It is not impossible for a path to lead to the surface that somehow avoids the flat cavern above."

It sounds hard to believe, but I've already seen the inside of the Void Fog, so it isn't unimaginable. Still, it feels like a bit of a stretch as our only option.

"There's really no other way?"

Remus avoids eye contact and acts like he hasn't heard me.

"The monsters," Tetsu says in his place. "We could lure one of them into reopening the entrance."

"No. If we do that, the likelihood something will go wrong is enormous. We can't risk it."

That sounds terrifying. But if it is a way out, it's definitely worth considering.

In the corner of my eye, I spot the hovering glow-bugs start to thin.

Remus notices too. "We should get moving. For now, we'll continue to look for a way up and only consider baiting one of those things if we have no other option."

I cling to Grímr and we dash away from the area of dwindling lights.

CHAPTER THIRTY-TWO

Bug Trap

Despite the brightness of the glowing bugs, the surroundings don't light up near as much as they should. A faint blue outlines rocks and stalagmites nearby, but neither are illuminated.

I stand on Grímr's back to look over the layer of glow-bugs. They span far into the distance in every direction, leaving dark spots in many areas. The bugs keep their distance from us, indicating that each shadow isn't representative of the size of what is hiding within. So, not every dark area will hide one of those massive egg-laying monsters. Well, hopefully.

Remus's plan leaves me rather uncomfortable. At the moment, it seems like all we're doing is wandering aimlessly. We've avoided the dark spots for now. Instead, we amble our way through the sea of glow-bugs looking for a wall. Even after days of walking, we've yet to come across one.

Bats screech overhead. Occasionally, they swoop down to consume swathes of the glow-bugs without warning. When they dive, they are silent, only noticeable by the disappearing clumps of glowing specks. They steer clear of the dark areas, so we've had no need to worry, but the entire fact that there are creatures above my head that I can't see approach is bothersome.

I want to light up the area with my fire, but Remus told me not to. He's worried that I might attract the monster we have no chance of facing. Honestly, I think it would be worth the risk. We need information, but it's hard to learn anything if we can't see. If that creature does attack, then great; we can direct it to the ceiling and I'll have a way out again.

Nothing but my freedom matters.

A deep growl thunders through the air and the five of us freeze. The glow-bugs all stop in midair. Constant interweaving movement forgotten. The presence is back, undiluted and bearing down on me. It feels like the creature is watching, right over my shoulder and ready to consume me whole.

A loud bang echoes from far ahead of us. It sounds like that monster is tearing through the ceiling again.

None of us speak. Unanimously, we switch direction.

Even an hour later, everyone is still looking over their shoulder and jumping at shadows. Or, more specifically, the patches lacking glow-bug light.

"How much longer are we going to do this?" I can't help but ask. "Shouldn't we try something different? Those creatures can't be hiding in each of those shadows, can we light them up just to check?"

"I understand your impatience, Solvei, but we cannot rush," Remus says. "This place is unfamiliar. I've already put us in enough danger. I don't plan to take unnecessary risks."

"But we've seen nothing new for days! How long do you want to keep us down here?"

"As long as needed to get you out safe." His eyes stare into me, lacking any of his usual amusement. Absolute seriousness and dedication. Without words, he tells me it's a promise he would die to keep.

I shut my mouth, stifling any more complaints. I don't like it. It feels like we're not even trying to get out at the current pace. What if we miss out on an exit because we are being too cautious?

I want to believe Remus. I want to believe in his apology and that he wants to get out, but the longer it takes for results to materialize, the more I doubt his sincerity.

I'm finally feeling better.

Not about being stuck down here. No. My sickness has finally receded to the point where my body fully listens to me and I actually have energy again.

It surprised me that Remus packed iron ingots in his and Grímr's pouches. Apparently, he knew enough about my people that he could treat me when I was unconscious. I packed only the three ingots for myself, thinking it would be enough. But Remus seemed to pull more out of nowhere.

The underground area we're in is far warmer than outside and there's no snow on the ground for me to worry about. For the first time in a while, I walk with my own strength. Even before I got sick, I was either riding Grímr or flying.

It's been years since I got sick like that. The last time was in a particularly cold winter with my tribe. Back then, I had to ration how much energy I used to keep warm. I couldn't just burn through all the local resources as I've been able to lately.

Jav hasn't been flying around as he usually would. The amount of things in the dark—especially above us—holds him back from looking around. Not that there is anything for him to see in the dark except the glow-bugs.

"Hmm, that's odd." When Remus stands tall on stretched limbs, he is easily the tallest amongst the team. He stands above the layer of glow-bugs and watches something in the distance.

Grímr pushes himself to stand on his hind legs, clearing Remus's height easily. It looks uncomfortable for him, but it lets him see whatever is going on. I retract my statement about Remus being the tallest.

Crouching low on the soft soil, I look underneath the blanket of floating bugs. It's not hard to spot what the others have seen. Swarms of the small lights are flowing toward a single point. The density of the light grows to a much greater brightness, but somehow still refuses to illuminate the surroundings.

At the point of highest concentration, the glowing spots float down to the ground before disappearing from sight.

"What do you think it is?" Grímr asks as he falls back on all fours with a thud.

"I'm not sure. I guess we'll find out."

I was worried Remus might want to stay cautious about this, too. Maybe the bugs will show us a way out.

As we get closer to the strange-acting bugs, the soil underneath our feet changes to a spongy surface with hundreds of plate-like mushroom growths. Somehow it's even softer to walk on than the soil had been.

The glow-bugs don't seem to react to our presence as we move in closer. Instead of keeping a good few meters distance from our group, they hover ever closer as the density of lights around us increases.

We are close enough now to see the fungi growths spiral around a central point. It is here that all the bugs seem to be attracted to. They all swarm around an opening in the center of the mushrooms.

What are the bugs so attracted to? We get closer, taking careful steps until we're right on top of the opening. The thing hasn't reacted to our presence, so I doubt it is anything more than a normal plant.

We all take a peek inside at the deep hole that must run far into the ground. Thousands of the glow-bugs rush inside the opening and fly at the walls, getting themselves stuck. The light inside is so intense it's almost hard to look at.

Before I can react, the tunnel of fungi convulses and I'm tugged backward.

I land on the soft ground and look up, only to be splattered by some liquid. I panic, thinking that I've just been drenched in water. A flame flares out and the substance ignites. It burns off quicker than anything I've ever seen. In barely a second, all of it is gone.

One moment, the sticky substance covers my face—that I now realize did not sting like water—the next, I'm engulfed in a fireball.

I gather my feet underneath me and push myself up. The others have all been lathered in the goop as well. Well, everyone except Jav. Somehow, he avoided any of the sticky liquid from hitting him.

"Ugh, yuck." Remus tries to wipe the substance off his body, but he achieves nothing besides spreading it further.

"What is this stuff?" Grímr has a similar issue, unable to get any of it out of his thick fur.

The hole where the goop came from doesn't seem to move anymore, so I walk up to them. "Should I burn it off?"

"No," Remus responds immediately. "We can't risk attracting attention."

Well, if he wants to stay all sticky, then that's on him.

A single glow-bug lands on his head, sticking itself to the dripping ooze.

"You two, don't get distracted," Tetsu says. "Look up."

Around the three of them, a cloud of the glow-bugs condenses. Attracted to whatever substance is coating the three tallest members of the team, the bugs swarm. For a moment, it just seems like a neat sight; the tiny creatures must really like the smell to close in like that after they've kept their distance for so long.

It seems completely harmless . . . until it isn't.

"Ouch." Tetsu swats a bug off her arm. Her eyes widen visibly as she looks at the spot where she was bitten. "We have a problem; they can pierce my skin."

The situation immediately becomes serious. No longer are these tiny creatures harmless insects, but a threat considering the innumerable quantity.

Remus and Tetsu take to swatting thousands of them out of the sky before they reach them. The wind created with each swing sends many more spiraling away. Even so, the glow-bugs get closer. An ever-growing number swarming in droves.

Jav flies through the densest parts, but can only ever stop as many as he can cut.

I look to Grímr to see him rolling around on the ground, crushing all that latch onto his hide. Uh . . . I guess that works just as well.

Despite how many of the bugs are being killed by the second, the density of the lights only ever increases. We need to get rid of that substance coating them or they will never stop coming.

Remus catches sight of my flame the moment its light comes into being. "Stop, Solvei. You'll do nothing but attract that monster."

Even as he says so, he swipes away at the bugs digging into his flesh. He doesn't bleed, but in the moment before the bugs can latch back on, I see the deep purple welts marring his skin.

None of the others are faring much better. Grímr is even leaving clumps of fur on the ground behind him as he scratches and rolls, trying to get rid of the bugs.

This is hardly the time to care about some bigger what-if. These bugs are going to eat their way through the team if I do nothing.

I disregard Remus's orders and flare my flames out to the bugs and the goop coating the three. As my fire touches the swarm, I can't help the gasp of shock that escapes my lips. Not only do my flames incinerate them with ease, but each of them contains a similar amount of energy as the average, non-enhanced soldier.

Every single one.

Gluttony overcomes me and I spread my flames as wide as I can to consume as many as possible.

The liquid coating Grímr, Remus, and Tetsu ignites, enshrouding each of them in a massive fireball that creates huge plumes of smoke above. I'm not worried about them; they've already shown how resistant they are to my flames. While the heat of my fire increases when burning through the gooey substance, it isn't too much hotter than what I can normally attain.

I'm lost in the indulgence of these impossibly nutritious bugs. The feeling overwhelms any thought of keeping my flames contained. I spread them as wide as they will go, and consume everything I can. Remus shouts for me to stop, but the feeling of satiation is too good to stop.

That is, until a terrifying hiss rips that feeling out of my chest. I freeze on the spot. The hiss reverberates through every part of my body.

A quaking crash shakes the ground under my feet. My legs wobble as the tapping returns, sounding more like a cratering impact with each tap.

A massive creature moves into the flickering light of my flames. Its large, bulbous body towers ten meters over us. Several long, spindly legs carry the being forward, shaking the ground with each step.

Its next growl snaps me out of my reverie. I try to pull my flames back to myself, to hide us within the darkness again.

I should have just extinguished them where they were.

My flames pass over the hole between the mushroom like growths. The fluid coating the tube inside ignites. In hardly a moment, the entire hole explodes. A pillar of flames rocket into the sky, lighting up much of the cavern.

There is only enough light to see for a moment, but in that time I spot at least two more of the monstrosities clinging to the ceiling in the distance.

Hisses resound from everywhere in the cavern, drowned out by the screech of the monster right on top of us.

My flames continue to burn down into the earth, far deeper than I ever expected the mushroom thing to dig. My eyes snap to the opening. It's tight, but it's our best hope of escape. I felt the explosion travel deep into the ground.

"The hole!" I shout to the others. "It's a way out." Of course, I don't know that for sure, but it's better than any other option we have at the moment.

Not even taking a moment to doubt my words, Remus orders everyone inside. Jav is the first in, flying straight down the tunnel and I chase not far behind. I try to turn back to watch, but Tetsu jumps in after me and pushes me deeper.

My flames still burning along the spongy ground of fungi let me see as Remus and Grímr dash toward the hole. The crashing sound of the monster's mighty heft closes in with each moment.

Grímr rams his head into the back of Remus, sending him flying toward the hole. One of the sharp, spindly legs smashes down on Grímr, piercing through his back without so much as an ounce of resistance. His spine is severed, and the momentum of his upper body tears away the last muscles connecting his body around the claw and tarsus that are piercing through his chest. His body splits in half.

The remaining upper half tumbles toward the hole. Remus pulls Grímr's head down into the hole after us, his hind legs abandoned. Remus squeezes through the tight tunnel with an ease none of us can compare, tugging what's left of Grímr down with us. The tunnel is far too tight for the panther.

The ground quakes and rocks fall from above.

"Keep moving down!" Remus shouts.

The hissing of the creature above continues as it digs after us.

Thankfully, the monstrosity cannot dig as fast as we descend. After we drop what must be a hundred meters, the sounds of digging above ceases.

I look at Grímr. A pang of dread floods my body. Crushed between the far-too-tight stone surrounding us, he is unresponsive.

I don't want to lose another person I'm close to. I place my hands on the side of his head and hope to see life in his eyes.

Instead, a tear opens in the back of his neck and tiny, sharp, spider-like legs pierce outward. A tiny black arachnid with ten spindly legs crawls out of the cut.

"Grímr?" I ask, slightly bewildered.

The small thing pushes its body up and down, which I guess is a nod. Huh.

"Nice to meet you," I say.

CHAPTER THIRTY-THREE

Adaptation

This is not what I wanted.

I was hoping for a way back up, not to move even farther from the surface. Now, we have no option but to continue downward. Our path back, blocked by that monstrosity. At least we'll be progressing and not wandering around aimlessly. Hopefully, there will be a way to loop around to the surface down here. I'm relying on Remus's word that space can act odd around the Alps, as impossible as it sounds.

That is, assuming this tunnel doesn't just end.

"Solvei! What were you thinking?" Remus doesn't yell, but with the tone he uses, he might as well be. "I told you not to use your fire. So what made you think erupting like that was a good idea?"

"Should I have left you to be eaten by the glow-bugs?" If I didn't do what I did, they would've continued to bite away at their bodies. Why is he mad I saved them?

"Compared to what you brought down on us, yes. Those flies would have posed no problem."

The bluish membrane of his skin is still littered with blisters and welts, so I can't help but doubt his words. We got out alive, so is it that big of a deal?

My eyes fall on Grímr, reduced to an arachnid smaller than Jav. For what happened to his body, I do feel a bit guilty. But if it's to escape, then I don't care about the cost.

I don't care?

I wouldn't care if they died? For me to escape? That sounds so wrong . . .

but I can't say I'm not willing to do anything for my freedom. Keeping my freedom is the greatest desire I have, but I never would have considered sacrificing others for my selfishness. At least, not intentionally. I've only thought this way after being trapped down here, haven't I?

Remus sighs as he watches me devolve into thought. "Just be careful from now on. We are unfamiliar with the environment, so being impulsive is dangerous."

I don't respond. These thoughts of mine have inflicted far more worry in me than I could have expected.

They betrayed me . . . but I don't want to lose any of them. I don't know if I want to stay with them after they dragged me down here, but they don't deserve death.

Now that I think about it logically and not with the fear clouding my judgment, they were trying to help me. Even if their method of 'helping' was horrible. Their intentions were good, and it was because of the blizzard that they were forced to act, but they still chose to take me into the caves rather than escape along the surface.

Even as I think that, a part of my mind combats the thought. They are the ones who put me here. They are the ones who trapped me. Now that I'm aware of it, it's easy to push it to the side, but it's concerning that it's there at all.

I close my eyes as I crawl after Tetsu. Remus follows behind me and Grímr sits on my shoulder. Bizarre how our roles are now reversed.

As my body moves through the tunnel, I focus inside myself. The rope of my thoughts and desires appears before me, as tightly bound as it was after the Fog. I inspect the knots within. The twists in the threads that cause the greatest conflicts of interest. Where my smaller, individual desires go against the greater direction of the rope and snap away from the direction they once wished to move.

The knot that once represented—or maybe caused—my intense phobia of being trapped has snapped. The loose threads retie themselves in a knot completely different from the original. Some threads have yet to bind with the rest of the whole, but it is obvious something has changed.

My fear of being trapped is no longer there, instead something more complex has taken its place.

Is it possible that under the intense mental strain caused by constant fear, the knot snapped and was forced to evolve into something that wouldn't kill me? My phobia kept me from acting rationally to escape, which forced me into an inescapable loop. Since the reactionary fear did nothing to help me escape, it has changed.

The only issue is . . . what has it changed into?

I can think straight now, but I seem to be flooded with thoughts of choosing the most excessive methods to escape. Including sacrificing those I care for.

So because an entirely emotional response was ineffective in helping me escape, my rope of desire has decided that a purely logical response is a better replacement? No morals? No interest in the things I care for? That's an obscene overadjustment.

Well, it's good that I know what's changed. Now, I just need to find a way to avoid hurting the others when my mind forces those ideas upon me.

Should I tell them?

Of course not. Think about how they used the last sensitive bit of info. I don't trust them not to betray me again.

Before I have the chance to think more on it, Tetsu drops into an opening ahead of us. I fall after her and land in her arms. She places me on the ground, ignoring the other two who crash beside us.

It's another tunnel, traveling horizontally instead of vertically like the one we came from. The ceiling is low, so I need to bend my neck, but it forces Tetsu and Remus to crouch. It's still better than crawling, so neither of them complains.

Did that mushroom plant dig all this, or did it just grow in the tunnel already there? Charred earth mars the walls even all the way down here. Soot doesn't continue long through the larger tunnel, so I assume this was here before the mushroom.

I wonder if I can get any of that sticky substance? It would be an incredible weapon. Even my team's bodies were burned a bit from the explosion. Not even my hottest flame can do that yet.

Also, being able to attract those juicy bugs would be amazing.

The tunnel we've fallen into has two ways we can go; straight ahead, or where it curves out of sight behind us. We all follow Jav when he points to walk straight ahead.

We don't walk through the tunnel long before it branches into two paths. Jav leads us down the left without pause.

"Be careful. There are scratch marks along the ground. Some creature frequents this tunnel a lot."

I look down and sure enough, they are there. But I have no idea how he can tell they belong to a creature rather than just the natural shape of the cave. I don't doubt him, but I would have ignored them if I were alone.

Tetsu takes the lead, with Remus following behind me. Jav sits on Tetsu's shoulder, rather than the dohrni for once. As probably the only one of us who still has his bearings, we rely on his directions to find our way out.

I keep close behind as Tetsu picks up her pace. The tunnel curves often, bending down and to the side. As we pass, the thickness of the cave changes, but mostly stays wide enough for us to move without trouble. The path branches again. We have two possible paths to follow.

"We should veer to the left from here, but only a single set of scratch marks lead that way. I can't see a returning set," Jav says.

"How many go the other way?" Remus asks.

"It's hard to say, there's no way to tell the scratches apart. Either we have a single creature moving back and forth many times, or there are over ten that have passed this way."

"So either follow the well-beaten path and come across whatever these creatures are, or head into the tunnel that we know one of those creatures hasn't returned from." Remus leans over my head as he has a look for himself. "Can you tell how old the scratches are?"

"No."

"Then I think it's best to follow the scrapes. Let's hope whatever leaves them isn't too strong."

We continue for hours, coming across many such branches in the cave system. Each time we come across a fork, we always avoid the paths that don't have a returning set of scratches. Some trails split, only to combine again when the tunnels reconnect.

There are plenty of caves that either don't have any scratch marks or have two sets, but every time we check those paths, we come across a dead end. So, regardless of what danger the creatures that leave these marks might pose, we continue to follow their trail.

Grímr cannot talk without a body to use. So whenever I ask him questions, he's limited to nodding or shaking his body.

"So, how do we go about getting Grímr a new body?" I ask the team. It isn't something I'm all too clear on yet.

"We will subdue an animal and hold it still while he digs his way into their brain." Tetsu taps the back of her own neck. "Most creatures get quite restless when they feel it. It's a good challenge to keep them pinned as he does his thing."

"Unfortunately, we don't have the luxury of choosing or planning our fights. Everything down here is still unknown, so he'll have to settle with whatever we can manage for the time being."

I look down at Grímr. He raises two of his front limbs in a "what can you do?" gesture. It's hard to imagine what it would be like to lose my body. I can't imagine it's an easy thing for him to adjust to; to lose the strength that body contained would be rough.

If the team wasn't here to help him find a new body, how would he be able to do it himself? There's no way he'd have the strength to compete with anything, right? Could he do it if he caught something off guard? But if he has to dig into their head, there is no way a creature wouldn't feel that. They would do everything they could to stop him.

Now that I think about it, we're heading along a path we know leads to unknown creatures, and yet we are down a good portion of our fighting strength. Without Grímr, we'll have to rely on Tetsu and Remus to take the brunt of anything we face. With Jav taking stabs whenever he can get the chance. Although, from how I've seen Jav fight so far, I don't know how well he'll do in this tight space.

They need someone to pick up the slack, right? I never got the chance to fix my spearmanship.

"Tetsu?" I ask. "Can I have my spear?"

She unlatches it from the bundle with ease and passes it back to me. Not saying a word.

"Solvei, I don't want you joining any fights for now," Remus says from behind.

"What, but why?" I turn to him.

"Because I don't know what to expect. Stay at range and use your flames if you have to, but keep your distance." He places two of his limbs on my shoulders and I'm pleasantly surprised I don't feel the tension that rises anymore. I still don't want them there. In fact, my desire to whip them off is just as strong. Only now, it isn't an emotional response tearing my gut apart until he lets go.

"I need you to protect Grímr while we fight. Can you do that?"

"Okay," I concede.

Even if I can't try out my spear, I can still see if I can burn these creatures. My flames have only gotten stronger recently. I'm just not sure if it will be enough.

I grip my spear as tight as I can and focus on my bodily control. Instead of only pushing my body to where my flames lose their brightness and become indistinguishable from fleshy skin, I go further. I push the physical flames to the limit of what I can achieve, and then I push harder.

I have no idea how effective it might be, but I hope it gives me added weight behind my swings. It's a struggle to be focusing as hard as I am and get no visual response. I can feel my flames getting denser, but I'm unsure how much that is actually helping.

I want to ask Tetsu to take one of my hits and tell me how much better it is compared to what I was doing before, but now is not the time. She is busy watching ahead of us in case anything appears while we're making our way through.

"Hey, do you hear something?" Jav asks suddenly.

I look at Grímr, who usually has the best hearing, but he shakes his tiny arachnid body at me. Right, that hearing must have been from the panther ears.

"What is it?" Tetsu asks.

"I swear I heard . . . talking."

CHAPTER THIRTY-FOUR

Mermineae

There are people speaking ahead."

We creep forward, as quiet as possible. My footsteps are light, but I can't help but wince whenever my boots scuff against rock.

The tunnel splits in three paths. The one on the right—with all the scratch marks—also splits farther in.

"The voices are definitely coming from where the scratches lead." Jav's voice is almost too quiet to make out, even as close as I am.

The volan turns his head back, looking over my shoulder at Remus. The dohrni nods to Jav in some unspoken agreement before we walk toward the voices.

The moment Jav passes into the right tunnel, he stops and tilts his head, listening for what I still cannot hear. He leaves Tetsu at the front and dashes back to the branching section.

"The voices are coming from this way as well," he says. "They are quieter, but I can hear them."

Without even turning to see if we are following, he begins his trek through the tunnel unmarred by scratches. The order we walk in flips, and now Remus is ahead and Tetsu is behind.

As we creep through the tunnel, a faint murmur tickles the back of my ears. The indistinct echo of voices finally becomes audible. High-pitched and squeaky, the chorus of conversation amplifies with each curve in the tunnel.

I clench my fingers around the shaft of my spear. Each step taken with the utmost care. I hold my breath and breathe through my flames, doing my utmost to keep them as physical as I can. The last thing I want is to give off light now.

The cave narrows as it inclines upward. I cringe as Tetsu squeezes her way through the tight passage, dragging her body across rock.

I can hear individual voices now. They are all high-pitched, but there is a distinct difference between some of them. They laugh and joke and speak in rapid sentences, but I still can't make out their words.

This isn't some animal's squeaks or barks. Despite it not yet being distinct enough for me to hear, it clearly has the structure of speech. These are people ahead of us.

I haven't heard any race speak with such shrill voices, but there is no doubt in my mind that whatever is down there, they are intelligent.

I thought nobody had been down here before us? Did these people leave that pie back at our entrance?

Tetsu knocks a rock loose from the ceiling and I freeze at the loud clank sound it makes as it clatters along the ground behind me. I'm not the only one to do so; both the two at the front and Tetsu herself stop, cringing at the sound.

The sound of chatter stops.

None of us dare move. We remain motionless for a good minute before the conversing starts once more. Although it is stays somewhat subdued to before. No longer do the high-pitched voices laugh and joke; they keep their volume restrained.

Remus raises a limb at Tetsu and while her face drops with a frown, she nods in acceptance. The two ahead of me continue on, leaving her behind. I scuttle after them, not wanting to miss out when I hadn't been told to stay behind.

Past Remus, the tunnel opens up. He stops just before the tunnel drops into a cavern. The voices are loud now, echoing off the walls and amplifying their words. I peek around the other two as they look down into the cave.

Our tunnel ends at a five-meter drop. From our vantage point, five short figures are . . . well, not clear, but visible. The darkness shrouds them too much to make out any details, but their slender forms are about the same height as me.

I strain my hearing, trying to make out the words over the intense echo and their companions' constant interruptions.

"—hate these tunnels. They creep me out."

"I know what you mean. I'm seeing shadows in the corner of my eyes."

"And to think we still have to wait months down here. I'm gonna go insane."

"Stop complaining, you lot." A sixth figure appears from seemingly nowhere. They march out of the shrouding darkness toward the five other figures huddling around each other. "We haven't lost near as many as expected. You should celebrate that these tunnels are safer than the plains."

"Safer? You're joking! We know nothing about what's down here. Someone disappears almost every other branching tunnel. At least on the surface, we can run and hide. We know what we are dealing with up there. If anything wanders into this cave, we have nowhere to run!"

The sixth sits amongst the others. "You believe our task is noble, do you not? A bit of time in an eerie cave is nothing if we can succeed. Or you consider yourself more important than our cause, do you?"

"O-of course not, Forvaal. It's just hard to imagine the beyond as anything but folktale."

"Fear not; it is real. Even with these rotted eyes, I saw it for myself. Under the deep blue sky, I stood unobscured. And yet, here I stand." The speaker takes a moment before continuing. "The calamity has given us this path. We must secure it before the all-powerful Kalma returns. Even she will not touch us should we persevere."

The response to his fervent speech is subdued, but I can still hear murmurs of agreement.

Where are these beings from? They can't actually be from the other side of the Alps, can they? Maybe there is somewhere in the mountains they come from. But . . . what is their goal? Some place called the beyond? Unless they mean the Stepps and the land back that way. If that's right, then they might know a way back up.

I glance over at Remus to see what he thinks. We can't just go down and introduce ourselves. I've seen enough of the races to know it isn't uncommon for them to be hostile toward the unfamiliar. Actually, I wouldn't say it's unlikely for them to be aggressive to those of their own. The Empire showed no hesitation in Zadok.

Remus is still watching over the group. All five of them continue to talk amongst each other.

Wait, five? What happened to the sixth? As I peer into the dark, I notice the one they called Forvaal has gone missing.

If only it was a bit brighter, I could see where they went. The voices continue talking, either ignoring their missing friend or not noticing their lack of presence.

"So, Piiv. Are your kits joining us anytime soon?"

"Riis will. I haven't heard from the other three in a year."

"Oh, that's horrible. I really liked Iraas. That hob hated when it was his time to become independent."

"Yes. I just hope it wasn't the centzon or revontulet. It would be horrible if they had to suffer before their end."

Remus backs away from the ledge, snapping me away from eavesdropping further. We ever so slowly move back through the tunnel until we reach Tetsu. Remus makes a motion with his limb and she crawls back the way we came.

As soon as we are far enough away not to be heard, Jav speaks.

"Have you ever seen one of those beings before?" he asks, angling his head toward Remus.

"No. Never," he says. "I never thought it was possible, but I think they are from the other side of the Alps."

"What should we do?"

"We need to report this," Tetsu says, only to receive an annoyed glance from Jav.

"And how do you propose we do that? In case you've forgotten, we still don't have a way to get back to the surface."

"Yes, we do." Remus's eyes stare through the darkness toward the camp of strange creatures.

His words make me narrow my eyes and I glare at him. He knows a way out? And he hasn't said it until now?

Before I can jump to any more conclusions, he continues. "Those beings. They mentioned they'd seen our side . . . assuming 'the beyond' is our side of the Alps. If we follow them, we might find our way out."

That . . . might work, but didn't they mention they would be there for months? I'd really rather not be down here so long. How long would I last before the knot of my psyche makes me do something excessive?

"That might take a while, and none of us are adept at skulking. Also, there's something else I should say." Jav waits until he has everyone's attention before continuing. "I've been keeping track of our position. Right now, we should have been well above the ground near the crevasse. I'm not sure whether the world here acts stranger than the Middle Elevation, or that group of creatures is between us and our home. Either way . . . I'm lost," Jav struggles to admit.

"So we'll have to find our way around them if we want to determine if these tunnels open into the crevasse. Could that be how they made it to the surface?" Remus ponders.

"Like I said, I don't know. If my senses were accurate, we should have breached the surface days ago."

Remus's eyes flicker to Grímr. "Whatever we decide, we shouldn't rush. I think it's time to search some of those tunnels those beings haven't charted. Maybe we can find Grímr a body."

With our objective decided, we move out once more. Tetsu takes the lead and we carefully look down the scratched tunnels for any of those creatures before we sneak through them.

We move away far enough that my body relaxes, the beings behind us too far to hear even if we make a ruckus. As we trek through a slightly wider part of the tunnel, I feel something odd above me. Even as I look up, I can't tell anything different about the stone ceiling, so I return my attention to Tetsu's back.

I'm just about to practice thrusting my spear again when a crash booms behind me. A rush of air billows my outfit and dust spreads around us.

I turn. Not fast enough. It feels like I'm moving in slow motion. Behind me, one of those beings I overheard before has Remus pinned to the ground. Its sharp fangs dig into the dohrni's head as he struggles underneath the creature.

It is an extremely slender creature with four legs and a tail. Its forelegs have each of Remus's limbs trapped, unable to strike out. Its fur is oddly the same color and texture as the stone ceiling above us.

I'm snapped out of my stupor as Tetsu tugs me away, brushing past me with a short sword raised to strike at the ambusher. The creature snaps its head to her, releasing Remus from his bite but not the pinning grasp.

Its eyes are a cloudy gray, but as it stares at Tetsu bearing down on it with her blade, they glow. The gray light intensifies the closer she gets.

Her short sword comes down on the creature, but it doesn't flinch. I feel a rush of shock as the blade bursts into dust the moment it strikes the beast's fur.

Before she can adjust to the loss of her weapon, another of those creatures drops on Bunny from above. I can't help but doubt my eyes as she struggles against the wiry looking form of the creature that drops on her. Bunny grapples with it, but it's obviously comparable to her in strength.

"Solvei, go! Take Grímr and run!"

I don't even think twice. My feet take me away without a moment's hesitation. I can't even turn around to watch them being overwhelmed.

My mind is in conflict. I want to go back and burn through those that would harm my team. But at the same moment, my mind won't risk it. My legs are snatched away and make me sprint through the tunnels against my will.

Tiny, hurried taps scratch at my neck. I look down at Grímr, who frantically gestures behind me. I turn to see one of the creatures rushing me down faster than anything has a right to.

The being cuts the distance between us faster than I can take a step. Its claws pierce through my chest and I can feel it tearing through the back of my outfit.

The creature's intelligent eyes stare into my own with surprise, but no remorse.

Flames explode out of me, engulfing the slender creature with intense heat. They incinerate the creature's fur, but its skin is tough.

The creature squeals. A high-pitched shriek that almost competes with that of a bat. It pulls its claws back to itself and desperately tries to put out the fire.

I use its moment of distraction to run. I can't continue down the tunnels with their scratch marks, they'll just catch up to me once they realize the fire isn't going to kill them.

They were hidden along the ceiling. That's how they caught us off guard. Their fur blends perfectly against the rock they clung to, so there is no way to see them. If there are any ahead of me, I need to make sure before I get ambushed.

My flames spread over every wall through the tunnel before and behind me. I'm indiscriminate. I don't know if their camouflage can hide from my probing flame, so I scorch every surface I come across.

Ahead of me, I feel the tunnel split three ways. Behind me, the creature has finally shaken off its fright and has resumed its chase. There is no time to waste; it'll be on me in moments.

I dash down the tunnel with only a single set of scratch marks. One of them came down here before and didn't return. I can only hope that whatever killed it won't be dangerous to me.

My flames reaching ahead of me burn through roots dangling from the rock above. It's strange, but the roots seem to angle toward the heat of my flame. They grasp at it and try to hook into it, but my fire burns through it with ease.

I realize the familiarity of this taste almost too late to stop it. Thankfully, I pull the heat out of my flames before they follow the fuse-like roots through the ceiling. Any later and the entire tunnel would be engulfed in an explosion. A waste for it to go off before my pursuer reaches me.

I grab Grímr off my shoulder, uncaring how rough my grip may be. I push him under my hood and tighten it closed. It's about to get rather sticky, and I don't know how well his small body could handle an explosion of that intensity.

The roots grab at me, showing far greater strength than their thin width would suggest. I burn them off each time they grab me, but only as far as they can reach me. The more there to slow the creature behind me, the better.

When I finally reach the base of the fungi tube filled with sticky substance, I risk a glance behind me. The being rushes around the corner with terrifying speed. What's more terrifying is that it is no longer alone. Two more of its brethren follow in its steps.

I pull myself into the tunnel above, covering myself in the viscid liquid as I worm my way up. Without a second of hesitation, the creatures follow me.

I sneer at them. They better hope their ugly snouts can handle some heat.

CHAPTER THIRTY-FIVE

Merminea Trap

Behind me, the creatures claw at the walls. The tight, sticky tube cakes them in a flammable substance. The first one looks like a naked jerboa with its fur burned off. Those scrambling after it find the liquid soaking their fur.

"Give up. We won't kill you," the one closing in on me yells.

"You think I'll believe that after you shoved your arm through my chest?" I shout back, incredulous.

It's fortunate that they aren't as fast moving vertically as they are on the ground, otherwise they would have caught me already. The farther I can get them through this tunnel, the less space they'll have to escape.

"Your friends are dead. Don't think they're coming to help you."

"Grímr, make sure you're hidden," I murmur just loud enough for him to hear before raising my voice. "You think I need help?"

I stop where I am in the tunnel and glare down at them. They are close now, but that's fine. They won't be getting out unscathed.

"Do you not see where you are?" The corner of my lip raises in a sneer.

They seem to realize—their widening eyes and immediate halt in their climb more than clear to my burning eyes—but it's too late.

In the narrow tunnel, I engulf everything in flame. The viscous substance explodes without effort. My flames spread with the explosion, farther than I can usually control. A chain reaction amplifies the flames as they rush both above and below.

It takes all my control to stop the heat escaping through the exits in both directions. I guide all that explosive power on the three below me. Every bit of power within my grasp enhances the heat within the tunnel. The flame twists and burns through each contour and opening I can find on the creatures below. Intense heat burns their lungs and stomach just as much as it does their skin and fur.

Their screams combine in a high-pitched squeal. No longer do they care for me. The only thing they can focus on is scrubbing away at their simmering skin. They fall down the tunnel, uncaring to grasp for a handhold. The sheen of bright yellow liquefied rock coating the tube does nothing to slow their fall.

Far above, I feel the energy flowing into me from the glow-bugs caught in the explosion. As much as I'd love to revel in the feeling and grasp for as many of them as I can, I need to make sure of this. I don't know how resistant their bodies are to heat and fire, so I need to put my all into it.

I take a hold of the goop-enhanced blaze above my head and force it down. It passes my body, and only because I know Grímr is still with me do I not relish in the heat. I push it down in a raging torrent toward my pursuers.

Well, they aren't really pursuers anymore.

I watch as they fall against the ground in the tunnel below, my flames never relenting with their intention to cremate these—now furless—beasts alive.

Their screams and desperate pleas are music to my ears after they tried so hard to catch me. After they ambushed my team.

I don't believe their words about having killed Remus and Tetsu. Those two are far too tough to be killed so easily. No, I just need to make some distance and they'll find their way back to me.

The one I'm most worried for is Jav. These tight tunnels are the complete opposite of his favored environment for fighting. Not to mention he doesn't have anywhere near the strength of the other two to fight in close quarters.

The screams have gone quiet. I let out a sigh of relief and calm the rapid breaths I hadn't realized I'd been taking. The energy from the dead creatures below trickles up to me, filling me with power comparable to the dahu, if a bit lower.

The strength of their energy is intense, but still beaten by the sheer quantity of glow-bugs I burned through above.

Even with the explosive power of the substance lining the walls of this shaft, I hadn't been sure if it would work. People enhanced to that point just seem so untouchable. My flames themselves couldn't come close to hurting them. Well, unless taking away their fur coat and leaving them bare to the world counts. But once past the surface layer, I can't burn further.

Still, despite my weakness, I beat them. I may have had to use the environment to my advantage, but I won. It feels good.

And that thought immediately makes me feel guilty. The others are still stuck down there with who knows how many of those creatures. Three made it past them, so it's hard to believe they are still holding a strong defense. I hope they made it away okay. If they made it away with Jav, I'm sure they'll be able to track down where I've gone. I just need to trust in them for now.

I take out the heat from the walls so I don't have too much trouble climbing up. There might not have been much magma, but it still makes a layer between me and the hard rock that I can actually grasp.

Just as I'm about to resume my climb, the ground shakes and a loud bang crashes through me from above. Not long after, a familiar screech echoes down to me.

That monstrosity, again? Seriously?

I can't help but lament my fate as the giant above lumbers around without care for who might be in a hurry to leave these tunnels. It tears through the earth above, but there is a long distance it needs to dig before it can reach me. In no time soon will it reach me, but it's only a matter of time before more of those slender rodents chase me up from below.

Hopefully, they'll be hesitant to chase me once they see the still burning corpses of their comrades below.

For now, I can do nothing but wait for the giant arachnid above to leave. The earth shakes around me. Will it leave before the beings below me chase me up? Without the help of the explosive liquid, there is no chance I'll be able to fend off any more.

Every second that passes feels like an eternity. I can feel the giant above continuing to investigate what must have been a bright flash of light. What's below me is unknown. Are they sneaking up on me? I saw how effective their camouflage was; could they be closing in on me in this very tunnel without my knowledge?

I blast a jet of flame through the chute below just to be safe. I don't feel the stealth-rats— for lack of a name—but it doesn't reassure me much.

The shaking from the arachnid above recedes. It is finally moving away.

Slowly and quietly, I creep up the tunnel. I pull back on my flame, letting the tunnel go dark. Aware that danger is both above and below, I keep my eyes peeled.

Nothing makes a noise as I breach the surface into the enormous cavern, to my relief. No scraping from below and the monstrosity has lost interest, returning to the darkness out of sight.

I pull my hood down, letting Grímr escape from the tight spot at the back of my neck. He looks around at the far swathes of glow-bugs before looking back at me. His small face isn't exactly expressive, but the way his front legs softly pat me, I'm sure he's trying to be supportive.

A wry laugh escapes my lips. I don't deserve his sympathy. I ran without a second thought, not even considering the possibility of helping. If I'd lit the stealth-rats alight, while I probably couldn't have hurt them, the shock of their burning fur could have given my team the time they needed to escape.

What am I supposed to do now?

I know I need to move away from this tunnel. I can hope the stealth-rats don't follow me up here all I want, but it's best not to leave it to chance.

Like the last time I was in this cavern—I assume it's the same one—Grímr and I avoid the dark spaces empty of glow-bugs. As we move between the swathes of flying insects that keep their distance, I can't help but be tempted. If I could eat all these lights bursting with energy, I'd grow faster than I'd ever thought possible.

If I can just get my flames hot enough to burn through the stealth-rat's skin, I won't need to worry.

Of course, I can't just spread my flames wide and reach for them. That would be just asking for those monstrosities to swarm. So, until I figure things out, I'll have to abstain.

Do I leave clear markings of the path I travel? Or do I hope they can find me without it? If I make the path I've taken too clear, the stealth-rats could use it to track me as well.

I do not know where to go, so I just pick a random direction and walk.

"Solvei." I hear Jav's voice behind me.

They found me far quicker than expected. I turn as Jav lands on the ground before me. A clear lack of the other two following him.

He looks relieved to see me. I sure feel the same way. "You got out safe," he says with a sigh.

"Where are the others?" I ask. Grímr crawls up my arm and with the way he looks at Jav, I'm sure he's as concerned as I am.

The scornful grimace that graces his features is not the response I wanted to see.

"They're not dead," he says, but despite his words, he still looks frustrated. "Those things took them as captives. They are strong, all of them. They overwhelmed us. It's only because of their unfamiliarity with the dohrni and volans that I could escape. Remus flung me away before they could grab him again."

They are alive at least, but being taken prisoner sounds just as bad as death.

I mean, my interaction with the stealth-rats was enough for me to know they were strong, but it's hard to believe those two could really be beaten.

"We have to get them back!" Jav raises his head to look me in the eye. His tiny hands clench by his side.

"How?" I ask. I want to get them back as much as Jav, but they beat our strongest team members. How could the three of us hope to take them on? Seriously, I'm the biggest amongst us now.

Jav turns his head away. "I . . . don't know." He looks off into the distant glow-bugs before snapping back to me. "First, we should find a body for Grímr. Those shadows we've hesitated from approaching, we'll have to enter them, hope there is something usable."

I glance at the closest of the dark spots. This is something I wanted to do before we split with Tetsu and Remus, but doing so with only our strength makes me hesitate.

"How well can you fight without being thrown?"

"Decently. The added momentum from Remus's throws is incredible, but don't doubt for a second that I can't fight without him."

Okay, that's good to know, but my own strength is still a problem. If whatever we face is immune to my flames, then I might as well not be here. I need to get my spearmanship to where I can actually be effective. How much time do we have to get our team back?

I clamp my fists over the pole of the weapon in my hands. There's no point pondering. I need to practice immediately. The less time wasted, the better.

We are still too close to the exit of that tunnel that leads to the cave system underneath us. I'll create some distance, then get my spear to the point where it is usable.

"Hey, where are you going?" Jav calls as he scrambles up my leg and sits on the shoulder opposite where Grímr perches.

"You think we should stay near the exit of that tunnel?"

"Ah. Right," he says dumbly. His eyes drop to the tear through the chest of my outfit. "What happened?"

I trace the tear in the fabric with a finger. "One of those stealth-rats shoved its arm through my chest," I say. "Sorry for damaging your gift."

"Don't worry about it. Once we have some time, I'll fix it up for you."

I nod in thanks. We are going to free Remus and Tetsu. We will as soon as I figure out how to stop my head from screaming at me to abandon them and run.

I hope nothing bad happens while I prepare.

CHAPTER THIRTY-SIX

Grímr's New Body

I focus on my body. The flames of my very being twist and condense under my will. With a deep breath, I push my body further than I have before. As long as my flames weren't visible, I'd never had a reason to reach beyond. Until now.

When my body is in this controlled state, it expends less energy, but pushing it this far has never been worth the mental strain, despite the possible increased efficiency.

Another breath and I wrestle with my control to push myself one step more. It's hard. I can feel a headache coming on from the strain, but I need to try. I don't need to reach the same strength as the others, just enough to pierce the skin of whatever creature we find hiding in the shadows.

With all my concentration, I condense my body, but even swinging my spear in this mental state might be hard. I don't really need to worry about slipping to where my flames become visible; I've grown enough that it isn't an issue anymore. Unless I push myself now, I won't be able to manage this level of control in a fight.

The goal is to pierce the stealth-rats' skin. If I can do that, then I'll have nothing to worry about. I don't need to worry about being hit. In fact, I can use their attacks to my advantage. I doubt they'll expect their attacks to be pointless to me. The only one of them that knows is nothing more than a pile of ash.

I don't need to be the most skilled spear-user. I just need them to think they got me so I can pierce them before they realize their mistake.

No! There's no reason to risk myself for those two. Just leave them and find another way.

My focus collapses at the intrusive thought. I'm not sure how I'm supposed to move forward with their rescue when my own mind refuses to agree with me.

I try to enter my mind and forcefully unravel the knot in my mental strands, but it is a wasted effort. I can rearrange some of the loose threads that represent many of my thoughts or desires in line with the rope's overall direction, but the knot remains stiff.

I can hardly leave my team behind. If I am the only one to get out, I would feel horrible.

Why? I'll be free. Who cares about those who put me in this position in the first place?

I know they did, but I don't want to leave Remus and Tetsu behind. Nobody deserves to be trapped. They don't deserve to be imprisoned by those stealth-rats.

But helping them doesn't help me escape. So there is no point in doing so.

Yes, it does. There's no way I can escape with my strength as is. I need them for their strength at the very least.

The knot is quiet. Does that mean it's finally agreeing with me?

I sigh in relief before returning my focus to my body. There's no time to waste.

I return my body to the same level of physicality as before. With my spear in hand, I strain my mind to keep my body steady as I strike the weapon forward. The bladed tip bounces off the stalagmite I used as a target. I leave only a scratch on the rock.

There has to be something else to it. My swing is definitely stronger, but it still doesn't come close to what I need. I've a few ideas if I could practice with my flame, but those monstrosities are attracted to any light I give off, so I can't try them out.

I close my eyes again and bring my body back to the limit I can continually manage. The strike with my weapon is momentary. I don't need to hold my body in its extra physical state for any longer than the attack takes to hit.

Once more readying my weapon, I step forward and command an impulse through my body. For an instant, I feel the spear move with an ease I couldn't have managed before. Again, the blade rebounds off stone. With the impulse of control ending, the spear jerks my arms wide.

A jolt of pain runs through my mind from the backlash of the sudden, explosive push past my limit. My control is lacking, but this is still far more than I could have accomplished back in my tribe.

The stalagmite has a rather large indent marring its surface now. It's not the clean cut I was hoping for, but it's still pretty good progress.

"Can you not be quiet with your practice? What if you bring down one of those massive things?" Jav complains as he looks nervously up at the ceiling.

He's almost a completely different person without Remus by his side. His nervousness and impatience are almost contagious, but I can't let myself fall victim to those if I want to have a chance of escape. It's something that the knot is actually useful for. I can feel a catalogue of emotions—primarily fear—that I'm able to work around because of the knot. Something far better for my survival than the amplification of those feelings as the last version of the knot caused.

"What's a bit of training going to help right now? We should be looking for a body for Grímr."

"No. A few hours won't make a difference if they've taken Remus and Tetsu captive. I need at least enough strength to not be worthless in the fight. Or do you think you can take on whatever's in those shadows alone?"

"It's not like we can't escape if things get tough."

"Do you really want to stake our lives on that?" I ask. "We need to be as prepared as we can. At the moment, I won't be able to pierce most creatures' skin. If I can get to that point in only a few hours, don't you think that's worth it?"

He grunts and digs his feet through the loose soil, but says nothing. That's enough of a confirmation for me. Time to push that impulse as far as it can go. I'm not looking forward to the headache that's coming.

"So, what do we have to do for Grímr to take a body?" I ask as we creep toward an area void of glow-bugs that isn't so large as to hide one of those arachnid monstrosities.

"Incapacitate, but don't kill it. Doesn't matter if we cause some damage, as long as it can't scratch at Grímr."

"What if I burn it?"

He glances up at me as he crawls along the ground. "No fire. We don't want to attract anything that's not what's in front of us. Let loose only if there's no other option."

We still have no idea what we're sneaking up on, so we split to approach from differing directions. As I move to the side, I notice something strange. The bugs that should be visible on the other side of the dark area disappear. The glowing lights dim as I put the darkness between me and the bugs.

Is the darkness not caused by a lack of bugs? The light doesn't cut off immediately, so I don't think it is something solid blocking the way.

Whatever it is, I'll figure it out when I'm closer.

I approach with my spear raised, ready to strike at a moment's notice. I keep my eyes peeled for anything that might attack. From the corner of my eyes, I notice that the light behind me dims now as well.

I stop and check the darkness again. The way everything goes dark reminds me far too much of the Void Fog for my liking. I stare into the darkness. No matter how much it worries me, I know this isn't the Void. It doesn't have that same feeling. This darkness doesn't have that intense emptiness I've only ever felt from the Void Fog.

I can't see Jav through this darkness. Hopefully, we'll reach the creature at the same time.

A rustling noise of something sliding across soil and stone reaches me. The darkness suddenly intensifies to where the bugs behind me disappear.

I hear a startled yelp from Jav through the darkness ahead of me. I rush forward. Jav must have been attacked before I was ready.

My feet almost stumble right into him when he finally comes into view. The shroud surrounding us makes it so I can barely make out his outline. In fact, the only reason I can see him is because he's moving. Wait, no. As I look closer, I realize there's something moving under him. Somehow, even though it's as close as Jav is, it is almost impossible to see.

"Sit still," he grunts at the creature underneath him. "Solvei, bring Grímr here. It's not ideal, but it'll do for now."

I do as he says and carry Grímr closer to the creature Jav is struggling to grapple with. It's a rather strange sight; Jav obviously has far more strength than whatever it is, but considering it is three times larger than him, it throws Jav around. He tries to dig his feet into the ground, but the loose soil hardly helps.

I crouch down over the creature and put my weight into holding it still. Now that I know my weight increases with greater control in my body, it makes this easier, but the lizard below me still jerks me around with strength I can't compete with.

Grímr crawls down my arm and up the spine of the creature. Only now that I'm as close as I am can I see it properly. A pale, white lizard with short legs wriggles under my arms. Its head is wider than its body and has what I think are gills at the back. Aren't gills only for fish? There isn't any water around, is there?

Jav lets me take over the job of pinning the thin lizard. Instead, he grasps its head and front legs and holds them tight. I realize why the moment Grímr cuts into the back of its neck. Its struggles until then feel like token efforts in comparison. It bucks me off and I'm forced to dive back on it in an awkward position to keep its back legs from clawing at Grímr.

Grímr himself is fast and efficient. Somehow avoiding many of the blood vessels as he cuts a path into its spine. Once he has dug deep enough, he slides each of his thin legs into the cut and buries himself inside.

The lizard's desperate struggles collapse into disorderly twitches. It continues sporadically twitching for almost a minute before it stops moving.

Jav lets go and I follow his lead, giving the white lizard space. The first thing I notice is that the darkness has receded and I can see the glow-bugs again.

The lizard's body jerks again. I look to Jav, but as he does nothing but watch, I remain still. A few more twitches along its body and I watch as it rises to its feet. The lizard's head twists to look our way and I notice for the first time, it doesn't have eyes.

"Everything good, Grímr?" Jav asks.

The lizard, no, Grímr, opens his mouth and hisses in response. Upon hearing himself, he stops and settles with a nod of his head.

"All right. We'll have to look for a stronger body. Something you'll actually be able to fight with. But for now, you'll have to settle with that."

As I watch the lizard that Grímr has taken as his skin, I can't help but think about the darkness it could shroud itself in. "Hey, Grímr. Do you think you'd be able to recreate that darkness?"

I'm not sure whether it's possible. Grímr might be able to take over its body, but does that mean he can replicate their abilities?

He tilts his head at me, but he doesn't move, so I can only imagine he is trying. His white, scaled tail twitches and his back legs jerk forward, sending him toppling. Just as I'm about to drop to my knees and see if he's okay, the area around him darkens.

The darkness only surrounds Grímr. Not nearly as wide-spanning as the lizard managed, but he succeeds in shrouding himself in a black mist that makes him almost impossible to spot in the dark cave. It's quite the amazing ability. It's hard to say whether this would beat the camouflage of the stealth-rats.

"Looking for a stronger creature might be unnecessary for now." I try to look Grímr in the eye before remembering he doesn't have any. "What do you think about sneaking into those stealth-rats' camp?"

CHAPTER THIRTY-SEVEN

Scouting the Captors

Getting Grímr a body that can actually fight takes far more precedence at the moment," Jav says. "How could we help Remus and Bunny without the strength he can give? What would sneaking in help, if we can't fight our way out?"

"Any creature that could have a chance against those stealth-rats is not something the two of us could hold down long enough for Grímr to take over. Did you not see how we were tossed around by a lizard as weak as that one?" I gesture to Grímr, before putting down my hand, realizing I might as well have called Grímr weak.

"We're better off getting reassurance that they are still okay first before we enact any stupid frontal assault," I say.

Jav grits his teeth as he considers my words. "And what if he's discovered? He won't get out in a body like that."

I hesitate. I'd been so focused on actually moving forward with my plan, I hadn't considered the danger Grímr would be in.

This knot . . . I really need to get a proper awareness of how it is influencing me.

At a tugging on my leg, I look down to catch Grímr winding his way up my body in his new, lithe form. Similar to a snake, he wraps around my torso and rests his head and forelegs on my shoulder.

Is this his way of agreeing with my idea?

He nods his head to me, reading my thoughts. I don't want him to risk himself, especially against the competent hiders he'll be trying to sneak past, but I don't have a better idea.

Jav lets out another frustrated grunt and paces back and forth before us.

"Even if that's what you both think is best, we'll still have to wait until Grímr can control that body well enough for him to actually go through with it. If we need more strength by then, it'll be too late to get him something better."

"I still think this would be better," I say. "We can hardly attack them head on. You two could sneak in and free Remus and Tetsu while I distract them. If we can find another of those fungi bug-traps, I might even hurt some of them while you and the others run."

I'm really liking how this plan is looking now, but we still need to get information first. Grímr needs to sneak in so we can learn where they are being held. I also want to know about that stealth-rat that could destroy Tetsu's weapon with a glance. Is it unique to that one or are more capable of doing it? I didn't see any mage markings on him, so it might be something different.

Wait, Grímr still can't talk. So how will he tell us of what he sees?

"How are we going to communicate?" I say to the lizard resting on my shoulder.

Grímr just shrugs at me.

"Give it time," Jav says. "He can make some slight alterations to its biology. I wouldn't at all be surprised if that's the first thing he's working on, considering he's not practicing his walking or that darkness-creation ability."

Grímr tilts his head away slightly. Somehow, he manages to look sheepish even without eyes.

Well, if we have to wait for Grímr anyway, I might as well get back to it. With my spear grasped tightly in my hands, I thrust forward at an imaginary enemy. I try to synchronize the sudden, intense increase to my physicality as best I can with the moment it is supposed to hit. I'm getting better, but I still have a long way to go.

I didn't think I'd be so worried for him. After he left, I couldn't stop thinking about all the things that might go wrong sneaking into those stealth-rat's encampment.

This new body of Grímr's can climb walls with almost more ease than it can walk along the ground. Combined with the shrouding ability it has to hide itself, there should be no chance of him being discovered.

But I can't help but remember the stealth-rats hiding along the ceiling to ambush us. What if Grímr walks over one of them without seeing them? I very much doubt he'd be able to stay hidden if he's literally touching one.

I am glad that the stealth-rats don't make fires. If they light the cave even the slightest, they would see the abnormally dark patch crawling along the stone ceiling.

It took a good few hours before Grímr was confident enough in his body to head down into the tunnels below. In that time, I've improved to where I can slice through stalagmites. It's still to be seen whether it's enough to pierce the skin of those with a decent enough enhancement.

Any attempt to push my control further is like hitting a stone wall. It will be a long-term effort to improve. In the meantime, I'll have to try some other ways to better my fighting ability. A few of my ideas will have to wait until we're out of this cavern, though; the monstrosities lurking above aren't as ignorant to bright lights as they are to sound.

Jav, being the only one amongst us with nothing to do in the meantime, struggled immensely with impatience. Many times as Grímr and I prepared ourselves, he would pressure us to hurry, but would achieve nothing other than disrupting our focus.

I may have gotten annoyed at him at some point and told him to go for a walk. It was probably not a good time for him to be wandering by himself, but by the time he came back, Grímr was ready.

I look down the tunnel once more, worried about how long Grímr is taking. He's been gone near two hours now. Longer than I expected him to be gone.

"I've got good, bad, and worse news." Grímr pops out of nowhere, the shadow of the shaft receding before my eyes. "From what I heard, they are both still alive. Unfortunately, they haven't been kept here. They are being sent back through the mountain, toward the mermineae homeland. That's what they call themselves: mermineae."

Grímr's voice sounds strange now. Not the familiar deep growl of his panther body, but a much lighter hissing tone. It's hard to pin the voice as Grímr's after I got so used to his last one.

"That's great! We can catch them off guard in transport." Jav grins for the first time since we landed in this mess.

"And that's where the worse news comes in. There's more mermineae that way. A lot more."

That wipes the smile off Jav's face, but after a moment of thought, he doesn't seem too disappointed. "That's still good. It doesn't matter how many there are, there's no way they can cover every tunnel. As long as these caves branch as often as they have, we'll be able to find a place to ambush them."

"How are we going to track them?" I ask. We can't just walk along the path that the mermineae frequent. I'd rather not be found out before we can help our team.

"Grímr and I will find where they're heading. We'll worry about how we're going to free them once we've decided on a place for the ambush."

"What about me?" I ask, but Grímr turns and speaks to Jav before he can answer. I wonder why he even bothers turning his head if he can't see in that body?

"I don't like the idea of leaving her alone. You should stay with her."

Jav frowns. He obviously doesn't like the idea, but he doesn't outright refute it.

To be honest, I don't like it either. I want them to believe I can take care of myself. It's true that each of them are stronger than me, but that doesn't mean I can't survive on my own. Also, I haven't really forgiven them for what they did to me. The altered knot has let me push past it, but what they did was horrible.

"I'll be fine by myself. You two should find the rest of our team."

My biggest concern at the moment is Jav. He's been acting far more agitated than I've come to expect from him. I'm worried about being alone with him. I don't know if he might lash out from the stress or chase after Grímr when he leaves.

Jav jumps at the chance to go after Remus. "She'll be fine. We go find the two, then we meet up with her before hitting them."

Grímr looks at me, unsure . . . or at least that's what his body language expresses. The lizard face doesn't seem to move much. "Are you sure, Solvei?"

I nod to let him know I'll be fine.

"All right. We'll find a route that the mermineae don't use and come back for you. We'll be quick. Stay here and wait for us."

Jav tugs his tail, and they're heading down the vertical tunnel before I can say goodbye.

Well . . . now I'm alone for the first time in a while. I can either wait here and practice my spear some more, or I can go for a bit of a wander. They won't be back for a good few hours. Will that be enough time for me to find another mushroom tube?

I lick my lips in anticipation.

I shake my head at the greedy thoughts. We need the explosive jam to help fight off the mermineae. I can't be thinking of eating now. We especially can't afford to have one of those giant monstrosities forcing me into the lower tunnels right now.

I'll just find one of the fungi traps and take some of the viscous substance and that will be all. No burning through the immense swathes of nutritious, tasty glow-bugs. No matter how tempting it might be.

I avoid the dark patches as I look for my target. Those lizards might not be the most dangerous, but there's no reason to believe they are the only creatures lurking in the shadows. It's possible we got lucky and found the only non-deadly creature when we got that body for Grímr. It doesn't help that many of the shadows move, so I have to keep an eye out in case something is sneaking up on me.

I trek forward, looking for any signs of another bug trap. A good hour passes before something finally catches my eye. The glow-bugs in the air have an ever so slight bias of moving to my right. It's unnoticeable if you look at the bugs themselves, but it becomes apparent when I cast my focus wide along the clouds of glowing lights.

As I walk with the bugs, they gradually increase their speed until they're all moving in cohesion toward a point ahead of me.

I've found another fungi trap. The flat, plate-like mushrooms grow out of the ground in a good five-meter radius of the funnel the glow-bugs flow into. I step on the mushrooms, and they are just as soft and springy as I remember.

When I make it above the hole, I have to hold myself back from flaring out at the bugs surrounding me. Having so much energy around me, but being unable to take a bite, is almost torturous.

I must have forgotten what happened the last time we came so close to this thing. Distracted by the surrounding bugs, I'm splattered with a face full of goop.

Only barely do I stop myself from reacting instinctively and burning the substance. It's a liquid—even if viscous—but it doesn't hurt like water.

With my hands, I wipe the explosive jam off my face. The glow-bugs are swarming already. Their tiny maws biting at both the substance and my body underneath. As their mandibles pierce through my solid flame, they pop. Their tiny bodies exploding from the flames they try to eat.

Even as hundreds of crackles declare the death of bugs over my arms, chest and face, I clamp down on my inner flame. I can't let the explosive liquid go up in flames right now. Both because I need it for our fight against the mermineae and the monstrosities that crawl over the ceiling of the cavern.

I snap off a few of the platelet mushrooms below my feet and wipe the jam off my body. Taking a few more of the mushrooms, I reach into the tunnel and pull a thick layer off the walls. I use a few more of the fungi to create a makeshift container. Hopefully, the bugs won't be able to eat through it before it can be of use.

With my goal in hand and a continual intake of energy in the form of tiny zaps around my body, I head back to the tunnel I was told to wait in.

As I walk, swathes of the bugs follow in my trail, each of them attracted to the smell of the jam I'm carrying. It's worrying; the mushroom seems rather resistant to their mandibles, considering they could pierce through the enhanced skin of my teammates, but they still find their way to the viscous liquid. If Grímr and Jav take too long, I might not have any left.

I drop into the tunnel. Low enough that the creatures above won't see the light from my fire, but high enough that I'll have time to react to anyone coming from below. While I wait, I'm treated to a decent flow of lights that feed themselves to me.

I can tell immediately when Grímr and Jav are back. Despite the light of burning bugs, the tunnel goes dark. The cloud of darkness deepens around me before receding and leaving Grímr in view.

Just Grímr.

"Where's Jav?" I ask as I get up, ready to head down into the tunnels.

Grímr hisses. Upon hearing himself, he stops and tries to speak again, his voice still layered with an annoyed hiss. "Jav is an idiot."

CHAPTER THIRTY-EIGHT

New Plan

The idiot didn't stick to the plan. Jav jumped to try to free Remus the moment he thought we were alone with them."

"Were they expecting you? How did you get out?" I ask.

"I don't think they were, but they camouflage themselves when they're resting. Jav succeeded in nothing but getting himself caught. They didn't even need to put in much effort. I stayed out of it. I should have helped, but there was nothing I could have done."

A groan escapes my throat. I knew Jav was wound up, but I never thought he would do something so stupid. We already had a plan.

"Why would they capture them? Why not kill them?" When the Henosis imprisoned me, it was for a very specific purpose. But the mermineae didn't even know we were down here with them until we dropped on top of their camp. What could they want from them?

"Information, I'd guess," Grímr hisses. "I overheard something about orders from a Viisin, but I'm not sure what to make of that. With how close the mermineae encampments are to the nations of the pact, they would be after any source of info they can find. But this is concerning; what are their intentions on this side of the Alps?"

We remain quiet for a time, mulling over the loss of another member of our team. It's just the two of us now. It's almost funny how the ones who betrayed my trust and thrust me down here in the first place are the ones who have been trapped themselves. Like the world itself is punishing them.

Without Jav, the chance of us freeing our team is slim. As small as he was, he was still our strongest fighter. At least, while Grímr is stuck in this body. Even if we were to find a stronger creature now, my flames can do nothing but destroy any body we intend to use. At least Jav could have cut their tendons without making the creature unusable.

No point thinking about what might have happened had Jav not been a fool.

"What do we do now?" I'm not about to make the same mistake as Jav and throw what freedom I have away. I'd only been able to consider the thought because we might have actually stood a chance of freeing them if we were smart.

Only if we were smart.

There was no way we could have fought the mermineae. If we had Jav with us, escaping to the large cavern was possible. It's not like we needed to fight the mermineae to free Remus and Tetsu. A decent enough distraction would have been good enough.

"I don't know," Grímr starts. "I can keep following them. This creature's stealth works well enough, but there's not much we can do to help them."

I should just leave them down here.

The twist in my desires decides to show itself again. As much as I'd love to leave Jav to the fate his own impatience brought, I don't want to abandon them.

I still need a way out. There's no way for me to free them, but if we follow the merminea captors, they'll eventually lead us out of this labyrinth of caves and tunnels back into the open air.

My argument appeases the knot of my psyche. Despite how it can twist my thoughts in ways that disgust me, I prefer this so much more over the uncontrollable fear that used to be in its place. With its cold logic, I can actually argue my point.

I'll just need to see whether it remains tied to my surface thoughts after I escape, or recedes like the phobia did. It'll be nice if I can actually enter buildings now.

Still, I'm not looking forward to the time it doesn't agree with my arguments. I can only imagine it's as cooperative as it is because I do not know any other way. Would it force me to abandon Grímr if the opportunity presents itself? I can't help but worry about the possibility.

I glance up at the wall of flame burning above. The flow of glow-bugs suiciding into my waiting stomach has slowed, but many still chase the sweet taste out of their reach.

I joined this team to get strong, to grow my power. Even if it's not the way they expected, nor the way I wanted, they've brought me to the perfect place to achieve that promise.

"Do you think you could follow them and guide me along the cavern above?" I ask, not turning from the crackling bugs. "I might as well make use of the time we're stuck down here."

"I can, sure. But is there even any point? I doubt the two of us could do much to help."

"Not as we are, no. The mermineae are traveling to the other side of the Alps, right? That will not be a short trip. What's to say things won't change by the time we reach the other side?" I know he can't see me, but I give him an earnest stare. What I'm going to do may or may not be entirely intelligent, but it's the best option I have.

"What are you thinking?"

"We never got around to doing the ritual on them, but did you know those glow-bugs give an insane amount of energy?" A slight chuckle escapes my lips. "I'm going to be detonating every bug trap I can find."

I was determined when I made the declaration, but now that I actually have to go through with it, I can't stop my growing wariness. I'm excited to burn through another bug trap, but also terrified of the arachnid monstrosities that follow.

Those things give me the same feeling I got from Hund. Even able to deform into intangible flames as I can, the monstrous beast would have no trouble killing me.

After all the time I've spent in the cavern, I've learned they don't react to sound. I can make as much of a racket as I want and yet they never drop to look. Still, they are up there, somewhere, so I'm always nervous they might drop unexpectedly.

When I reach the fungi tunnel, I dive in. I get the goop all over me, but it hardly matters when it'll explode in a few moments. I wriggle down as far as I can with the substance slowing my movement.

As soon as I let my body relax, the tunnel explodes around me. A thrum of power blasts through me and I relish in the heat that results. So much hotter than anything I can yet make. Hopefully, that changes soon.

I'm already far stronger than I should be for my age. My flames are already growing to a lighter shade of orange. Soon, I might even reach a bright yellow; the color of a warrior. If this works out the way I hope it does, I wonder how hot I'll get? Maybe my flame will reach the same blue that only Elder Cyrus could reach.

I wonder how other áed would react to me? The binding I have isn't something any but the most dedicated achieve, but I was able to improve it in an incredibly roundabout way. The heat of my flame is far greater than should be possible for my age. I've consumed many a strong creature, but the wasteland isn't exactly empty of its own nourishing beasts.

Isn't it too strange that I've grown as I have from so few creatures and people? Chameleons and colossal-worms wouldn't be short of energy, and while we avoided them in most circumstances, there have been occasions where one would be taken down. Why were there so many adults who could only manage a yellow flame and nothing more with those creatures around?

At the growth rate I've experienced in the past months, there should have been more with greater flames. Is it just easier to reach the golden flame than anything higher? Do the creatures out along the Titan Alps just give more energy than those back in the wasteland? Or has the Void Fog changed more than my mind and binding?

I'm snapped out of my thoughts by the loud pounding of the arachnid above. This one is quite determined to dig out the source of flames.

The ground quakes and loose rock tumbles on my head. I pull back on the remaining flames, snuffing the light from the tunnel. The monstrosity continues to tear through the ground after me. Nervous that it'll get close soon, I drop farther down the shaft.

Despite how similar it feels, I'm glad this thing isn't actually a Titan. It can't devastate the earth with its sheer presence like the truly incomprehensible being did.

I shake my head at the thought. Why am I comparing the capabilities of monsters? It's a bit like putting a dingo and a colossal-worm next to each other while I'm a jerboa. Either would squish me.

The arachnid eventually loses interest and the sounds of its heavy limbs tapping against the ground fade. I count out the next ten minutes before I risk climbing up.

I say it's nothing similar to a Titan, but it's hard to think that when looking at the damage it leaves in the wake of its attempt to dig me out. A good one-hundred-meter deep crater is all that's left of the mushroom ring. Although, it's hard to prove whether the monstrosity or my explosion destroyed it.

No sign of the arachnid, thankfully. If I can replicate this as many times as possible on the chase after my team, I might even stand side by side with them in a fight.

Well, one can hope.

I'll need to see if even a small flame will attract those arachnids. If I can switch forms and fly around as a bird, I could reach many more fungi traps than only walking would allow. It might be harder for Grímr to find me, but I can always make regular trips back to see if he's looking for me.

Well, no time like the present. I move back down the crater until I feel safe enough, then send out some of my inner flame in the shape and size of my falcon form. It flies away from my hiding spot as quickly as I can manage. My control is what lets it fly, not the wings, but I still make it flap to at least give it the appearance of a living creature.

Far from what I expect, nothing drops from above. Instead, in moments of flying above the swarm of glow-bugs, something absolutely massive rockets through my bird. My flames scatter over the creature's exoskeleton and the picture it paints does nothing to reassure me.

A centipede. But somehow far larger than the ones we'd seen in the higher cavern and on the surface. No, this is bigger. Ten times larger, at the very least.

It doesn't make a sound after decimating my flames. Something that big should shake the earth when it falls to the ground again. But no, there isn't so much as a whisper.

Even disregarding its silence, there's no way that thing should have been able to hide. None of the shadows I've seen would be large enough to hold it. There's not a chance it could hide under the swarm of lights; its massive size wouldn't allow it.

Has that thing been there the entire time I've been moving through this cavern? Where has it been hiding?

I'm suddenly overcome with dread and hesitate to move forward with my plan. What else waits to crush me in a lapse of awareness?

The feeling doesn't last long. My psyche's knot of desire quickly suppresses the tightness in my chest. I let out a calming breath. It doesn't matter what else is invisible to me; this is the only plan I have. I can't give up on it just because there is another creature I have to add to my list. I'll get nowhere if I hesitate at every obstacle. Especially when the obstacles are likely to punish me for that hesitation.

Still, it's probably better I wait down in this hole of mine for a bit.

Too bad flying is out of the question. That would have sped up progress immensely. I shouldn't be surprised the world doesn't want to make my life easy. It hasn't so far, why would it now?

CHAPTER THIRTY-NINE

What Lurks in Shadows

Three days and ten explosions later, I worry how long Grímr is taking to join me. It shouldn't be hard for the little blind lizard to follow my trail; his nose is good enough to pick out the burning remains of my . . . exuberance, from hours away.

It shouldn't be a challenge for him to find the scorched base of the tunnels that have been detonated. And yet, he's late.

I continue forward, looking for more fungi tubes to blow up. The energy I've gained from the glow-bugs so far hasn't been enough to leave a visible change to my flame, but I can feel the incremental growth with each firestorm.

Without Grímr by my side, I've felt far more lonely than I expected. The knot suppresses my emotions from influencing my actions, but walking toward the unknown alone leaves me with a tension in my chest that I can't ignore. It won't stop me from advancing, but I still feel uncomfortable. The only time the feeling recedes is when I'm enjoying the intense heat. If only it lasted longer.

As I continue forward, toward what I think is the other side of the Alps, I spot a strange dimming in the wall of lights before me. The density of glow-bugs decreases. Curious but wary, I approach slowly. It's not a shadow like I'm used to seeing, just a gradual reduction of lights the farther forward I travel. I've seen too many dangerous things in this cavern, so I approach with as much care as I can.

Beyond the lights, there is nothing. A vast expanse of darkness that expands as far as I can see. Not a single glow-bug within the darkness. It's almost like an invisible wall prevents them from passing a certain point.

A well of dread rises in my chest as I peer into the darkness. Is there something in there? Another massive creature that the glow-bugs know to avoid?

I stumble backward before catching myself. Not panicking, I ever so slowly back into the embracing swathes of lights. That monstrous centipede could hide amongst the lights somehow, despite its size. I don't want to know what doesn't even bother hiding.

I return to the last tube I exploded. The darkness expands so far in each direction, it will take days to move around it. Probably. I also want to be near my hiding hole in case it moves. The arachnids above react incredibly predictably and that centipede hasn't shown itself other than that one time, but who knows how this third giant might react?

For now, I'm just going to wait right here until Grímr is back.

Grímr is late.

Each hour that passes—or at least what I assume is an hour—I grow more agitated. Doing nothing like this is a waste of time. I want to get out there and continue my growth, or progress through the Alps. Anything to make it feel like what I'm doing actually has worth.

I've been practicing my spear, but I've hit a wall. No matter how hard I try, I can't push my control any further. My swings refuse to hit harder. What I really need now is something to practice on. I can't do much more just swinging at nothing.

As much as I dislike the idea, I'll have to approach one of those shadows eventually. If there are creatures I can handle in them, it will be an incredible help to my improvement. I still have fought no one other than Tetsu with my spear. Before I'm forced into an encounter with those mermineae, I want to be comfortable with my weapon. As it is, I'm not even confident I'd be able to scratch them.

"Solvei."

I jump to my feet and point my spear toward the voice, before realizing my mistake and lowering it. The black mist disperses around Grímr's body.

"Don't do that. I could have stabbed you," I grouch.

"You haven't moved as far as I expected." He brushes off my gripes. "Why'd you stop moving?" he asks as he tilts his head toward the massive shadow.

"There's something ahead. Something huge. I wanted to wait for you before trying to move around it. What took so long?"

"Ah. I found another of those tunnels you've been exploding. I was hoping to catch you after you blew the one I found. Anyway, come. There's a path to the next one with no scent of the mermineae." He drops into the vertical shaft.

I follow close behind. I'm glad to see he's still okay and hasn't been discovered.

"You've been loud lately. I'm surprised the mermineae haven't been able to hear you. I can almost feel the ground shaking from your explosions." He says as he crawls into the tunnel below. "You'll be careful, won't you? Don't do anything reckless."

"Grímr, look where we are. Simply being here is reckless. Anything could be hiding where we can't see." While my mind jumps to the immense centipede I'd seen, there's no reason to worry him further.

"I still don't want anything to happen. I've overheard some of the mermineae's conversations. It's clear they aren't native to these tunnels, but it'll be a good couple of months before they reach their destination. Promise me you won't take any rash actions."

I nod seriously to him before realizing the pointlessness of the action. "I'll be careful," I say. "But you have to promise the same."

He lets out an amused breath. "Of course."

I know I should get used to it, but I don't like being alone. It's only been a few days and yet I'm already feeling incredibly relieved to have Grímr at my side again. I have my own task to accomplish. If I can't handle a bit of time by myself, how am I going to handle the next couple of months?

"We'll probably have to keep our meetings as sparse as possible from now on," Grímr says after a moment of silence.

I expected it. Having Grímr run between me and those he's following would be nothing if not time consuming. If he falls too far behind the mermineae, we might lose them. I knew it was coming, but it's still disappointing to hear.

Well, at least without him around, there's no chance the knot will force me to betray him. That's something, right?

Really, I just don't want to experience that same isolation as in that oven. But, there are more important things going on than my own issues. The rest of the team probably are in a far worse situation than my solitude.

"How are they being treated?" I ask, trying to distract myself. I care about them, even if I still struggle to forgive or forget what they did.

Grímr stumbles, tripping over his own feet. He hesitates before responding. "They are being treated fine. Nothing to concern yourself with."

Grímr is as bad a liar as he's ever been. I don't ask any further. I don't want to feel guilty for considering this their punishment for betraying my trust.

How Grímr can find his way through this maze without sight, I don't know, but without any backpedaling, he leads me to the familiar sight of a tunnel filled with roots.

No, not roots. Now that I don't have to run for my life, I see they are a whitish-brown fungi that hang from a hundred points in the tight tunnel. A dim blue glow emanates from the hole in the ceiling. I'm surprised the glow-bugs come down this far. The tubes are at least a few hundred meters deep.

"Don't worry about waiting for me. I'll find you when I need to. The mer-mineae have been traveling that way almost consistently." I note the direction he points his head. "Take care of yourself. I'll see you in a few weeks or if they change their course."

The black mist shrouds him once more and I can barely give a "goodbye" before he's gone.

A sigh escapes me. Well, I might as well get back into it. I ignite the fungi tendrils around me and watch as they burn into the ceiling, leaving small holes in their place. They burn like fuses through the earth until they reach the tube that contains all that explosive jelly. As in the many times prior, I let the comfortable heat wash over me.

I watch in curiosity as the jets of flame travel through the deep tunnels. They bend and follow the branching caves for quite a distance, charring stone as they blow their way past.

It doesn't take long for a giant arachnid to attempt to dig for my flame. Really, I'm so thankful it's as dumb as it is. If it didn't give up, it would get to me in no time. If it were smart, it might even wait in ambush.

Even though I've experienced it so many times now, the thrum as its legs smash through the earth still unnerves me.

As always, it gives up before it even reaches half way down the tube, returning to the darkness of the cavern and opening my exit. I wait a good half an hour to begin my climb. Just in case.

Upon breaching the cavern, I'm welcomed by the sight of glow-bugs . . . on only one side. This tunnel has only led me to the very edge of the massive shadow.

No. As I look around, I realize that I'm well within the expansive darkness.

I'm sprinting for the safety of the swarm before I even realize my legs are moving. Ten meters, thirty, fifty. After running over a hundred meters, I finally reach the safety of the blue bugs. It's only after I'm within that I remember the bugs don't offer any true safety by themselves. Only the awareness they give of the other creatures in this cavern.

I twist on the spot, expecting something unthinkable to be bearing down on me. Nothing. It's all in my imagination.

I shake my head at my impulsive actions. I'd already seen the shadow, so why did I react with such panic? Why didn't my knot suppress my instinctual terror?

Whatever. I'm out now and there's nothing coming for me.

I remember Grímr's directions and immediately set out. I don't want to stay around here regardless if something is chasing me or not. It is behind me now. As long as I keep moving, I don't need to worry.

In my haste to move away from the extensive darkness behind me, I almost stumble straight into a comparatively tiny shadow in front of me. Not so close that whatever is hiding can see me—I hope—but close enough that I can see it isn't the shrouding mist of darkness. Instead, I can make out the silhouette of some beast ahead of me.

It's big, but not the same scale as the arachnids, especially not that giant centipede. It's about the same size as the panther body Grímr used to have. Definitely not the same shape, though. While the silhouette isn't exactly clear, there are two large shapes at the side of a smaller central body.

Slowly, I back up. I don't want to deal with this now. Not while the massive shadow still looms behind. I take another step back and try to circle around the creature, losing sight of the silhouette.

I may not see it anymore, but the loud snap that rings out halts my next step. Before I even realize why I'm doing so, I throw myself out of the way as something rushes forward before slamming shut.

I spring to my feet before the creature can attack again. As I take a step away and ready my spear, I finally get a good look at what attacked me. A pincer about the size of my body opens to reveal two lines of jagged teeth. It must have clamped closed as it sprung toward me.

The pincer hovering in the air pulls back as the arm and body it connects to come into view. Considering the size of its claws, the body is rather small. About equal to the creature's oversized pedipalps. The only reason the thing can even keep its balance is the long, thin legs that stretch wide off its body.

Looks like I'll be practicing my spear earlier than expected.

CHAPTER FORTY

Pseudo-Scorpion

Now that I have a better look at it, the creature looks like one of those tiny scorpions I used to see in the desert. Only cut in half and enlarged. It doesn't have a tail and its midsection is far smaller—in relation to the claws—than that of a scorpion.

I tighten my grip on my spear and take a step back to open some space. A glance over my shoulder shows nothing but the darkness behind me. Nothing is charging out toward us after the loud echoing snap from the half-scorpion.

That short moment of distraction costs me. As I turn back, the claws of the creature fly toward me and I'm unable to jump away fast enough. It slices through my hand, sending my spear flying off to the side and tearing right through the sleeve of my outfit.

The claw doesn't leave any lasting damage to me, of course, but I'm now disarmed and my snowsuit is torn above the glove.

I take another step away. The scorpion retracts its pincers to its side, ready to burst forth with its next strike. It scuttles forward, trying to get within attacking distance again. The darkness is still behind me and my spear is on the other side of the scorpion, so I try to back away to the side.

The scorpion keeps at the same pace as me as I try to circle my way around. As soon as I have a clear path to my spear, I abandon all caution and dash toward it. The scorpion's claws explode forward, barely grazing past my head.

I pick up my spear without issue. Now that I'm on the other side, I can easily just run off. I don't need to worry about the darkness looming behind it if I don't engage. But isn't this the perfect opportunity? The scorpion isn't anything dangerous. Well, not to me. My snowsuit might say differently. The next patch without glow-bugs I try to run into might hide something I can't fight. Or maybe all I'll find are the blind-lizards, which won't be much of a challenge.

Against my better judgment, I raise my spear again and wait for the half-scorpion to approach. It does so slowly, almost seeming unsure of how to attack. The pincers on its long arms sway from left to right and brush across the ground.

Well, if it isn't going to attack, I might as well take the initiative. I thrust straight forward, hoping to pierce it with one blow. The sharp tip of my weapon grazes off the scorpion's carapace, leaving nothing more than a shallow scratch on the hard surface.

I realize the folly of my decision to attack it head on almost too late. I've put myself right between its pincers. There's no way I'll be able to back up in time to avoid them snapping at me, so I go the only other direction I can think of: right between its legs. I crawl under its body as I hear two loud snaps ring out one after the other.

It knows I'm under it and immediately tries to scuttle backward to keep me in front of it. In a moment of inspiration, I wedge the back of my spear into a rock and angle the sharp end into the joint between its body and pincer. The creature backs up with enough force that the spear pierces right through the hard carapace and into the vulnerable inside of the limb.

The scorpion screeches and twists away from the sharp pain in its joint, but only pulls the spear along with it. Before it can move too far away, I clamp down on my control as hard as I can and slam my entire body onto the spear, jerking it down and through the bottom of the joint.

Another screech escapes the scorpion as it backs away. One of its pincers now drags along the ground, limp.

I spring to my feet and rush around to the side with the injured limb. If it can't attack me with that pincer anymore, I should be able to attack it without worry. I can't risk using my flames, so I need to use anything that might give me the advantage.

It tries to spin and face me while backing away, clicking its remaining claw to threaten me. It is in pain and feels in danger, so it wants to scare me off.

If you didn't want to be in danger, you shouldn't have attacked me.

I run around its side faster than it can spin. Once I'm near its back, I rush in and bring my spear down in a downward swing. I push a heavy impulse through my body, trying to put as much weight behind it as I can as the sharp tip comes down on the center of its body.

I'm rewarded with the bladed tip slicing into the carapace. It doesn't dig in deep, but it's proof that this method works. I doubt anyone else in my team would have any issue cutting this scorpion up—except Grímr in his current body—so I still have a long way to go before I'll be able to pierce the skin of the enhanced creatures, but this is a good start.

I jerk the spear out of the scorpion and move around its back again before it can spin on me. The next swing is aimed at the joint of between a leg and its body. Even if I can pierce its carapace, it'll take too long to fell if each strike is shallow. I need to slow its movement.

Instead of the joint I was aiming for, I hit slightly lower on its leg. I put in the same amount of effort as what let me break through its back, but the angle of its hard leg ricochets the blade down into the soil.

The scorpion spins on me and snaps out once more. I expect to tug the spear along with me and dodge with ease, but the spear doesn't budge. My strengthened blow wedged it in the rock beneath the soil. With my unenhanced tug, I'm sent off balance and the pincer slams closed around my head.

I apply the proper strength to free my spear and back up. An annoyed glance is all I give the remains of my hood. I need to be more careful; I still need this outfit for when I finally escape these caves. Wading through snow without its protection does not sound fun.

The scorpion snaps its pincer a few times, confused how it didn't catch its prey.

Determined not to make any more mistakes, I dash toward its weak side again. As soon as I run, it turns to me, but it is too late. My spear thrusts straight into the joint of its front leg. I glide my hands up the shaft of the spear and push another impulse through my body. I twist, severing the leg entirely as I continue running behind it.

Before it stops screeching and can turn on me, I bring my spear down on the rear leg I missed before. This time I hit dead-on. The blade cuts through with ease, removing another leg.

Without two of the three legs on its weakened side, it can't keep its balance. The scorpion collapses as it tries to turn.

The opportunity presents itself, so I take it. I chop off the remaining leg before it can push off the ground again. Like the last swing, I feel the carapace shattering beneath the weight of my spear.

The scorpion can do nothing but squirm on the ground now. With its remaining legs, it drags itself away from me, trying its utmost to put its claw between us. It screeches. I'm not sure whether it's in fear, pain, or just from the futility it must feel. Maybe it's all. Maybe it isn't even capable of those thoughts and it is just instinctual screeching.

Whatever the case, it would be cruel to extend this longer than it needs to be.

I jump on its back, careful not to be knocked off by the jerky movements of the dying creature. Once I'm above its head, I ready my spear and thrust down. The spear really is better for thrusting; while the swing earlier only barely got through the carapace, my thrust pierces through the bottom of its head.

The half-scorpion doesn't die immediately, so I pull back and spear through its head once more. Its struggles slow, but many of its limbs still twitch. The pincer opens and clamps closed in a loop. One more thrust stills it for good.

I drop to the ground and look over the motionless scorpion. It's the first creature I've killed without relying on my flames. I definitely have a lot to work on, but to know my practice and training with the spear hasn't been for nothing feels great.

My outfit could have been spared the damage, though. Besides the hole in my chest, both the hood and one of my sleeves have been severed. I pick up both from where they lie on the ground and shove them into a pocket. When I rescue those three, I'll make sure Jav fixes it up, just like he promised.

My eyes hover over the corpse before rising to the void. Luckily, whatever is hiding in there has shown no intention of interrupting our fight. But I won't be able to just burn through this corpse as I normally would; even if whatever is in the massive shadow doesn't react, those arachnids above definitely will.

I lug one of the severed legs over my shoulder and move on for the next fungi trap I can find.

While I did fairly well to disable the scorpion, I realize I need to be faster. It could only hit me when I was caught off guard. In a fight like that, I need to react quicker so I won't be hit even if I'm surprised.

The first pincer that hit me caught me when I was distracted by my surroundings. While I can't say being aware of my surroundings is bad, I'll need to make sure it doesn't come at the cost of my awareness of the enemy before me. I should have at least created more distance and gauged the scorpion before worrying about the shadow.

The second hit was entirely on my unfamiliarity with the spear in an actual fight. Whether or not I should have abandoned the spear after it didn't come out isn't something I can know for sure. In a more dangerous fight, leaving myself unarmed might be just as bad as letting the enemy get a hit on me. What I can improve is my understanding of how my spear might react when different strength is applied to it. I had no idea I lodged my spear in the earth until I tried to tug it. I feel like the only way I can improve this understanding is to just use the weapon more. Become more familiar with it.

As I walk, I continue to replay the fight in my mind and think of ways

I could be better. Opportunities I'd missed in the heat of the moment and pointless movements that I'd have been better without.

Eventually, the slow biased movement of the glow-bugs becomes apparent once more and I follow them to my next meal.

I hear the squawking of the bat before I see it. The outline of the creature is visible within the blue glow of the innumerable lights. It seems I'm not the only one who uses those fungi bug-traps to have an easy feast. The bat crawls along the ground, jerking its head into the swarm of lights every few moments.

The bat approaches the hole in the center of the fungi growths and throws its head in the stream of bugs. It's obviously enjoying the meal, but I'm curious how it will deal with the jam that the fungi tube spits out when you get too close.

As expected, the viscous liquid spurts out and covers the bat. It screeches; the ultrasonic noise loud to my ears even this far away. The distance stops it from disturbing my flames, fortunately.

The bat mustn't have had a plan to deal with the substance. It stumbles back and tries to wipe at it with its wings, to no effect. The glow-bugs soon swarm the creature, intent on the delicious juice coating the bat's body. Another screech rings out as the bat realizes their roles are reversed and it is now the one being eaten.

With a flap of its wings, the bat launches into the air. It flies right through the thick layer of bugs. As it breaches the top, a wave of the blue lights follow after it. It looks like every bug in the area chases the bat into the air. Millions of tiny glowing dots chase after a single creature. The light intensifies around the flying bat as the bugs swarm.

That terrifying, chest-shaking growl rumbles through the cavern a moment before the bat disappears along with a large section of the swarm. The earth shakes as an arachnid monstrosity crashes to the ground. Only visible from the outline of the many glow-bugs still spread through the air, the creature looms tall.

I freeze, hoping it won't notice me.

Barely a second passes after it crashes to the ground before a bang tears through the air, far louder than even the impact of the arachnid. As difficult as it is to see, I can still make out the arachnid being launched a good hundred meters. Almost as if it appears out of the swarm, the giant centipede rushes the arachnid and slams its forcipules into its side.

I don't find the heavy impacts shaking the air anywhere as frightening as the silence in which the centipede closed the distance. Its weight alone should rattle the earth. It is unsettling.

I flinch as the arachnid slams many of its front legs into the centipede. The echoing clatter of metallic reverberations is almost too loud to handle. With impossible ease, the centipede lifts the arachnid off the ground and slams it down on its head before twisting around it.

The centipede constricts around the arachnid while it tries in vain to slam and bite its way out. But the centipede has the weight advantage by a factor, so it is all but impossible for it to escape.

I make myself as small as I can. Their fight—if one can even call it that—has taken them to the edge of where I can still make their outlines. Should I make a run for the fungi trap? Or should I just wait and hope they don't crash their way over here?

Before I can make my choice, a deep cracking and groaning echoes through the cavern chamber. The arachnid's terrifying screech shakes my body before cutting short. A wet crunch accompanies the deformation of the arachnid's silhouette.

The glow-bugs return to their normal height and I lose sight of the centipede uncurling from the dead arachnid. The remains of their fight disappear into the darkness. Nothing makes a noise.

I think . . . I'm just gonna lay here for a bit. I don't want to be the first creature to make a noise after that. Getting a taste of that arachnid's corpse would be nice, but there's no chance I'm risking any proximity to that centipede. As soon as I can, I'm diving down that tunnel and running far away.

CHAPTER FORTY-ONE

Growth

I've been down here for months. Thankfully, I never got caught in the middle of the fight between giants. In as long as I've been traveling through this cavern, not once have I seen the giant centipede again. While the arachnids will often drop on the creatures after they get swarmed by the uncountable bugs, the battle between giants was a one-off.

It's surprising how common it is to find bats or the residents of the shadows trying to feed from the fungi traps only to find themselves as paste under the giant arachnid's massive weight. I catch sight of it at least once a week on my journey.

After burning my way through hundreds of the fungi tubes, it has become routine. Despite the immense strength they show and the instinctual fear I feel in their presence, the arachnids are predictable. Not once have they acted different than what I've come to expect. They always react to bright flashes of light and chase them down. They will usually ignore flashes of less-illuminating light, but will chase it down, regardless, if it stays lit long enough.

I may have done some experimenting once I'd become more comfortable with their predictability. In the hidden depths of a fungi trap, I'd had a flame bloom far above until an arachnid attacked.

My goal had been to see if explosive-enhanced flame could damage its body. I might have been trying to push above my level, but after all the energy I'd been raking in from the glow-bugs, I wanted to see if I could take on something bigger.

Of course, I never should have been hopeful. Even at the hottest temperature, my flame could not scorch a single thin hair.

Engulfed in flame as it had been, it never changed its actions. It tried to dig to me, so I simply dropped deeper into the tunnels below. Despite the terror its screeches inflict upon me, I treat the monstrosity as nothing more than a nuisance.

Because of the arachnid's inflexibility, I've become so accustomed to detonating the fungi tubes that I've been able to increase the number I hit per day to fifteen. I can leave the safety of my hole only a few minutes after it gives up digging without worrying that it'll come after me.

The only thing that takes time anymore is running the distance to the next mushroom trap. While I don't think there is any true pattern to the layout of the tubes, they always grow about the same distance away from each other, so it is always easy to find the next. Just run in the direction I need to travel and veer off whenever I notice the strange behavior of the glow-bugs. It's no more difficult than that.

The immediate benefit of constantly eating these nutrition-dense bugs is that I always have the energy to push on. I need far less sleep than normal and I can run almost nonstop at my top speed without issue. It's not even close to the speed I can reach with flight, but it's something.

I don't need to be running as much as I have been. The mermineae Grímr and I have been tailing aren't in any rush to get through the tunnels. But sprinting around lets me gorge myself as much as possible.

It's insane how far the Alps extend. I'm sure I would have run Zadok Kingdom's length twice over by now. Maybe even three times. And yet, the mermineae have shown no sign of rising to the surface, according to Grímr.

It feels like every visit from him is less frequent than the last. I always look forward to his return. It's the only time that is broken up by the monotony of running and detonating.

Hmm . . . maybe monotony is the wrong word. I really enjoy blowing up those fungi tunnels.

Disappointingly, even with all the energy I've gained in the past weeks, my fire has only gotten a bit hotter than what the explosive jelly could reach. It's a significant improvement over what I could do, but my flame is still a bright orange rather than anything more impressive. I was really hoping to at least approach the golden hue many of my tribe could achieve. Instead, the amount of flame I can influence has exploded.

It's hard to measure my capabilities as many factors influence the strength or intensity of my flames in any circumstance, but using a general standard can help track my improvement. Where before I could probably have filled a five-meter radius sphere of flame for an hour before exhausting myself, I can now fill almost fifty meters for the same time. At least, that's how it feels. I've hardly had the chance to experiment except when exploding the fungi trap.

The range at which I can control has stretched farther from my body as well. I never truly had a maximum distance, but the farther my flame is from my body, the harder it is to influence. Before, ten meters would have been my effective maximum for full control. Further than that, the flame would react with less precision until about a hundred meters, where I'd only be able to feel the flame.

This is, of course, assuming that my fire is isolated. Should my flame rocket out two hundred meters, I would still have been able to feel through it and control it to some extent.

Now, my range has multiplied near tenfold.

I'm almost certain none in my tribe had a range as far as what mine has become. Elder Cyrus definitely had the widest, but his effective range wouldn't have been over fifty meters. I'm already double that.

The range has made searching the lower tunnels almost easy. Even if I don't travel down there often, I can just send out a wave of flame and I can see all the branching tunnels.

Another change I've noticed since my energy has exploded in strength is that I can feel sources of heat in the cavern. As long as they are within my effective range, I can feel the temperature of the bats. No other creature down here seems to give off any heat, but it explains that odd feeling I had when the mermineae ambushed us.

While it was subdued before, now I'm able to make out individual limbs from the thermal sense. If I'd realized what I'd sensed back then was the heat of a warm-blooded creature, then my team might've never gotten into this situation.

The wave of flame I sent through the tunnels didn't reveal any sign of the mermineae. Hopefully, I haven't wondered offtrack without noticing. I've already been stuck down here far longer than I ever wanted to. Only the promise of an exit has halted me from doing anything excessive.

Should I have any reason to believe those I'm following don't actually have a way out, there is no doubt in my mind that the tangle of my psyche will push me to do something drastic. Even though it is almost a death sentence, it might even push me to fly to the ceiling, relying on the chance that I won't die from the impact before the monstrosities tear through the two layers of ranked stone.

I last met with Grímr only a week ago, so there isn't anything for me to worry about as of yet.

Beside my—numerous—gorging sessions, I've made time to look into the shadows that hide both the blind-lizards and pseudo-scorpions. Other creatures hide within many of them, but none have been much of a challenge. Beating them with my spear has been easy.

Well, except one. But that never attacked back, so I was given free rein to use its shell as strength practice for my spear. Even after months, I'm yet to pierce it.

My technique has improved immensely. After that first fight with the pseudo-scorpion, I have kept my outfit from tearing much more. There is a tear over my chest and my other glove is gone, but the rest is still mostly intact.

On the other hand, the amount of force I can push into my thrusts and swings has stagnated. Actually, I think with the amplified energy within me, my control has worsened. Any improvements or gains from practicing my spear and control every day are offset by how far my capacity has grown.

Now that I think about it, how did the amount of my flame increase so drastically without the temperature following suit? I'd always been told it would grow naturally along with my capacity. Is that wrong?

My circumstances are unique. I am very aware that my recent growth is not natural, so is that why my heat is lagging? Or do I have to figure out the proper method to increase it?

It's improved to the same temperature the explosive jam used to push it to, which should be just enough to fight against the mermineae. I'm worried that it still won't be enough to fight against the more enhanced of their race. At the very least, I hope the expanse my inner flame can now cover will be enough of a smokescreen to let my team escape.

I detonate another tube of explosive jelly and relax into the heat as the heavy thuds pound through the earth. At this point, I could just cast out my fire to reach for the glow-bugs myself, but I enjoy the extra boost the substance gives my flame.

Even after all this growth, I've settled into a loop of doing the same thing every day. After looking down on the arachnids for their predictable actions, I've gone and become the same. Well, I've not changed my actions simply because they are so effective. I hardly have to worry when I've done the same action a thousand times prior, but becoming complacent isn't doing me any favors.

But . . . how can I increase the number of bugs I'm consuming without putting myself at immense risk of retaliation from the giant centipede or arachnids? I already leave immediately after the arachnid stops trying to dig me out, but maybe I can increase my running speed somehow. A way to know for sure which direction the next fungi trap is would be nice too, but I'm not sure how to approach that.

If I can apply extra strength to my spear strikes by focusing on my control, then I should be able to do a similar thing with my running, right?

As I climb out of the crater that used to be the top of the mushroom tunnel, I push into a run. First, I try to increase my physicality. Rather than speeding me up, it does the opposite. With my control at the limit, it makes me feel like I'm pushing against a strong wind compared to before.

From the obvious negative results, I change up my approach. I still need to be careful not to become visible, so I pull back on my body until my flames are on the border of emitting light. I'm sure this point between physical and not looks strange; the surface of my body ever so slightly flickers, but the light usually partnered does not appear. Nobody looking at me closely would mistake me for an albanic now.

My eyes glow when I'm like this, but it isn't any more intense than the surrounding bugs' light.

I'm faster than usual, but not by much. As I transition between the two states, I notice that while I don't feel like I'm pushing against a wall anymore, I can't push the same amount of strength into my legs. Is this a balance thing? Do I have to figure out the sweet spot between the extra strength I get from more weight against how much that weight works against me?

I play around with my control for the time being. There isn't anything else I need to worry about until I reach the next fungi trap. My weight changes back and forth, but it seems I was wrong; there is no 'sweet spot.' Only reducing my weight seems to increase my speed.

That is . . . until an idea passes through my mind.

I come to a halt, dropping my shoulders and tilting my head back. Why didn't I think of this weeks ago?

I run again. This time I keep my upper body on the verge of flames, but solidify my legs to the most I can push them. It makes controlling my body harder, as I have to split my focus away from just keeping a grip on my form, but it's manageable.

My speed increases by a good twenty percent over my previous maximum.

Why did I never think to split my focus between different parts of my body? It's not like I didn't know I could do so; I've changed my hands into claws without changing the rest of my body. Whatever. I know I can now. I should be able to improve my spearmanship again with this.

As I run, I experiment with the most effective distribution of control. Quickly, I find that I can't push my body to the same maximum mass with my mind split between so many areas. It doesn't matter so much for running, but I can imagine it might become a problem when using my weapon. The more weight I can put behind my spear, the better, after all.

As obviously beneficial as this is, it does nothing but make me want to change my form. If I don't have to worry about the light I give off when not in my standard form, I could extend the length of my legs to give me a longer stride or lengthen my arms for better reach. Wait, Tetsu taught me to use the spear in my default shape, but why do I need to keep the same form as her? Could I not just grow an extra set of arms and use two spears?

So many ideas to explore. So many I can't because of the monstrosities I'll attract doing so. If I want to experiment with these improvements, I'll need to spend more time in the tunnels underneath. Doing so will cut into the amount of bugs I can consume, though.

The solution is simple, and yet difficult. I need to improve my control so that I can hide my flame even with a morphed body. This will solve almost all my problems; I'll be able to fly again, increase the force behind my spear, and it'll give me the opportunity to practice and try new things, all while still hunting down the swarms of bugs.

Of course, if improving my control was that easy, I would have done so already. I'll need to figure out a way to push it to the next level.

"Solvei." I jolt as Grímr's voice breaks the silence.

"Stop doing that!" I say, embarrassed at being caught off guard. "You're back early. I didn't expect you for at least another week." Not that I'm complaining.

Grímr drops the cloud of black around him. He looks exhausted. Now that I think about it, he must have been moving incredibly quickly to catch up to me while I was running.

"The mermineae." He pauses for a breath. "They've reached the exit."

CHAPTER FORTY-TWO

Ascend

R eally?" The news excites me. "Finally?"

"Well, yes," Grímr says. "But there are a lot of mermineae crowding the path. Even alone, I don't think I could sneak by them."

He looks up at me in concern, but even with his worries about the number of enemies we will face, I feel nothing but giddiness now that we are so close to getting out.

"Well then, let's go. There's no reason to wait."

"Wait. We still need to prepare. I need a stronger body than this if you are going to get through. Nothing good will happen if we go as we are."

I spare a glance over his pale lizard body. "Nothing in this cavern would be too helpful. Well, except for the monstrosities, but there's no chance of touching them. You are better off keeping the stealth ability than switching."

Grímr cuts off a hiss as it leaves his throat. "You've been looking through those shadows? I told you to be careful," he chides before pausing for a few seconds. "Solvei, I don't know how we are going to get past them."

I know the knot in my psyche is influencing my thoughts right now, but this is my first opportunity to escape in what feels like forever. There is no chance I'm passing this up.

"Let's go check it out. What other option do we have?" I try to keep my tone serious, but I'm not sure if I truly hide my exhilaration.

Grímr gives me a worried glance before he turns and leads me away. "It's a few days' travel."

I last met Grímr a week ago, so we shouldn't be this far away from the mermineae. Did Grímr direct me to the side before, or is he leading me away right now? He wouldn't be leading me away from the exit now, would he? No. Out of our team, he's the one I trust the most.

I can't wait to get out of this horrible underground cave system. The swathes of glow-bugs I've gorged on have got me through, but I miss the sky. I want to smell air that isn't stale. Once more, I'll be free.

It doesn't matter what I need to do, I'm getting out.

"So, in those areas devoid of glow-bugs, you faced nothing too dangerous, did you?" Grímr asks as he crawls along the ground beside me. "You didn't go looking down in the tunnels below?"

I send a questioning gaze to the lizard, who cannot notice it. "No. Nothing too strong. A few tears in my outfit are all I needed to worry about."

"That's good," he says.

Is it? It would have been better if there was something strong enough for Grímr to take over. If that was the case, we might have better options before us than simply sneaking by.

I realize that what we're doing will be dangerous. The mermineae are strong enough to beat the enhanced members of our team. No matter how much fire I have at my command, I'm never going to push my way through too many of them.

Well, unless the three mermineae that I already killed in the center of a fungi tube explosion were the strongest of their race. Then, this might be easier than I could have hoped for. But I'm not about to put all my hopes on that slim possibility.

I want to look at the exit the mermineae are guarding before I decide on any plan.

We spend most of the next few days in an uncomfortable silence. Grímr stays in a state of thought for most of the time and any time he goes to say anything, the words die in his throat. I try to start conversations on my own, but they always fall off after a few terse exchanges.

Still, his presence makes the trip more comfortable than before. Loneliness isn't enjoyable.

Eventually, we reach another of those massive shadows that cover everything from one side to another. Grímr walks straight toward where a giant monster is obviously hiding without even hesitating.

I grab his tail before he can leave the safety of the glow-bugs. "What are you doing? We don't know what's hiding in that darkness."

Grímr looks back at me oddly and I let go of his tail immediately; I hate when people hold me like that. I shouldn't do the same to others.

"The exit is ahead. This is how they reach the flat cavern above," he says and waits for me.

The monster is covering the path out? I shouldn't even be surprised that the only place I refused to check is the way up.

"Okay," I say. If these mermineae can get past whatever hides in the shadow, then I'll just have to do the same. Better than waiting down here. The lack of worry Grímr expresses about what lies ahead also gives me a reason to push on.

Instead of continuing forward like I expect, Grímr jumps on my leg and climbs up my body until he's wrapped around my neck.

"There are mermineae ahead. I'm going to cover you in darkness, all right?"

Before I can even question him, the black shroud wraps around us and I can no longer see.

"You'll have to point out where we're going if you plan to keep the both of us obscured like this," I say and Grímr simply nods once before snapping his head forward.

I was already worried enough about going into the giant shadow, but now I don't even have the reassuring light of the glow-bugs at my back. Each step I tense, expecting something to jump at me. Or to stumble over the sleeping form of some Titan undisturbed until now.

I'm about to speak up and ask exactly what I should expect ahead of us when Grímr interrupts me.

"I smell them; they aren't too far ahead," Grímr whispers in my ear. "Be quiet from now on."

How am I supposed to avoid them if I can't see them?

I almost vocalize my concern when I feel something that answers that question for me. A hundred meters ahead, there is a patch of heat far warmer than any of the surroundings. Last time I felt this, I didn't know what it was. Now? My heat sense has improved that I couldn't mistake it for anything but what it is.

A merminea.

The first I've seen in months. Well, I still haven't seen it, but the point is the same. I can tell where it is just from the body heat it exudes. No longer will their camouflage let them ambush me.

I divert my course to avoid it, but soon notice it isn't alone. As I push farther into this darkness, a few more appear in range. Each keeps a good fifty meters between each other, but they all remain motionless. As I move closer, the detail improves and I can distinguish each limb. I creep past the first, only twenty meters away. The merminea doesn't move. So much so that if it wasn't giving off so much heat, I'd think it was dead. Not even its chest moves to show breathing.

I move between the merminea, careful of any motion around me. It's unsettling walking through the pitch black and knowing there are enemies all around. Has Grímr felt like this the entire time we've been down here? The constant stress must have been hard.

Soon, I notice something strange. Ahead of me, I can feel the heat of a few mermineae, but they aren't on the ground. They seem to be suspended in midair.

Curious, I creep ever closer. More appear above the others, almost vertically. After the point where they rise into the air, I can feel none.

I cast my gaze upward, pointlessly looking for the mermineae through the darkness. Do they have ropes to the ceiling? Is that how they get out? But why would they put them within the shadow that doubtlessly holds some terrifying existence?

I come very close to slamming my head into the stone wall that appears in front of me before I can react.

For a moment, I just stand there, passing my hand over the surface that extends out of my reach and sight. I struggle to suppress my groan. Of course. I'd gone and misled myself.

There was never a terrifying monster hiding in this shadow. It is dark simply because there is nowhere for the glow-bugs to travel this way.

The cavern wall. That's all that hides within.

I feel foolish. After seeing the arachnid and centipede, I went and fabricated some imaginary monster. I could have risen to the upper cavern at any of the walls I now know I came across on the way through the Alps.

A tap from Grímr snaps me out of my ruminations. He jerks his head up above us, obviously thinking I don't know where to go. Rather than letting him know how stupid I feel for my mistake, I push on.

The wall is smooth. Few places to grab and pull myself upward. With no other option, I look around to make sure Grímr's darkness shrouds me completely. The last thing I want is for those mermineae to see the light I'll give off.

Limiting it to only my fingertips, I push the heat of my flames until I know I'll be able to dig through the rock. Grímr twists his head as he feels the heat from my glowing orange fingers. He digs his claws into my shoulder, obviously questioning my action, but I don't have an option if I want to climb the wall.

I try my hardest to keep my flame hidden as I amplify the temperature, but it seems as impossible as hiding my flames in bird form. I'll have to rely entirely on Grímr to keep us hidden.

My fingers sink into the stone with ease. After the past few times climbing this way, I've learned that putting too much heat into my hands will do nothing but melt away the handhold I'm trying to rely on. By keeping the heat high enough to slice through stone, but only limiting it to my fingertips, I can lift myself with the rest of my hands without worry of slipping.

I wonder about the walls. Do they encircle a massive cavern or are they more like pillars that can be walked around? Whenever I came across one of these massive shadows, I always descended into the tunnels underneath and sent my flames in search of the next fungi tube to rise to the surface again. Not once did I try to go around.

I can no longer feel the heat from the mermineae on the ground below, so I should be near the halfway point in my climb. It's not hard to find how far I am from the ceiling. When I'm in range to sense, it would be impossible not to feel it. Above me there are tens of mermineae climbing around and through a vast hole.

The hole is about twenty meters away from the wall, but many mermineae move from the ceiling of this cavern into the flat surface of the cave above. I can't make out the full size of the hole from where I am, but it's big. Obviously a hole made by an arachnid.

I have to stop before I reach the top of the wall. A large heat signature moves into the edge of my sense range. It gets closer while I remain motionless and I realize it's a swarm of mermineae. The detail improves as they move toward the ceiling hole and I feel at least a hundred moving together.

As much as I want to stay still to limit the risk of being seen, I'm too close to the direct path down the wall. With as much speed as I'm willing to risk, I scale the wall until I'm well off to the side. And it's lucky I put some haste into my movement; the group of mermineae flood through the hole, not stopping for a second before they race down where I was not a moment ago.

They don't seem all that quick while climbing upside down, but the moment they reach the wall, they rush down with speed I couldn't hope to compare.

I wait, still, until they are all far below before continuing up. Not wanting to remain in a position to be found, I don't approach the hole directly. Instead, I curve up the wall, planning to climb around to the other side of the massive missing section of the ceiling and enter that way. I'm much more likely to be noticed going in directly.

I reach the ceiling and push my fingers into the rock to melt a grip for myself. Or at least, I try. The rock doesn't melt under my heat. I can't even feel it warming up.

Right. Ranked stone. Of course, I can't burn through the rock that Remus and Tetsu couldn't smash their way through.

Instead of digging my own handholds, I'm going to have to rely on the stalactites that drop from the ceiling. They will not be easy to climb across. I doubt my grip strength is enough to carry me to the hole before I fall, so I need to do something else.

Fortunately, Grímr's shadow leaves me with an option I haven't really been able to make use of in the past months. First, I grow claws on the tips of my fingers. I would lengthen my arms, or maybe change my body to imitate a dohrni, but I'm not too sure if the shadow can hide all the light I would create. After watching Remus, I know dohrni bodies could traverse this obstacle without issue.

Instead, I settle with changing only my hands and feet. I morph my feet to allow myself to grip the stalactites without dangling from only my arms. Before long, I've changed them to be rather similar to the talons I'm familiar with, only with more surface area to grip. I can't dig in with my talons, so it's best not to rely only on the grip I can get from their sharp points.

It isn't long before I'm ready. With glowing hands and feet, I grasp the first of the stalactites only barely visible through the dark shroud. I tug at the rock formation to make sure it'll remain attached to the ceiling and my grip won't come loose. Before I reach with my other arm, I focus on my body and make sure I weigh as little as possible without becoming visible.

There might have been a better way to do this; trying to push my legs higher up the wall while I slowly creep backward along the ceiling is far harder than I expected. I'm not at all worried about the fall. Even before all my improvements, falls were never too damaging. What's actually worrying is the mermineae couldn't miss us if we did fall.

Awkwardly, I hang from my hands and talons and make my way around. I was right to think the other side of the hole would be less populated. There's a few I have to avoid when I climb over the edge, but I get into the shallow cavern without issue.

Now I just need to hope my luck keeps up.

CHAPTER FORTY-THREE

Supersized Angling

I stumble away from the hole, moving toward the space with no thermal presence. Talons are not very comfortable to walk on, and I struggle to move without staggering. Thankfully, none of the mermineae have noticed my presence yet. I can only be thankful that they don't have a fire to light their way. It's understandable down in the cavern below, but if they had a source of light up here, then Grímr's shadow would stand out.

Grímr points his head in the direction we need to go, but even without his input, the higher number of merminea that way would be enough of an indicator. The slender creatures are far less wary than they were down below. They all move around together and talk without restraint.

Despite the increased number of mermineae, I feel much better walking around knowing that they aren't all that alert. There mustn't be too much danger in this cavern for them to be this lax.

I follow along the congregation of merminea, keeping them at the edge of my sense range while I weave through individuals that lay unmoving at the peripheral. It takes a while, but I know I've found the exit as soon as the number of mermineae exponentially increases. The point they surround is far out of the range of my sense, but there's no doubt in my mind that is where the mermineae are coming from.

That's my exit. My escape. I will finally be free.

Thankfully, even my psyche knot knows that rushing forward will achieve nothing. I need to get a better idea of the layout to think of a way past them.

I feel Grímr tightening around my chest, either from distress or an intentional warning. Whatever he wants, I ignore it. I push closer to the mermineae than I've dared before, coming within meters of the nearest. The hum of chatter through the cavern is more than enough to cover any sound I make as I crawl forward. Several mermineae hide along the low ceiling, but they are easier to avoid than the ones on the ground.

I wonder how they're able to cling to the smooth surface of the rock without digging their claws in. They aren't digging their claws in, right? It'd be horrible if all of them can easily pierce the ranked stone that even the strongest attacks of my team hadn't been able to do much more than scratch.

Without being able to see for myself, I have no way of knowing. My thermal sense is good, but nowhere near detailed enough to see the individual claws or fingers. The cold stone is completely invisible.

When the tunnel above finally reaches my sense, Grímr is squeezing tightly around my neck. Amongst the many hundreds of heat sources ahead of me, there are some moving through a spot where there should be stone. I quickly lose track of them, the stone between us preventing me from feeling the heat, but it is enough to know I've found my target.

Grímr digs his claws into my shoulder. He only barely holds himself short of snapping at me. It's obvious I'm too close to the surrounding mermineae for his comfort. I do feel anxious myself, but I'm so close to getting out. Just a hundred meters forward and I'll be on my way out.

To Grímr's displeasure, I press on. There has to be some way to pass. Something to give me a method to get through them.

Right now, the only options we have are to sneak by without their notice . . . which will be near impossible, or attack them head on and break our way through . . . which is just as impossible. I could also get a stronger body for Grímr and use him as a distraction to get through alone.

My psyche sneaks in that last option, but the likelihood of it working is so low that it doesn't even argue when I refuse it.

As I look over the dense crowd of the mermineae, I feel a grin coming over my face. I have it. There is a way I can get through with little . . . well, maybe a lot of risk, but it's guaranteed to work.

I finally relent to Grímr's silent protests and make my way out of the pack of mermineae. Really, we are lucky to not have been noticed. Their eyesight mustn't be all too good if they don't realize they can't see parts of the tunnel they could before.

Well, I'm not about to question what goes my way.

First, I need to find another hole to the cavern below. I could use the one

I entered through, but the less mermineae around, the better. Choosing a random direction, I move away from my exit. In a short while, I'll be back.

Once we are a respectable distance away from the mermineae, Grímr hisses in my ear. "What were you thinking, Solvei? Do you want us to be caught?"

I did get a bit overwhelmed in the moment; I admit. The exit attracting me like a glow-bug to explosive jelly. Never should I have got as close as I did to the swarming mermineae. "I'm sorry, but I got an idea. I know how to get us out."

Grímr perks at that, his anger all but forgotten. "Really? How?"

I avoid looking at the lizard on my shoulder. There is no chance he will like what I have planned.

I couldn't find another hole to the cavern below, so I settled on returning to the one we entered through. Traveling the hundreds of meters along the ceiling is hard, but eventually I reach my goal. I can't feel the heat of the mermineae through the stone above me, but I should be close enough for what I have in mind.

Grímr didn't like my idea. Actually, he vehemently refused to let me go through with it at first. But with my freedom in sight, I wasn't willing to let this go. When I moved to do it by myself, he relented.

"It would be safer if you wait a distance away until I'm done," I say as I adjust my grip on the stalactites I hang from. I'll be able to handle a few hits, but if Grímr gets unlucky, he'll be dead in one.

"No. This plan is already far too dangerous. I'm not leaving you in more danger than absolutely necessary."

There aren't any mermineae crawling on the ceiling this far from the wall, so it's not like I'll be spotted. My glowing hands and feet might give me away to the monstrosities, but considering my plan, it's a small risk to take. Grímr would have been safer keeping his distance, but refuses to leave me visible when I do what I'm about to do.

Well, there's no point holding off for longer than necessary. The constricting pressure of Grímr's body mirrors my nerves. The quicker I do this, the sooner we'll be out in the sunlight once more.

I focus on my target fifty meters ahead of me, right below where the tunnel leading upward should be. It takes almost all my focus to ignite the tiniest fire from this distance. I would have no trouble creating it next to me and then sending it away, but there is no point risking myself.

In moments, I amplify the flame over the ceiling. It burns a bright yellow and lights up everything around as it spreads over the stalactites. I'm unable to even char the rock, but that's not my intention. My flames light up the massive cavern below like a miniature sun.

It doesn't take long for the screeching to start. I grip tight against the ceiling and double-check that the flame is far enough from me. An arachnid monstrosity's bulky body scuttles along the ceiling with far too much speed to seem natural.

It slams its front legs through the rock. The impact quakes through my hands and before I can tighten my grip, my fingers slip out. Dangling from my legs, I don't relent on my flames. I keep them burning around the arachnid until it is joined by a second. The tapping of its legs across stone and the tearing through rock threatens to loosen the grip of my legs as well.

A chorus of high-pitched shouts of terror reaches my ears. The arachnids have found the mermineae. From the light of my flames, I can see the pedipalps of the arachnids grasping at the slender creatures before swallowing them whole. My flames spread into the cavern above, but each of the mermineae are already fleeing at an incredible speed.

I feel around with my flame and realize I missed the tunnel by a rather extensive distance. The flames along the ceiling slide into their new position where I want the monstrosities to dig. One follows my flames, but the other continues tearing through the rock as it chases after the screaming rodents within.

This works far better than I expected. If I keep going, I should be able to lead the arachnids to dig right through to the tunnel above and clear any opposition we'll face.

It works, but their screams reverberate through me. Somehow, their voices seem louder than the immense quakes of these near-Titan existences.

No. I'm so close to freedom. They are in my way, so I need to remove them. If they don't run away, they will have nothing but the might of these arachnids to deal with. But . . . I still hope they choose to run away.

With one arachnid tearing into the tunnel above, similar to how it would chase me down into the fungi tube below, I finally decide to pull back on my flames. But in the last moment before my flames go out completely, a glint from below catches my attention.

My eyes widen and I immediately grasp tighter on the stalactites. A tremor stronger than anything the arachnids have caused rocks the world. Even putting an impulse of strength into my grip, the shaking of the earth nearly tears me right off.

The giant centipede has slammed into the ceiling. Without my flames, I can't see how much damage it unleashes, but the sound of screaming mermineae quickly dies out. In their place, the arachnids screech at the new rival to their hunt and launch themselves at it.

I hear a crunch as an arachnid is caught in the jaws of the centipede. It shrieks in pain as the second arachnid slams into the centipede from its other side, knocking it loose from the ceiling. A few seconds pass before the tremor of the three monstrosities hitting the ground reaches me.

The sounds of their brawl rumble through the cavern. Grímr's claws dig into my shoulder again, but I don't complain. I need to get out now.

If I wait to be certain that those giants won't come back up, then I'm just asking the mermineae to block my way. I need to use their confusion and terror to escape while I can.

I clamber along upside down until I come across a new entry to the cavern above and pull myself up. It is only once I'm on solid ground do I realize a problem I didn't think of until now: the ceiling above me doesn't have stalactites for me to climb across. I have no way to get up to the tunnel above now that the ground is destroyed.

The stone under my feet shakes from an impact below. I put my hand on the ground to steady myself while the earth settles. There's no time to worry about whether I'll be seen or not. I need to act now.

I settle to change into my falcon form for the first time in months. I will my body to morph as fast as possible. Surprisingly, my flames are more willing than ever to do as I want. It's still not fast, but it's far better than before.

"Keep your darkness as thick as possible," I tell Grímr.

As my body size shrinks, I notice Grímr weighing me down far more than before. There is less of me to grasp onto, so I feel him grasping at places that restrict my movement.

"Don't grab my wings," I say, and he quickly obliges.

It takes five minutes to change. Far too long with the constant tremors from the brawl going on below. When I'm finally done, I'm only slightly bigger than Grímr, which isn't great, as I need to lift double my body weight. I give an experimental flap of my wings and find that while it's a struggle, I can lift us off the ground.

Before I can throw myself into the air and fly through the tunnel, an explosion of rock pelts me. Stone shrapnel tears through my side, and I feel the plane of stone under my talons drop away. I spread my wings wide, hoping that the monstrosities throwing each other across the cavern can't see my flame through Grímr's darkness.

I beat hard, fighting against our combined weight to drag us to the freedom I've longed for. The screech of the arachnids behind me feels so close. Just like the other times, the only sounds coming from the centipede are the devastating impacts as it smashes against the arachnids or the stone of the cavern.

Grímr has kept my view clear of darkness, but the angle I have to see is only enough to keep the tunnel above in my sight. The colossal fight is all but invisible. I can only hope the same is true for me. The flames from my head light the way, and I dart forward with as much speed as I can gather.

I move past the cratered remains of the tunnel just as another quake shakes the earth and air around me. No mermineae block my path to the wide tunnel above. I break out into the large tunnel of black rock. Despite my mindless state the last time I was up here, I recognize this as the tunnel under the Titan's path.

I'm so close now.

Another tremor loosens the dark rock, and I'm almost hit by a chunk that falls in front of my face. I can see movement in the distance. Most likely, the mermineae that ran away are waiting for the monstrosities below to stop their brawl before they approach again.

I turn to the side where it looks like there are less of them and fly forward. It'll be hard to sneak by them, so I'll just have to fly past and find an exit before they realize what's going on.

The open air calls me.

CHAPTER FORTY-FOUR

Freedom

The tunnel is thankfully tall enough that I can fly over the heads of the mermineae without issue. Black stone above lets me shoot past them without notice. While there are a few of the mermineae active in the center of the tunnel, most hide themselves along the walls of the cavern.

I need to be able to see the exit, so Grímr leaves a small gap in the darkness ahead of me. It is only a matter of time before one of the svelte creatures notice me through that tiny opening. I push my wings to the limit, flying as fast as I can past the many camouflaged mermineae I can sense hiding in wait.

Hopefully, the fact that they are hiding doesn't mean they are expecting me. It's concerning; why else would you camouflage yourself except to ambush someone?

I finally spot a break through the walls. There's no doubt in my mind that is the path to freedom, the number of unhidden mermineae before it is telling. Well, those mermineae are going to be a problem. There's no way I can fly into that narrow passage without them noticing. Not when I'll have to weave my way past them to get through.

There are few options for me; I either pass this opportunity up and continue down the tunnel until I find a better, less populated tunnel, or I brute force my way through them.

My impatience to reach the surface might be influencing my thoughts too much. Without much consideration, I blast the group with my flames and incinerate the fur off their skin. Each of them shrieks and scratches at their body to free themselves from my flames.

I use the distraction to dart between them and through the breach in the wall.

No longer do I have stealth on my side. The screams of the rodents behind me attracts the attention of every mermineae in the crevice to me. All that's separating me from the surface is this fissure and the enemies within.

The light shining through the split in rock above is blinding. It leaves the black cloud I'm shrouded in exposed like a blemish on the world. There are a lot of mermineae camouflaged along the walls above. I can feel them. Each one looks squarely at me.

I don't have time to back down now. Finally, I completely unleash all the power I've worked months to build up. The tunnel explodes in a cascade of flame. I replicate the intensity achieved by detonating the fungi traps entirely with my own strength.

Many of the creatures above me scream and flail like those before, but there are exceptions. Three of the mermineae clinging to the walls ignore my flames even as they scorch their skin. One throws themselves at me, and only the cover of flames allows me to curve out of the way of its strike before it plummets below.

The next two are less willing to throw away their positions. They wait until I fly close enough to strike. I try to do the same thing with the second; blind them and jerk my body around their extended arm, but after seeing what happened to the last of its brethren, it instead snaps out and grasps my wing. His hand passes right through and my momentum carries me up to the third.

I need a second to recover the physicality of my wing, which stops me from dodging the third's claws. They pass right through my fiery plumage and chest. If that physical strike is all it could do, then I have no need to worry. At least I think that until the weight on my back dislodges.

Grímr slams into the wall. Hard. A snap resounds and his body goes limp. I quickly pull back on the flames around him before they burn him like the mermineae underneath me. Thankfully, he lands on a protruding rock away from the mermineae. I'll be able to pick him up without issue.

I flap my wings and gain more height. So close. I'm so close to escape.

What? No. I need to get Grímr. Why am I flying away?

I breach the surface and find myself in the bright blue sky. The moon high in the sky and the Titan Alps welcome me. Euphoria floods my chest. I'm finally free.

The feeling lasts for only a moment before it drains to dread. I snap my neck down to the fissure beside the familiar sight of the Titan's path. How could I? How could I abandon him? I toss my bag with my outfit and spear to the side and dive back down, willingly throwing myself back into that horrific tunnel.

The moment I fall below the surface, I recoil at the mental backlash. The knot screams at me to get back to the surface. My wings jerk in an attempt to pull myself back up, but I have too much momentum.

I drop like a rock toward a motionless Grímr and the merminea holding him by the tail. My talons pierce right through his eyes and the fire in the crevice reignites with greater intensity than before. The merminea tries to pull me off, but each time his clawed fingers try to grab at me, they do nothing but slide through my incorporeal form.

My talons and beak are the only things left physical as I claw and strike at it. I continue to amplify the heat around it until the merminea finally releases Grímr.

If you don't let me grab Grímr, I'm just going to keep coming down here.

The threat only works somewhat. It gives me enough fight against the knot's control to fall to Grímr and pierce my talons into his back. I don't have the time or mental control to care about how I get him out, just that I get him out.

Now, with every part of my mind collaborating, I rocket upward. Away from the mermineae still struggling against the cinders burning through their skin.

I wasn't able to kill any, most swiping away my flames before they became fatal. But none got away without deep burns through their skin, which is incredibly encouraging. I'm not helpless against them.

Once more under the open air, I let out a sigh of relief and look down at Grímr. The lizard is still not moving. Lacerations litter the pale body, many of which couldn't be only from the mermineae. Shrapnel from the cavern exploding around us must have hurt him without my notice. As long as he's still fine on the inside, we'll be okay.

I soar down and pick up my bag before darting away. The mermineae scatter across the ground below. There are almost as many as in the tunnel below, but I can't see a single one. Even with the light of the sun and knowing exactly where they are with my thermal sense, I still can't spot them. Their fur takes on the color, pattern and texture of the snow and rock around them with uncanny precision.

We are obviously not in the same place we entered. While still at a high altitude of the Alps, the land far below is not familiar in the slightest. From my vantage point, the land appears far flatter than I'm used to. As far as I can see, there are no major hills or mountainous terrain beside the Titan Alps itself.

Actually, the appearance of the Stepps lacks many of the trees that populated the other side. It's hard to tell from this distance, but direct channels leading away from the Alps discolor much of the land beyond the Stepps. Mostly, they are straight, but sometimes the lines of damaged land curve or widen.

I stretch my wings wide and just enjoy the moment. Feeling free once more is amazing. I'll need to find where my team has been taken, but for now I just want to relish in the calm that I'd all but forgotten about in my long stint within the Alps.

The moon ahead of me looks higher than I remember, and there's a faint vertical line below it, like a scratch mark in the sky.

I feel an ever so slight tapping on my talon and look down to spot Grímr in his tiny spider-like appearance, half-protruding from the back of the lizard.

"Is the body dead?" I ask, slowing.

He nods to me and climbs the rest of the way out and clings to my talon.

"Do you need it?" If the body is of no use to him, I might as well.

He shakes his small body and gestures with a leg to the limp lizard.

With his permission, I burn through it, thankful not to have to deal with all the extra weight anymore. After months of glow-bugs, it's rather underwhelming. Though, the flavor is decent.

I'll have to find Grímr another body. A task that might be rather hard, as much of the open plains before me appear uninhabited. There might be no other option at the moment to fly until I find something. Landing in the snow with my torn outfit isn't something I want to do.

Remus, Bunny, and Jav will have to wait until we get ourselves sorted before we can even think about freeing them. Hopefully, Grímr has some idea of where they might have been taken, because I wouldn't know where to start.

Now that my mind is free from the influence of the knot, I realize my actions in the tunnel were rather horrific. Hundreds of mermincae were killed by leading the monstrosities to them. I don't truly regret what I did, as it led to my freedom and those that entrap and imprison others deserve nothing less. But the mass slaughter by incomprehensibly strong beings reminds me far too much of the fate that befell my tribe. As much as I hate that they would imprison rather than kill, they are still people. I've seen their sapience. To cause the same sort of devastation that killed my family is not something I want.

Even as I consider how horrible it is to murder all these people, I know I would do it again to protect my freedom and the freedom of those I care for. While I don't know if I could ever forgive those three for what they did, I don't want them to suffer that fate.

Death would be a better outcome.

Light scratching at my feet has me look down at Grímr, who jabs a leg backward, gesturing behind me. I twist my neck to find what he's indicating to and my flames chill the moment I spot it.

High on the Titan Alps is the mountain's namesake. A titanic buzzard perches between mountains that appear minuscule beneath it. Even so far away, it is still far too close. How did I miss it as I came out of the tunnel?

Despite its brown and black feathers, the avian Titan appears to shimmer in the sunlight. Visible distortion warps the entire outline of the creature, but nothing stops me from seeing it twist its head. The air seems to freeze around me as the eye of the massive bird locks onto me. My breath catches and wings lock. Even as I lose altitude, I don't adjust my flight. I don't dare make any motion that might keep its attention on me.

The Titan's eye peers right through me. It feels like it sees much more than that which is visible. My entire being is exposed. My past, my thoughts, my fears. The Titan tears me apart piece by piece until there's nothing left. The world around me fades out and I can't see anything but that giant eye piercing through me.

Until the eye turns elsewhere.

The world returns to me and I feel like I've been twisted inside out. My wings snap wide and I forcefully pull myself back into stable flight. The snow awfully close for comfort.

I glance back to the Titan once more, but it is looking somewhere far to the north. It's okay. It's not watching me anymore. I calm myself and check to see Grímr clinging to my talon. I offer my other taloned foot and he quickly scurries inside the bag with my outfit.

Didn't Jav say the Titans were all on the other side of the Alps? Was that true? There aren't more Titans in the plains below, are there?

Now that I think about it, where has the crocodilian Titan gone? Its molten path has gouged just as much out of this side of the Alps as it has near the pact nations. The remnants of its path move out of sight far in the northwest, toward the moon. At least it's far enough away not to worry about, which is far better than the Titan behind me.

Still, the mountainous buzzard doesn't move from its perch, so I should count myself lucky.

I move away from the croc Titan's path. The mermineae populate the area far too much for me to be comfortable staying near. They all stay hidden, but I'm not willing to risk staying near them now that I'm so visible.

Wait, why are they staying hidden?

Even as the thought goes through my mind, I'm too late to react. Before I can process what is happening, my entire body is torn away from physicality and my flames are dispersed so wide I'm unable to even think straight.

When my mind stops spinning, I feel my body separated into several balls of flame careening toward the ground below. I spread my internal flame and connect each of my separated parts, but my body is slow to come together again.

Whatever hit me was moving far too quick. I couldn't get a proper look even as it shot through my flames. Whatever it was, I can't find it. But that is hardly my biggest concern right now; the frozen water below is approaching rapidly.

I won't be able to pull myself together quick enough to avoid the snow.

CHAPTER FORTY-FIVE

Enantiorn Eagle

My body snaps together a moment before I crash into the snow. I'm already dropping too fast. There's no way I'm pulling out of this dive. The only thing I can do is clamp down on my form and try to cool my exterior as much as I can without chilling the heat within. If I can keep all my heat inside, I should be fine.

I smash headfirst into the thick white cover and find myself buried deep. The layer of snow rises well over my short stature while in this form. I flail with my wings and drag myself on top of the white powder. Despite my best efforts, the snow melts around me. A sheen of water stings as it rips energy from my flames. On top of the snow, I hold myself up with the tips of my wings. I try my best to keep my talons from sinking. My bag with Grímr has fallen fifty meters away. I need to get over there.

I try to minimize how much of my body is touching the snow, but even with only my talons and the tips of my wings, the speed at which it is melting is concerning. The longer I stay still, the greater the pain becomes. I scuttle along the surface while I look up; I need to find what attacked me. There's no point taking to the sky again if I'm going to be hit with such intense force again.

With wings spread wide, a large bird glides through the air far above. My first thought is that the Titan has chased us down in the moment I stopped looking, but the plumage of differing shades of blue says otherwise. The Titan buzzard is still far away on the Alps.

The bird above has four long wings that allow it to twist through the air at incredible angles. The eagle curves up, flying upside down and in the opposite direction after an impossibly sharp turn. It doesn't seem to have any more difficulty flying inverted than it did upright. Angling its neck, the bird looks down at me before falling into a dive. Its beak appears more like an axe-head than something that should be on the head of an eagle.

It accelerates far faster than should be possible simply with the help of gravity. From hundreds of meters in the air, it takes barely a second for the four-winged bird to run its talons through me once more.

Five meters long and a wingspan nearing twenty, the eagle dwarfs me. Its talons run me through, but don't split me apart like the last impact. I hold onto my physical form for as long as it takes for the bird to return to the air, taking me away from the melting snow. I tear my body past the claws and I'm hit by a throbbing pain through my chest. My torso takes far longer than it should to pull together. There's something more to the blades on its feet than a simple physical attack.

Before the bird can whip its head around to bite at me, I spread my flames wide and climb out of its reach. The intense wind catches at my wings as I try to climb up the leg of the eagle. As my flames spread to cover the bird's entire body, I notice I can't reach its feathers. Not only that, my flames intensify and burn brighter as we twist through the sky, leaving a trail of fire far behind us.

The eagle twists once more and brings its beak down to bite at me, but as it closes down on me, my flame explodes outward completely involuntarily. It blows me far out of the maw bearing down on me.

It takes a moment to adjust myself and catch the wind under my wings again, but I'm fortunate to have been blown toward my pack and Grímr.

I skim the snow and scoop up the bag as I pass by. As fast as I can, I fly toward the path left by the Titan. The mar on the landscape only a few hundred meters before me. With a twist of my neck, I monitor the eagle that seems to have gained an incredible amount of height in the moment I lost sight of it.

It twists its body and dives again. Even with almost five hundred meters between us, I don't hesitate to throw the bag into the snow once more. I brace and force my body as intangible as I can.

The sharp axe-like beak slices through the right side of my body and dismembers my wing. I tumble through the air and crash into the snow once more. Agony jolts through my body. This isn't something I've felt since I fought the general.

The flames of my wing don't return and I'm forced to regrow it. Unlike my fight with the general, I don't feel near as drained from the loss of a limb, but that doesn't change the fact that without my wing, there's no way I can reach the fissures beside the Titan's path. No chance the bird leaves me enough time to regenerate.

The bird is resetting itself for another dive. I don't know how I'm going to deal with the next one. Without my wing, I can't fly. All I can do is pull myself along the snow that melts below my fiery feathers.

A few minutes. That's all I had to enjoy the freedom of the sky before it was taken from me again.

The air around the bird is just like that when I faced the general. If I don't figure a way out of this, I might not survive. What can I do? My spear? No, that along with my bag and Grímr are too far to reach. Not to mention it'll be hard to use without arms.

My flames have already shown to be ineffective. They can't even touch its body. The strange bending of light around its feathers, while they seem to amplify my fire, completely blocks the bird from being damaged.

The only option I can think of is to unleash. Burn everything in the surrounding air. It might not hurt the eagle, but there's a chance it will scare it off. Doing so will almost certainly melt the snow around me and I'll be left dealing with a pool of water, which is just as bad.

I don't have the time to come up with anything better; the four-winged creature far above twists into a dive. I stumble toward my bag while a firestorm erupts from me. A twister of fire spins up toward the incoming projectile of a bird. In seconds, my flames meet the falling bird and leave no room to dodge the intense heat.

Instead of being scared off as I'd hoped, the eagle flaps its wings and my body is flattened against the ground. A gust of wind stronger than I've ever felt pins me to the earth. I stare in disbelief as my flames burst outward in every direction except where I intended. The intense wind blasts away not only my flames but also the surrounding snow.

At least I don't have to worry about water now. I try to move my wing and talons, but the pressure is too strong. Somehow, even while incorporeal, I'm still pushed back. As tightly as I can, I grasp at the flames still spreading with the gust and pull it back. It's the only option I have left. The eagle is closing in faster than I react.

My flames won't be enough. The firestorm burning through the air rushes back toward us, but it won't reach in time. There's nothing left I can do.

Seriously, I struggle for months to get back to the surface and I get taken out by the first beast I come across out here. If the Eternal Inferno wasn't an apathetic existence, I'd assume it was messing with me. No one else could be this unlucky, right?

What will Grímr do without me? I can't imagine it'll be easy to find a new body by himself.

The eagle bursts through what little flame I could put up in the time I had. It doesn't even blink. My greatest strength, nothing more than a slight annoyance.

I notice movement in my peripheral, but I can't look away from my death as it speeds down to me.

What am I thinking? Am I just going to lie here and accept what's coming? Of course not! There's one thing I can do. It'll hurt, but pain is better than death.

I mix the fire of my body with my inner flame and push it out the side of my body. The agony is as unbearable as losing my wing, but I achieve my goal. I rocket off to the side. My small falcon body is flung out of the way of the eagle's path.

It hurts as much as it does because I'm essentially cutting off my body to do this. I haven't been able to make my inner flame solid yet, but using the mass of my body, I'm able to push myself out of the way.

The eagle screeches, sounding like it is in pain. I'm not sure how. Did I hurt it somehow? Did the firestorm break through its defenses when it slammed back together? No, I can still feel my flames burning around it. The bird's defenses haven't been breached . . . so why?

It continues to shriek and I turn my head to watch it fly to a high altitude once more.

What just happened?

Before I can question further, I feel a hand wrap around my neck. I'm pulled to the rough, furry side of my captor and the land blurs around me.

I focus on the one holding me and realize it's a mermineae. They run along with three legs while holding me and my pack with the other.

I'm extremely uncomfortable in its grasp, but I hold myself off from squirming. For whatever reason, one of my enemies wants me enough to jump in the giant eagle's way. I'll do everything I can to stop it from keeping me captive like its race is my team, but until we are away from the bird, I can hold myself back.

The merminea dashes around, showing incredible speed that none in my team could come close to beating . . . except Jav after being flung. It digs its claws into the hard earth and cuts near all our momentum. In a moment, we slam down into a tight crevice I hadn't even noticed.

I fall out of the speedy creature's grasp and fall to the ground as the merminea digs its legs into either side of the fissure and stares to the sky. The eagle passes over our haven.

While the merminea holds still to the walls above, I open my pack to make sure Grímr is all right. He moves to climb out the moment he sees my missing wing, but I shake my head and push him back inside. I do not want the person above to know Grímr is here.

The fact that the merminea didn't hold on to me any longer than needed is a good sign, but it is still a part of the race holding my team captive. I don't know what it wants, but I'm not trapped here yet.

"You are intelligent, yes?" The merminea twists its head to face me while clinging to the walls above.

There's no more sign that the eagle is coming for us, but I wouldn't be surprised if it is still in the air above, just waiting for me to rise to the air once more.

My wing regrows outward from my chest, but I'll have to wait a while before it'll be usable at all. For now, I'm stuck with this merminea.

"Yes."

At my confirmation, he drops to the ground beside me. I scramble back slightly, placing myself before the pack as I observe him. His eyes are a cloudy gray with a slight glow that dims with each second. So that merminea I saw turn Bunny's weapon to dust a while back isn't the only one. Assuming the glowing gray eyes actually represent that power.

He stops a few paces from me, looking down at my regrowing limb.

"You are from the beyond, yes? Your friends came here before you?" he asks with his shrill, male voice.

I warily nod. He knows of my team that is held captive. Will he try to make me join them? If so, I'm not about to let him take me. Flames churn within me, ready to burn him should he try anything.

Thankfully, he keeps his distance. On his hind legs, he stands far more still than I thought possible for a living creature. His foggy eyes inspect me with an unreadable expression.

"You and your friends, I want to ask of your assistance."

I tilt my head in confusion. The mermineae already have them captive. Why is he coming to me to ask for help?

"You people already hold them prisoner. Why ask me?"

The merminea doesn't shake his head, keeping still despite the furrowing of his brows. "No. Not those ones. Your strong friends."

"The people you hold are the only people I know." Who is he talking about if not for the three of my team?

"Not me. Traitors. They doom all mermineae with their blasphemy."

So he's not a part of the group that holds my team? Maybe we can work something out. He might help Grímr and me free the others.

"What do you need help with?" I'm not sure who these "other friends" are, but if I can do what he needs, we should be able to come to an agreement.

"Stop them fleeing. Mermineae cannot leave the plains. Divine wrath will punish all for their cowardice."

CHAPTER FORTY-SIX

Caavaa

What do you mean? How are we supposed to help with that?"

He wants us to stop the other mermineae moving through the Alps. That they are trying to reach the other side—the "beyond," as they call it—isn't surprising. We've passed thousands of them on our way through the mountain, after all. But I don't know how he expects us to stop so many.

Instead of answering, he climbs the narrow walls of the fissure. "Come. We will assist with freeing your friends, then you can return the favor. That is what you want, yes?"

The merminea stops before breaching the surface and glances around with his camouflaged head.

He knows what I want, on top of appearing to know where my team is being held. But the entire fact that he's so willing to help me free them makes me suspicious. Why would he be so open to betraying his own kind?

Not that I have many other options than to follow him now. That eagle attacked me after only a minute of flight. I have no choice but to assume that is the standard out here. I'd been so happy to return to the sky after so long without it, but I'm now in another environment where flying is too dangerous.

This merminea knows how to traverse the surface. Hopefully, moving with him will let me learn how to avoid the predator of the sky. The most concerning thing to me is the high likelihood of this merminea being exactly like the others. If he has woven this idea of the ones holding my team being traitors, then I might be just following him into a trap. Maybe my flames scared them enough that they didn't want to take me head on.

I have to discard the possibility after a second of thought. Why would this merminea save me from the eagle if he just wanted to lead me into a trap? It wouldn't make sense.

So, despite my better judgment, I decide to trust him for now. Whether he wants to help me free my team or not will become clear soon enough. I just need to make sure not to give him too much information. Nothing could have missed the firestorm I unleashed through the sky. There's no doubt he knows how strong my flame is after that . . . I'd like to call it a fight with the four-winged bird, but "struggle" would be a more appropriate word.

I could stay in my falcon form and pretend to be unable to change my appearance, but I'd have to give up on the protection my outfit would offer. I'd rather not face the elements when any benefit I would get is limited.

As long as they don't find out that most physical weapons have no effect on me, I should be fine. Hopefully, those eyes of theirs will be the only thing dangerous to me.

With my mind decided, I change the focus of my morphing. Instead of trying to regain my wing, I let my body return to my default form.

Despite asking me to follow, the merminea doesn't seem to be in any hurry to move. His body remains stiff as he peeks out over the land. As he remains still, his fur visibly changes. The snowy white darkening into a gray and black to reflect the stone beside him. It's quite incredible. Even as I watch him closely, he disappears against the stone he rests upon. Not even the outline of his body is visible.

He doesn't complain that I take my time, patiently waiting until I've changed and donned my outfit.

Once done, I climb up the wall below him. I can feel his heat, but seeing his head move from what appears to be nowhere is rather unsettling. He fixes me with a stare as he inspects my body. I have my spear in hand and Grímr hides within the pack strapped to my lower back.

The merminea, appeased by my readiness, reaches his arm out to grab me. I drop off the wall before he can reach me. I'll follow him, but I'd rather avoid his grasp if I can.

His hand freezes as I fall away from him. Gray eyes watch me with an intensity that doesn't suit the cloudy, unfocused gaze.

"You are not able to hide, yes?"

I just stare at the merminea. What does that have to do with him grabbing at me?

"Great birds attack on sight. I will hide you so the enantiorn eagle does not hunt." He reaches his hand forward once more, inviting me into his hold.

I groan. I'd really rather not, but if he's right and the eagle above attacks anything it can see, that would explain why all the mermineae I've seen remain hidden.

With a sigh, I reach my arm forward, inviting him to grab me. In moments, I'm tugged to his chest and we are speeding along the surface again. It might have been easier on him if I'd remained in my smaller bird form, but with how much snow we're running across, I'm glad to have the protection of my outfit, regardless of how many holes it now has.

His fur is rough. It feels like I'm being held against the grainy bark of a tree, but instead of the pleasant smell of wood and nature, he reeks of decaying meat and filth. This might be a weird thing for me to say, considering I've never done so myself, but when was the last time he bathed?

I'm bigger than I was the last time he carried me—nearly as tall as he is if he were to stand upright—but he has no issue holding me against himself as he sprints along the surface. My knees squeeze at the sides of his thin torso to keep me steady. It is uncomfortable in his grasp. My knot doesn't flare and force me to fight my way out, but I can't help but squirm.

To distract myself from the uneasy feeling, I speak up. "So, what's your name?"

"I am Caavaa. Forvaal."

Caavaa? Forvaal? Are they both his name? Forvaal sounds familiar.

"Caavaa, why do you call the other mermineae traitors?" I ask.

"They go against the will of Kalma. All mermineae shall be punished for their hubris."

"Kalma?"

"God of decay. We are her servants. When she learns mermineae flee the Buzzard's Hunting Grounds, her wrath will not stop at only those that run. They are foolish to fight against fate."

God? Does that mean this Kalma is like the two beings Ash told me about? Belobog and Chernobog, the gods of light and dark known to the albanic. Well, if she's anything like Hund, I can see why they'd be worried. I'm not sure why a few mermineae leaving their homeland for a safer place would make this Kalma angry. It's not like their entire race would travel through the mountains at the word of somewhere safer. The tunnels are far too dangerous to risk that.

"How do you plan to stop them?" I ask. It's not like we can just kill them all, they are still his race after all. I doubt he'd be willing to go that far. Killing a few that are in my way isn't above me, but I wouldn't go killing them in the hundreds just for the sake of it.

"Close the entrance. That is why I want your friends; they opened the way, they can close it again."

"Wait, what?" It wasn't one of the mermineae that tore those holes in the enhanced stone? Is it the same person who left that pie?

"A year ago. Warriors with strange abilities took down great birds as they descend the mountain. Outsiders. Yet not hostile. They do not listen; not to our requests, nor our threats. You and your friends, we need to request your aid."

We are moving quite far from the Titan's path now. The land is near perfectly flat as far as I can see. Unlike the other side of the Alps, the mountains and hills seem to have ground down into a gradual slope over the Lower Elevation and the Stepps. No wonder those birds are so deadly; beside the fractured earth provided by the path, there is nowhere to hide.

If there were people from the pact nations that moved here, then they'd have to be at a level of strength greater than my team. There couldn't be all too many of those, right? Maybe Remus will know who they are.

"You have powerful people of your own, don't you? Can't you seal the opening yourself?" I ask.

"No. Those of us with strength can only destroy. Gifted the decay eyes by the great Kalma, Forvaal can remove any boundary, but not rebuild it. Outsiders are needed to seal the passage, while we kill all the Forvaal traitors that may reopen the way."

Forvaal must be a name for those with those cloudy, gray eyes. How could someone just be given power? I assume the decay eyes are what destroyed Bunny's weapon. It must also be what Caavaa used to scare off that eagle. How powerful must this Kalma be to gift others with such strength?

The ones he calls outsiders . . . I wonder why they don't respond to the mermineae. Assuming there were no lies in his words, he thinks that only those from the same place as them could convince them. If that's true, he has a reason to try to free my team even without me requesting so.

But there is a flaw in his thinking. Even if the people who came here are from the nations we came from, that doesn't mean they will listen to us. There is no guarantee they'll hear us out if they have ignored the locals.

Is this some misunderstanding of culture? I've seen plenty of differences between races and people as I've traveled, so I know that something that might be natural to one might as well be taboo for another type of people. Is this merminea projecting his assumptions on how others will act?

If so, I have no plan to correct his mistake. If he knows that people from across the mountain aren't all friendly with each other, he would be far less likely to help.

We speed along the snow for a while longer. It's a struggle to be held as I am, but I push through the tension until the light disappears. I watch the path ahead of us, but we are already inside the hole in the ground by the time I notice it.

A shallow cave within the hard packed soil. The sunlight filters through the entrance behind me, lighting the small space. It's more of a burrow, with enough space to fit only a few mermineae. Mermineae I can feel along the walls, but unable to see.

I'm unceremoniously dropped to the soil. It'd be annoying if I wasn't so happy to be out of its grasp.

"Caavaa, what is this? And why have you brought it here? Does it don corpse-skin? Did you bring one of the centzon to us? Are you trying to doom us more than we already are?" a feminine voice squeaks from the wall as a merminea moves out of concealment.

"Fear not. It is an outsider, not centzon," Caavaa says. "There was an explosion at the hole. I followed this one away from it. The quakes rumored to follow the outsiders; this one is the cause." He gestures to me with a clawed hand.

Wait, they've been hearing my detonations? I guess that's why he assumed I was intelligent and not some beast when we met.

"They will help?" The female merminea turns her attention fully on me. "It's small, no? The other outsiders were larger."

"Yes. We free the outsiders, then they assist us."

"I'm Solvei." I introduce myself, somewhat annoyed at being called both 'it' and small.

My attention drags away from the two visible mermineae and lands on the one still hiding along the wall. I can feel the heat of its body, but still can't spot its outline.

"Oh, I'm so happy you're with us. The traitors don't understand how much danger they are putting all of us in. Many of them have never met our god, so I can sympathize with their ideal, but the Forvaal should know better." She speaks with such expressive words that her lack of body movement seems odd. "May the great Kalma's wrath never curse our meeting. Solvei, it's great to meet you. I'm Aana."

As we lock eyes, I notice that while hers have the same shade of gray as Caavaa, they are nowhere near as cloudy. Her gaze is focused and intense.

"So," I start, sending a glance to the merminea still hiding in the corner of this burrow. They know there is someone there, don't they? "How do we plan to free my team?"

Caavaa opens his mouth to speak, but is interrupted by the third merminea finally coming out of hiding. "Wait. We have no assurance that they will return the favor once we free them, no?"

"A favor in return for a favor. You think otherwise, Muuro?" Caavaa asks. "Both would murder a merminea before the chance arose."

"And yet both are intelligent species. These outsiders are different, how?" Caavaa frowns, but doesn't respond.

"This is still the best option we have, so I'm not against the idea," Muuro says. "I just want some assurance that they will reciprocate the assistance we give them." He stares at me. His gray eyes not as cloudy as Caavaa's, but still far more than Aana's.

What does he want from me? I push the bag holding Grímr out of his sight and grip my spear. His gaze immediately snaps to the motion and I realize my mistake. By trying to hide it, I've done nothing but attract his attention. I take a step back under his scrutiny.

Thankfully, he doesn't push the issue, but he definitely knows I'm hiding something now. "Don't worry so much," he says. "Let's just get to know each other first. The more we understand about each other's intentions, the better off we'll be."

I don't know how to feel. His smile is as fake as Gloria's once was. My first impression of the other two has been . . . at least not bad, but Muuro sends off warnings in my mind. There is something off-putting about him.

"I'll start then. I am Muuro, from the far western plains. Our goals are twofold; stop mermineae fleeing the plains and prevent our god hearing about their attempt. The three of us are here to infiltrate the traitors and work with the Forvaal clergy to save our race."

He turns to the other two. "Is there anything you want to add?"

Aana speaks up. "I'm a local. I'm intimately familiar with the Euroclydon winds and how to survive them. Please rely on me if the Titan begins a hunt."

Uh, what's this about a Titan going hunting?

"No," Caavaa says.

Are we not going to acknowledge what she said?

"Well then, it's your turn, Solvei." I can't help but narrow my eyes at the way he says my name. He sounds friendly, but I feel daggers hidden in his tone. "You saw me while camouflaged, how?"

The other two mermineae turn their heads in surprise, but I know I wasn't all too subtle with my gazes earlier. "I couldn't see you. I felt you."

"You . . . felt me?"

"Yes. I can feel the heat you give off."

"Huh." Muuro seems slightly off-kilter, but recollects himself rather quickly. "Then. Next question." His eyes narrow at the bag on my lower back. "You are hiding something, yes? Show us."

CHAPTER FORTY-SEVEN

Traitors

I try to say I'm not hiding anything or any other lie, but the words freeze in my throat. I've not needed to lie in such a long time that I'd forgotten the changes made by the Fog prevent me from saying anything but the truth. Of course, misleading by limiting the information I give has worked, but how can I do that in this situation?

I can't show them Grímr. Not while he's in such a vulnerable state.

"I'd rather not." With a hand over my bag, I step away from Muuro and make sure there is nothing to block an escape attempt should it be required.

"Come now, we can hardly work together if you're not willing to trust us." He steps toward me, rising to his hind legs, and looks down on me.

The other two mermineae stand off to the side, thankfully not getting in my way, but also not opposing his actions. My flames churn beneath the surface, ready to retaliate should he attack. I'd rather have their help to free my team, but I don't need them. It isn't like they are the only option I have; Grímr and I could figure a way eventually, but that will take time.

I've been out on the surface for barely any time at all and I can already tell it is just as hard to survive out here as down in the caves. The mermineae have camouflage for a reason. It might take me far too long to figure a way to safely traverse these plains before I can reach Remus, Jav, and Bunny.

Just as I'm about to refute him once more, I watch his eyes slide to my right. There, standing on my shoulder, is Grímr.

"What are you doing?" I blurt. Why would he come out now? Doesn't he realize how dangerous this is for him? What if they decide to use him as a hostage? There's no way he can defend himself as he is.

I try to grab him and push him back in my bag, but he just scurries over my fingers and gives me a glare.

Ah. It's too late to hide him anyway. The mermineae have already seen him, there's no point hiding now.

"This is Grímr. He's a friend." Grímr waves as I introduce him. I open my bag to show that it was only him hiding within. "Happy?" I glare at Muuro.

"Uh . . ." He stares dumbfounded at the portian. "Not what I expected, but we can work with that."

Each of the mermineae seem rather disturbed at the sight of him, having taken a step away from us since he'd shown himself. How rude of them.

"Your tiny friend," Caavaa starts. "He was with you the entire time?"

I nod before bringing the topic back to what is most important. "So, how are we going to free my team?"

Muuro inspects me and Grímr with his gray, unfocused eyes. "You can both fight, yes?"

Before I can answer, Caavaa does for me. "This one made explosions that spooked the traitors. Fire does her bidding, and she transforms into a bird; like a tiny vermilion," he says. "The insect, I do not know."

I look at Grímr, silently asking whether I should tell them. He bobs his body in affirmation.

"Are there any creatures in this area that are strong, but not impossible to subdue? Grímr can make use of them if we give him the opportunity."

"Sure, there's plenty," Aana says. "But make use of them, how?"

I hesitate and look down at Grímr for a second time. I know he doesn't like people knowing what he can do. He gives me a serious look and nods again.

Well, if he's fine with it. "He can take over their bodies by digging into the back of their heads."

Each of them takes another step away and their faces twist in disgust. Aana even reaches for the back of her neck in a display that clearly shows what she's thinking. The excessive reaction is shocking. I know he was worried about people's reactions in the past, but I thought it was mostly his own self-consciousness. It's not that horrible. There are plenty of dangerous things in the world. The Titan watching over the plains at this very moment is at the top of the list.

Grímr slumps on my shoulder before the light taps of his feet climb up my neck. He settles in my hair and none of the mermineae take their eyes off him. It takes a second for them to realize their mistake, but they don't close in again. Even Muuro, who was in my face only moments ago, now keeps a wide space between us.

"We need time to prepare, an alicanto is perfect," Caavaa says. "Strong. Big. Not impossible to beat. Will make the plan easier."

"We'll have to wait for the night. Do keep your distance until then," Muuro says and moves back into his corner of the small burrow, blending back into the wall.

"Wait, what's the plan for freeing my team?"

"Your friend gets his body tonight, then we tell you." Caavaa walks to the exit of the burrow. "Traitors will become suspicious if I'm gone much longer," he says and rushes out.

"Where's he going?" I turn to Aana, the only one still visible.

"He's spying on the traitors. The clergy doesn't have the numbers to oppose them directly, so we have to wait for our opportunity. We are here to forward information home."

"Sure, tell the outsider everything." Muuro's shrill voice grouches from the wall.

"She's gonna tell who?" Aana snaps back. "Two minutes ago, you were spouting about being open with each other. This is different, how?"

Muuro doesn't respond, so she turns back to me with a huff. "Well, Solvei, I'm glad to finally meet someone from a race that isn't hostile. I've heard stories of people like that in the far west, but it's great to know that the beyond has some too. I guess a peaceful land is bound to have peaceful people."

Peaceful people? That's quite the bit of misinformation. Although, compared to this side of the Alps, ours might actually be more placid. I won't know until I see more of the plains for myself.

"Do you mind telling me about the beyond?" Aana asks as she sits before me, keeping a decent distance between us . . . or between herself and Grímr. "I've grown up hearing tales about it, but nobody had been there before this year. Is it true the moon doesn't bleed at night?"

"The moon bleeds?" I ask, but Muuro interrupts us once more.

"You are asking about the beyond. Why? Now, more than ever, it is blasphemous. Some might assume you are a traitor yourself if you are too curious."

She doesn't move, but her eyes turn to the hiding merminea. "You are curious too, no? There are many stories, but which are true?"

"Curiosity is fine as long as you do not act upon it. The world is harsh, but the great Kalma is harsher. If she were to learn of your disloyal thoughts, death would be a blessing," Muuro says.

"I know!" Aana snaps. "I know how terrifying she is. I'm trying to stop the traitors right now, no?"

"You still do not know the true lengths her spite can reach," the bodiless voice says. "Our eyes are not the only thing she can change."

Aana grits her teeth and stares off into space. She's obviously done with talking.

This Kalma sounds horrible. I hope I never meet her.

When Caavaa finally returns, the light of day has disappeared. He takes one step into the tight burrow, says "Come," and leaves.

I'm surprised by the simplicity of his command, but the two mermineae don't hesitate to follow. Slowly, I creep out after them. I'm worried the eagle will dive after me in the dim moonlight.

"Don't delay, Aana. Cover our guest," Muuro says.

"Me? Why? You should carry her."

"You're the jill. She will be more comfortable with you, I'm sure."

Aana casts a wary glance at Grímr where he sits comfortably on my head.

"Worry not." Caavaa holds out a fur blanket that blends with his own hide. "I pilfered a cover from the traitors."

He hands it to me and I immediately cringe from the texture; it's sticky and hard, not at all like any cloth I've felt before. As I look closely, the fur is all held together by some type of hardened sap. Against my better judgment, I give the blanket a sniff and almost retch. It smells worse than it feels.

"What is this?" I ask warily, holding it at arm's reach.

"Merminea fur. You can hide with that," Caavaa says.

Ugh. I guess the mermineae aren't very good craftsmen. With a feeling of disgust, I look down at the sheet of fur. Once Grímr has climbed off my head and wedged in the crook of my neck, I toss the heavy blanket over my head like a cloak.

I shiver as the slimy coat sticks to my hair and shoulders. This better not be the only way to survive the plains. Even as I stand here, the fur changes color to reflect the snow my feet sink into. It's a good thing that I avoided getting the boots or lower half of my outfit damaged while I was in the caverns. As long as I don't fall over for long, I should be fine.

It's strange that the mermineae's fur retains its camouflaging characteristic. Maybe when we free the others, Jav will repurpose their fur into an actual bit of clothing for me.

Without waiting so long as to confirm that I'm properly hidden, Caavaa drops to all fours and skulks away. Both other mermineae follow suit and I'm left to catch up, hoping that their gift is enough to hide me from anything above.

I glance into the sky, looking for any birds flying overhead, but the moon captures my gaze. The faint line I noticed in the sky earlier now glows as bright as the moon itself. It reaches from the horizon in a perfectly straight line until it reaches the moon. A tear in the sky. There is no other answer; something has cut the sky between land and moon.

Did it happen while I was in the Alps? Was it the Titan? I don't know if anything else would be strong enough to do such a thing. The path of the crocodilian Titan leads that way, so it must be.

What does this mean? Is the world going to fall apart?

The mermineae around me don't seem to consider it worth any attention, so has it been like this for a while now? At least it doesn't seem immediately dangerous.

I shake my head. There's no point worrying about it. I wouldn't be able to do anything about it, anyway. I just need to focus on the task ahead of me. It's time to get Grímr another body. Hopefully, this one will be strong enough to last.

We travel in silence for nearly an hour until we reach the largest disruption in the constant slope I've yet seen. Where the snow thins, I can see smooth gray stone curving over the landscape for quite a distance. A shallow dome that expands above the plains.

Beyond the field of stone, I see the familiar sight of a glacier. Further down the Alps, it expands to the sides and takes up much of the land as it had on the other side. So, we are on the Lower Elevation. Then, after I free my team, as long as we head below the Stepps, we won't be in danger of dangerous beasts like that eagle.

I'm not going back. My friends are back on the other side of the Alps, but I cannot put myself back into those entrapping caves. If the team wants to head back after we rejoin, then they'll do so without me.

A glint catches my eye from ahead of me. At first it looks gold, but somehow the color is green the second time I spot it.

"We are lucky," Caavaa says. "An alicanto. At the first mountain we check."

I glance over the area before us once more. Mountain? What mountain? At most, this mound of stone can be considered a large hill.

"Solvei," Caavaa calls to get my attention. "We will assist, but don't expect us to decay our eyes for you. We can hold the alicanto only if you bring it to the ground. Whether your tiny friend succeeds is up to you."

What does that mean? They won't decay their eyes? Do they mean they won't scare that bird with that eye power he used when he saved me?

"Okay. Should I know anything for the fight?"

Caavaa hums. "The alicanto's first reaction when caught digging is to fly off. You will need to fly." His eyes drop to the spear in my hands. "It is covered in metal, so that will have limited usefulness."

I nod and toss off the sticky cloak with a glance upward. Relieved that there are no birds diving for me, I grow my wings.

I don't have any time to experiment with any forms that might let me use the spear while I'm flying, so I settle with the familiar falcon form I've used so much now. But, I don't want to take this fight without the benefit my weapon can bring, so I'm going to have to rely on something I learned to do only earlier today.

I light up the surroundings like a burning pyre amid darkness. As the flames of my arms morph into wings, I engulf my inner flame around the weapon and slowly let go.

Rather than falling to the ground below, the spear floats within my fire. A mental tug rolls the pole in a slow strike, speeding up into a spin as I become more comfortable with this new feeling.

It was painful earlier, combining the fire of my body with my inner flame. But doing so finally let me realize what I was doing wrong for so long.

Physicality isn't directly related to how far I push my control. Sure, having better control over my flame helps, but I could have an impossibly excellent control and I never would have been able to force my flames solid.

The flame of my body is just somehow . . . different. It would be impossible to reach the same corporeal state with my inner flame. It also explains why my body is so slow for a fire.

To give physicality to my inner flame, I have to cheat. Instead of just burning through air to empower myself and my flames, I need to use the weight of the air itself.

Of course, the air doesn't weigh that much, so mass I can supply from other sources helps as well. I can burn through the earth to give my flames weight. To give them grip where they never used to.

The downside of this is that I need to rely on my own supply of flames rather than the flames that might be created by burning through things. After months of munching through those glow-bugs, though, this is not much of an issue.

I take to the air, my spear following in a cradle of flames.

I am ready.

Alicanto

Controlling my spear without my hands is far harder than I expected. Even the lazy twirls around my body feel like I'm trying to balance it with a foot. It's a bit like when I first grew my wings; the unfamiliarity of using my flames to grasp makes my actions feel alien.

Cycling through strikes and thrusts of the variety of styles I know helps me gain familiarity and speed in my actions, but it doesn't stop feeling strange. Doing so while focusing on flying only amplifies the feeling. I realize now the importance of the balance training Bunny had me do. I need more experience splitting my focus.

I fly toward the flickering gold and green glint until I can make out its avian shape. The grounded bird is digging through the earth. It mines into the stone amongst piles of boulders and loose rock. Metallic scrapings echo through the air as its beak, talons, and wings grind through the earth.

I cast a glance down to the three heat signatures following close beneath me. They are blending with the ground, but it doesn't seem like they are going to back out now.

The grinding cuts off and the bird rises from the hole. Moonlight bounces off the creature's shiny body, the light as bright as if it were day. Its feathers glimmer and shift between gold and green. The alicanto's wings snap wide and it screeches up at me. I guess there's no hiding my approach when flames writhe around me.

The bird's screech doesn't sound natural. Like when it was digging, it sounds more like the scraping and grinding of metal. As I close in on it, the alicanto doesn't wait for me. It flaps its large fifteen-meter wingspan and takes off.

I'm surprised and somewhat thankful it doesn't take me head on. I'm still carrying Grímr in my pack, so I'd rather avoid any heavy impacts. It'll be especially bad if this bird can hit as hard as that four-winged eagle could.

Now that I think about it, why am I holding the bag? I quickly toss it into the surrounding flames to be carried alongside my spear. Grímr should be fine floating around until I need him.

Unlike the last avian I had to deal with, this one is slow to rise. It takes multiple flaps to pull itself into a stable flight. Despite the slow movements, the amount of turbulence the bird stirs through the air says much about its strength. The thing must weigh tons.

The alicanto gradually speeds up, but it is no trouble for me to catch. Other than its large wingspan, the bird has a long rope-like tail of feathers. Feathers which, as I look closer, are far more inflexible than they should be.

I glide behind the bird for a few seconds, waiting for the perfect opportunity to present itself. The longer I wait, the faster the alicanto becomes. It's impressive how fast this creature is moving, considering how slow it was to get off the ground.

Impressive as it is, I can't wait any longer. It might get faster than me if I wait for an opportunity that won't present itself. I cut the distance between us in a moment. The alicanto twitches and I only barely halt my momentum in time to prevent the bird's tail smashing through me. The tail whips through my wing, which quickly reforms.

It's a relief it doesn't possess that same ability as the other bird to tear me apart without regard for the incorporeal state of my flames.

There was something I noticed when the tail tore through my flames. Even the way the tail flicks around for another strike only confirms what I felt. The feathers are all metal. The tail acts more like a chain than anything natural, with movements that bend only at joints.

What with how slow it was to start its flight, its entire body might be metal, not just the feathers. Will Grímr even be able to take over a creature like this?

Well, no point having doubts now. I shoot a jet of flame out of my back, pushing me under the second tail-swing in a way that would be impossible for a normal bird. For that instant, I use the new mass-carrying inner flame to propel myself while removing the physicality of my wings.

As soon as the sharp chain of metallic feathers soars over my head, I snap my wings back to corporeal and give myself a boost with a jet of flame. I rocket toward the metal bird faster than I've ever moved.

With my inner flame grasping my spear, I launch it forward. The weapon bounces off its metallic feathers without leaving so much as a scratch. I'm not surprised; it's too difficult to put much weight behind my flames to breach the bird's defenses.

To stop me from reaching its back, the alicanto twirls in the air. Razor feathers slice through my body without resistance, but it does nothing to me. Not needing to worry about Grímr—who still floats amongst the trailing storm of fire—I slam into the metal breast of the bird without a touch of damage to my body.

As fast as I rocket into the bird, it means nothing in the face of the weight it possesses. The alicanto stops its twirling and levels its flight again, but that doesn't mean I have nothing to worry about. As I cling to the underneath of the metal bird with my talons and clawed wing tips, its feathers buzz as they oscillate.

I watch in surprise as the feathers leave their natural position. A metallic scraping scratches at my ears as each feather weaves past one another. In seconds, the plumage moves at a terrifyingly dangerous speed. Feathers cut through my talons and wings and before I know it, I've lost my grip.

Unwilling to let the bird take the advantage, I bring the firestorm down upon it with an intensity I'm still not used to. I can feel gold and silver along with more common metals and some that I don't recognize. If I can burn away the feathers defending it, I can make an opening for Grímr.

The bird hardly reacts to the flame spreading over its body. Curving its wings, it soars high. It gains altitude quickly, but its momentum dies with altitude. I trail behind it, but keep some distance between us; I don't know what it's planning.

The alicanto slows to a stop in midair. With a mighty thrust of its wings, it plunges toward me with near max speed. I'm right below it and there is no mistaking that I'm its target. The bird has finally given up running and plans to take me head on. It's an intimidating sight; so much weight nosediving toward me.

This is an opportunity, so I resist the urge to dodge.

I cast the flames holding my bag away from the incoming beast and grasp my spear in my talons. I can't put much weight into the weapon with only my inner flames physicality. It'll be more effective to hit it myself.

With flame jets bursting from my wings, I rocket up into the plummeting mass. I doubt my spear can do any damage if it is a glancing strike, so I need to make sure it's a direct hit. The alicanto dives with its razor-like beak first. Dangerous talons poise to pierce me.

Its body has too much sloped armor. Nowhere I hit will give me the purchase I need to pierce. Not with the limited weight I have in this body.

Nowhere except the eyes.

It'll be difficult to hit, but that's the only place I'll be able to do any damage. I line up my spear, twisting in the air so I'm rising with my talons ready to thrust the spear through the bird. It leaves me exposed to being run through by the alicanto's beak, but I should be fine.

The metal bird falls with insane momentum.

I rise with explosive thrust.

The impact sends me sprawling. It takes a few seconds for the flames of my body to come back together enough for my thoughts to be comprehensible. Quickly, I look below. My spear is missing, and the alicanto continues on its spiral toward the ground.

Did I get it? Did my spear pierce through its head? Or have I flung it into the distance somewhere?

Even if I missed, I don't have the time to waste searching for my weapon. I pull my wings to my side and chase after the falling mass of metal. My flames have been trying to burn through its hard feathers this entire time, but I still haven't succeeded.

An explosion of sound rocks me as the alicanto impacts the earth. Dust rises from the crater it leaves, but the crash wasn't enough to end the bird. It screeches to the skies. The metal grinding sounds rougher this time, like scratching rusted metal.

The spear is there. Wedged deep in the creature's eye socket is the shaft of my weapon. The wood is in splinters, but there's no doubt I hit my mark.

The mermineae, still hidden, rush toward the crash site of the alicanto. I beat them there, slamming into the head of the bird, trying to push the spear deeper. I achieve nothing but scattering my body. The bird doesn't even flinch.

The alicanto is glowing. Not only from the reflection of the moonlight, but also the heat of its feathers. A deep red glow rises beneath the gold and green shimmering. It should be far hotter than the melting temperature of most metals now, but I've only been able to heat it to this point. Regardless, its exterior is softening now. It shouldn't take too much longer before Grímr's opportunity will present itself.

I'll have to protect him from the heat while he digs in.

The mermineae dash forward, their fur darkening under the illumination of my flames and the alicanto's reflection. They grab at the creature's wings and tail, their claws dig into the metal and pin it to the ground. The razor feathers zigzag along the bird's surface, trying to cut through the offending claws, but they fail to inflict significant damage.

The alicanto jerks, trying to pull its extremities back to itself, but while the mermineae stumble and struggle against its efforts, they keep it pinned for long enough for me to get to work.

I stand on top of the metal bird, its feathers tearing through my talons, but that does nothing to stop me. With a hop, I land on its head. It snaps around at me, but with its wings pinned as they are, it cannot fling me off. The metal around the shaft of my spear is the first of the creature to melt. It's only a matter of time now and the rest of the metal will melt.

I'd rather Grímr not have to recover from entirely melted plumage, so I decide this is good enough an entry. My talon grabs the spear and I jerk it out with as large of an impulse as I can push through this body.

The weapon can hardly be called a spear anymore. Snapped near the tip, it's a disappointing sight. Well, now I got something for Tetsu to do when I get her out.

My flames tear through the cavity and the bird shrieks once more. It looks like there is flesh inside the creature. Only the feathers and a thin outer layer are metal. I float the bag with Grímr down to my side and hurriedly open it. Thankfully, he jumps on my offered wing without delay and I bring him to the cavity, where he disappears.

The alicanto's struggles escalate. A flurry of movement whips the wings and tail out of the grasp of the mermineae. I can't have it getting rid of Grímr, so I wrap myself over the missing eye.

The razors of the alicanto tear into me as it tries to remove me. I hold tight. As long as it's trying to get me off rather than dig Grímr out, we'll be fine.

The mermineae try to regain control of its limbs, but the freed tail whips them all off their feet. The creature twists and flails in its panic. My eye twitches as the mermineae back away from the beast. They give up far too early for my liking. I can understand self-preservation, but we only need to last a little longer.

The shadow-lizard didn't take near as long as this is taking. I know this bird is larger and far stronger, but my grip will not last forever. Not while the alicanto rolls around and scratches at me with its sharp metal talons and wings.

Each feather is fast approaching its melting point. My flames covering the huge bird slowly bring the temperature higher. Far higher than should be required to eat the metals lining its body. It's hard to think that not long ago, I hadn't even been able to melt iron.

Despite the feathers' refusal to melt, they are softening. Each time its wings or tail slam into the stone or its own body, the feathers bend. The grinding sound only grows louder and more grating as the feathers scrape along one another with heavy resistance.

With nothing able to dislodge me from its head, the alicanto changes its approach. Its wings and talons dig into the earth before it slams its head into the ground. The impact dislodges me immediately, but the bird doesn't seem to notice. It continues to smash its head against the stone until the soft metal bends and the creature's head twists at an unnatural angle.

I worry that its desperate actions will crush Grímr as he's wedged deep within the flattening metal head, but the alicanto's actions slow. A few more stone shattering impacts and the bird collapses. The grinding feathers come to a halt.

I jump on top of the creature's head while extinguishing the inferno. I'm sure Grímr has succeeded, but I'm still worried he's hurt. The eye cavity is nothing but a mess of blood and flesh, no way to see Grímr inside. With how much damage the bird caused itself before it lost control, I wouldn't be surprised if it killed itself.

"Grímr? Are you okay?" I ask, not sure if he can hear me through the thick head.

I wait for a moment before the body jerks underneath me. After steadying myself, I let out a sigh of relief. I don't know if that was him trying to respond to me or just making himself familiar with the new body. It's similar enough to the way the lizard acted after Grímr took hold that I'm confident he is fine.

CHAPTER FORTY-NINE

Preparation

I poke at a feather on the alicanto's neck. Despite it no longer spinning around the bird's body, the plumage remains sharp. The bird twitches again. Grímr must be having trouble learning to control this beast. While it took a few moments to put the reins on the lizard, he has yet to achieve more than spasms even minutes after entering the alicanto.

I twist in my mounted position toward the merminea trio closing in on the downed bird. I spare them a suspicious glance. They said they would help once the bird was grounded, but the effort they put in was minimal at best. Were they hoping Grímr and I would fail? Or were they trying to gauge what we can do? Whatever their intention, they've only succeeded in making me annoyed at them.

Much of their hides are scratched up with shallow cuts. Their arms and claws are damaged by the grinding feathers when they tried to pin the bird. A gash in two of their sides and one's chest from the chain-like tail. As bloody as the wounds look, they are only skin deep.

As irritated as I am with their lack of help, the alicanto they lead us to is the best I could hope for. There aren't too many things that'll come out unhurt from a dive from this heavy bird. It's strong and, while slow to accelerate, its powerful wings can push it to incredible speeds.

"Your friend succeeded, yes?" Caavaa asks as he approaches the twitching bird.

I watch him carefully, uncertain he won't pull something before Grímr can control his new body properly. The mermineae stop a few meters from us, thankfully. They inspect the still hot, deformed feathers along the wing of the downed beast.

"Yes." I don't tell them any more. If they know it'll take time for Grímr to learn to adjust to his new form, they might take advantage of that. Their actions in that fight remind me that while we are working together, I shouldn't expect much from them. They care more about achieving their goal than helping me. If Grímr and I were to die, it would be a setback at most for their plans.

The wings of the alicanto finally move with structure and not the twitchy jerks it had until now. Their long, fifteen-meter wingspan stretches wide. Metal groans under the effort. The wings freeze in place and the singular remaining eye of the bird opens up before me. Grímr's new eye seems to wander randomly until it lands on me.

A swirl of green and gold light glistens in the moonlight's reflection, almost like they are lights in of themselves. Considering the power of this beast must sit near that of the dahu, I wouldn't be surprised if they are glowing all on their own.

Grímr winks at me. I take that to be his confirmation that everything is all right.

His eye rolls forward and his wings grind as they clamp closed to his sides. I have to lean forward and hold on to the neck feathers as Grímr slowly brings his talons underneath him. He stumbles around for a while until he steadies himself and steps forward without falling.

The mermineae back off, their faces unable to hide their revulsion. I don't really understand it; it's not like it's them being taken over. Is this sort of reaction normal to Grímr? It would explain why he was so hesitant to tell me what he was when we first met.

"Your races are common in the beyond, yes?" Aana asks with hesitation.

I turn to her before Grímr tries to follow suit. His head twists in the right direction, but his feet aren't quick enough to account for the change in balance and we topple to the ground.

"Yeah, I think so," I say, trying to ignore the many-ton bird flailing beneath me.

The mermineae exchange glances. It's obvious they are hiding something. Whatever thoughts they've had amongst each other, they don't share it with Grímr and I.

I narrow my eyes, but before I can question them, the feathers beneath me buzz. They tear through my talons, and I realize I'm still in my falcon form. I should change back before Grímr is ready to leave.

"So, what's the plan to get our team out?" I ask as I glide off Grímr's back.

They're still yet to tell me what they have planned. I haven't questioned their lack of openness until now, what with Grímr's new body taking precedence. If they still don't answer even now, I think it's time we part ways. I don't want to work with people who will try to lead me on.

"A few days we have to wait." Those are not the words I want to hear, but I hold myself back from interrupting. "I shall infiltrate the holding camp and remove restraints. You can create a distraction, yes?"

"Uh, sure." I lower my eyes to the spear-tip, which is all that remains of my weapon. "Do you just want me to spread fire through their camp? Your people will be hurt and I don't think I'd be able to tell you apart from the others." I'll do what needs to be done to free my team, but I doubt Caavaa will be fine with the slaughter of his own people.

"That is fine. Traitors deserve no mercy."

I can't help but stare at him. Our goal is only the freedom of my team. He should consider the deaths of his people as something to be done only if necessary. Well, if he has no issue with it, I probably shouldn't hold back. Who knows what kind of counterattack might reach me if I'm lenient on my enemies.

"I'll give you the signal to start once I'm at a reasonable distance. Take care not to be seen." He points to his eyes. "The Forvaal, those with decay eyes, will not let you off."

Yeah, he doesn't need to tell me. I already know to be careful around the mermineae that can turn things to dust. Thankfully, it doesn't seem all-powerful. Caavaa could only send away that four-winged eagle for a few seconds with his. Then again, that bird brought me close to death, so being able to scare it off even a moment is impressive.

My body finally finishes changing back to my natural shape and Aana tosses the sticky cloak of shed fur. I grumble, but pull it over myself. Even at night, there must be things to hide from. Grímr's shiny plumage isn't exactly well hidden, so I feel the disgusting cloak is rather unnecessary.

"Your friend will collect the captives in the commotion," Caavaa says.

"And what will Aana and Muuro be doing?" I ask. It seems like Grímr and I will do all the work. Sure, they have the information we need, but considering they expect us to help them afterward, they aren't participating much.

"They'll be waiting to hide you after your escape."

It is obvious they are putting all the risk on us. If this fails, only Grímr and I will be in any real strife. Even so, I won't complain. But they can definitely expect me to reciprocate; neither me nor my team will risk ourselves when we look for those outsiders.

"I must head back," Caavaa announces. "Muuro, Aana, please lead them to the observation point near where the outsiders are being held. You know the one, yes?"

"Of course." Aana lowers her head. "May you remain hidden on your journey."

Caavaa returns the gesture. "To you as well." And with that, he runs off, fading from sight in moments.

Aana turns to me. "Get some sleep. We'll head out at first light."

And with that, both she and Muuro skulk away until they come to a stop nearly at the range of my sense. I'd think they might be planning to run off if they hadn't gone in different directions. Actually, just because they've gone to rest apart from each other doesn't mean they won't run off. Well, they're hardly going to run off now; they've already helped Grímr get a body, they'll be expecting something in return soon enough.

I make my way to Grímr. The massive bird is far longer than the panther he used to inhabit, but with his wings at his sides as they are now, he is only a fraction larger than he was. Beak to talon, he's only three or four meters. The chain-like tail is about as long as both wings; fifteen meters, and the feathers flare out at the end, creating a remarkably sharp blade.

The moonlight dims and the reflections off his new shiny plumage die along with it. As the metal bird fades into the darkness of night, I notice an ever so faint light from its sole remaining eye. I was right in my assumption that like the dahu and Forvaal, the creature's energy burns through its eyes.

Do all creatures get this glow when they are strong enough? Or is it just some? No, it is definitely only some; Hund's gaze was powerful, but his eyes didn't glow. Not even slightly.

Do the glowing eyes represent some ability or power that is unique only to them? It would fit with what I've seen. The dahu could control forests of rock and the Forvaal can do that weird dust thing they call decay. Is the ability of the alicanto to spin its feathers? Or is it simply how its outer body is replaced by metal?

It looks like Grímr has finally got the hang of walking on his massive talons and has moved onto stretching his wings and tail with dexterous motions.

"Doing all right in there?" I ask. I know the brain of the bird can't have been left in a good state after the amount of knocks it took. The head is still bent out of shape. I'm not sure if Grímr can fix the deformations.

He nods to me without a break in his movements. He keeps his focus on balancing with his heavy wings and tail stretched to their limits. I guess he considers mastering his body important to do right away, rather than morphing his throat to allow speech. We are still out in the open, so I don't blame him for his choice. He's not as lucky as me. He doesn't have one of the mermineae's cloaks.

One of the sticky, stinky, rotting blankets made from the horribly rough fur and some unspeakable substance that I'm not even sure I want to know where it comes from . . . Wait, why did I think I was the lucky one in this situation?

The Ember Moon's flames ignite and cover the plains in its familiar red glow. The bright shine from the alicanto's body returns, but this time it is a deep crimson, not the gold and green color it previously took. Grímr's eye lands on me and I'm glad it's my friend in there, not some beast. The glowing bloodred eyes are rather eerie, especially considering Eldest Ember's light has changed this bird's appearance entirely.

I can't tell if it's the light playing tricks on me, but the feathers and maw of the bird seem far more intimidating than before. The feathers are more jagged and the beak opens for a line of sharp teeth I swear weren't there a few minutes ago.

It is only when I see the spiky metal ball of feathers at the end of his tail, do I know for sure that his body has changed with the Ember Moon.

Grímr opens his razor-toothed beak and takes a single step toward me before his limbs lock up and he slams into the ground. I wait a few moments, but he doesn't move.

"Are you all right?" I ask.

Grímr winks at me—is it a wink or a blink if he only has one working eye?—and I take that to mean everything is fine. Maybe he's just trying to control a new aspect of his body he found. I don't know. But I'm sure he knows what he's doing.

I'll leave him to it for the night.

In the morning, we move out before the sun rises. Grímr is back to the same way he looked before the Ember Moon, for which I'm thankful.

"What was that last night? Did your body change with the Ember Moon?"

"Ember Moon?" Grímr asks before shaking his beak.

With my merminea cloak, I'm riding on the back of Grímr as he flies after the two running below. Apparently the birds of prey in the area are hesitant to attack other predators of the skies, so riding Grímr is far safer than flying with my own wings. Which is rather frustrating. Maybe I should cover myself in flames to make myself look bigger than all the other birds. Would they attack me then?

"The midnight light seems to send this body into a frenzy. I was receiving signals of intense hunger that didn't make sense and the body began moving entirely on reflexes, so I had to lock down the muscles and joints. I've never seen something like it in any of the other creatures I've been in. The closest would be the instant reflex of some bugs."

"What about the changes to your body, though? The jagged feathers or spike-ball tail?"

"The what?" Grímr tries to turn his head to me, but the still-deformed shape of it prevents him getting an eye on me. "I didn't notice any changes. The body didn't recognize anything was different."

"Huh, well you definitely changed. You became a far more intimidating bird there."

"I'll have to look into it tonight."

The sun finally breaks past the horizon and I cover my eyes, expecting to be blinded by the reflection off Grímr's shiny plumage. But . . . nothing. It's like the metal doesn't reflect the sun's light at all. The green and gold sheen remains, but it is dark, like it's in the shade rather than direct sunlight.

This new body is incredibly curious. I can't wait to help Grímr figure out its secrets.

But first, we need to free our team. Only a brief trip and we'll see them again.

This mission is going to go perfectly.

CHAPTER FIFTY

Remus

Remus had experienced many things in his life. He'd met many races and been to places most couldn't fathom. Despite how much he'd seen, he knew that there was always something more waiting out in the world to discover, but never did he think he would see the other side of the Alps.

It had been a good decade since he'd been on his last travels, and while he'd considered a vacation sometime soon, he never expected to be thrust into these new lands in the way he had.

The Alps were impassable. That fact was common knowledge for centuries. You can't travel far through the Middle Elevation without breathing equipment, not to mention the ever-increasing dangers one faces as they climb higher. In comparison, the journey through the tunnels beneath the mountains was incredibly tame.

The whole idea of a cave system running through the entire Alps still boggled his mind. There were plenty of mining operations in the Alps that had never come across the underground caverns. It was unthinkable they'd always been there.

The journey to this new land was not exactly . . . comfortable, in any sense of the word. He was usually fine with a bit of discomfort, and if it weren't for his junior team members, he might have even treated it like a holiday. But the treatment of the mermineae toward his compatriots left nothing but a foul impression of his captors.

The mermineae's method of torture was the same as the way they lived;

primitive. It was almost a walk in the park compared to his time in the war prison of West Henosis. The mermineae's attempts relied heavily on their claws or blunt force, nothing creative at all.

The most frustrating part was that he gave them the information willingly; there was no reason to hide what he knew. The sensitive information he could never disclose was never asked of him. He gave up information like strengths of mercenary members and important locations with hardly any hesitation all to prevent them hurting his team, and yet they did anyway.

The information was public anyway. They'd be able to find out everything from asking any member of the Mercenary Order they picked up along the way, so he never held back.

Remus tugged at the bindings locking his tentacles together, made of a thick sap-like substance that wouldn't loosen no matter the force applied.

The mermineae were incredibly uncivilized. Not having even the most basic of amenities for a comfortable life. They hid themselves with their camouflaging fur against predators and hunted with their teeth and claws, not even assisted by weapons. He could hardly consider them more than beasts.

The only thing that might indicate potential sophistication was the rotten rug tossed over Remus and his two teammates, with the sap that held the furs together being the same that bound his limbs.

The warmongers of the warring isles would be considered an advanced civilization next to these mermineae.

And yet, despite their lack of advancement, they had strength significantly greater than Mercenary Order median, each one of them equivalent to a lower Luis-ranked mercenary.

Remus looked over his two comrades with frustration. Their own limbs were locked and weapons confiscated. He had seen none of the mermineae carrying them on their travels, so he had to assume they didn't bother bringing them along. They didn't use weapons themselves, after all.

Bunny was as strong-willed as her father. Her eyes glared at any mermineae that glanced her way. There was no reason to hide any information she knew, especially after Remus told them in front of her, but she held back anyway.

Jav . . . had not lasted so long without problems. He had been loud and aggressive against their captors for a few weeks after his questionable attempt to free Remus and Bunny, but after that, he'd pulled into himself. He only talked now when absolutely necessary. It was both sad and infuriating to watch his young friend's fall.

A bundle of leaves landed on the ground before him. Remus looked up to a set of gray eyes. The Forvaal were the strongest of the mermineae. Even without that strange ability of theirs to reduce an object to dust, they have the strength to go toe-to-toe with the best of the Luis mercenaries. He didn't doubt there were some amongst them that could compare with the Beith ranked.

"Rub those into the bindings. Be subtle. Do not move until the bird arrives." The Forvaal blended back into the earth after murmuring his piece, the words barely loud enough to register.

Remus stared after the Forvaal. "Huh."

Bunny inclined her head in question.

"It seems we have a benefactor." Remus knew that if this merminea represented a group opposing their captors, the only reason they'd have to free them would be to gain information themselves. Well, he wasn't about to ignore this gift.

He squirmed his way over to the pile of long dry leaves. The restraints made movement difficult. He pressed the sap-like substance into the pile left between them and tried to rub them in. There was no guarantee that these leaves could somehow remove the sap, but Remus would risk himself before he let the other two try it themselves.

Bunny looked like she wanted to jump on the chance, but her own restraints and biology stopped her from moving. For now, she'd have to be patient; something he was surprised she still struggled with, despite being stuck so long.

Jav huddled into himself, ignoring anything happening in the real world. Remus's body wrung every time he looked at his friend. It was times like this that he wished he'd focused more on increasing his strength rather than exploring the world. Many of the Beith mercenaries he'd once stood side by side with were now leagues ahead of him. If he had replicated the effort they put in, his team would not have fallen into such a situation.

Remus rolled back and forth over the long leaves. A buildup of dust piled around the leaves as they ate away at his restraints. Eventually, he felt the sap drying up against the membrane of his skin. It only took a small tug with his limbs to crumble the bindings that had locked him away for months.

Without being obvious to any watching mermineae, he stretched his muscles that had become stiff after so long being unused. He moved on to freeing Bunny, who was squirming where she lay as she watched, envious of his freedom.

Jav didn't notice what was going on until no sap remained on his limbs.

"What?" He looked down at his now free hands with confusion.

There would be no easy escape for Jav this time. They had torn his wingsuit to shreds after his capture. It was good to see him react to the world once more. Remus had been afraid that he would remain a shell if they'd ever escaped, so his immediate reaction was rather relieving. Even if he didn't think the volan would be okay for a long while.

This whole situation, Remus felt responsible for. He'd treated the search through the caverns as another of his exciting adventures through an undiscovered place. He should have pulled back when half his team showed heavy resistance to push on. But no, he'd just gone and put everyone in even more danger.

Jav's father, his old teammate from decades ago, he wasn't sure he could face him should they ever return. He'd let his old friend's son fall prey to such horrible treatment.

Bunny peered out from under the cover of shed merminea fur. She looked to the sky, obviously looking for the bird mentioned. She turned her gaze back to Remus with a raised eyebrow, remaining quiet.

"I'm not sure how we'll get out." He answered her unspoken question. "But we'll need to wait for the signal before we make any attempt. Let's hope they have a decent plan."

Jav was still looking at his hands.

Remus touched the tip of a limb on the small volan's back. "We're getting out. You think you can push through for a bit?"

"Huh?" Jav's eyes didn't seem to focus, but he responded regardless with an affirmative hum and a nod. "Mm."

As soon as Remus got his team out of this mess, he was going to make sure they were fine. He'd already underestimated the effect of mental health when he'd sent Solvei into a prolonged panic attack. He wouldn't make the same mistake.

Once out of the mermineae's clutches, he needed to find Grímr and Solvei. They must still be trapped down in the depths of the Alps. He could only hope they were still hale and surviving. Maybe they found a way up in his absence.

There was no point in worrying now, not when he still needed to get these two out of danger. He'd seen the girl's eyes; she was a survivor. No matter how much she feared, he didn't doubt she'd find a way out.

He knew from the start the young áed had the determination to push onward. Her desperate gaze in that first spar he'd had with her had shown him not to treat her as a child. Doing so would have been an insult to the challenges she'd already faced.

Despite their ages, Remus believed Solvei had a far better chance of escaping than Grímr, assuming she got a proper grasp on her terror. Grímr was far less likely to take any risks to reach the surface. That also meant he was likely to survive longer down there, even if it meant becoming a part of the ecosystem. Remus hoped the two of them could rely on each other until they reached safety.

As the sun lowered in the afternoon sky, Remus felt the tension exuding off Bunny beside him, her impatience doing her no benefit as they waited for the signal. Jav didn't really seem to process what was happening, but he was aware, which was good enough for Remus.

He put a tentacle around the volan and lifted him to his head. Jav twitched at the touch, but didn't fight his grasp.

A flash of light shone from the north. Remus's eyes swiveled in the direction as Bunny twisted her neck. For a moment, he doubted his sight. The unforgettable burning falcon flew toward them.

Remus couldn't help the chuckle that escaped him. It was so relieving to know she was all right.

"I guess the bird we were waiting for was Solvei, after all." He felt giddy for the first time in a while. Hopefully, she came with a plan and wasn't hoping to take on the bunch of mermineae alone.

The áed wasn't heading directly for them, instead she seemed to aim for the area Remus knew most of the mermineae were hiding. How she knew they were there, he didn't know.

Well, she was the signal, so he might as well follow their plan. He tossed the cover off their heads to the confused squeaks of the nearby mermineae. Bunny wasted no time throwing herself at the nearest of the sounds, snapping one's neck before it even realized what happened. She was best with a weapon, but that didn't mean she couldn't fight without one.

Unfortunately, they could only get the jump on one. The next arm wrestled their way out of her grasp as she tried to do the same to them.

The snap of Remus's whiplike limbs sent a few mermineae sprawling, but they quickly faded from sight, camouflaged against the ground. He grunted, passing his gaze over the surrounding, knowing that they would sneak up on them in a moment of distraction.

He needed to ignore these and get his team to safety. There was no way the three of them could take on the entire congregation of mermineae.

His eyes fell back to Solvei, to see what her plan was and to be sure she was okay. But he could hardly believe what he saw. As the áed in her falcon form closed the final distance to the camp, the flames surrounding her exploded. In moments, a flashover of bright yellow fire smothered the camp.

This was far greater than anything she'd been able to achieve the last time he'd seen her. More than that; this was more fire than he'd seen any other áed achieve. The golden flickers hugged his form but did not burn. They were hot, of course, but not enough to breach the enhancement of his outer membrane.

The same was not true for the mermineae around him. High-pitched screams met his ear. After all they had done to his team, he could not say he cared all too much for their pain.

The flames were difficult to see through, but the mermineae visible before him were no longer covered in the fur that made them so hard to spot. Remus took advantage of the creatures' pained flailing to take the offensive. He shattered spines and crushed the heads of those too busy crying in pain to defend themselves.

A laugh echoed above Remus's head. "You get what you deserve, bastards!" Jav didn't move to join the fight, but he seemed to enjoy the retribution laid on those who'd caused him so much pain.

Of course, not everything could go perfectly.

Bunny, who'd been beating on a merminea, was blown into Remus. A powerful strike by one of their captors as they flew in through the cover of flames caught her off guard.

Remus absorbed the impact and dropped her at his side. The new merminea crouched on all fours glared at them with its glowing, cloudy gray eyes. Flames licked across his skin, where no fur remained, boiling the surface of its body. Despite the bubbling skin, its focus was entirely on Remus.

The merminea bared its fangs and hissed, the sound a combination of a whistle and a growl. The glowing of its eyes intensified, and Remus felt a deep, sharp pain through one of his foremost limbs. He dodged to the side before flinging himself toward the Forvaal.

Even as fast as he was, it wasn't quick enough to hit the merminea. It scampered to the side and dashed toward Bunny, who stood ready to retaliate.

Remus peered down at the throbbing pain in his tentacle, only to find it gone. Reduced to dust and spread through the flames. The fight was still going. He couldn't focus on it now.

He rushed back, hoping to get the jump on it while it was engaged with Bunny. It was not to be. As soon as he came within striking distance of the merminea, it dropped to its forelegs and kicked at Remus, its claws cutting deep into the limb he'd flung forward in attack, before scurrying out of the range of retaliation.

Remus stood beside Bunny, prepared to rush forward once more. He couldn't afford to let the Forvaal attack them with those eyes again. With no clear way to stop it, he needed to put all his effort into not giving the merminea a chance.

"Weren't you told to wait for the giant bird?" a familiar voice asked from the shroud of flames.

Not a moment later, golden chains materialized out of the flame and wrapped around the Forvaal, tripping it mid-step. The burning bird flew in with talons poised for the merminea's eyes before it could regain its balance. A wet squelch and a screech announced that she'd hit her target.

The giddy feeling was overwhelming now, and he couldn't help but let out a guffaw. "It's great to see you again, Solvei." Despite the pressing circumstances, it really was.

The Forvaal was quick to gain distance as it clutched a hand over its bleeding eye. Unfortunately, there was still another glowing orb to worry about.

Now, all they needed was Grímr, and the team would be united.

CHAPTER FIFTY-ONE

Rescue

Did Caavaa not tell them they were supposed to wait for Grímr? Their early escape has already thrown the plan into disarray. Mermineae across the camp have taken notice. The Forvaal I got the drop on is only one of many able to ignore the pain of their burns; I'm sure there's plenty now on their way to stop the escape attempt.

Through my flames, I can feel three already circling us, waiting for the opportunity to strike. More are heading toward us through the smokescreen provided by my flames.

If they hadn't brought attention to themselves, I could have kept the mermineae's focus entirely on me while they escaped with Grímr. Where is that metal bird, anyway? He should have been here by now.

There's no point lamenting the plan's collapse. I can only adapt to the situation. Too many mermineae have already stopped bothering to attack my distractions and are making their way toward us.

I did not want their entire focus on me when I attacked, so, flying amongst the flames, imitations of myself appear, flickering in and out of existence. As far as I know, the mermineae have no way of discerning my true body, so many will attack these birds and be shocked at the ineffectiveness of their actions.

Of course, it is not the attacks of the normal mermineae that I'm worried about, but the Forvaal. I've not yet seen if their decay eyes can harm my body, so I'd rather not take the risk.

Thankfully, my inner flame seems wholly immune to whatever their power is. I felt nothing, so the only reason I knew they attacked me was the shocked response of one of the Forvaal that failed to damage one of my fake falcons.

Only two mermineae have been able to swipe my flames off their bodies, but it never takes long for the firestorm to close back in. These two are the ones I'm paying the most attention. They are likely the strongest mermineae in the area and our greatest threats. One moves toward my team while the other thankfully runs off in the opposite direction.

I feel a shift in my flames. "Bunny, behind you!"

She spins on her heels and smashes the instep of her foot into the face of the merminea leaping toward her. It had tried to attack her while her back was turned, but unluckily for it, I can feel their movements.

Blood gushes from its snout as it lands on its back. The merminea scrambles to get its feet under it again, but Bunny's boot slams into its head, crushing it into the stone beneath the puddle of wet snow.

The one-eyed Forvaal glares daggers at her. Worried that it might be attacking with its remaining decay eye, I dart forward once more, aiming to make the creature symmetrical again.

It isn't to be. The Forvaal, aware of my existence now, dodges my swooping talons and retaliates. His claws bisect me, but I'm quick to regain myself. I turn to attack it once more, but his eye locks on me and shines gray.

An instant of unbearable pain assaults me. Agonizing. It's like being doused in an ocean of water.

I am forced entirely incorporeal, and the pain abates. Belatedly, I realize I am screaming. I shut myself up. Now's not the time to be yelling. My body is still in one piece, although I feel smaller. I need to kill the Forvaal before he can do any more damage.

The fogginess in his eye spreads as we lock gazes. Without the physicality of my flames, his decaying eye can do nothing. I can do nothing but wait until he's done. My flames already surround him, but they cannot burn through him fast enough.

"Die already!" the merminea shouts as his face scrunches in pain.

The glowing gray of his iris leaks into the pupil and white of his eye. His gaze grows ever more cloudy and unfocused as he tries to use the ability on me, to no avail.

He finally pulls his sight from me, his hands grasp over his remaining eye as he grunts in pain. With a jet of flame behind me and a flap of my wings, I jerk forward, ready to tear his other eye out.

Before I can, Remus and Bunny slam into him, hitting the Forvaal with coordination so that the creature isn't able to make space for itself. Now that it cannot evade their strikes, the brutal pelting it receives ends its life. We have more mermineae surrounding us, but they continue beating into its head until it is nothing but paste.

"Solvei, are you okay?" Remus asks as he steps away from the burning remains.

"I'm fine," I say. "We just need to hold out until Grímr gets here."

Those eyes were painful. I felt much of my body disappear in an instant under his gaze, but I can still fight.

The mermineae around us are using my flames to hide, likely waiting for a perfect opportunity. I can feel my flames sizzling their skin, but I cannot see them with my heat sense. My own flames are near-blinding compared to their tame body temperatures.

Remus and Bunny stare into the flames wearily. The surrounding crowd has grown to seven now and plenty more are on the way. I push my flames outward to give my team visibility on those around us, but that was a mistake. Without the cloaking flames, all mermineae dash in together.

We struggled to take on even one, how are we meant to take on all at once? Thankfully, most aren't Forvaal, but that they can still think about attacking while the skin burns off their backs means they are all stronger than average.

I shoot out of the way, not willing to take them on. Thankfully, it seems both Remus and Bunny are of the same mind. They jump, trying to throw themselves out of range. Jav clings to Remus's head like usual as they soar over me.

While I'd been hoping the mermineae would collide against each other now that their targets have disappeared, it was too much to ask for. They halt their momentum and dash after my team, ready to attack them the moment they land.

A massive displacement of my flames warns me of an incoming threat from above hardly a moment before it slams into the ground. I rocket into the still-airborne Bunny's arms as the giant metal bird tears along the ground, sending up a spray of water and rock. The mermineae are too slow to notice their incoming death. The red and yellow flames reflect off the shifting golden and green feathers as the alicanto slides across the stone, pulverizing each mer-minea in its way.

I'm impressed Grímr knew where to aim. He obviously came in at full speed, so how did he see through my flames and time it so perfectly? Do ali-cantos have another sense they can use beside sight for precise targeting?

Grímr grinds to a halt, covered in merminea blood. I jump out of Bunny's arms, thankful for her protection from the spray of water and snow. I wave them toward Grímr's hefty body.

"Go to Grímr. He'll get you out."

Once I'd known what was going to happen, I'd pulled back on flames, not wanting my inner flame to sizzle from the water. But now that my firestorm is gone, every mermineae around us can see. Grímr slaughtered a few with his landing, but there are far more around.

Remus doesn't even hesitate. "Grímr, that's an amazing new body!" he shouts as he rushes ahead.

Bunny climbs on top of the alicanto after Remus and Grímr rises to his feet. The bumps and dents from the last fight remain, but there are no new ones from his landing.

It's frustrating how slow he is to get in the air again. The mermineae rush us in droves. I recreate my inferno around us, blocking the sight of the Forvaal and hopefully terrifying those who'd been burning from my previous attack.

Many flee, but the stronger of the lot still close in. Grímr's wings create intense gusts as he slowly gains air. The wind pelts the mermineae, mixes with my flame, and crashes through them. They lower their chests to the ground and scamper forward, uncaring for the wind or flames that cut over their heads.

I recreate the chain of flames I used to trip the Forvaal, using it to grab at their feet. A couple stumble, but the rest either notice the grasping flames early and evade or break through them. The low center of mass allows the mermineae too much control of their movement for my weak inner flame chains to stop them.

As I fly over Grímr's head, I realize he's moving too slow. The mermineae will be on top of us if he takes any longer to rise. As heavy and powerful as the alicanto is, mermineae know how to take one down. We don't have time to waste.

My gaze lands on the gash in the stone where Grímr's landing threw away all the snow and water. The alicanto is an extremely heavy bird, so I don't know if my plan will work, but it's worth the attempt.

I focus my flames on the gouge through the snow and melt my way through as much stone as I can. Rather than burning it for energy or leaving the molten rock, I take in the mass, and add weight to my flames. It doesn't bring my fire to the solid presence my body has, but it is enough to carry momentum.

The first of the mermineae throws itself on Grímr's wing, and I see him tilt as the creature tries to bury his wing in the ground. Grímr's tail sweeps around and knocks away the next three closing in, while Remus whips a limb into the head of the one grasping the wing.

Unfortunately, the disruption to his flight has brought Grímr's glide back to the ground. His talons scrape against the earth as he tries to regain height.

The only way for him to gain air before the rest collapse on him is if my plan works.

I hope it'll be enough.

I direct the mass-carrying flames underneath the giant bird and blast him. My flames roll along beneath him and continue to roast the underside with jets of flame. He'll have to forgive me if it gets too hot.

I try to cycle the heavy flames, but I find with each impact against Grímr, I lose some of the weight. We are quickly approaching a distance too far for me to continue extracting mass from the stone. Unless I burn through the snow and water below, I'm stuck with what I've already taken.

Despite these problems, the fires blasting into the underside of Grímr's wings work far better than I'd expected. Even as the mass dies away from my flames, there still seems to be an effect. Curious.

With a few mighty beats, Grímr pulls the team out of the range of the mermineae jumping in the air after us.

As I pull away the last of my flames covering the mermineae below, I feel the strongest of them come to a stop. I'd been monitoring this one ever since I noticed it wipe off my flame with ease. The moment I look down at it, the bright gray glow of its eyes pierces my flames.

I force my body incorporeal. Despite acting before I felt it, the sting of the Forvaal's eyes still pounds through my body. It was only for an instant, but it's still too much.

Directing the mass of the burning air into a jet, I throw myself amongst my team. My wings don't work when they are immaterial, after all.

A hand from Bunny holds me steady, and I let out a sigh of relief to be out of that Forvaal's sight. I'll need to figure out a way to fight them without leaving myself vulnerable.

A short, grinding screech from Grímr alerts me we are not yet out of danger. I snap my head around and quickly realize what is wrong. The outline of his wings is decaying. Not only that, his tail is rapidly losing length. The Forvaal has not stopped its offensive.

"Keep moving!" I shout and engulf Grímr's body in fire.

How far does that ability work from? We're at least a few hundred meters away now.

My flames burn underneath Grímr's wings again, hoping for that same effect I'd noticed before where he seemed to get more lift even without mass pelting him upward. In the meantime, I spread my flames wide to hide our exact position from the Forvaal's eyes.

It doesn't seem to work. Even blocked from sight as we are, Grímr's wings still fall away to dust. I push the mass from the air into the flames. Maybe it is a reckless action, considering how much it hurt to feel the decay of my body, but I have no other ideas to protect Grímr.

As soon as the thin barrier of physical flames is in place, I feel pain. It's not as bad as if it were my actual body, but it still hurts to hold on. Thankfully, the decay Grímr experiences stops and he can focus on getting us out.

Far too long does the ache through my inner flame continue. Grímr has almost reached my fastest flying speed by the time it stops.

I flop on my back now that I don't have to worry about protecting us. There is a lot of energy at my beck and call now, but it is mentally draining to control it all. It would have been easier if I hadn't tried to split my focus so much.

"Wow, you two. I'm not complaining at all, but what happened in our time apart?"

Remus seems to be as cheerful, as always. Although as I look closer, Jav huddles into himself and isn't looking around. Bunny seems fine, but she's not speaking. Maybe Remus is trying to keep a strong front for them or at least cheer them up.

I feel a bit bad for considering their entrapment a good punishment for how they dragged me down into the caves. While we never needed to enter the tunnels, the blizzard did rush their decision. I still have reservations about what they did to me, but I've worked so hard to get them out. We should all enjoy our regained freedom and worry about what we are going to do later on.

Despite my conflicted feelings, it really is good to see them again.

CHAPTER FIFTY-TWO

Reunion

A h, so it wasn't you we were supposed to wait for?" Remus asks.

"No," I say. "The plan was for you three to not attract any attention until Grímr could swoop in and pull you out." Now that I think about it, we're lucky he was quick to realize what was happening when he came crashing down. "Good job, Grímr. How'd you time your attack so perfectly? I didn't think you could see through my flames."

"Attack?" Grímr tilts his still-deformed head back. "Oh right, yeah . . . my attack . . . I, uh, just figured that was the right time."

I stare at the back of his head for a good moment before letting out a laugh. He's still such a horrible liar.

"You crashed, didn't you?"

I burst into giggles at the wordless glance he sends back. It's been ages since I've felt this relieved. The constant pressure and worry I've been subject to pops like bubbles with each laugh. I may hold reservations for what they did, but I'm glad we are all finally free.

"Flying is harder than you think," Grímr rebukes, only to send me into another fit of giggles. He realizes his mistake quickly. "Well, flying this bird is. I was too far away when you started your distraction, so I tried to hurry. By the time I was close enough, I couldn't slow down."

The last streaks of twilight dim and leave only the moon to light the land beneath us. Grímr's metallic sheen glows, but the outer edges of his wings lack the same luster. It's a good thing Grímr doesn't feel the pain of his body in the same way a normal creature would. I'm sure it would be excruciating.

"I'm going to take us down, all right? This body is starving, and I'd rather not lose another so soon."

"You're not going to crash land again, are you?" I tease.

"Probably. I can't feel my feet."

As Grímr slowly lowers his speed and altitude, Remus takes the opportunity to speak. "I need to properly thank you both. I appreciate you coming for us over such a long distance. There's no doubt in my mind it must have been difficult. Solvei, even after my poor decisions, I owe you everything for getting these two and myself out."

Bunny nods seriously, but Jav still seems mostly unfocused. He's looking out over the landscape, but isn't paying attention to the conversation.

I'm sure whatever they went through must have been hard. I feel asking about it would be the wrong choice. After escaping the Henosis soldiers, the last thing I wanted to think about was what happened while I was with them.

True to his word, Grímr doesn't land softly. He slows himself enough, but his chest and head still slam into the ground. We grind to a halt after a few meters. I throw myself off to check his condition, but the underside of the alicanto is in a far worse state than the upper side we'd been sitting on would indicate.

The Forvaal tore away his entire metallic protection. Not a feather remains down there, and each taloned foot has all but disappeared.

Despite the critical state of his body, Grímr drags himself a few meters from where we landed and slams his beak into the stone. I'm worried he'll hurt himself even more, but soon, he's dug a hole deep enough to bury his head. His movements change and a grinding crunch accompanies the bobbing of his head.

I guess he's found something to eat.

Thankfully, Grímr had the awareness to drop where there is no snow cover. I'd change back now, but as a show of faith, I left my bag and snowsuit with the mermineae we are supposed to meet later tonight. Okay, maybe I didn't really care about giving them any assurances, but risking my outfit while I was the focus of hundreds of mermineae wasn't something I wanted to do. It was just easier to leave it with them.

Bunny and Remus both stretch. Sighs of contentment come from each as they stroll in the open.

I know Aana said that the birds of prey won't hunt near others, but it's concerning how visible we are. We were originally supposed to fly immediately to the meeting point, but I don't blame Grímr for taking a break after the amount of damage he's sustained. I hope he can get his body fixed up; finding another one as good as that might be hard.

I planned to set Jav and Bunny on their tasks to fix my outfit and spear as soon as they were free, but seeing their current state stops me. Making demands now would be inconsiderate. I'll give them some time before letting them pay me back.

My eyes fall on Remus's missing limb. During the fight, I had felt it fall away into dust through my flames. It is good he's still alive, but if I'd been quicker, he might have come away unharmed.

Strangely, as the dust remnants of his limb passed through my flames, not a single fleck burned.

Remus's eyes roll back in his head and he catches me staring. He wiggles his stump and gives me his usual eye smile. "Don't worry, Solvei. A quick visit to the Lu-Lum family will get this fixed up as if it weren't ever gone." His eyes rise to the ever-watching Titan perched on the Alps. "Well, that might take some time, but don't think I'm any weaker without it. This is hardly a scratch to me."

I don't comment. I'd actually thought it would be easier for him to recover from a missing limb. To know he needs to meet with someone to regrow it is an awakening. Áed can regrow limbs by eating. After watching Grímr's speedy healing while he was a mountain panther, I'd assumed all fleshy creatures were like that.

Is there any other assumption I've made that is simply wrong?

"What happened since we were separated? You have grown like a wildfire." His eyes grin. The word choice obviously amusing to him.

"Grímr followed you. I ate bugs."

He gives me a perplexed look at my excessively brief explanation. I let out a chuckle at his expense before going into more detail. I tell him of the lurking monstrosities, my spear fights with the creatures in the shadows and the massive amount of energy the glow-bugs provided.

"So that was you?" Remus asks, and at my confused gaze, he continues. "Our assailants were becoming increasingly nervous as we moved through the tunnels. They'd been hearing the quakes through the earth and let their fears run wild with what it might be. It was particularly bad for the group watching over us, as it always seemed near. They'd come to think we were cursed."

Remus lets out a chuckle. "It's amusing to know it was you the whole time."

I smile hearing that. It hadn't been an easy trip for myself, so to know I made it worse for the ones we were following is satisfying.

Bunny sits down and listens in halfway through my retelling. She looks around, obviously searching for my spear once I tell them I'd learned to carry it in my flames, but I soon tell of the fate that befell it.

"We need new weapons," she speaks for the first time since we freed her. "I'm uncomfortable without one. I'll make you one once there are materials for me to use."

I follow her gaze over the plains beneath the Alps. There's no obvious trees anywhere to use in creating the weapons she might want to make. Bunny probably wouldn't have an issue using entirely metallic weapons, but that would most likely be far too unwieldy for me.

Grímr is still gorging in the hole he's dug himself. He must have a smell for metals in that body, which will be incredibly helpful for both me and Bunny.

"So what about those mermineae? I assume you were working with the one who freed us from our restraints. Are they truly on our side?" Remus asks.

"I'm not sure," I say. "They seem determined to oppose the mermineae that captured you. They call them 'traitors.' Though, as much as they say they need our help, they don't risk much in their support."

"They need our help?" Remus asks.

"Yeah. Apparently we aren't the first to cross the Alps. The ones that came before us don't listen to their requests, so they want us to talk to them on their behalf."

His eyes widen. "Did the mermineae not try to force them?"

"I think they were too strong for them. Caavaa said the outsiders ignored their threats. They were quick to move from the Alps, but the mermineae couldn't stop them."

Remus's eyes lower in a frown and he goes quiet in contemplation.

"Do you know who they are?"

He raises his eyes to meet mine once more. "I have a hunch." He pauses before continuing. "Actually, there is only one group it could be, but I don't want to believe it. It means they've abandoned their oath and left the pact nations undefended."

Now that I think about it, Remus is supposed to be one of the stronger mercenaries, right? Who are these people that can brush off the mermineae when not even he can?

"Who?" I ask.

Remus absently pokes at the stub of his limb. "The Beith mercenaries. Many of which I am friends with . . . or at least I was. I'd known some were missing, but I never thought they would leave the younger generation to defend against the Alps alone."

So the elite mercenaries that are meant to remain on standby for major threats are on the opposite side of the Alps from the land they are supposed to protect? Are my friends no longer safe where I left them?

"Will the people of the pact be okay?"

"I . . . I don't know. Without the Beith mercs to defend them, I'm not sure the Mercenary Order will hold off the mermineae invasion."

"Invasion?" I ask. I knew they were trying to get to the other side of the Alps, but there is plenty of land along the Stepps that I thought they'd settle in. Was that too naive of me?

Remus glances up at Jav, who's still to react to my existence, lost in the starry sky above. "I'm afraid our interrogators made quite clear their intentions. Besides, there is almost no chance the countries bordering the Alps will cede the land. The wealth of resources they'd lose would be astronomical. Thankfully, those in charge of their invasion are the last to push through the Alps. There should be a few months before war ignites."

"The last? No, Caavaa said there were still far more coming. They are running from their god. From what I understand, every merminea not part of Kalma's clergy is on their way to reach the 'beyond,' as they call it."

Remus's eyes fall on me. His intense gaze searching for any fabrication in my words. "If that's the case, then we need to find my old friends, not to help this clergy, but to prevent the destruction of every pact nation. Why does this Caavaa want to stop his own race?"

"Fear. The three I've met that oppose the mermineae trying to cross the Alps are all terrified of a being they call Kalma. They believe if she finds out the merminea race is trying to flee, they'll face a horrible fate. Even those who don't run."

"Damn." Remus turns to watch Grímr climb out of the deep hole he'd excavated in the stone. The alicanto appears in far better shape than when he started his feast. So eating metals can recover his body? That's helpful.

"We're going to be busy for a while."

"You want to work with the clergy?" I ask.

"We have little choice. We don't have the time to solve this ourselves. If our goals are aligned, we might as well."

I still don't like how they have refused to take on risk themselves. It makes me feel like they consider us disposable. "Just be careful around them. I don't trust them."

"Of course." Remus nods.

I'd wanted to just live again once we freed the trio. If the mermineae expected me to risk myself for them after this, I would have just walked. This side of the Alps might be dangerous, but it's a whole new world to explore. If it means I have to go through the Alps again, there isn't a chance I will return.

I was content to leave my friends in the safety of the pact nations and go traveling. Maybe I'd eventually find another path around the Alps and I'd be able to return. But now that I know they are in danger, I'm forced to get caught up in all this mess with the mermineae.

The clergy better live up to their goal. Just as the Beith mercs better return to the pact nations. I didn't leave my friends there only to be thrust into the midst of war. I've seen how that destroyed Leal's life. If I can prevent the same happening once more, I will.

About the Author

J. B. Oro is the author of the Young Flame series, originally released on Royal Road. He is a massive progression fantasy and xenofiction fan. Oro finds that the more unassuming and visibly contradictory to their strength characters are, the better.